MURDER

IN A WALLED TOWN

The Private Memoirs of Wayne Armitage

New Mystery Writer

Katherine Woods, author of *The Other Chateau Country*, will make her debut as a mystery-story writer when Houghton Mifflin Company publishes early in October her "Murder in a Walled Town." The background is not Paris, and not the Riviera, but the real "French" France of the provinces, which Miss Woods knows from first-hand experience. She spent last summer in the "Neyronnes" of *Murder in a Walled Town*, and the last two winters in Aix-en-Provence. When not at her typewriter, Miss Woods can generally be found at the wheel of her car.

(1934)
Gastonia, NC, *Daily Gazette*

MURDER
IN A WALLED TOWN

The Private Memoirs of Wayne Armitage

Katherine Woods

COACHWHIP PUBLICATIONS

Greenville, Ohio

ISBN 1-61646-332-5
ISBN-13 978-1-61646-332-8

CoachwhipBooks.com

CIVILIZED MURDER: KATHERINE WOODS AND *MURDER IN A WALLED TOWN* (1934)

CURTIS EVANS

Murder continues to fascinate the intelligent reading public. . . . It is essentially a "refined" taste, a
taste sophisticated but not decadent, a taste for inexplicable strangeness in human behavior, for the
unraveling of curious puzzles and the presentation
of queer characters, for odd stories well told. . . .

—excerpt from Katherine Woods's
review of *More Studies in Murder*
(1936), by Edmund Pearson

Best known today for having produced the much admired original
English translation of Antoine de Saint-Exupéry's beloved novella,
The Little Prince (1943), Katherine Woods (1886-1968), in addition to writing columns for the *New York Times Book Review* for
three decades, also published a mystery novel, *Murder in a Walled
Town: The Private Memoirs of Wayne Armitage* (1934), and a
travel book, *The Other Chateau Country: The Feudal Land of the
Dordogne* (1931).[1] Though well-reviewed at the time of its publication, Woods's *Murder in a Walled Town* was never reprinted,
and today the book most regrettably is essentially a forgotten work.
Moreover, despite the familiarity of Woods's name to English-
language readers of *The Little Prince*, little is known about her
interesting life. Happily, Coachwhip Publications's reprinting of

Murder in a Walled Town has provided fans of vintage mystery with an opportunity to read this unjustly neglected work and to learn something about the accomplished woman who wrote it.

Katherine Woods was born Mary Katherine Irvin Woods in 1886 in Merchantville, New Jersey, where her father, Matthew Cooper Woods, a Presbyterian minister and graduate of Princeton seminary, served as pastor for three years. After her father's exceedingly untimely death at the age of 32 in 1889, when Katherine was but two years old, she and her mother, Nancy Irvin Shaw Woods, moved to Clearfield, the northwestern Pennsylvania native town of both of Katherine's parents. Nancy, whose paternal grandfather, businessman Robert Shaw, had been one of Clearfield's most prominent residents, would later marry Abraham Bowman Weaver, a well-off Clearfield lumber dealer.[2]

Decades later, in 1942, Katherine Woods recalled that not long after she and her mother had gone to Clearfield, where they were staying at her maternal grandmother's home, the town, which is bisected by the Susquehanna River, was hit by the Great Flood of 1889 (aka the Johnstown Flood). As water inundated the first floor of her grandmother's house, a family cousin made a timely arrival in a rowboat and rescued his imperiled kinfolk. Bestselling mystery author Mary Roberts Rinehart, who was a decade older than Woods and grew up in Allegheny City (now part of Pittsburgh), for her part vividly remembered watching with her mother during the aftermath of the Great Flood as the Monongahela and Allegheny

CATHARINE WOODS — Our time and space are too limited to say all we would. Go to Catharine herself for all information. Office hours :   7.00 A.M.–10.30 P.M.

1904 Mount Holyoke yearbook photo of Katherine Woods (whose first name is spelled differently), with a wry caption emphasizing her highly developed work ethic.

Rivers, swollen with water, carried dead bodies from Johnstown past their house.

Woods was educated at Abbot Academy, in Andover, Massachusetts, Blair Academy, in Blairstown, New Jersey, and Mount Holyoke College, one of the so-called "Seven Sisters" of elite northeastern women's colleges (the others being Barnard, Bryn Mawr, Radcliffe, Smith, Vassar, and Wellesley). After her graduation from Mount Holyoke in 1908 Woods worked for a few years as a reporter and features writer for *The Philadelphia Press* before being hired by the *New York Times Book Review* in 1912. She would write columns for the *NYTBR* over the next thirty years. During the 1910s Woods also was active in the woman's suffrage movement.

By 1920, Katherine Woods was living with Edith Huntington Snow, daughter of the late Francis Huntington Snow, a professor of natural history and chancellor at the University of Kansas. A decade older than Woods, Snow had attended classes at the University of Kansas and Stanford University before moving to New York, where she trained as an artisan weaver. After successfully implementing a weaving program at the Marblehead, Massachusetts sanatorium as therapy for convalescing Great War veterans, Woods with Beatrice Vail Abbott established in New York the Snow Abbott Looms (later the Snow Looms School of Weaving and Crafts). During the 1920s and 1930s Snow frequently accompanied Woods on the latter woman's trips to France and in 1934 Woods warmly dedicated *Murder in a Walled Town*, which is set in France, to her longtime companion: *To Edith Huntington Snow Who Shares with Me the Charming Secret of the Real Neyronnes* (the titular "walled town" of Woods's novel). In her *NYTBR* review of Vera Brittain's *Testament of Friendship: The Story of Winifred Holtby*, Woods took the opportunity to observe and to praise the existence of what she termed "strong friendship" between women:

> . . . . while strong friendship between men has been intelligently celebrated in history and legend, strong friendship between women has been scarcely even believed in. It has been regarded as something

Katherine Woods at the age 35 in 1921,
the year she made her first trip to France.

shallow and jealously-ridden (not to say feline), or else unhealthily emotional (not to say abnormal); whereas, as most sensible people know, life abounds in women's sane, firm comradeships.[3]

Murder in a Walled Town arguably was a natural outgrowth of Woods's earlier book *The Other Chateau Country*, published three years previously, in 1931. Not only was Woods greatly interested in France and the social history of small communities, she also was fascinated with both crime fiction and true crime; that she would pen a detective novel set in a small French town thus should not come as a great surprise. Woods was hardly alone in being an intellectual who was irresistibly tempted to try her hand at a tale of mystery during the Golden Age of detective fiction. For example, just two years before the publication of *Murder in a Walled Town*, the English physicist C. P. Snow, a fellow of Christ's College, Cambridge, had published a well-received prentice novel, the mystery *Death under Sail* (1932). At this time mystery fancying intellectuals around the world, such as T. S. Eliot, Ferdinand Pessoa, and Jacques Barzun, joined in lusty chorus to sing praises of the form.

In the pages of the *New York Times Book Review* Woods reviewed not only social histories of rural localities, such as Margery Allingham's *The Oaken Heart* and August Derleth's *Village Year* (books by mystery writers which lovingly detailed life in, respectively, Tolleshunt D'Arcy, Essex and Sauk City, Minnesota), but also books on true crime and crime fiction, including *The Anatomy of Murder*, a collection of essays on real life murders composed by members of Britain's celebrated Detection Club, a social organization of distinguished detective novelists; Dr. Joseph Catton's *Behind the Scenes of Murder*, a psychiatric analysis of homicide; Edmund Pearson's *Trial of Lizzie Borden* and *More Studies in Murder*; and Howard Haycraft's *Murder for Pleasure: The Life and Times of the Detective Story*.

Evident in these reviews is Woods's intense interest as an intellectual in what she termed, in her review of Edmund Pearson's *More Studies in Murder*, "the unraveling of curious puzzles and the presentation of queer characters." "Although [the detective story] may sometimes be the object of cold intellectual scorn," Woods noted in her *NYTBR* piece on Haycraft's *Murder for Pleasure*, "its criterion of real excellence is uniquely intellectual." Her respect for the mental and artistic acuity of the Detection Club is clear from the praise she afforded the seven contributors to *The Anatomy of Murder* (Margaret Cole, Freeman Wills Crofts, Francis Iles/Anthony Berkeley Cox, E. R. Punshon, John Rhode/Cecil John Charles Street, Dorothy L. Sayers, and Helen Simpson):

> Held within the limits of fact, these novelists have made fact as entertaining as fiction, and much more broadly and suggestively interesting than detective fiction can be. They are, of course, no mere purveyors of thrills at any time: sophisticated and scholarly as well as ingenious, they are all masters of their subject and their craft, obedient to the exactions of accuracy, insight, logic and finesse. Every one of them can write. And every one of them is quite individual in expression and attitude. . . . Every one of these stories has its own character and is in its own way brilliantly told. The members of the Detection Club handle murder, in fact as in fiction, neither sensationally nor sentimentally, but intelligently, realistically and with unfailing interest.

Starkly contrasting with Edmund Wilson and other literary pundits who vocally turned decisively against the detective novel in the 1940s, Woods in 1941 avowed that the form "begins its second century in a maturity of muscular vigor, audacious experimentation, and adroit finesse."[4]

Woods's passion for mysteries, both imagined and factual, peals most powerfully in the opening lines of her review of Pearson's *Trial of Lizzie Borden*:

It is a story which has more than classic perfection to recommend it: within a flawless frame of incident, character, background and chance it holds to those strange contradictions and inconsistencies, those small illogical particulars in action and observation, which are the marks of human reality. It becomes, thus, the more completely and astoundingly perfect; and because of its perfection it has a quality of fascination which will probably never die.

It was, and is, a mystery story. . . .[5]

Woods's own mystery story received strong praise upon its appearance in 1934. In the *New York Times Book Review*—admittedly friendly ground for Woods—mystery critic Isaac Anderson conceded that *Murder in a Walled Town* did "not belong to the rapid-fire school of mystery fiction," but he lauded the novel's atmosphere, pronouncing that "no intelligent reader" would not wish to linger in "so charming a place as Neyrolles," the author's fictionalized French walled town. Similarly, in *The Age* a Melbourne, Australia, reviewer praised Woods's "skill in characterization" and her novel's "admirable setting," adding: "The story is told with a quiet charm, and a feeling for subtleties of character, which are quite rare in a murder mystery story."[6]

Murder in a Walled Town is set in the fictional *bastide* (fortified medieval settlement) of Neyronnes, which Woods probably based on Domme, a village built in 1281 on a rocky outcrop overlooking the Dordogne River and later fortified in 1310, to which she had devoted laudatory words a few years earlier in her book *The Other Château Country*. The Knights Templars were imprisoned in Domme in 1307 during their persecution by King Philip IV and the town several times changed hands between French and English forces during the Hundred Years' War (1337-1453), but by the spring of 1933, when the events in *Murder in a Walled Town* take place, Domme had enjoyed many years of tranquility, to which Woods alludes when writing of Neyronnes in the novel:

> One of the most picturesque places in France. . . .
> Unspoiled. Cheap. No Americans there, no English.
> A tiny walled village on a hill, with a good little inn
> where you could live for only a little over a dollar a
> day. And study . . . absolutely quiet, remote from the
> tourist trails and from all the currents of modern life,
> and nothing ever happened to disturb you or inter-
> rupt your work, for weeks on end.

Of course all this glorious placidity soon suffers considerable
disruption.

Murder in a Walled Town is subtitled *The Private Memoirs of
Wayne Armitage*, its being narrated after the event by Wayne
Armitage, a young man who is employed as a teacher at a boys'
school in Paoli, Pennsylvania, near Philadelphia. (Woods seems
to have drawn Wayne's background from that of her long-deceased
father, Reverend Matthew Cooper Woods, who during the last year
of his life, when Katherine was but a toddler, had been the Presbyterian minister at Parkesburg, Pennsylvania, not far from Paoli.)
Wayne Armitage, who is taking a long-cherished summer's vacation in Europe, has traveled to Neyronnes not merely to bask in
the village's calm, unspoiled beauty, but to take advantage of its
low cost of living. As Wayne explains in the novel, the new United
States presidential administration of Franklin Delano Roosevelt
had recently taken the country off the gold standard, causing the
value of the dollar to drop relative to foreign currencies, a serious
matter for American tourists in Europe.

Wayne finds to his initial chagrin that additional American
tourists have made for Neyronnes with the same economizing
notion in mind: Margaret Hamilton, a forty-something decayed
gentlewoman with a beautiful voice ("Many American voices are
unpleasing, I know, just as many English voices are unpleasing;
but the English language as spoken by an American of cultivation
and good breeding is certainly as fair-sounding a thing as the
English language can be.") and a handsome Kerry blue terrier
named Fergus; Mrs. Wilde, a neurasthenic invalid widow, and her

lovely, much put-upon daughter, Christine; John and Elinor Sherrill, old friends of Margaret Hamilton; and Horace Braye, businessman and outsize example of the "ugly American," and his "nincompoop" wife, Rosalie. Along with these Americans, there is additionally a courtly Frenchman, Henri de Brassac, who is also staying at the inn at Neyronnes.

When Mrs. Wilde is found dead in her bedroom from an overdose of morphine it soon comes to appear that someone badly wanted the hateful matron to check out permanently from earthly life; and there is no shortage of plausible candidates for the role of murderer. Wayne himself is deemed not to be above suspicion, especially since he by his own admission has fallen in love with Christine Wilde, to whom a substantial income is now due with her mother's death. Before the truth behind Mrs. Wilde's demise finally is brought to light, there will be a second shocking death at the charming inn.

With *Murder in a Walled Town*, Katherine Woods gave Golden Age mystery readers a well-plotted novel peopled with intriguing characters in a fascinating and beguiling setting. Mystery fans of today should enjoy these same qualities, as well as Woods's pungent observations concerning social and economic conditions in the United States and Europe following the onset of the Great Depression, which seem surprisingly timely in 2016. At one memorable point after the murder of Mrs. Wilde, fraying tensions snap, leading to a confrontation between Horace Braye, a true "America First" type who condemns all things French, and the other, worldlier, guests, who seem, unquestionably, to represent the author's own view of things. As one of the cosmopolites explains to an interested bystander:

. . . . [Horace Braye] has been providing our comic relief here in Neyronnes since Saturday evening. He has his American bootleg bar with him, and he thinks all foreigners are robbers, and he doesn't see why the old houses of Neyronnes aren't torn down to widen the road—you know the type. He is one of those coarse, clownish, ill-tempered, incredibly ignorant bounders that you read about, and that occasionally you do actually meet. Foreigners hate them, of course; but no foreigner can possibly hate them with the concentrated fury of aversion which they inspire in their suffering fellow-Americans— their squirming fellow-Americans, I might say. Horace is one of those kingfishes, and we laugh at him and loathe him and wonder what offensive imbecility he is going to bring forth next. But all the same. . . . Horace is no imbecile. . . . he knows his own stuff, and I think he has a pretty keen brain, of his own kind.

Observers of the current American political scene may well murmur, *plus ça change, plus c'est la même chose.*[7]

Endnotes

[1] On the controversial modern colloquial 2000 translation which replaced that of Katherine Woods, see David Kipen, "A Charmless New Version of 'Prince'," *SF Gate*, 21 June 2000, at http://www.sfgate.com/books/article/A-Charmless-New-Version-Of-Prince-2753877.php.

[2] Biographical information in this paragraph and the two which follow is drawn from records at Ancestry.com and from the *Clearfield Progress*, 17 October 1942, 1.

[3] *NYTBR*, 14 January 1940 (review of *Testament of Friendship*). On Edith Huntington Snow, see Census Records at Ancestry.com and "Edith Huntington Snow," Cooper Hewitt, Smithsonian Design Museum, at https://collection.cooperhewitt.org/people/18046231/. Woods's feminism and dubiousness about

women's emotional need for men is evident in her scornful remarks concerning Margaret Lawrence's *The School of Femininity: A Book for and about Women as They are Interpreted through Feminine Writers of Yesterday and Today*:

> Its generalizations are for the most part bio-logical (the word "biological" is never long ab-sent from these pages) but beyond its preoccu-pations with women as females the book has no coherent argument. In so far as it attempts any, it seems to be the not startlingly-original contention that women cannot escape from their racial burden of gestation and birth, and that for this reason they "take to writing" only to compensate for biological frustration or to ease some biologic hurt, giving it up again, "by the rules of their nature," as soon as they "find a man." *NYTBR*, 1 March 1936.

[4] *NYTBR*, 2 February 1936 (Review of *More Studies in Murder*), 18 July 1937 (Review of *The Anatomy of Murder*), 14 September 1941 (Review of *Murder for Pleasure*). Among the contributors to *The Anatomy of Murder*, Woods singled out for especial praise Anthony Berkeley Cox, dubbing him "that mercilessly intelligent novelist whom we know as Francis Iles." Under the pen name Francis Iles, Cox at this time had published a pair of highly-regarded psychological crime novels, *Malice Aforethought* (1931) and *Before the Fact* (1932).

[5] *NYTBR*, 14 March 1937 (Review of *Trial of Lizzie Borden*).

[6] *NYTBR*, 21 October 1934; (Melbourne) *The Age*, 25 July 1936.

[7] "The more things change, the more they stay the same." "Kingfish" was the nickname of Huey Long, a famous and controversial populist politician in Depres-sion-era America whose colorful career was cut short when he was assassinated in 1935.

MURDER
IN A
WALLED TOWN

To Edith Huntington Snow
Who Shares with Me the Charming Secret
of the Real Neyronnes

NOTE

All the characters in this story are imaginary. And I hope that the scene is sufficiently disguised as to be unrecognizable. With the exception of one great historic event, that picturesque and delightful village on its hilltop has known no form of battle, murder, or sudden death, so far as I have been able to discover, for at least three hundred years. Since the end of the Wars of Religion, I feel sure that nothing but the French Revolution has disturbed its calm. And, like the narrator of my story, I hope to go back to it, and find it still unspoiled.

K. W.
Hôtel du Roy René
Aix-en-Provence
March, 1934

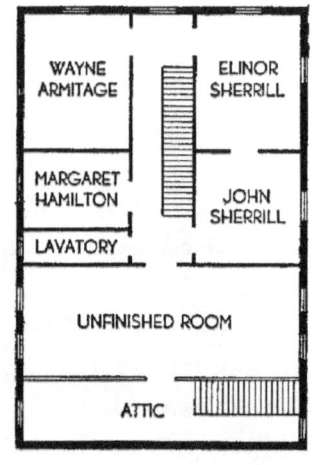

2ND SLEEPING FLOOR

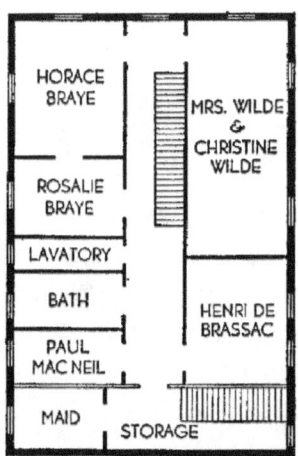

1ST SLEEPING FLOOR

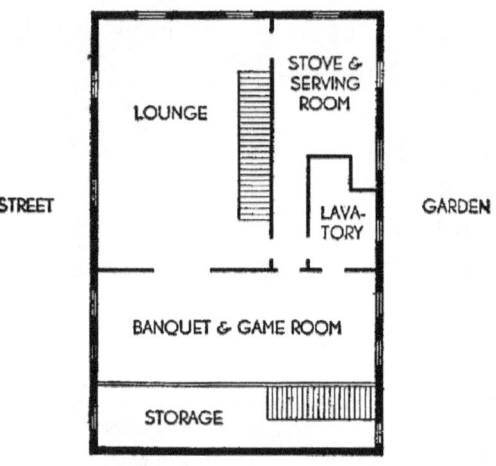

GROUND FLOOR

PAVILLON ANNEXE

Auberge de Vieux Neyronnes

I

I COME TO NEYRONNES

People say a great deal, I've noticed, about large events that result from small causes: a woman rushes back to be sure she has turned off the hot water, and misses the train that is swept off the bridge in the flood—that sort of thing. Life and conversation are full of it. But it seems to me that the resultance of small events from large causes is just as interesting—only 'small' and 'large' are not really the words I mean. What I am thinking of is the momentous, indeed the all-important, personal consequences which may spring from broad impersonal movements, situations, affairs. It was this kind of thing which happened to us all, that summer at Neyronnes.

On the nineteenth of April, 1933, the United States of America went off the gold standard. And because of that incident in international finance, life and death and romance and mystery and tragedy and renewal came to a group of ordinary individuals in a small village in central France. Because our country 'went off gold,' our strangely assorted group of Americans gathered at Neyronnes in the first place. Because we came there and stayed there, all our lives were changed and for some among us life ended; but hope and happiness came to others—new happiness and new hope. In the long run that curious story of Neyronnes is a good story, a story that 'comes out well.' Christine, thank God, is happy. It seems to me that that is all that really matters, but of course I know that my point of view is completely biased where Christine is concerned! And I am really thinking of everyone when I say that the story ends well. Justice triumphed: of that I do feel convinced, for all the strangeness and the dreadfulness of what happened to us there.

But of course at the beginning no one could have guessed that there was going to be a story at Neyronnes at all. . . .

I was on the high seas when the United States went off the gold standard. In that, I was like Monsieur Herriot: he was voyaging westbound on the *Ile-de-France* and I was on my way to Europe on the *Paris*, and the ships passed and saluted somewhere toward the middle of the Atlantic. But unlike Monsieur Herriot, I didn't take the matter of the gold standard itself very seriously.

As a matter of fact, I was thinking very busily about other things. I was on my way to Geneva to do a bit of research work at the International Labor Office, and of course I just went ahead. My job is teaching history, but I have always been interested in labor matters, and when this chance came my way I had jumped at it, naturally. And I was so interested in everything that was going on there—in the Labor Office, and the League, and Geneva itself— that it just didn't occur to me to think of international finance in any personal way. In spite of the fact that I teach history, I haven't traveled much abroad, and foreign exchange was just foreign exchange: if the Swiss franc was twenty-three cents instead of twenty, it didn't mean a lot to me. But by June the dollar was really dropping.

Long before the nineteenth of April, I had planned a summer's holiday: I was going to France, and England, and maybe Italy, too. I had worked out what a trip ought to cost, and I thought I could manage it. And what I wanted to see, what I wanted to learn about, was the real country. I knew Paris, and London, fairly well; but what I had a yearning to become acquainted with was the provincial towns, and the villages, and the long stretches of road between the trees and hedgerows; I wanted to see terraces, and vineyards, and arcades, and ancient tumbledown houses, and little old narrow winding streets; I wanted to feast my eyes on feudal castles, and mediæval abbeys, and Gothic churches, and to watch the country people gathering in the little towns on market-day. I wanted a lot . . .

I had been teaching history in a boys' school near Philadelphia; I hadn't had much money, ever; and what with paying back what I had had to borrow to get through college, and taking care of my mother through several years of invalidism, I had never had anything extra: I had never been able to see the things I had been teaching about. Now my mother was dead. My debts were paid. I had had this bit of a job at Geneva, with two months added to my time off from school and my steamship fare paid one way: when I finished the job I was through, on my own, free, for the rest of the summer. But when the dollar began to show that it was dropping, I had to reconstruct my ideas: it looked as if I should have to go straight back home . . .

Well, I didn't want to do that. I had already bought my return ticket, tourist, with American dollars in America. But I didn't want to use it right away. I didn't want to give up my hoped-for glimpse of the 'real country' in foreign lands.

And then, all of a sudden, I thought of Neyronnes, and remembered what an artist friend had told me about it. One of the most picturesque places in France, he had said. Unspoiled. Cheap. No Americans there, no English. A tiny walled village on a hill, with a good little inn where you could live for only a little over a dollar a day. And study. He said it was absolutely quiet, remote from the tourist trails and from all the currents of modern life, and nothing ever happened to disturb you or interrupt your work, for weeks on end.

I realized that I should have to give up the summer's travel that I had planned, but I could still have an interesting European holiday, quiet, unusual, 'real.' I cashed a good deal of money in French francs, before the dollar should drop farther, and I crossed the border into France.

On a map of Europe, or even a map of France, it doesn't look to be a long distance from Geneva to Neyronnes, because Neyronnes (although of course it isn't on any map smaller than the large-scale Michelin) is not far from the center of France. But central France is a pretty big locality. And when I talk of it, I am no more definite than that about the whereabouts of this little walled village of ours.

I love Neyronnes, and I want to go back to it and find it still unspoiled. It is all that my painter friend told me—all that and more;
but although murder couldn't spoil it, tourists could. Not from me—
nor yet from Christine—are any tourists going to find out where it
is! And all that I need say here about its situation is just that I had
to change cars a lot, and wander around in a surprising fashion
over the map of France, before I ever got to the place at all.

Finally I decided to spend the night in the nearest city and go
out in the morning by a fairly early train. Not that there was a train
to Neyronnes itself. The railroad station was at a little town in the
valley, several miles away. But I had a leisurely breakfast, trying
to get used to the French way of doing things and not to feel guilt-
ily lazy over having breakfast in bed; and then I picked up my old
Gladstone and got into a third-class compartment on a little train
and traveled along—still in the utmost leisure, as if the train were
just having a pleasant stroll—for some time; and when I got out at
the station of Jeanniot, I was ready to walk.

Here was I, then, on a beautiful June morning, with my bag in
my hand and francs in my pocket to a tune somewhat less gay and
affluent than the rhythm of twenty-five to the dollar, and I was
stepping out of the railroad station into Jeanniot's Place de la Gare.
Here was I, Wayne Armitage, not many years out of college and
as poor as a church mouse, knowing perfectly well that with the
dollar falling I ought to be going home and absolutely determined
to do nothing of the kind.

As I went out past the exit barrier, it occurred to me that I'd
better ask the way to Neyronnes; and then—this seems ridiculous,
but it's true—it burst upon me for the first time that I knew almost
no French! I simply hadn't realized it before. I'd got along with
English everywhere, without any trouble. . . Well, now I was in the
country—the 'real country' that I had always wanted to see and
learn about. I should just have to use what brains I had and what
French I could remember. There was a man with an automobile,
near me at the curb, and a man with a donkey-cart. I felt less
shy of the carter, and I went up to him and waved my hand toward
the right.

"Neyronnes?" I said inquiringly. *"Là?"*

The carter's gesture embraced all the landscape to the left, and he shook his head with emphasis.

"Pareecy!" he replied; and then, before I could puzzle out what that was, he poured forth a torrent of directions, of which, not unnaturally, I could understand not one word.

"Houp-la!" cried the man in the automobile. He got out of his car and approached me, and from the moment my eye fell upon that jovial, friendly countenance I liked that man. He was young, and good-looking, and broad-shouldered, and gay; he had a big hearty voice and a big hearty laugh, and I felt as if he might once have been a famous college athlete, if he had been an American. He came up to me now, and addressed me in slow, bookish, perfect English—the English of a man who has studied it conscientiously and successfully, but has never spoken it much.

"I am going to Neyronnes," he said. "You will come with me?" And he picked up my bag, set it in the tonneau of his sedan, and waved his arm in a broad gesture to indicate my place beside him in the car. "I live in Neyronnes," he explained, as I tried to thank him for his kindness. "My father has been interested in the restoration. I," he added simply, "I keep the inn. If you wish to stay at the inn, my wife and I shall be most happy to receive you. If you do not wish to stay, we shall be glad to help you to see Neyronnes in the time at your disposal."

It was a formal speech, but he made it with unconsidered ease; and it gave me my first experience of the perfect naturalness of French courtesy—although I realized then as later that my host, whose father had been 'interested in the restoration' of the old *cité*, was no ordinary hotel-keeper! Of course I told him that I was planning to stay at the inn, and was delighted at the prospect. And so I rode like a prince into Neyronnes.

We hopped out of Jeanniot and turned from the highway into a byroad that wound around between hedgerows. There was nothing spectacular about it, but it had charm—a gentle country scene. Then we swung around at the foot of a little hill, and my host pointed upward: there were the crumbling thirteenth-century ramparts, there was the broad grassy space that had once been the Lists where tournaments were held, there was the church-tower.

We turned away, lost sight of the citadel, seemed to pass it by, swung back again, and suddenly began to climb steeply, and then passed through a narrow old arched gate. We were in a space between fortress walls now, and the narrow road, still steeply mounting, turned sharply at a right angle within that enclosure. On our left was the doorway of an ancient church built into the fortifications. On our right, touching the ramparts, was the wall of a house with beautiful Renaissance windows, a house that had been a very noble dwelling centuries ago. Straight ahead of us the road narrowed still more to go under a portcullis and through a tower which formed, with its two pointed arches, the double inner gate of the *enceinte*. And just inside that was another Renaissance house, with windows more beautiful still.

The whole thing made the most picturesque scene that my eyes had ever fallen upon. And it was all so *real*. All the mediæval history that I had ever studied and taught had come to life before me. Here was the Europe I had come to see. . . . Brinton Elliott, my painter friend, had told me that this fortress-village was almost a 'little Carcassonne'; like the peasant in the song, I never have seen Carcassonne; but as we drove through the triple gate of Neyronnes I felt that I need ask no more of perfection. This was enough.

And I was so fascinated, so absorbed, as the little village street stretched its short length before me between ancient tumble-down cottage walls, that I never saw a plain and prosaic building on my left, just beyond the little gardened space near the church that surrounded the tiny community's monument to its war dead. It was a building larger than the others, scarcely more than two hundred years old, not at all quaint, and in perfect repair. I saw it, as it happened, soon enough. And of course I did not know that Christine Wilde was standing in one of the upper windows of that plain building, telling her mother that Monsieur Delande seemed to be bringing a new guest to the inn. . . .

The car made its way slowly down the little street, honking as it approached a corner where it seemed to my unaccustomed eye that no turn could possibly be made. But my host swung quickly and easily around the curve and into an even narrower bit of road under the overhanging beamed façade of an extraordinarily fine fourteenth-century dwelling-house. And then, as we entered the Place des Halles of Neyronnes, I knew that my enthusiasm at the gate had been only a dim foretaste of the rapture which awaited me here. I have come to know since that, although mediæval town gates are no great rarity in France, such a *place* as that of Neyronnes is almost unique. At the time I just felt that this was too good to be true.

In the center of a broad cobbled square rose an enormous linden tree, outspreading its perfectly proportioned branches to form a thick canopy of protection as well as shade. Rustic chairs and tables looked homelike and inviting under the tree, but they were not what held my attention. On the opposite side of the square, as we turned into it, was an ancient crooked building with a wide beamed gallery like a veranda, and across a little cobbled alleyway from this engaging structure was a beautiful thirteenth-century house, perfect with its beams, its corbels, its small-paned windows, even the vines that grew in profusion about the entrance, and the girl in white lace cap and fichu who was leaning against the lintel of the door. At right angles, and farther back, was a smaller, plainer building, also beamed; and next to it stood another good old dwelling-house, with vines and a sundial; the narrow street by which we had entered ran along the side of this house. Behind us, too, was a row of three or four picturesque ancient houses, at the architectural details of which I did not then glance. Only on the fourth side of the *Place* was there any intrusion of the commonplace; and even here the heavy stone houses were not new, although the hand of 'modernization' in the way of doors and windows had not been arrested in time, and the buildings had probably never been as fine architecturally as their neighbors.

And yet, I felt then, and I have never ceased to feel, that the more or less ordinary quality of the fourth side of the broad *Place* at Neyronnes gave its own *cachet* of reality to the whole extraordinary scene: this was no show-piece, but the central square of a village where people lived; these houses were their homes, their shops, the inn, the museum. And later, as we visitors used to sit, according to our custom, in the roomy gallery under the overhanging upper story of the building that was the museum, we scarcely saw the 'modern' houses at all. We looked out at the *Place*, and the streets and paths which came into it, and the roofs of other buildings where the roads sloped downhill, and everything that we saw was picturesque to the point of being theatrical. Even to the movements of the peasants crossing the square with an occasional donkey, the old women and children who came to get water at the fountain in the corner farthest from us, the whole scene was like the stage at some fascinating play.

My host, whom I now knew as Monsieur Delande, drove around the square and stopped his car in front of the charming thirteenth-century building, which, to my astonishment and delight, I saw to be the inn. The girl with the white fichu had disappeared, and in a moment a buxom and very pretty young woman appeared in her stead. She was plump and smiling, like her husband, but what with him was heartiness became with her an unswerving calm; I never saw Madame Delande ruffled or harassed; neither she nor her husband ever looked tired. And yet, how hard they worked! And how much they had to try them, that summer when the United States went off the gold standard and a miscellaneous bunch of American tourists sought cheap living under their ancient hospitable roof!

Monsieur took out my bag. He drove his car into the mediæval building at one side, which was, I now saw, the inn's garage. The girl with the fichu came back, and it was explained to me that the single rooms with hot and cold running water were in the *pavillon annexe*, a few steps back, near the church, and that she would escort me there. It was also explained to me that if I stayed eight days or longer the rate for room and board complete would be thirty francs a day. And when I had signified my assent to all this, the girl with the fichu picked up my old Gladstone as easily as if it had been a woman's overnight bag and led me up another street, no wider than an alley, that wound between some fine old houses and the ruins of other fine old houses and then in a few yards came out somewhat surprisingly on the other little *place*, just inside the gate.

Here, facing the gate and the war memorial, and at right angles to the back of the church and the funny little *Mairie*, was the *pavillon annexe*. It was the plain, large, unromantic structure, probably of the early eighteenth century, which I had not noticed when we came in. Nothing could have looked less like my idea of a pavilion than this solid rectangular building; but it looked, as it was, comfortable. With its heavy walls within and without, it looked quiet, too.

The front door opened directly into a big uncarpeted room that had some good furniture in it, a center table with writing-materials, and on one side, under a window, a phonograph. The stairs led up from this room, and we climbed two flights. The maid showed me into a small, simple, neat, and not uninviting bedroom, set down my bag, and opened the shutters of the two windows. And even as she went out of the door I hurried to the front window and stood there for a long time looking at the view. Then, with the conscious deliberation born of deep satisfaction, I began to unpack. . . .

This was what I had been longing to find. It was genuine. It was interesting. It was peaceful. It was cheap. Here I would stay, and read, and study, and take long walks, and enjoy a real vacation, in solitude. It came over me suddenly that I had never had a 'real vacation,' in that sense, in my life. There had always been some worry, some burden, some distraction, the intrusion of some troublesome event. Here there was nothing. In spite of the fall of the dollar, there was nothing to worry me now, in this fascinating mediæval village where I could live in sufficient modern comfort for thirty francs a day!

I went back to the window, and looked out at the fortress gate, and the old church, and the ancient stone cottage with its outside flight of steps, across the way. Beyond the gate-tower other hillocks raised their soft green heights above the valley, and far away the distant mountains marked the horizon with their hazy blue rim. Peaceful. . .

And as I stood there drinking in the charm and restfulness of it all, a big automobile came from the direction of the inn, turned sharply into the little *Pace*, and stopped under my window, at the *pavillon* door. I looked at it idly; but I have the American's instinctive—I fear, irremediable—interest in motor cars: I had never been able to own one, but I had long ago learned to drive; and when I see an automobile I know, without stopping to think how, what kind of car it is. I had a queer little feeling, now, that my peace was threatened, that my remoteness was somehow broken in upon. It was a Packard car that was standing under my window in Neyronnes.

Of course I told myself at once that it was silly to be disturbed by that: an American make of car was no sign of the presence of Americans! A great many French people had American automobiles. Besides, Elliott had told me that Swiss travelers sometimes came to Neyronnes, and of course Switzerland teemed with American motor cars. I repeated to myself that there was no sense in being afraid that my solitude would be sacrificed to the presence of my fellow-countrymen. And just at that moment a girl stepped out of the car, a girl who was unmistakably American, and whose appearance filled me, astonishingly, with delight instead of a selfish dismay.

She was tall, and slender, and young, and very pretty. Soft hair caught the sunshine in golden lights in its masses of chestnut brown, and waved in graceful natural curls on a beautifully modeled sunburnt neck. Strong sunburnt arms were as firm and able-looking as they were well-formed and comely in her sleeveless dress of burnt-orange stuff. From the curve of her head to the line of her perfect ankles and her slender feet, every contour was lovely. And she was as unconscious as Queen Victoria, standing there.

I don't know exactly why I was so sure she was American: it may have been her ankles, and her feet in those well-cut sport shoes; it may have been her air of independence, along with competence and charm; when I looked more closely at her face, as she continued to stand there at the doorstep, I saw that her expression held none of the carefree happiness one likes to associate with pretty and well-to-do young American girls. Her big brown eyes troubled me: they not only looked anxious, smitten with a chronic anxiety; they looked somehow unnatural, as if she were trapped or caged. Independent, yes, in a sense. But not the happiest sense. Independent by nature, but certainly not free.

She just stood there quietly, for several minutes, while the engine of the car purred in its opulent quietness behind her. Then she spoke, raising her voice just a little to reach someone in the house.

"Aren't you ready?" she asked. "Do you want any help?"

On the floor below me a window opened, and out of it came a voice. "Oh, I've changed my mind," it said. It was a woman's voice, and it continued: "I don't want to go, after all. We couldn't get back in time for lunch."

"But I thought you wanted to lunch at a restaurant," the girl said. "And we had made the appointment at the hairdresser's."

"Well, I've changed my mind. Go and unmake the appointment. And will you tell Monsieur Delande that I cannot eat *écrivisses* with all that pepper in the sauce? I simply will not stay here if I can't get the food I want. But I feel tired. I don't want to take that long drive to the city. Put the car away."

The girl half-turned, hesitated an instant, quickly turned back.

"I might go anyway," she said. "I might take Miss Hamilton. She'd like it."

"And leave me to lunch here alone? Good Heavens, Christine, are you crazy? Anyhow, you've got to talk to Monsieur Delande about the food. Besides, Miss Hamilton is going to play Russian bank with me right after lunch. She couldn't go to the city and get back in time. You know I need someone to put me to sleep: she could not go, possibly. As for your going without me—I never heard of such a thing! You put the car away this minute, and then telephone to the hairdresser that I'm not coming. Then I think it wouldn't be a bad thing if you did my hair yourself, with that dry-shampoo stuff. Hurry up."

"All right, mother," the girl said, in an amiable, matter-of-course fashion, and turned toward the automobile again. But before she got into her luxurious equipage she walked around the engine and looked at it, not lifting the hood, but just regarding the front of the car; and the thing that I saw in her face was tenderness. It made me think of Lindbergh's 'We.' But it made me think of more than that. She was alone here, this girl Christine, with a selfish pig of a mother, and all she really had to love was her car.

And it did not occur to me to lament, now, that the solitude of Neyronnes was non-existent, and that there would be at least three English-speaking females living in the same house with me and chattering all over the place. It is quite true, and I confess it without shame, that at that moment and from that moment I had forgotten all about solitude, in thinking of the strange look in a girl's eyes—eyes brown and wide and unnaturally bright, set far apart below a broad forehead in a lovely pale face. If she had been happy, she would have been very beautiful, this girl Christine. As it was, she was a troubling creature: there was something about her that, in this first glimpse certainly, I could not understand.

II

I GREET OTHER REFUGEES

By the time I had finished unpacking, had filled in the police blank
which took the place of hotel registration, and had written a note
to Geneva to have my box of books sent on to me here, it was after
twelve o'clock. Except for Christine's appearance under my window, there had been nothing to molest the quiet of the morning: a
few cars had passed, some low French voices had sounded
undisturbingly from outside, there had been a few barely audible
movements within the house. At noon the bells in the church-tower
rang, with a deep, musical note, and in the fields out beyond the
ramparts I could indistinctly see people moving about.

Shortly before half-past twelve I locked the door of my room
behind me and walked down the street and around the sharp corner under the handsome fourteenth-century mansion, and so into
the *Place*. Madame my hostess was sitting at a table in front of the
inn door, and although she spoke no English she made me understand, as I approached her, that I might have luncheon either in
the house or on the veranda opposite, which she called the *galerie*.
I chose the *galerie*, and she said, "*Tout de suite*," and signaled to
the maid. And I went into the veranda and waited while my table
was being set.

It was not a veranda at all, but a broad space, as wide as a good-
sized American porch, under the built-out upper story of a six-
hundred-year-old house. The floor was of hard pebbled dirt, and
on the outside, between the supporting pillars, a wall had been built
up knee-high and set with bright geraniums in pots. Nasturtiums

33

grew in a bed along the veranda, and vines clambered up the side
of the house, with its plaster wall and old red beams. Sitting in the
wicker chairs of the *galerie*, behind that flowered proscenium, it
was exactly as if one looked out from a box at a play!

But when I went in to have my luncheon, there was no one there.
A table laid for one guest only stood at the far end, next to the
house wall. My own table was being set near the end closest to the
entrance, which was the end closest to the door of the inn. And I
was well along in my hors d'œuvres before the occupant of the
second table appeared.

I was thinking about the girl Christine, and not unnaturally I
was wondering whether I should see her at lunch, and also how
long it would be before, in the etiquette which obtains among traveling fellow-countrymen, I might venture to introduce myself to
her, when I heard a little scuffle on the dirt floor quite near me;
and, looking around hastily, I saw a dog. If I had been surprised
by the sight of the opulent Packard car and the lovely American
girl in the simple fastnesses of Neyronnes, I was scarcely less surprised by this dog. For I had never seen a dog quite like him; I had
rarely seen so noble a dog before.

His body was built much like an Irish terrier's, although a little
larger, but his hair was not rough and reddish, but almost silky,
and blue-black. He had a 'boxed jaw' and a handsome squared
beard, and about midway in his long and shapely head his eyes
looked out upon the world with an expression of deep thoughtfulness and the kindliest good-will. He had none of an Irish terrier's
look of pugnacity nor a Scotty's air of impenetrable reserve nor
the curious childlike attractiveness of a Sealyham, nor was he big
and powerful like an Airedale; but he seemed to me to possess the
most admirable charms of all these breeds; and he was far more
beautiful than any of them. I like dogs, and I've known a good many,
but this one was new to me. In any case, however, I was his firm
friend at first sight. He stopped, looked at me, wagged his tail, and
approached closer. From around the curve of the cobbled *ruelle*
someone spoke to him.

"Fergus," said a woman's voice, "you must remember that not everyone likes dogs."

"I do," I said, and jumped to my feet as the dog's mistress came into the *galerie*.

As I recall my instantaneous recognition of Miss Hamilton's voice as American—the natural instantaneous recognition of any American voice—I am conscious of a little wave of irritation over the so frequent implication that an 'American' voice is a voice which is uncultivated or harsh or drawling or in some way necessarily ugly. Many American voices are unpleasing, I know, just as many English voices are unpleasing; but the English language as spoken by an American of cultivation and good breeding is certainly as fair-sounding a thing as the English language can be; it was such a voice that I heard speaking now. The girl Christine and her mother had clear and well-modulated and attractive voices, too, even though the older woman's tones broke into such peevish notes. But Miss Hamilton's voice was really beautiful, and I expected to see a very personable, not to say impressive, individual come into the *galerie* in the wake of the handsome dog.

What I saw was a middle-aged woman of average height, insignificant features and coloring, tired gray eyes, dressed in an old-fashioned jacket suit that was actually ragged. Naturally I did not observe many details about her in that first moment, but even then I noticed that her coat was threadbare and had been darned. And even in that first quarter-hour I felt, rather than saw, that she was completely indifferent to her shabbiness. I had never seen an American woman who looked so poor, and I had never seen any human being who seemed more of an aristocrat.

She answered my somewhat impulsive remark.

"I'm glad you like dogs," she said, "but you mustn't let Fergus and me interrupt your luncheon. Sit down."

I continued to stand, and patted the dog's head.

"Won't you let me introduce myself?" I asked. And at that she smiled.

"They can't pronounce your name," she told me, "but I already know something about you. You are an American. You have just come from Switzerland. You like Neyronnes. You are going to stay awhile. Aurélie has told me all that already. Aurélie is the plump maid. She has also told me that you are *très gentil* and that she hopes Mrs. Wilde and Miss Wilde and I will find you *sympathique*." She laughed. "You didn't expect to meet any other Americans here, did you?"

"Well, no," I admitted. And she chuckled again.

"If you will have your table moved up to the other end, near mine," she suggested, "I will tell you about us while you eat your luncheon—while we eat our luncheon, I should say."

Whereupon, naturally, I picked up my little table and moved it myself. The waitress (there were only two maidservants in constant attendance at the Auberge de Vieux Neyronnes, and this was the other one) brought my neighbor's hors d'œuvres and rearranged my *couvert*. The dog stretched himself out beside his mistress's chair; and our tables were close enough together for conversation but not close enough to feel crowded. I thought it a pleasant arrangement.

"My name," said my neighbor, "is Margaret Hamilton. I fancy that I am perhaps a very little less than twice your age, and I come from New York. My *carte d'identité* declares that I am a woman without profession."

"My name," I responded, in the same Arabian-Nights fashion, "is Wayne Armitage. I am twenty-seven years old, and I teach history in a boys' school in Paoli, Pennsylvania."

"Ah," she remarked, "you are a little older than you look. But in the Middle Ages I might well have been your mother. As your history will have taught you, we married young in those days."

Her directness, and her little air of impersonal amusement, robbed this speech of any challenge to gallantry, and she did not wait, indeed, for any reply. She changed the subject, and went right on:

"Your compatriots in Neyronnes number three at present. All females. All stuck."

"Stuck?" I echoed. And she chuckled again. I was beginning to realize that amusement was never far from those gray eyes that looked so tired beneath her lined forehead and her graying drab-brown hair. And when she talked in her odd, gay, individual fashion, her mouth, which in repose was merely nondescript, became somehow almost fascinating, so alive was it, so alive did her whole face become.

"Stuck," she repeated. "Stranded. How are the mighty fallen—I mean the mighty dollars, my child. They are dropping to a new low . . ."

"Oh!" I cried, in sudden understanding. "That's why I'm here, too!"

"I thought," said Miss Hamilton, "that that was possible." And the tiny wrinkles played about her eyes and mouth as mirthfully as if they had been dimples, as mirthfully as if she had been care-free, and pretty, and young. Here was someone, certainly, who could contemplate the fall of the dollar, even the fact of being 'stranded,' with genuine amusement.

And then she held her hand aloft for a moment in the consumption of an olive, and I saw, more clearly than I had yet seen it, the fringiness about her cuff. I saw, too, that at the elbow the sleeve of her jacket would soon be worn through completely where it was already darned. I felt a little embarrassed all of a sudden, and, as so often happens in such cases, I took refuge in talking about myself. I told her about my stay in Geneva, and my hopes for a summer's traveling, and my selection of Neyronnes as a haven when the dollar went down; and she was sympathetic, and serious.

"You couldn't have made a better choice," she assured me. "I know France pretty well, and I don't know any place where you could get more real reward for so little money—in the kind of reality you want. Neyronnes is a perfectly fascinating spot; I come here often. And the inn is admirable: it is well-kept and comfortable, and the food is delicious. The Delandes are very nice people, and very kind. You'll love Neyronnes, I know, and everything about it. And, speaking of food, here come the *écrivisses*."

It was my introduction to those craw-dads of the mountain streams of France, which are served in so many different ways according to the specialty of the region, and I found them very tasty.

But at the moment I did not give this *pièce de résistance* the attention it deserved. The appearance of the *écrivisses* made me think of Christine's mother, and I found myself wondering, for the sake of Christine's peace of mind, whether they would be peppery. Mine were. And my new neighbor noticed that, too.

"They have two ways of doing the *écrivisses* here," she said. "This way uses a lot of pepper. But if there is too much for your individual taste, all you have to do is to say so, and the next time yours will be cooked with less seasoning. Almost all Mrs. Wilde's food is cooked specially for her. Mrs. Wilde," she added, "is an invalid."

I thought of the Packard.

"Stranded, too?" I asked.

"Oh, yes," Miss Hamilton answered easily. "The Wildes are stranded, too. The Wildes are 'absolutely broke.' If there is one thing that this *crise* has probably taught you already, Mr. Armitage, it is that there are marked degrees to absolute 'broke-ness.'"

Her voice was whimsical, but it was kind as well. I confess that for the moment I did not feel quite sure what she was talking about. All I could think of to say was that it must be very hard to be worried about money when one was ill.

"Yes," she said, "it must be. Mrs. Wilde is a very pathetic woman. I am hoping," she went on, in her lovely voice, "that your being here will pep her up a bit."

What I felt was a quick resentment at being expected to pep up Mrs. Wilde. From what I had heard of her conversation, from what it had told me of her attitude toward her child and her neighbors, I wished only to give Mrs. Wilde a good hard slap—and since that was manifestly impossible, a good cold shoulder. But of course I could see that she was pathetic: an invalid, in exile, suffering, suddenly poor . . .

"I had hoped," Miss Hamilton continued, "that Fergus would entertain her. But unfortunately she isn't interested in dogs."

At the sound of his name, Fergus looked up and yawned pleasantly. And as I agreed that it was indeed unfortunate for anyone not to be interested in canines, I took the liberty of asking what kind of dog Fergus was.

"A Kerry blue terrier," his mistress answered. "I got him in England five years ago. I'll spare you the list of his ancestors' and relations' championships, and just tell you at once that he himself has never been shown. He is simply my pet dog, and a good one—though he's a trifle big to live in one room in a hotel. When I got him my life was—er—less confined. But," she added cheerfully, without a pause, "he is very adaptable. He is always well-behaved, and I think he is happy."

Well, I thought to myself, Miss Hamilton loved her dog. The girl Christine loved her car. And Christine's mother? Christine's mother loved nothing in the world but Mrs. Wilde, I was already prepared to guess.

A few cars were driving one by one into the *Place*, coming by the narrow street which was the only entrance for vehicles, circling the big linden, parking on the grass plot by the fourth side of the square, and depositing their passengers to go into the house for luncheon or pause under the tree for *apéritifs*.

"Neyronnes is famous among the French, although very few foreigners know about it," Miss Hamilton remarked. "There are often a good many people here on Saturday and Sunday, and after the fourteenth of July—or rather, beginning with the fourteenth of July—there is a real 'summer season,' and the *auberge* is usually full. But now it is very quiet: nobody at the inn except us poor Americans. We have some interesting resident neighbors, though. That beautiful house on the corner, as you come into the *Place*, is the summer home of a very charming countess who was born near here. It is the realest restoration I have ever seen—if only they could have done Carcassonne like that! And on the *chemin de ronde*—"

She broke off suddenly. Christine Wilde came out of the inn, brilliant in her orange dress against the shadowy interior, and crossed the cobbles and the *galerie*, swiftly, to our tables.

"Miss Hamilton," she began, without apology, "mother says, will you please come and play Russian bank with her just as soon as you finish your luncheon?"

"Certainly," said Miss Hamilton, and rose at once. "Is she ready now? I'll come right away. May I present Mr. Armitage? Miss Wilde will tell you more about Neyronnes, Mr. Armitage. I was just beginning, Christine, with some of the handsome houses on the *chemin de ronde*."

"Oh." Miss Wilde's monosyllable sounded absentminded, and, I thought, none too pleased. Miss Hamilton went into the inn, with her dog at her heels, and Christine sat down abruptly.

"Miss Hamilton is awfully nice. She is so kind to mother," she said. "My mother," she added, "is an invalid. And naturally she gets a trifle bored in a quiet little place like this. She will be glad to meet you, I am sure, Mr.— what is your name? Oh, Armitage? Thank you. As I was saying, Mr. Armitage, I am sure she will be glad to meet you. It will give her a new interest."

I felt, this time, quite definitely annoyed. It was not that I was unwilling to be kind to a chance acquaintance who was so unfortunate as to be an invalid. It was that both Miss Hamilton and Christine spoke as if entertaining Mrs. Wilde would naturally constitute my first and keenest desire . . .

Had I come to a walled village in the middle of France to give a new interest to a selfish sick woman, I asked myself? I'd be hanged if I had! And I was about to change the subject as pointedly as politeness would allow, when I caught again the troubled look in the girl's bright eyes.

"I shall be very glad to meet your mother," I said, instead. And Christine answered as if that were a matter of course.

"Oh, yes," she said, "everyone is. My mother is very charming, Mr. Armitage. Everyone adores her."

I though of the conversation I had overheard.

"Perhaps she will let me keep her company sometimes when you are out in your car," I ventured. But at that Christine looked puzzled.

"Out in the car?" she echoed. "But I don't go out in the car without my mother, except for little errands, and they never take long. It is quite true," she added weightily, "that mother doesn't care much for going on little drives herself, so we don't use the car a great deal. But of course I never take it out for pleasure unless my mother goes along."

"Well," I began, knowing that what I wanted to say sounded silly, but feeling that Christine's entertainment was almost as important as her mother's, and determined to put my oar in somehow, "I confess that when I saw that big car of yours, and saw that you drove it, I was seized with the feverish hope that you might be so kind as to show me a little of the country—with Miss Hamilton, if your mother didn't feel like going, too . . ."

"Oh, no!" cried Christine. Then, showing a little normal embarrassment on the heels of this almost automatic reaction, she gave a rather awkward little laugh. "Please excuse me. I didn't mean to be rude. Of course I see your point of view. But of course I couldn't go for a drive without my mother, and, as I told you, she doesn't enjoy motoring very much. Mother doesn't like me to take Miss Hamilton, even when I go on an errand," she added in a matter-of-course fashion, "because, you see, that leaves her quite alone, and that is so hard for her."

I gave up.

"If there is any way in which I can be of service to your mother, I shall be very glad," I lied, and I was rewarded by a hint of real friendliness in Christine's absent-minded smile.

But, needless to say, I was not enjoying this conversation! I was glad to welcome another interruption. This was the appearance of Miss Hamilton once more in the doorway, and with her a radiant vision: a woman whose age might have been anywhere from twenty-five to forty or so, whose chestnut-brown hair waved back beautifully from a broad, low, unlined forehead, whose cheeks and lips were barely touched with make-up that was applied with an artist's hand, and whose exquisitely smart blue frock brought out deep and lovely tones in her gray-blue eyes. French, of course, I said to myself—frankly glad to see anyone so vivid and attractive, for as a companionable neighbor Christine had proved a disappointment—a French fellow-boarder, and a very charming one. . . And then the newcomer spoke one word.

"Christine," she said.

And as I got to my feet I actually stumbled in my astonishment. That was the voice that had spoken from the window. This was Christine's invalid mother . . .

She came into the *galerie*, followed by Miss Hamilton—who, it is unnecessary to point out, looked more than ever shabby and middle-aged and insignificant—and by Miss Hamilton's handsome dog. And although she had spoken to her daughter, it was toward me that she advanced, and to me that she held out her hand, while her face lighted up with the most cordial and animated of smiles.

"I am so glad to meet you, Mr. Armitage," she said. "I introduce myself, you see, and I welcome you to Neyronnes. I have just been hearing about you from our other compatriot"—she indicated Miss Hamilton with an affable gesture—"and I am sure you will agree with me that we must all be friends together, we forgotten Americans." She paused rather dramatically, and Miss Hamilton gave a deprecatory chuckle.

"Oh, come now," she interposed. "It isn't so bad as that—'forgotten Americans . . .'"

Mrs. Wilde raised her hand and let it fall again, both to command silence and to emphasize her pronouncement.

"Oh, yes, it is!" she declared. "We are all forgotten Americans together, Mr. Armitage. It may not be so bad for you—you are a man. But the rest of us are forgotten women, Mr. Armitage, forsaken and stranded by that mad Democratic administration, in this beastly country that defaults on its debts."

Miss Hamilton had ceased to chuckle. Her face was set in rather hard lines, and as I glanced at her standing there behind the radiant vision that was Christine Wilde's mother, I was surprised to note that her cheeks were flushed, and that she looked as if she were having a hard time to disguise her feelings. It came over me for the first time—and I remembered it later—that self-control, for Margaret Hamilton, was not so easy as she made it appear.

"Don't let us begin with controversial subjects," she said very quietly. "I am sure that Mr. Armitage doesn't want to plunge into an international argument before he has been in France twenty-four hours. And you know that I don't agree with your feeling on either of those points, Mrs. Wilde." She smiled now, gaily again. "Let's keep the peace," she concluded. And Mrs. Wilde smiled too.

"Oh, I always want to keep the peace," she averred. "I am a most good-natured woman, Mr. Armitage, and absolutely unbiased in my judgments. But I really must warn you, in the most good-natured way, that Miss Hamilton is positively pro-French; I tell her it is nothing short of unpatriotic. But I will tell you right in front of her that I never allow her wrong ideas to stand in the way of our friendship. I always make a point of looking at both sides of a question, myself. Don't you think that is best, Mr. Armitage? Indeed, as I sometimes say to my little girl, I don't know how I could endure my sad life if I hadn't cultivated the power to see other people's points of view. And I want to tell you that I am very fond of Miss Hamilton, even if she does stand up for Roosevelt and actually like the French!"

I really felt very much embarrassed, and rather put upon; and I decided that the best way for me to receive this silly speech was to treat it as a joke. All the same, I wasn't going back on my convictions nor yet on Miss Hamilton. So I laughed, and said, "So do I," as lightly and as firmly as I could. And then I added, "And I hope that you will be generous enough to like me, in spite of my opinions, too. Are you," I went on, before she could interrupt me, "staying long in Neyronnes?"

"I fear so," she said. "I am the prisoner of poverty. I am absolutely broke. I am one of the victims of this terrible depression, Mr. Armitage. I am staying for some weeks at Neyronnes because the inn is cheap. Of course it is not at all what my little girl and I are used to, as I am sure you understand. But my little girl is happy wherever I am—she is one of those fortunate children whose mother can be a real companion to her, Mr. Armitage. Don't you feel sorry for children whose mothers cannot share their youth? When my little girl says that her mother is her best friend, I know that she is telling the simple truth. And of course that makes it easy for her to endure life in this place. But it is not so easy for me, Mr. Armitage. If I were not naturally unselfish and uncomplaining, I really do not know how I could stand my misfortunes—I really do not know . . ."

She went on and on. Her voice flowed like some unceasing stream of bright, hard, molten metal. It had no softness in it. I had the feeling that it had almost no sense. And of course it had become apparent to me that Mrs. Wilde was as far from being 'absolutely broke' as she was from being unselfish and uncomplaining.

As I set down even this much of our conversation, I realize that it may seem altogether trivial and irrelevant. But it is not that, really. For in those first chatty exchanges we all learned a good deal about each other, became fairly well acquainted. And I do want, if I can, to present some picture of us first comers as we were at Neyronnes on my first day there, before anyone had any inkling of tragedy. For when tragedy came it engulfed all four of us—Mrs. Wilde, so utterly selfish, so obvious; Margaret Hamilton, who seemed not to be selfish, and who was certainly very far from obvious; the girl Christine, whose youth was being crushed out of existence by her mother's steam-roller egotism; and even the innocent and puzzled stranger that was myself . . .

III

I OVERHEAR A CONVERSATION

Naturally enough, I took a dislike to Mrs. Wilde, with her smart clothes and her well-cared-for complexion and her 'animated' ways. Self-conscious, self-righteous, self-centered, absolutely self-absorbed, she seemed never to give a thought to her daughter, or to anyone else. Christine existed merely, one would have concluded, to wait upon her mother, and to flatter her at the same time; and the real tragedy of the situation lay in the fact that Christine seemed long ago to have reached that conclusion herself. Even Miss Hamilton seemed to me to exaggerate Mrs. Wilde's helplessness and pathos, the necessity for being 'kind' to her, for indulging her constantly.

I was forced to admit to myself that Mrs. Wilde had a certain attractiveness; no one could deny that she was 'easy to look at'; and she had a kind of vividness, along with her self-assurance, which gave her naturally the center of the stage. If she had not been such an egotist, she might have been really charming, I thought, in a superficial sort of way. But I did not find her pathetic: I found her detestable. She was worse than a steamroller. She was a vampire.

But, mercifully, she troubled me very little. The worst of my selfish fears were not realized: I was not called upon to supply Christine's mother with a new interest, nor even to pep her up. We got acquainted with each other, as I have said, in the middle of my first day at Neyronnes. But when Mrs. Wilde and Miss Hamilton went off to play Russian bank, and Christine announced that she was going to oil the car, I was left to myself, and I continued to be left to myself through the next few days. I strolled out, that afternoon, to 'poke about' in Neyronnes, and I had a magnificent time. When I came back to the *Place*, at half-past four or so, Christine, in overalls and a jumper, was coming out of the garage, and she laughed in a girl's gay, unself-conscious fashion as she held out grimy hands for me to see.

"I've just finished," she said. "It's only the little five-hundred-mile oiling, but it's a dirty job. I love it," she added. "Don't you like to get good and dirty, fussing around a car?" And when I admitted that I didn't share that ideal of pleasure, she said, quite simply and naturally, "I adore it. It makes me feel so free."

This, certainly, was a different Christine. This was the real one, a thoroughly normal human being. . . I should have liked to go on talking with her now—an oil-stained girl in overalls—but she remarked immediately that she must go and clean up, and she slipped into the side door of the inn and disappeared.

There were several unexpected passages and ways in and out, around that *auberge* at Neyronnes. I took the more obvious route, by the curving *ruelle*, and I did not meet Christine, nor see or hear her in the *pavillon*.

And the days that followed were quiet and charming. I almost always met Miss Hamilton at mealtimes, and we chatted pleasantly on subjects that were usually completely impersonal. The Wildes ate in the picturesque low-ceilinged room that was the *salle à manger* of the inn, and I saw them very little and spoke with them scarcely at all.

A good many French people came and went during the daytime, and three days after my arrival a scholarly-looking man with the ribbon of the Legion of Honor in his buttonhole came to stay. He drove up in a small roadster, before luncheon, and settled himself in one of the first-floor rooms of the *pavillon*. Miss Hamilton told me that his name was Henri de Brassac, and that he was very particular about having a room on the garden side of the house—not on the street.

"So Madame has put him in the double room next to the Wildes," she said. "It's a big quiet room, under the unfinished part of the second story, and they have taken out the other bed: I hope that he is paying an extra price for a double room and staying an extra long time. It seems that the single rooms on the second floor, the only single rooms that would have suited him, are both engaged from tomorrow. As a matter of fact," she added, "it will be much quieter for Mrs. Wilde to have just one man next to her, unless he turns out to be noisy. He doesn't look noisy, does he?"

He didn't. He looked, and was, almost completely silent. Miss Hamilton, with her perfect French and her friendly manners, exchanged a few formal sentences with him on the day after his arrival. But although polite he was certainly not gregarious. Mrs. Wilde ignored him. I think she was prepared automatically to dislike whoever had the room next to hers. She and Christine had the biggest room in the hotel, an enormous chamber with two windows on the garden and one on the street, and to the moment of the Frenchman's advent they had been alone on the first floor.

And yet, on one of my first nights at Neyronnes, I could have sworn that I heard sounds in or near the empty storage-loft on that floor, in the middle of the night.

There was a glorious full moon, and I had taken to strolling around Neyronnes fairly late, to get the effect of the walls and the gates and the old buildings in the moonlight. On this particular evening there was a party of some sort in the main building of the inn, and there were a good many people moving about the little citadel. But along about half-past ten it suddenly came on to rain; there was a scattering of the party's guests and a sudden procession of cars out of the village; and I, having been down on the hillside, well below the ramparts, had a steep run to get home.

As I passed the kitchen, I saw both the maids cleaning up after the party, and, as I looked up at the windows of the *pavillon*, I happened to notice that they were all dark. From the street there was a side door into an ancient building which adjoined the *pavillon* and was used as a sort of storage annex to it, and I had

already learned to use this as an entrance to the *pavillon* garden—
one could go straight through a stone-flagged room where the garden furniture was stored, and out another door into the garden
itself. And I remembered Miss Hamilton's telling me that there
were stairs from the ground-floor up to a somewhat neglected storage-room on the first story of the ancient annex, and that there a
door had been cut in the house wall into the first-floor corridor of
the *pavillon* itself. The room occupied by the maid Aurélie also
opened out of this storage-room in the older house.

By the time I approached the *pavillon*, it was raining so hard
that I wished I knew how to find that sheltered short-cut. But it
seemed best not to risk explorations in the darkness, so I went
along the street side of the house as usual and around to the front
door. I looked up and saw that the Wildes' room was unlighted.
Inside, even the hall light had been turned out—that surprised me—
and I had the feeling that everyone in the building was sound
asleep. But as I climbed the first flight of stairs, I thought I heard
the sound of someone, or something, moving at the back end of
the house.

It seemed to me that there was a person there who was trying
not to make a sound, and who was almost, but not quite, succeeding. At the head of the stairs I stopped and listened, but the slight
noise had ceased. I walked down to the door that led into the older
building, and stood still. There was no longer any sound of movement, but it seemed to me that I heard heavy, troubled breathing
somewhere. I almost tried the door in the house wall, or the doors
of the nearest bedrooms. But after all, I told myself, there was nothing alarming in these sounds—neither the actual suggestion of a
marauder nor anything that might be taken as an appeal for help—
and this was a hotel . . .

Besides, the maid Aurélie would have had plenty of time to
come in by the back way from the kitchen, and these were just the
kind of sounds that she would make if she were out of breath from
hurry and trying not to disturb anyone—I did not realize, then, how
thick those walls were! I decided that I should only make myself
look foolish if I tried to butt in anywhere, and I went back along

the hall and up the stairs toward my room. I am not afraid of burglars or of ghosts, but I do hate to look absurd! I felt more sure of myself when, as I passed Miss Hamilton's door on the way to my own, I heard the dog Fergus give a low growl. And I went to my room and went to sleep.

But the next day I did go to the trouble of finding out that there had been no extra guest in the inn that night. And Miss Hamilton happened to mention that Aurélie had complained of having been kept working in the kitchen until after midnight. I ended up by reminding myself that a stranger could not feel called upon to explain every sound he might think he heard in a hotel at night, especially if the hotel were an old and oddly planned building, as this one was.

And then the next day, on a morning which had dawned fresh and lovely after rain, as it often did at Neyronnes, the Frenchman Henri de Brassac came. And on the afternoon of the day after that, we welcomed the Sherrills. I never mentioned to anyone the sounds of the night. And in a few days I was ready to admit that I must have imagined them.

The arrival of the Sherrills was pleasantly dramatic. It was Friday, always a quiet day at Neyronnes, and I had taken a notion to have tea under the linden tree and had asked Miss Hamilton to join me. Miss Hamilton continued to be a good deal of a mystery to me, moving like a princess in her complete unconsciousness of her poverty-stricken appearance, and giving out so much information on the subject of everything and everybody except herself. I enjoyed talking with Miss Hamilton, and I had told myself that I wanted to talk with her further about Neyronnes—the history, or legend, of the grim towered structure, for example, that was known as the prison-house.

But as we sat down to our agreeable little English tea, I realized that the subject I truly wished to discuss was Christine Wilde. I had seen her very little, and thought about her a great deal. I was terribly puzzled and distressed about her. Not Miss Hamilton's own untold story, not the picturesqueness nor the past of Neyronne's, held my imagination as did this lovely caged bird of a girl . . .

"How long has Mrs. Wilde been an invalid?" I asked abruptly and without apology.

And somewhat to my surprise Miss Hamilton answered, "I don't know."

"I never saw the Wildes until eight weeks ago," she went on. "During the last two summers I have spent a good deal of time at Neyronnes, and just after I got here this spring Mrs. Wilde and her daughter came. Mrs. Wilde was very much upset about her financial losses, and then the fall of the dollar on top of that. She said the state of her health was such that she did not want to take the long journey to America, so she was looking for some place where she could live cheaply in France. It seems obvious, too, that she has lived so long in Europe that she has got out of touch with things in the United States, and she seems to have no friends or family there now. She is one of those passionately patriotic expatriates who is always bragging about her own country and hating the country she's in; but that," Miss Hamilton commented, "is just a type. One is always stubbing one's toe on them in France. Mrs. Wilde seems to have been in poor health for some years. So far as I have gathered, she is the widow of a naval officer. Christine, it seems, was taken out of school four years ago, when her father died—she was sixteen then—and she has been wandering about Europe with her mother ever since. They both speak four foreign languages fluently, and they are well acquainted with every fashionable health resort on the continent of Europe. They don't go to England, because they don't like the climate. Now, you see, they are economizing."

"But Christine!" I ejaculated. "How frightfully rough on her! The poor child seems—"

I never got the words out, about what Christine seemed; and perhaps it was just as well. At that moment a small motor car came into the square, and a woman's voice cried out, above the gentle sound of the engine,

"But, John, this isn't *possible!*"

The car came to a standstill behind Miss Hamilton, and I could see what she could not an exceedingly charming woman, dark-haired, youngish, and very much alive, who put her head out of the car window and looked about her, without moving, otherwise, at all.

"There is no such thing!" she cried, again. "We're dreaming it!"

The Kerry blue terrier, who had been lying quietly, as usual, at Miss Hamilton's feet, jumped up, surprisingly, and made an almost puppyish dash toward the strange automobile. And,

"Why, here's a dog like Fergus!" the charming young woman said.

Miss Hamilton sprang from her chair, turned around, and flung herself toward the newcomers as rapturously as had Fergus himself. The young woman jumped out of the car. A man's voice cried,

"Hullo! Hullo! Hullo!"

"It *is* Margot!" the strange young woman exclaimed, and threw her arms around Miss Hamilton's neck.

"It *is* Elinor!" Miss Hamilton laughed, and there was a personal happiness in her lovely voice that I had not heard there before. "How do you do, John?" she went on, and the man got out of the automobile and shook hands with her, less impulsively, but with a pleasure that was just as plain to see.

He was a tall, spare, dark-eyed man, who looked distinguished without looking conspicuous, and I was instantly glad to see him. And, from that first moment of their arrival, the Sherrills were good for us all.

It was good for Miss Hamilton to be with her old friends—friends of the days when she had not been shabby, when there had been no incongruity in her possession of a magnificent thoroughbred dog, when her hair had not begun to turn gray. It was good for me to have another English-speaking man to talk with. And it was the Sherrills who succeeded in providing Christine with a little holiday. What Mrs. Wilde would never have thought of granting to Christine's own request, what she would have refused to concede to Miss Hamilton's pleading or to my argument, she gave readily enough to the first suggestion from the well-known novelist John Sherrill and his exquisite wife: she let them take Christine with them to Tournus and Cluny.

But I am getting ahead of my story . . . What Mrs. Sherrill said next was that Neyronnes seemed incredible.

And Miss Hamilton answered, "Why, of course, Elinor, that is what everyone says!"

Then I was introduced to the strangers, and the suitcases were dumped out on the cobbles, and Madame and Monsieur came out to greet their new guests, and the smart little coupé was driven into the garage. But when Madame asked if the newcomers wished to go to their rooms, Mrs. Sherrill, whose French was as perfect as Miss Hamilton's own, declared that she didn't want ever to leave the Place des Halles, and couldn't they just have tea?

And Mr. Sherrill said, in English,

"We've engaged our rooms ahead, so why bother?"

So we all sat down together and fresh tea came, and we really had an awfully good time. Henri de Brassac strolled past us, coming up the steep path from the Lower Gate and the Promenade des Lices, but he did not speak to us, and I thought he looked bored at the sight of more Americans. The Sherrills explained that they had arrived on the *De Grasse* ten days ago, and had driven by easy stages to Neyronnes, where they intended to stay awhile.

"We had planned this summer in France and Italy, and when the country went off the gold standard we made up our minds to come anyway, and just stay put somewhere," Elinor Sherrill said. "John knew about Neyronnes, so here we are. Isn't it heavenly?"

She was younger than Miss Hamilton, and far, far more prosperous. Even in these last years of upheaval, life had been fairly easy for Elinor Sherrill, I guessed, where Margaret Hamilton had found it hard. But it was clear that these three Americans had come, originally, from the same stratum of American life: they were very different as individuals, but, as the saying is, they spoke the same language. And I was more pleased than I can say that they seemed to accept me as a real neighbor, almost as one of themselves. I wished that Christine might be having tea with us, away from her selfish, silly, impossible mother. But with that one cloud upon my contentment, I was well satisfied with our *partie carrée*.

And when the Sherrills met Christine, that evening, they liked her. And I could see almost at once that they were planning something that would give her a bit of a breathing-spell.

Before they had it, however, I had an embarrassing experience. I was the unwilling auditor, that very evening, of a conversation which, later, I would have given anything I possessed not to have heard . . .

It was simple enough, the incident. I was making one of my evening prowls about Neyronnes, and I sat down, as often, on the grass below the drop of the ruined outer rampart, near the arch of the Lower Gate. The Promenade des Lices lay between the gate and the crumbling outer wall, and often of an evening young men and maidens walked about there, or sat and held each other's hands on the bench near the gate itself. Although I knew I couldn't be seen, I never moved or paid any attention when people passed by or stopped near where I was sitting. Even if they talked to each other, I couldn't understand a word they said.

So, that evening, I didn't feel troubled when I caught the approach of light footsteps in the *Lices* behind me, although the hour was a little advanced for the home-keeping folk of Neyronnes to be wandering about. And when I recognized the voices of the speakers, it was too late for me to move. They were sitting on the bench just behind me. I was sheltered only by a bit of vine-grown wall. If I had stood up, or even tried to crawl away, I should have been seen; and it seemed to me important that the speakers should not know that even the first sentence had been overheard. Better to stay where I was, I told myself, and hope that they would move away, or change the subject, soon.

"So, you see, clothes don't matter any more, Elinor," Margaret Hamilton's beautiful voice sounded clearly in my ear. "When one is quite desperate, as I am, one just keeps one's mind on essentials, and gets along as best one can from day to day."

"Oh, Margot, dear—*desperate!*" cried Mrs. Sherrill; and Miss Hamilton went on, evenly:

"That's what it seems to me. I have an annuity of seven hundred dollars a year. That is all there is left, except a very small amount of cash on hand from the sale of the last of my bonds, and that is going fast. Everything else is gone. I don't know where it went. I wish to Heaven I'd spent it. If I had wasted my substance on riotous living, I should have some extra-special fun to remember, presumably. But it's all just gone, swallowed up, disappeared. The bank says that in time a little may come back on some of it, but that doesn't seem to me to be a very practical hope—it isn't a hope that the bank is willing to take any risks on, certainly.

"And you see, Elinor," Miss Hamilton added, "when you are forty-five years old, and prematurely gray, and not very strong, and have no profession and no business experience of any sort, you can't exactly hope to get a remunerative job. I haven't any rich relations who will remember me in their wills, either," she continued, speaking for the first time a little bitterly, "much less help me now. I haven't even any home to go to. The good old days are gone. I'm just finished, done for, Elinor, unless something turns up; funny, how one finds oneself waiting for something to turn up—and of course nothing ever does. But—well, one gets along as best one can. What was it young Jolyon said—'To be kind and keep one's end up, what else is there?' That's the way I feel. And it does me a lot of good to see you and John, Elinor, dear. I hope you'll stay awhile."

"I think we shall," said Mrs. Sherrill. But she did not allow herself to be led away from the subject in hand.

"Margot—I can't bear the thought of your 'waiting for something to turn up.' Isn't there anything we can do?"

"No, darling," Miss Hamilton declared firmly, "there isn't. I thank you with all my heart, Elinor. And I will promise you this: if I lose my seven hundred dollars a year and there is absolutely nothing between me and the bread-line, I'll come to you before I think of jumping into the river. But short of that, I'm not going to borrow money I could never pay back, and I'm not going to sponge on my friends, especially when they are hard hit themselves, as I know you and John are, though you are both such good sports you never say so. No, Elinor, theft or murder seems more self-respecting than that. And I've got to keep my self-respect," she added. "It's almost all I have left."

"Self-respect and courage," said Mrs. Sherrill softly. "I think you have a good deal, Margot. But that won't feed or clothe you, worse luck. And, tell me, too if you stay here month after month in a remote little place like this, doesn't the monotony and loneliness get on your nerves?"

"No, curiously enough, it really doesn't. I enjoy looking on, you know. There's a good deal to look on at even in a little place like this. And I love Neyronnes itself, and the walks I take; I never get tired of it, truly. So far, too, I've been able to get hold of a good many books—lucky I read French, isn't it? And, you know, Elinor, I've been pretty busy this last month just trying to be nice to that poor Mrs. Wilde and her daughter. I *am* sorry for her—for them both. One is glad to do what one can."

"I suppose so." Mrs. Sherrill was apparently not much interested in Mrs. Wilde. Then, to my surprise, she added, "I like that American boy, the young teacher who's stranded here."

"Yes, he's nice," Miss Hamilton agreed pleasantly. "Well, I certainly do hope that you and John will be able to endure our quiet life for a few weeks. *Courage, mes vieux . . .*"

"Courage"—Elinor Sherrill repeated the word in English.

"'Courage is but a word; and yet, of words,
    The only sentinel of permanence . . .'

That is just you, Margot."

"Thank you," Miss Hamilton responded, "but—'permanence': I'm not so sure, Elinor. What troubles me most about this—this turning upside down of all my world—is the effect it has on my mind and spirit, on the real me, you know. . . . I never thought of myself as dependent on money—I could get along on very little, I know, if I could just be fairly sure of firm ground under my feet. But this complete upheaval—it does queer things to me: it almost frightens me; sometimes I feel as if I understood the strangest depths of life, the strangest impulses. A sense of desperation seems to sweep away *everything*, somehow—not only material luxuries, material necessities, but one's sense of values, almost one's sense of right and wrong . . ." She broke off suddenly, and when she spoke again it was in a different tone. "Thank you for quoting Galsworthy to me, and for believing in me, Elinor. That helps—you don't know how it helps. I keep saying that I won't be downed by material things—you give me courage to say it again . . ."

She had risen from the bench, and I heard their light steps fade away up the hill as they walked back toward the village. I sat still for a long time on the grass below the rampart, thinking that I ought to try to forget the personal revelations I had heard, and knowing that I never could—that I really did not want to. At that moment, I felt glad to have got a better understanding of Miss Hamilton.

IV
I MEET HORACE BRAYE

The Sherrills asked Miss Hamilton to share a table with them in the *galerie*, and I was glad to see that they always had wine for luncheon and dinner, and that Mr. Sherrill always filled Miss Hamilton's glass. I drank the red wine of the country, myself, and it was only five francs a bottle. But Miss Hamilton had not been having wine, and I guessed that she liked it—that it was one of the amenities she had been used to. I had of course realized that Miss Hamilton had been accustomed to 'better days'—to far better days than I, for instance, had ever known. And for all her beautiful patrician dignity, I had guessed that she did not find poverty easy. As for the Sherrills, they had been forced to a new economy, too, and from being relatively rich they had now become relatively poor; but they never talked about it. The only person who talked about poverty was Mrs. Wilde.

In no conversation, however brief, did she neglect to mention the fact—or, I should say, the fiction that she was 'broke.' And yet, that did not prevent her speaking scornfully of people who were actually poor. She even made a condescending reference, once or twice, to the Sherrills' little Chevrolet, although she was enough of an intellectual snob to treat the Sherrills with great respect as a rule. To me, she paid little attention; after her first affable greeting she seemed to have dismissed me as of no account; and after that short exchange of a few words at the garage door, her daughter and I had no personal conversation whatever. Yet the Sherrills, like Miss Hamilton, were always considerate to Mrs. Wilde and her invalidism, and it did sometimes happen that we all had coffee together in the *galerie*. That was what we were doing on Saturday evening, and the rest of us sat silent and peaceful while Mrs. Wilde prattled of herself and her misfortunes and her opinions and her poverty.

After an afternoon given over to many rural sightseers, Neyronnes and its Place des Halles were quiet in the long evening twilight. And I, for one, was willing to let Mrs. Wilde talk on, so long as I might be allowed just to watch the scene before me. A woman drove a donkey-cart across the *Place*. Two little girls came in from one of the corner *ruelles* with a pot of milk between them, and carried it cautiously across the cobbles to one of the more beautiful of the mediæval houses on the other side of the square.

The big *Place* could be entered only at the corners: only one of these corner pathways was wide enough for a motor car, and only one other, the steep descent to the Lower Gate, would admit the passage of even a small donkey-cart. Peasants and villagers moved very slowly to and fro. And the whole scene, in the gently fading light, against the background of the noble old houses, was, as Mrs. Sherrill had said, "incredible." I even forgot to feel anxious about Christine Wilde: and I allowed myself to think that she, too, was enjoying this quiet immemorial pageant. To her mother, I simply was not listening; I think that no one was. Our peace was broken only by the arrival of a motor car. It was an enormous Lincoln, and it got around the corner and into the *Place* with some difficulty.

John Sherrill groaned. "Here," he announced, "comes another American family who crossed by the French Line."

"With a car like that, they won't stay in Neyronnes," his wife murmured comfortingly.

But Mrs. Wilde fairly shrieked in admiration. "Why, Mr. Sherrill, you're just like Sherlock Holmes! How do you know?"

He chuckled. "You do me too much honor, dear Madame Watson," he said. "I know they are Americans because they have the A.A.A. badge on their car. I know—or I guess—that they crossed on the French Line because they have the license letter and series number that the French Line gives you when you drive out of Havre. And I hope that Elinor is right and that they are too prosperous for Neyronnes. I don't like their looks."

Neither did I. The car had stopped in front of the inn now, and we could plainly see the man and woman who were its only occupants. And when the man opened his mouth and spoke, we liked him still less.

But to say that he spoke is to make an under-statement. He was purple with anger and exhaustion, and he bellowed.

"God damn this place!" he roared. "Why don't they tear down those good-for-nothing houses and make a decent road!"

"Oh, Horace," wailed a timid voice from this person's companion, "that would cost an awful lot of money. Don't you suppose they're just too poor?"

He was a bull-like individual, and this remark was a red rag. I jumped at once to the conclusion that remarks from his life's comrade often were.

"*Poor!*" he ejaculated. "*Poor!* The *French?* My God, you poor fish, the French are the only people on earth who have any money left, the bloodsuckers! And now that we've got to this God-forsaken place up this damned hill, I'll bet they'll hold us up for our last cent for a room with a bath, damn them . . ."

What with rage and fatigue, he snorted as he bellowed. But his speech, of which we could hear every word, affected his different listeners quite differently.

Margaret Hamilton gave an irrepressible little giggle and whispered, "There isn't a room with a bath in the place, thank Heaven!"

Mrs. Wilde, on the other side of me, said, quite audibly, "Oh, the poor man! What will they do?"

Mrs. Sherrill, Christine, and I all sat silent. But as Madame Delande appeared in the doorway and smiled her most gracious hospitality upon the newcomers, John Sherrill got up and walked very quickly to the car, from which the bull-like personage was now preparing to descend.

"How do you do?" he said, and his voice and manner were models of the most urbane affability. "Monsieur Delande, who speaks

English perfectly, happens to be away at this moment. May your fellow-countrymen welcome you?"

If the big man's rage had been funny, the complete and sudden transformation in his mood was funnier still. His wrath fell from him on the instant. From being tired and nervous and angry he became not only amiable, but definitely friendly, and positively content. His smile spread across his broad countenance with a joviality that was almost benign.

"Well, Heaven be praised!" he pealed forth his thanksgiving. "Americans! We *are* in luck!"

He did not even glance toward Madame his hostess, but addressed John Sherrill again: "Nobody here who speaks English, eh? Well, I say, can you talk their silly lingo? Will you ask this dame how much she'll rob me of for a double room and a bath?" He turned toward the group of us in the *galerie* and winked broadly. "She'll rob me all right. You can be sure of that. And how! Europe expects every American to pay double—how's that for a wisecrack?"

He was in high good-humor now. Miss Hamilton looked at him with the first expression of scorn and dislike that I had ever seen on her kind, plain face. But Mrs. Wilde laughed sympathetically, and called out, in a voice which she could make very sweet when, as now, she wanted to:

"It's a perfect shame, but there are no private baths in this hotel."

"There are no double rooms free at this moment," added Miss Hamilton; and her voice was not sweet.

John Sherrill spoke in a low tone to Madame, and turned back to the strangers.

"This is a simple country inn and it has no private baths," he confirmed the bad news. "And it happens that at present the double rooms with running water are all taken. Madame has a room with one large bed, for twenty francs. Or, if that won't do, there is another, smaller, room adjoining, which you can have, as well. The smaller room usually rents for fifteen francs; but since no double room is free, Madame will let you have the two single rooms for thirty francs, which is the price of one room with two beds."

The man grunted. "No bath," he growled. "My God, you'd have thought that all the Americans coming to Europe in the last ten years would have taught these people a little civilization . . ."

"No private bath," Mr. Sherrill answered with perfect gravity, "but hot and cold running water in each room, and a very good modern bathroom in the house. You can have baths for four francs apiece." He smiled. "I don't have to ask Madame Delande that." John Sherrill was getting some fun out of this stranger, I could see . . .

The woman in the car had not spoken, or moved, during this colloquy. She was leaving all the negotiations to her husband, and with his last growl he quieted down. I think that all would have gone well if the Frenchman, Henri de Brassac, who had been having a solitary liqueur under the linden tree, had not suddenly got up and walked, directly in everybody's line of vision, across the square.

Mrs. Wilde rose with the determination of one seized with a great idea. She was a little 'outside herself,' I think, with the exciting arrival of rich Americans whom she thought she could impress. She really had been bored in Neyronnes!

"If you really want a double room, I don't see why you shouldn't have one," she said. "That Frenchman has a big double room, and I don't believe he's paying any thirty francs for it, what's more. He ought to be willing to take a single room, and not inconvenience other people. I'm going to ask him." She smiled coyly. "You know a Frenchman will do anything for a pretty woman," she added. And before anyone could stop her she had stepped out into the *Place*.

Mrs. Wilde was undeniably a pretty woman. She was a woman of the world. She spoke French like a native, and she had lived in France and in half a dozen other countries of Europe. She made her undoubtedly astounding request of Monsieur de Brassac in a low voice and with a really charming manner. And the scholarly-looking Frenchman refused it politely but firmly, and in the English language.

"I regret infinitely that I cannot oblige Madame and her friends," he said. "I have come to Neyronnes to spend some weeks in literary work, and I have chosen my quiet room on the garden with great care. It is the only one which meets my needs, and I am sorry that it is impossible for me to surrender it to Madame's compatriots."

He bowed low, and walked away. Mrs. Wilde turned back to us almost at a run, and her face was scarlet. Christine looked stricken and sick. Miss Hamilton, the only one among us who could be said to be on any terms of familiarity with the Wildes, evidently thought that a little gay brusqueness would best ease the situation.

"I guess maybe it serves you right, my dear," she said lightly. "He's a stubborn gent, isn't he?"

"He's an utter bounder," Mrs. Wilde declared; and seemed to feel better.

"Well, never mind, mother," Christine murmured weakly, but she was interrupted.

"Of all the dirty brutes!" the American arrival began. "I'll be damned if I'll stay here and give up a room I want to a filthy foreigner!"

A wail sounded from the big car. "Oh, Horace, I'm so tired! I don't want to go on tonight. And you know you like it much better when we can get two rooms next to each other—usually there aren't any, or else you say they cost too much. Do let's stay, now we're here. I think it's kind of a pretty place and here are all these nice people from home to talk to." The voice ceased suddenly to wail and became practical. "Besides, it's Saturday night, and we've got to stay somewhere until the banks open . . ."

"Rosalie!" cried Horace. "*Haven't you any money?*"

"Oh, Horace, no!" The voice was plaintive again. "I know you told me to get some in Die-john while you were having the car oiled, but I forgot. I forgot you hadn't any either. We've got to stay somewhere until Monday, Horace."

I all but feared for Rosalie's life at that moment. But I did not know Horace. Instead of cuffing his wife over the head, as I had half-expected, or swearing at her, as I had felt sure he would, Horace burst into a roar of laughter. It was good-natured laughter. It was patronizing and affable. It was the laughter of a man satisfied with himself, contentedly indulgent toward the imbecilities of his spouse, and willing to be at peace with life.

"You poor simp!" he roared, in tones of delight. "I expect you are tired, after working your brain so hard. Of course we'll stay, you boob. We'll have two rooms when we can get them without busting a bank, and we'll have baths in a public tub at four francs a throw. Now let's everybody have a highball and drink damnation to all Frenchmen!"

With an enormous flourish and a really amusing burlesque of Henri de Brassac's ceremonious bow, he handed his wife out of the car, while John Sherrill told Madame Delande that the newcomers would stay until Monday and that the maids could take the luggage to their rooms.

"Oh, Horace," cried Rosalie gratefully, "I think this is lovely!"

She advanced toward the *gaterie*, a small blonde woman whose modish clothes did not make her appearance quite smart, and whose well-cut features did not make her face quite pretty. But if her blue eyes and Cupid's-bow mouth showed no intellect and not much character, they did seem to bear witness to a lazy good-nature, an easy-going amiability that would not grudge good-fortune to others as long as life was pleasant for herself. And her social sense, at this moment, rose to what she thought was expected of her.

"I am so glad to find other Americans in this out-of-the-way little place," she said, in a voice that was high-pitched and babyish, but not unpleasing, now that it had ceased to wail. "I am going to introduce my husband and myself right away, and I hope you'll all do the same. My husband is Mr. Horace Braye, and I am Mrs. Braye, and we would like you all to have a nice little drink with us."

We did introduce ourselves, while Mr. Braye guided his huge car not unskillfully into the garage, and when he came out his wife introduced us all over again. I noticed that he treated each of us to rather a hard look, as if he were in the habit of fixing people's faces in his memory, and when he came to Mrs. Wilde the hardness sharpened for an instant, as if he thought he might have seen her somewhere before. But Mrs. Wilde gave no sign of recognition, and Mr. Braye seemed to realize that he had made a mistake.

Watching him, I had the impression that he was not so stupid as he seemed; that against another background he would show more brains and more individuality than I had given him credit for.

As a matter of fact, this bumptious American was a type quite new to me. I had heard that some of my pupils had bumptious parents, but I had never met them. I had read about Americans of this sort, but I had never seen any, and I was inclined to think that they didn't really exist. To the end, Horace Braye did seem a little incredible to me. But Miss Hamilton and the Sherrills, who had traveled so much more than I, assured me that this big bounder was not at all the only one of his kind.

One met them, they said, on big transatlantic liners (sometimes on small ones, too), and at tourist hotels all over Europe. One disliked them. One was heartily ashamed of them. They gave the United States a bad name, wherever they went. But sometimes they were genuinely well-meaning, for all their ignorance and intolerance and vulgarity and bad manners and braggart jingoism. They were almost always 'good fellows,' and occasionally they were honestly generous and kind. With Horace Braye, one could not, as yet, say . . .

Certainly he was insistent in his hospitality about those drinks. We none of us wanted them. But when pressed, Mrs. Wilde accepted a Grand Marnier and Christine chose mere lemonade and Miss Hamilton had a Vieille Cure, while I followed the Sherrills' example and took a Bénédictine. Mr. and Mrs. Braye stuck to their demand for highballs.

"But I won't drink damnation to Frenchmen, Mr. Braye," said Miss Hamilton. "Why spoil a good drink with ugly sentiments? Let's drink a friendly toast to happiness at Neyronnes . . ."

A friendly toast to happiness at Neyronnes . . . I can see her now, and I can hear her voice with its high-bred haunting loveliness which no human being would ever forget, and again I feel that little sense of wonder that she should have chosen to propose just that toast, just then.

"A friendly toast to happiness at Neyronnes . . ." But except for her own old associates, Margaret Hamilton felt no friendliness toward these people, nor was she a woman who was hoping for happiness for herself or believing in it much for others. A queer shiver gripped my heart, in the strangest way.

And yet any stranger looking at us would have thought that we were all 'good fellows' together. I am sure that that is what Henri de Brassac did think, for instance, as he strolled again across the Place. And Horace Braye's next remark was certainly not fraught with tragic portent: it was almost unbelievably ludicrous.

"When I get a chance to open the case I've got in my car, I'll give you all a drink that is a drink," he said. "I don't trust these foreign concoctions. Slops, most of them. No, sir, when I travel I take my good American liquor along!"

"*What!*" cried Mrs. Sherrill. "Whatever do you mean?"

And Horace beamed at her proudly.

"What I say," he replied. "I stocked up in New York, with my own bootlegger. Had a special case made, to go on the back of the car—it looks like a trunk, but it isn't—and everything's O.K. I carry my own bar with me, wherever I go. And I'm telling you—it's the only way to do, if you can afford it."

He looked around at us, like a schoolboy showing off. And then a faint cloud seemed to brush across his contentment, and he added, hastily: "I don't want you to think I'm a hard drinker. I'm not. I don't go in for boozing. Not me. But when I do drink, I like to know what I'm drinking. You can't feel sure of this foreign stuff."

"Can you feel sure of American stuff?" asked John Sherrill, with a solemnity that matched Horace's own. "Until Prohibition is repealed, there will be no liquor control or inspection at home." He had struck just the right note to draw Horace out.

"Well, it's good home stuff," said that simple home-lover comfortably. "When I have good home stuff I know where I'm at. None of these thieving foreigners for me, not if I can help it. You never know what they've got up their sleeve—some new scheme to rob Americans, most likely. It's bad enough to have to eat their messy food, I'll say. But the Maddam here, she likes it. She's even got a sort of soft spot in her heart for these Frenchies. She thinks they're cute," and Horace's laugh boomed loud and hearty in the quiet of

the *Place*. "And what I say is, a man's got to please his better half."
He winked broadly at John Sherrill. "You know how that is, I'll
bet! She wanted to come to France," he added. "That's the only
reason old Horace left the good old U.S.A. She wanted to get some
Paris clothes, right where they grew, though God knows why. She
had this notion about our driving the car ourselves, too. And she
made me come on a French ship, what's more—that *Shamplane*,
we crossed on. She got it all worked out to go to Italy, too, and go
home on one of those swell Dago liners. But I says, Friend wife, I
says, there are limits even to what old sap Horace will do for you."

Rosalie giggled. The rest of us were spellbound. Horace's highball had apparently tapped bottomless reservoirs of small-talk.

"I says, No, sir. Not for me. I've had enough. We're going home.
And not on any Dago liner, you can bet your bottom dollar while
you've got any dollars left to bet. We're going straight to Mar-sails
and we're going home on a good American boat, you bet. We're
going back to where a dollar's a dollar, just as quick as an American ship'll take us there.

"Besides," added Horace, stimulated now by his highball to
what was obviously the repetition of his favorite creation in the
way of a joke, "I said to Rosalie, I don't mind taking a ship that's
named the *Sham-plane*, because a real plane might be too dangerous; but I'll be damned if I cross the ocean on any boat that calls
itself the *Wrecks!*"

Rosalie's giggle rippled more loudly across the quiet evening.

"Do you get it?" she demanded. "He means that new ship that
everybody's crossing on, the fastest one, the *Rex*, and *ship-wrecks*.
Isn't he cute? But he's so cute I tell him I'm afraid he's too smart
for most people—so I always hurry up and explain. But now," she
cooed, "he can't rush me away for two days. We've got to stay here
over Sunday, until the banks open somewhere, because we have
no money. And I'm glad. I think it's lovely here, with people to
talk to, and all."

"I'm glad you've come, too," said Mrs. Wilde graciously. "You
know, Mrs. Braye, I am not used to staying in a small place like
this, and I do get so bored. Ordinarily, I go to Biarritz, or Aix-les-

Bains, or Carlsbad, or Merano, or some place where there is some life, and where even a wretched invalid like myself can find diversion. But now I am absolutely broke, so I am staying here."

Horace Braye turned to her sharply. "You don't look broke," he said, and even through his effort at gallantry his manner had suddenly become that of the watchful business man. "You look like a million dollars, I'll say. What's put you in the red?"

Mrs. Wilde sighed prettily. "Oh, this terrible depression," she answered. "I am glad I don't look poor, Mr. Braye—I always feel that to look our best is a duty we owe to those around us—but indeed I am all but penniless. My dividends are away down, one of my banks has failed completely, and now comes this awful inflation. I don't understand it at all—I am only a poor sick forgotten woman—"

But Horace interrupted her rather rudely.

"Oh, everything'll be all right," he said. "You can't down the good old U.S.A. We'll show these Europeans what's what, yet—they may think we're busted, but they can't put one over on us! I expect you'll be on Easy Street again before you know it, Mrs. Wilde, and you'll forget you ever were worried. What was this bank that failed?"

"The Marquette Trust Company of St. Louis. I thought it was one of the best banks in the country, but they said it had got into wrong hands."

"Yeah, that does happen." Horace shrugged his big shoulders. "But I expect you'll get all yours back. I don't know that particular bank myself—I've never been in St. Louis, except passing through: I'm from New York, and I guess pretty nearly everybody in that burg knows old Horace Braye—but lots of these bank failures are just matters of readjustment. The thing for you to do, Mrs. Wilde, is not to worry—kind of take it in your stride, if you get me. Well, now, Rosalie, what about looking at those rooms of ours?"

I had not spoken a word through all these cross-currents of stupid conversation: I was stricken to silence in disappointment and resentment. Neyronnes—this ancient, romantic, unique Neyronnes, this tiny village on its hill—to be ruined by the intrusion of people like these! To be sure, I already disliked Mrs. Wilde. But even Mrs. Wilde had a certain urbanity, and her voice did not slam and bang and boom all over the place. Besides, Mrs. Wilde had a way of taking color from the people around her; and against the background of the Sherrills' charm and good-breeding and Miss Hamilton's unobtrusive poise, she became fairly inoffensive, even in her silliness; and I personally was willing to put up with Christine's mother for Christine's sake. But now Mrs. Wilde would probably take her tone from the newcomers—especially after having been humiliated at the Frenchman's hands—and would, so to speak, make herself one of them. Well, I tried to comfort myself, it was only for the week-end. That great ape and his brainless wife would be gone in a few days . . .

But that thought did not bring the solace that it should, and my *malaise* went deeper than mere sulks. The darkness was falling now, and I turned and looked at Christine, who was sitting beside me, silent and relaxed, her hands folded in her lap. And I had the strangest impulse, not in sentimentality nor romantic emotion, but in a kind of protectiveness, to reach out and lay my own hand over hers. I didn't do it; but I had to exercise a definite force of will to stop myself.

But out of the shadows on the other side of Christine Wilde's chair, Elinor Sherrill stretched out her hand with just such a gesture as I should have wanted mine to be, and laid it on the girl's two hands clasped in her lap. Here was protectiveness, understanding, tenderness.

"You are going with us to Cluny," said Mrs. Sherrill, in a matter-of-fact tone of friendly kindness. "We have asked your mother, and she says you may."

V

CHRISTINE GOES ON A HOLIDAY

Some spirit of sheer contrariness moved me to escort the new arrivals to their rooms, which were on the first floor of the *pavillon
annexe*, opposite the Wildes' huge chamber. They were attractive
rooms, with gay blue-and-white wallpaper which was also used
prettily to cover the wooden screens around the stationary wash-
stands, and the pattern of which was almost duplicated in the chintz
of window curtains and bed-coverings. The front room, which was
just under mine, was the larger of the two, and I was amused to
see that Horace Braye settled himself in this as a matter of course,
and left the small room, which had only one window and no view
at all, to his wife.

He grumbled a little over the discovery that there were no bells
to connect with the main house. But as the maid Aurélie was waiting to see to the baths and take the breakfast order, he was able to
make himself comfortable without much cause for complaint. I
went on upstairs to my own bedroom, turned on the light, picked
up a book, and then decided that I could not stay indoors and
started out again. By this time I had adopted what seemed to be
the general custom of leaving my door unlocked.

I started toward the stairs, and then—being restless—I took a
sudden notion to explore the unfinished part of the house and look
for that connecting 'back way' in from the village street. On the
long June evening the darkness had almost fallen, but not quite. I
paused at the head of the stairs, outside John Sherrill's bedroom—
the Sherrills were still over on the *Place*, with the Wildes and Miss

Hamilton—and took a casual look at the door of the unfinished room. Then I opened the door. And I drew back with a queer little catch at my heart, from something that was certainly shock, and seemed almost like dread. I had been thinking of an 'unfinished room' in terms of reasonably new houses, in America . . .

But this house was two centuries old. This room had once been lived in—lived in a hundred years ago, perhaps, and left since to neglect. On the east side—the street side—the windows were barred with heavy shutters of solid wood, but on the west side, toward the garden, the small dusty panes stood uncovered—uncovered save by dirt and cobwebs, through which the dim light entered crazily to fall upon the festoons of spider webs hanging from the ceilings, filling all the corners, making strange draperies around the baseboard to the unplaned floor. The walls were plastered white, and at some time within recent years someone had traced plans in blue crayon, to show how the wide space could be cut into rooms and finished, as on the floor below. Now, against the dead whiteness, these blue lines seemed eerie in themselves. And below the white walls spiders crawled sluggishly, or scampered, in the dust. No description, no listing of what was to be seen in it, can give any explanation of the ghostliness, the gruesomeness, of that room.

But I had come upon a tour of exploration. And across the vast and haunted expanse of that unfinished room was another door. As I write this, in the bright daylight, with sunshine and living trees and chintz-curtained windows about me, it seems strange to set down the fact that I needed determination to cross that room; but need it I did! A huge spider ran across the floor in front of me. Another, smaller but somehow more hateful in his deliberate voluptuous blood-thirstiness, made a slow and greedy movement toward a fly caught in his web. I stepped firmly forward, crossed the space in front of me, and opened the door.

There was nothing there but darkness, a clutter of old boards, the top of a rickety stair, a roof-beam that came down almost to my head. And I realized suddenly what I ought to have known before—that this upper space in the still older house, beyond the unfinished room in the *pavillon*, was merely an attic. The storage-room, the door that could easily be used from the old house to our annex, the passageway, was on the floor below. There was no need for anyone to enter that ghostly chamber; apparently I looked back across the unfinished room and saw the solitary and conspicuous marks of my footsteps in the dust—apparently no one ever did.

I went back the way I had come and walked sedately down the front stairs and out the front door.

It was absurd that I should feel a little shaken! In excuse, I reminded myself that I had been nervous and irritated to start with. But I felt in no mood, now, to meet my fellow-lodgers. And I did not go back to the central square and the lighted inn and the broad-beamed *galerie*. I did not even walk in that direction, down the village street. It was from this street that one turned off to swing around the narrow roadway into the *Place*. Or one could keep on it as the road sloped downhill, and so come out near the Lower Gate and the Promenade des Lices, or go on still farther and eventually circle back to the church and the Upper Gate.

For this was the *chemin de ronde* of ancient Neyronnes, the passage inside the double line of ramparts, on which the finest houses of the village had their entrances, to back up, on the other side, above the broad *Lices* and the far-flung open view. Neyronnes was very small, and on its little hill-top it was almost perfectly circular. I set out on the *chemin de ronde* in the other direction: I turned past the old-time Governor's mansion, near the Upper Gate, swung along a curving roadway lined with walled gardens and mediæval dwellings, and drew near, soon, to the grim and myste-rious prison-house where witches had been tortured in the fifteenth century.

The prison-house had been restored, and made into a really fine residence: it had good 'crossing' windows on the *chemin de ronde*, and above the inner rampart on the other side its gardens descended the steep hill in well-arranged terraces. But the regula-tions that governed all reconstruction at Neyronnes had forbid-den the cutting of windows in the tower itself, or the widening of the narrow openings in the outer wall of the ancient structure; so, although it was extremely interesting and in some ways beautiful, it was somewhat lacking in light and livableness. It seemed more like a museum than a dwelling; and perhaps it held too much of its old suggestion: that was certainly true now, when it was not occupied . . .

I stopped near the ancient well—bottomless, people said—on the triangular grassy space where other village pathways ran into the *chemin de ronde*. There was a short-cut, here, back to the Place des Halles and the inn, but I did not take it. I stood still for a few moments, and then went on down the road: I was not far from the Lower Gate now, and in this spot the tumble-down houses and the restored cottages made a sort of *mélange* together. I had taken only a few steps beyond the prison-house and the grassy triangle when I heard a voice, which seemed to come from that mass of low buildings.

There was nothing unusual about that, of course. Village people lived in these small houses on the narrow streets; and more than one family from some French city or other had restored one of the old dwellings as a 'summer cottage.' Neyronnes had a summer population of close to a hundred, all told, and of course there was nothing strange about hearing voices here. The strange thing was that I heard only one voice, and that I was almost certain it was speaking English.

I did not understand any words. I did not know where the voice was coming from. But the inflections sounded English, a kind of English sing-song, a monologue, a *recitatif*. And it was not the voice of any one of the English-speaking people whom I knew to be in Neyronnes. It was a voice of quite different quality, a man's voice, husky, a little labored. I stepped forward, past a lighted cottage. I stepped back, toward the shuttered empty prison-tower. The voice was neither louder nor less loud. I still could not tell where it came from. I still could not distinguish a word. I still felt sure that the language was English. I stopped and waited. And the sound of the voice stopped too.

I had some idea of going in search of it, but I gave that up as impractical. The only street lights of Neyronnes were a few low-powered bulbs set at wide intervals in mediæval lanterns, and although they were very attractive to look at, the illumination they gave was almost nil. Besides, the dwellings, the goat-sheds, the ruins, were all mixed up together here. I must put off my quest until daylight. And I had better ask a few questions before I began!

Moreover, I remembered, it was Saturday night, the time when the largest number of visitors came to Neyronnes. And I had already learned not to be astonished at the appearance of visitors who spoke English! The fall of the dollar was bringing a strange assortment of my own compatriots, certainly, to this supposedly unknown spot! I suspected that economy even had something to do with the Brayes' choice of a route and their decision to do without a chauffeur. It was likely enough that this mysterious voice merely marked the arrival of another 'gold-stranded' American. If he resembled the latest comer, Heaven forbid! Normal exasperation over Horace Braye brought respite to my wool-gatherings as I walked on down to the Lower Gate.

But the respite was brief. For as I sat there on the grass with my back against the outer rampart, and tried to collect my thoughts sensibly, all my fear for Christine swept over me again, a stronger flood than before. And after a little while I rose up wearily and started back toward my room.

Even now, I did not want to go by the *Place* and the lighted windows of the Auberge de Vieux Neyronnes. I stumbled back over the cobbles by the way I had come. And as I went I heard once more the curious sing-song voice, slower now, tired, mumbling. I hastened my steps. If only I could catch a word! And I did catch a word. One. There seemed to be a new beginning to the singsong. Then, suddenly, on an intake of breath, an upward inflection, the voice stopped, with a strange deep sigh. But I heard the last word, distinctly. It was the word *cherubim* . . .

I felt too tired, myself, to think, or puzzle, or worry. There was something odd and unnatural here. But I could not make it out. Not now. I waited a little, but the voice did not speak again. There was no sound of movement, anywhere. I went back to my room and went to bed.

But the night was not restful. I could not get to sleep for a long time. And when I did finally drop off into an unhappy slumber, I had a horrible dream. I dreamed that I heard Christine calling for help, calling as if she had a gag in her mouth and could not make an articulate sound. But I heard her. I knew that she was in the unfinished room; and although the door was locked on the inside, as I had known that it would be, I battered it down and forced my way in. And there, in my dream, was Christine, tied in some way beneath one of those dim haunted windows, while an enormous spider made its slow, voluptuous, blood-thirsty way toward her. It was as large as a man. It was a man. As I watched, the spider turned into Horace Braye, stretching out hands of destruction toward Christine. And as I tried to reach her first and could not, I saw something in my dream that seemed to me more horrible still. Quite close to Christine, white, expressionless, unmoving, Margaret Hamilton was standing. And she was making not the slightest effort to help.

. . . It was a dreadful dream, the kind of dream from which one wakes in sweating terror, torn in the wretched throes of formless suspicion and antipathy. Certainly, when the morning came, I felt the sharp injustice of such a sleeper's vision of kind, plain, coura-geous Miss Hamilton, and the incongruity of such a monstrous presentment of that jovial bounder Horace Braye. It was Christine's own mother, I reminded myself in the sane clarity of the daylight, whose vampire-like egotism brought an actual danger of stunting her daughter's development and injuring her life. Margaret Hamil-ton, for all the shortness of their acquaintance, seemed to be a real friend. And Horace Braye, with his puns and his xenophobia, was a mere passing stranger whose selfishness was not villainous and not likely seriously to inconvenience anyone except his wife. And as, glad to get up early in the bright morning, I sauntered out the towered Upper Gate and into the grassy *Lices*, I felt the pleasure of a return to frank, give-and-take normal life again when I saw Miss Hamilton ahead of me, with her dog.

And the sight was a pretty one. A herd of five goats was eating its luxurious way up the broad promenade, and, like all the goats of Neyronnes, they were handsome specimens, and as clean and well-cared-for as house pets. Fergus was making mischievous efforts to tease them a little, bounding up close to them and then backing quickly away. But the sportiveness of a terrier could not disturb these creatures' immemorial calm. One by one, as he approached them, raised its solemn bearded face and stared at him with its long eyes, then returned placidly to cropping the grass. Only one, a pure-white kid among his brown and fawn-colored elders, expressed any feeling, and that was not of fear or of annoyance, but of mere curiosity: he found Fergus mysterious and fascinating.

It was natural enough, I think, that this scene should have helped to soothe my unrest and chase away the cobwebs—the literal memory of cobwebs—of my bad night. Already, too, there was cheerful movement about the little walled village, people coming in from the valley and the farms to the neighborliness of early Mass, sightseers and picnickers arriving, as they always did on Sunday, to see Neyronnes, and to see it again and again. Everything seemed so bright and enjoyable that I could even almost forget, or explain away, the man who had chanted strange words in English in the darkness, and ended on a sobbing sigh . . .

"Did you know we were going to have a children's banquet in the *Place?*" Miss Hamilton asked, as I came up with her and we walked on together. She, too, seemed to be in a gay mood. Every year, she told me, sixty or seventy boys and girls from a near-by school came in big char-à-bancs, with their teachers, to spend a day at Neyronnes. Tables were set for them under the linden tree, and after they had eaten a bounteous repast they had songs and a few speeches. It was great fun.

"They come partly to work up their mediæval history," she remarked. "You'd better tag along, and see how it's done. You will enjoy it, and so shall I. And Mrs. Wilde will stay in her room and not be bothered much. But this tiny village is going to be thronged with French country people until sundown, and what do you suppose Horace will do?"

"He's got a car," I grunted. And Miss Hamilton clapped her hands a signal which brought Fergus quickly to heel.

"Fine!" she said. "Let's send him off for the day. Where shall it be? To Macon to eat? To Aix-les-Bains or Vichy to see the great world? To Lyon? To Geneva? To Le Puy? To Bourges? No, they'd never look at a cathedral, those two. To the château of Jacques Coeur and a fifty-franc lunch, at Roanne?"

"All those places are tremendously far away," I objected. But I had caught my neighbor's gay mood, and I joined in her laugh.

"Every place is tremendously far away from Neyronnes, thank God," she said. "But that hasn't saved us from Horace's visitation. What's a car like that for? I am sure," she went on, "that Horace's car has at least sixteen cylinders and a taxable horsepower of forty-eight and an easy loping speed of a hundred miles an hour. And if he can't run over to Vichy and show his wife the sights, what, I ask you again, is his car for? Is it only to lacerate us with his presence, and not offer us any relief? The Sherrills and Christine," she added, "are going to Tournus and Cluny today."

"Oh," I responded, rather blankly, "I thought it was later on."

"No, they decided last night that they would go today if the weather was good and Mrs. Wilde was well enough to be left. I have just been in to see Mrs. Wilde and she seems to feel exceptionally husky; so all is well. They will start before lunch, and they plan to get back tomorrow evening: it's a long distance, you know. Mrs. Wilde has said they may take her car, so Christine will drive; and she will enjoy that."

"Well, I hope we can get rid of Horace and Rosalie," I said.

And, somewhat to my surprise, we did. Egged on, I think, by Mrs. Wilde's references to the cosmopolitan world of fashion with which she was familiar and Mrs. Braye was not, our latest arrivals did elect to go to Aix-les-Bains for the day. They left at a very early hour—for Aix-les-Bains is far from Neyronnes—and we knew that they could not get back before evening. The Sherrills delayed their departure for the pleasure of seeing the children pile happily into the *Place*, but before eleven they were ready to set out.

"By the way, Armitage, our car is standing idle," John Sherrill said to me. "Why don't you take Miss Hamilton out to see the country a bit, this afternoon or tomorrow, or both?"

Christine had not yet come from the *pavillon*, but Miss Hamilton was there; and she shook her head as she smiled.

"Thank you so much. I should love it," she said. "But Christine's being away will leave her mother lonely, and I know she will be depending on me for company."

"She might go too," I suggested. And Miss Hamilton raised her eyebrows as she twisted her face into a funny little grin.

"In a Chevrolet?" she said. "With all due respect to your natty little car, John—"

The sentence went unfinished as Christine and her mother came down the little *ruelle* into the square. Christine had a small bag in one hand, and the other arm was around her mother's shoulders. They made a sweet and sentimental picture, the tall fresh athletic girl, walking along with her pretty, and always bright and animated, young mother, in such an attitude of protection and tenderness— sweet if one had not known that Mrs. Wilde was almost monstrous in her self-absorption, and that her daughter's devoted abnegation was too complete to be right or fair. As it was, one could only be glad that Christine was going to have a holiday, even for thirty hours or so. How long was it, I wondered, since she had left her mother for as long a time as that, since she had even slept in a room alone?

But she never spent any time with her mother again. Before Christine returned from her little outing, Mrs. Wilde was found dead in her room, with a hypodermic syringe that had contained morphine lying empty on the table beside her bed. I jumped to the obvious conclusion; and I was wrong.

VI

I SOLVE A MYSTERY

It seems more than a little strange to remember that during the time directly preceding the discovery of her death, I did not give a thought to Mrs. Wilde. And when Miss Hamilton found her body, my first feeling was a double sense of relief: a great and immediate relief, I confess it, that Christine was free; and, in the second place, relief that she was away from Neyronnes at this moment. It never occurred to me that Mrs. Wilde might have been murdered. I took it for granted that she had been a drug-addict, and that she had died as drug-addicts, poor wretches, often do. But I was glad that her daughter was not there . . .

It was the merest chance, I thought, that she was not there. For it was on the second night after Christine's departure that her mother died. The Brayes were still with us: they had returned from Aix-les-Bains Sunday evening and on Monday they had discovered that while the exchange was so uncertain they could not cash their letter of credit in the little Jeanniot bank; so willy-nilly they decided to stay until Tuesday or Wednesday while they waited for money to come from the nearest big town. Then on Monday the weather turned threatening, and John Sherrill telephoned from Cluny that they had decided to spend the night there, and would be back in Neyronnes some time the next day. Mrs. Wilde left the door open when she went into the telephone room, and I was just outside. I could hear her somewhat petulant assent to what John Sherrill was evidently presenting to her as a matter of course. He did not ask her permission for the extension of Christine's holiday: he made a courteous inquiry, I could guess, as to the state of her health, and then he told her their plans; and although her voice was fretful, she did not forbid the delay, nor did she ask to speak to her daughter on the telephone.

Miss Hamilton's prediction as to the claims upon her own time proved to be correct. That otherwise unoccupied voyager was pressed into Mrs. Wilde's service for all her waking hours. She played cards with her, talked to her, read to her, arranged her meals and sat at her table, ran her errands, did her mending, and even rubbed tonic into her hair. In everything but sleeping in Mrs. Wilde's room, she was apparently taking Christine's place. All the rest of that Sunday, while the children trooped happily all over Neyronnes, and hordes of country people drove up for luncheon and *gouter* and dinner, and the prettily costumed servants rushed competently hither and yon, I had no speech with either Miss Hamilton or Mrs. Wilde. The only one of my fellow-boarders with whom I exchanged a word was Henri de Brassac.

He was out and about all day, watching the children, looking on at the movement of the crowds—although not talking to any-one—and as I paused once in a walk across the *Place* toward the end of the afternoon, he suddenly came up and joined me.

"It is a pretty sight, is it not?" he remarked surprisingly, in his perfect English. "I believe that Monsieur appreciates our Ney-ronnes."

"Oh, yes, I do!" I cried, with emphasis, and wondered if I sounded like a gushing schoolgirl. This grave, firm, self-contained Frenchman made me feel *gauche* and self-conscious; and yet I was enormously glad to be able to speak even four words to a French-man about Neyronnes. Conversation with the Braye couple, here in this lovely spot, left a bad taste in my mouth; and really Mrs. Wilde was almost as bad. My thought of Christine was wholly per-sonal and greatly troubled—and I never had a chance to talk with her, anyway. Miss Hamilton and the Sherrills were, I was bold enough to put it, my 'own kind' of people, but they were almost too much my own kind. In their way they were typical Americans (as the Brayes, I was sure, were not?), and talking with them was like talking with friends and neighbors at home. Monsieur and Madame Delande, on the other hand, hardly counted: they lived here; they kept the inn; this was all in the day's work. In talking with a French fellow-visitor, in Neyronnes, about Neyronnes, I did get a new and distinct satisfaction. I even went so far as to tell him that I was interested in mediæval history.

And he was exceedingly affable, indeed almost friendly. One might have said that he was trying to make up for his rudeness of the day before, but I did not think that. I did not think he had any feeling of having been rude. But I did flatter myself that he was paying me a very real compliment, that he was differentiating between me and Horace Braye, for instance, and that he was welcoming me to his country because I was really interested in the treasure France had to give to the world.

Not unnaturally, then, I told him that Mr. and Mrs. Sherrill had gone to see Cluny and Tournus, with Miss Wilde.

"Ah," he said, "Miss Wilde? I should not have thought that Madame Wilde or her daughter would be interested in Cluny or Tournus."

"Mrs. Wilde is not. But I think that Miss Wilde may be," I assured him, with what I realized was a rather ridiculous earnestness.

And I realized something else, too: Henri de Brassac seemed to have acquired quite distinct opinions about us in a very short time. He must have overheard a good deal of conversation which we, in our stupidity, had taken for granted that he could not understand. And it was with some witless idea of doing justice to Christine that I added:

"I think Miss Wilde has never had a chance."

"One can believe that." He smiled lightly; and then his smile deepened and became quizzical. "Then Madame Wilde is alone for a few days?"

"Until tomorrow evening. But Miss Hamilton is staying with her all day," I answered.

"Ah," the Frenchman said again reflectively, "Miss Hamilton. She is kind, that lady. Why should she be so kind to this Madame

Wilde? She is the good neighbor, *n'est ce pas?* And she is very intelligent."

It was my turn to smile. "She is very intelligent," I echoed. "She loves Neyronnes."

"Ah," Monsieur de Brassac repeated, "then I shall have great pleasure in talking with her, also."

He left me with one of his courtly bows. And I find it a little curious, now, to recall that conversation.

There is something bizarre, too, in the remembrance of how Miss Hamilton and I tried vainly to stave off one of Horace Braye's puns when he returned from Aix-les-Bains that evening and said that he hadn't enjoyed his lunch.

"You should have eaten at Belley," Miss Hamilton told him, and realized too late the possibility of wise-cracking in the name of Brillat-Savarin's birthplace and the continuing fame of its food! Horace's pun we were obliged to endure.

And it seems strange that up to the very moment of the discovery of Mrs. Wilde's body, I was concerning myself with what I had come to call, in my own thoughts, 'the mystery of Neyronnes.' The mystery of Neyronnes, indeed! Within half an hour of my solving it, how unimportant, even in its pathos, had that little mystery come to be!

As I was left almost completely to myself over Sunday and Monday, I hoped that I should be able to find out the secret of the unknown man who was hiding himself somewhere—as I reasoned— in the tumble-town labyrinth of the ancient houses of Neyronnes. There were a good many of these houses, buildings that had been 'too far gone' for restoration when a group of public-spirited citizens set themselves to the task of 'saving Neyronnes' a number of years ago. The best dwellings on the *chemin de ronde* had been repaired, as private residences, at that time. The thirteenth-century house on the *Place* had been reconstructed, furnished to suit its period, made comfortable, and equipped as an inn. The old beamed structure with the *galerie* was an excellent local museum. The Place des Halles had been entirely restored, as had the fortified church in the ramparts; and the gates and the walls had been so repaired that there was no danger of further demolition at the hands of time. The village had been placed under the protection of the Ministry of Beaux Arts, and all the stones of Neyronnes were periodically inspected, to make sure that every wall was standing safely.

But on the narrow byways in the interior of the village there were many old walls to which nothing else had been done: here and there one could see a bit of good fenestration, the remains of a cornice, occasionally a niche, even a tourelle; goats lived in the best of these ancient sheds; most of them were mere roofless walls. Inhabited houses jostled the ruins, but there were at least a dozen mediæval buildings that were wholly deserted. Not even children's play enlivened those sad walls, and weeds grew in miniature jungles in their enclosures. It was in this labyrinth that I had heard the voice in the night.

That tangled mass of masonry, which constituted the 'poor quarter' of the little village, was only a stone's throw from the inn by the short-cuts. And it might be, I told myself, that an English-speaking stranger was boarding in one of the cheaper cottages. I could find out about that at once! So I began by asking Miss Hamilton, when I caught a moment of her attention on Monday, whether she knew of any such person in Neyronnes.

She looked at me blankly. "Why, no," she said, and added: "What possesses you to go prowling around at night, in those dark alleyways? You'll meet the ghosts of Neyronnes, if you don't look out—or the rats."

And that was all the satisfaction I got out of Miss Hamilton. I decided to do my investigating on my own and not ask any more questions. For deep in my heart I felt anxious: was there a maniac hiding here?

But Sunday had been wholly unproductive, and Monday almost completely so. I seemed always to be running into village people; and I did not want my purpose to be known. I was rewarded by finding an overgrown hole in the ground, which may well have been the entrance to an important subterranean passageway in the old days when Neyronnes was frequently besieged by warring feudatories or by the King himself. But of the twentieth century I discovered nothing, and I was keenly disappointed.

Then on Monday evening I heard the voice again.

It was about eleven o'clock, and the sky had clouded over so that the night was quite black. I have no electric flashlight, but I could make my way about by the slight illumination of the street lanterns, and I sauntered easily enough down past the old prison-house and along by a few lighted cottages. As before, I had just passed the grassy triangle with the ancient well when I caught once more the sound of English rhythms in a sort of chant. But the husky voice was stronger now. The speech was slower. As I stepped nearer I had no difficulty in understanding the words. And this is what came distinctly to my ear:

> "'In Xanadu did Kubla Khan
>   A stately pleasure dome decree:
> Where Alph, the sacred river, ran
> Through caverns measureless to man
>   Down to a sunless sea.'

"But I don't like the rest of it. I don't get much kick out of Coleridge, really. Here goes something with a better swing, once again:

> "'Thus said the Lord in the Vault above the Cherubim,
>   Calling to the Angels and the Souls in their de-
>   gree:
> "Lo! Earth has passed away
> On the smoke of Judgment Day.
>   That Our word may be established shall We
>   gather up the sea?"'

"That moves! Now for the best verse:

> "'Sun, Wind, and Cloud shall fail not from the face
>   of it,

> Stinging, ringing spindrift, nor the fulmar flying
>   free;
> And the ships shall go abroad
> To the Glory of the Lord
> Who heard the silly sailor-folk and gave them
>   back their sea!'"

There was a moment's pause, and then the voice went on, slower, and sadder: "'Gave them back their sea . . .' Ah,

> "'I must go down to the sea again, to the lonely sea
>   and the sky,
> And all I ask is a tall ship and a star to steer her by,
> And the wheel's kick and the wind's song and the
>   white sail's shaking,
> And a gray mist on the sea's face and a gray dawn
>   breaking.'"

I listened, there in the summer darkness, while every word of Masefield's beautiful 'Sea Fever' sounded from the otherwise silent ruins of the ancient houses of Neyronnes. And even as the poem was beautiful, so its recitation was beautiful, too. I knew now, of course, how it was that I had heard that strange word *cherubim* two nights before: this man who was pouring forth English poetry amid these fallen walls had begun Kipling's 'Last Chantey' and had stopped at the end of the first line. I remembered the suddenness of that sighing break, on its upward inflection, as if he were, on the instant, too tired to go on. And he was tired now. But his husky voice had exquisite intonations, a moving depth. And here alone in the darkness he was reciting poetry because he loved it. It was not often that one heard the English language like that . . .

He was silent for a while when he had finished the Masefield poem, and I stood where I was, afraid to move for fear of making my presence known, and anxious now, above all things, not to be discovered. For a matter of some minutes there was not a sound.

Then the voice began again, and the old familiar words were the last I should have expected to hear:

> "'When to the sessions of sweet silent thought
> I summon up remembrance of things past—'"

He went on to the final couplet, but his voice grew slower and more tired.

> "'But if the while I think on thee, dear friend,
> All losses are restored, and sorrows end.'"

I knew as he finished the last line that the Shakespeare sonnet had closed his recitations for the evening. I crouched down against a shadowing wall and stayed there for at least half an hour. But no other sound came from anywhere around me. It was midnight or after when I finally slipped noiselessly back by the short-cut to the market-place, and from there to the *pavillon* and my room.

The threatened rain began to fall as I got into bed, and I thought with a sick dismay of the man in the ruins. I even had a wild idea of going out to look for him, to make sure he was all right. But he surely must have some kind of adequate shelter, I reasoned; and he probably wouldn't take kindly to a stranger's interference. It was certainly no objection to getting wet that kept me in my own comfortable room, but my natural curse of shyness, the fear of butting in. And of course, without his voice to guide me, I probably could not have found him, in the dark. I tried to go to sleep, and I succeeded with remarkable promptitude. And although once I was awakened, unprecedentedly, by a loud and ugly growl from Fergus, who slept with his mistress in the small bed-room next to mine, I had a good night on the whole. When the dog's growl disturbed my sleep, it was still raining. But when I finally awoke, at seven or thereabouts, the day was fresh and clear and beautiful, and I jumped quickly out of bed, went over to the inn to get my breakfast, and decided to set forth in search of our mysterious English-speaking neighbor at once.

In the bright sunshine of that June morning I walked around
the ancient Governor's dwelling, down the *chemin de ronde*, and
as far as the prison-house. And there I stopped. In the shadow of
that dark tower a broad stain lay black upon the cobbles. And I did
not need to look twice to see that it was blood.

It was no mere scattering of drops of blood, such as might have
come from the wound of some animal. It was a great pool, and it
was fresh. No such animal as might have been housed within the
walls of Neyronnes could have lost as much blood as that, and continued to live, I guessed. Could someone have killed a dog or a goat
in the street of the village? I looked at the spreading stain, and
shuddered. And as I continued to look, I saw that drops of blood
led away, a trail marked upon the cobblestones, from that central
stain on down the roadway. Past the green patch with its old well,
I followed, and into the labyrinth of ruins; so into a tumble-down
shed in the midst of that labyrinth, on the inside of the narrow,
curving street. The trail was clear, and I went where it led me . . .

This pile of broken walls offered more shelter than most. There
was a real roof over nearly all of it. Several windows, on the east
and north sides, had been rudely shuttered, and thus were effec-
tively closed. And since the door by which I entered was low and
narrow, the result was to make the inside very dark, especially to
one coming from the brightness outside. I could not see, now, the
bloodstains which had led me to the door of this hut. But in the
most sheltered corner I could make out a camp bed, and a man
lying upon it, motionless.

I had a cold sense of dread, for an instant, of what I should
find as I drew nearer. But the man was alive. With another step I
could hear the sound of his labored breathing. And then he spoke
to me.

"Ah," he said, and his words were forced out with difficulty,
"I'm—glad—you've—come . . ."

"I've come to help you," I said. And making my way to the nearest of the boarded windows, I was relieved to find that its rude
covering was a shutter: I jerked it open and the eastern sunshine
poured into the hut. On the simple but adequate bed the man was

lying apparently as he had fallen when he stumbled into his refuge only a short time before; but in the torrential rain of the night the shelter of that refuge had failed him. The whole place seemed almost flooded. The man's clothing was soaking wet and his body was shaking. And there was blood all about: on the bed, on his coat, his sleeves, on the long white hand that was stretched out toward me; there was blood on his face, at his mouth. I knew, now, what had happened. This was a sick man; and he had had a hemorrhage. He had been drenched with the rain through that long night, in this wretched, inadequate shelter. He had gone out on the street with the first sunshine. He had been stricken in front of the prison-house, and he had crawled back to his hut, where he lay racked with a chill, able only to murmur feebly that he was glad I had come . . .

But on the instant his last force deserted him. My idea, naturally, was to get him to the house, to a warm bed, dry clothes, good care. But by the time I had crossed the hut, he was incapable of movement. As he heard my voice, apparently he had fainted.

I tried to lift him, but although he was light he was tall, and I could not manage the awkwardness of that weight alone. I went out into the village street, but no one was in sight who could give me any assistance. I was frightened now, afraid that the man would die before I was able to help him. If I had seen any of the villagers—the schoolmaster, the laundress, even the seamstress—I should have asked aid in taking him to whatever house was nearest: I could have made myself understood enough for that. But the roadway stared vacantly at me in the early morning, and only one thought came to me—Margaret Hamilton: Margaret Hamilton, who was kind to sick people, who knew her way about, who would tell me what to do . . .

I rushed back to the inn by that blessed short-cut, and as I turned into the *Place* I saw Miss Hamilton just coming out of the main door of the *auberge*. I did not see that Monsieur and Madame Delande were just behind her. I did not look at her face. I ran across the square as fast as the rough cobbles would let me, and when I got as far as the *galerie*, I called to her:

"Please send someone, quick! There's a man very ill, down there in the ruins. I need help—right away!"

But Miss Hamilton did not answer me. She did not seem to hear me. She looked at me with a strange wild stare in a dead-white face, and cried out:

"Mrs. Wilde is dead. She took an overdose of morphine. I've just found her body.

"I found her body," she repeated. "She took an overdose of morphine."

VII

CHRISTINE COMES BACK

Even then, my thought stayed with the man in the ruins. Mrs. Wilde was dead. But this man was alive—he had been alive when I left him—and he would die unless help came soon. Miss Hamilton was useless. I realized that the Delandes and the inn staff had enough to think of and to do. It was Henri de Brassac, at this moment walking sedately and unconcernedly around the corner of the *ruelle* toward the *galerie*, upon whom I called for aid; and it was Henri de Brassac and I who lifted the sick man and carried him as gently as we could up the sloping, curving roadway to the *pavillon annexe*. I was about to take him to my own room—I couldn't at the moment think of anything better to do—when Monsieur de Brassac stopped me.

"There is a small room opposite mine," he said. "I do not know if it is prepared for use, but it is unoccupied; and these rooms are never kept locked. We will give that room to our invalid." And when for the first time it occurred to me to wonder how I was going to pay for the luxury of entertaining a sick man, the Frenchman must have sensed my thought at once, for he said:

"We need not worry about the costs." He smiled at me, and his smile, though friendly, seemed again a bit quizzical. "The little franc keeps its same little value, so far," he reminded me. "I shall be glad to undertake the responsibility of this sick lad."

And I felt my heart warming toward this foreigner, who could be so frigidly remote and then become so sympathetic and so kind. We found the little bedroom in complete readiness for a visitor, and although it was cell-like in its narrowness and its simplicity, it was perfectly comfortable, and of course spotlessly clean.

I ran up to my room to get a pair of pajamas, and I was conscious of a shudder as I passed Mrs. Wilde's closed door. It looked, of course, just as usual; but there was a square of white linen lying on the floor near the corner; it must have been with some queer instinct of orderliness in the presence of death that I picked it up and thrust it into my pocket, bending over just an instant and then hurrying on up the stairs.

When I came back, Monsieur de Brassac was busy undressing the stranger and getting him ready for bed, and he did nearly all the work. He was very quick and very gentle. The sick man was half-conscious now, and had surrendered himself to our ministrations in dazed contentment. We had him in bed in a very few minutes, and the Frenchman said, "I will get the doctor."

I tried to thank him, and I did manage to stammer out something about his skill. But he stopped me with a shrug and a gesture.

"I was in the war," he said briefly, and repeated, "Now I will get the doctor."

He was gone before I realized that he probably did not yet know about Mrs. Wilde's death. . .

As for myself, I did not know what I ought to do. The man on the bed tossed about a little. He still shivered, and he had a fever. He coughed badly now, but there had been no return of the hemorrhage. I knew, of course, that he was very ill, and I did not think that I ought to leave him. He was a young man, not over my own age, I guessed, with a thin ravaged face and a body that was like a fleshless wooden toy, so thin and bony was it. He looked, I thought, like a person of gentleness and refinement; of fastidiousness, but not, perhaps, of much strength of any kind; a beauty-loving, futile person, who had been ill for a long time. Tuberculosis, of course—and at this point in my reflections Monsieur de Brassac came back. His face had become very stern, and he had brought a strange man with him.

"I found the doctor already here," he said. "The gendarmes, too, are at the inn *bureau*. I have just learned what has happened. We must all report to the gendarmes at once."

I wrenched myself away from my ponderings over the sick man—what he had been doing, hidden there in the mediæval ruins of Neyronnes—and pulled my thought back to the situation at the inn. Mrs. Wilde was dead. Christine was free from the bonds that had held her spirit and her too-sensitive young mind. Her mother had been a drug-addict, and now she was dead. And Christine, mercifully, was away at the moment. Now we must all go and make routine reports to the police, before Christine got back.

Monsieur de Brassac and I left the doctor with the sick man, and went over to the main building of the *auberge* . . .

In the big low-ceilinged room that served so picturesquely as café and extra dining-room—the room into which the front door directly opened—a serious-looking young man in the uniform of the *Gendarmerie Nationale* was sitting at one of the long oak tables, while his colleague stood near-by and eyed us all as we came in. The Brayes, Horace blustering and Rosalie scared, were seated near the door, and Miss Hamilton was talking in low tones with Monsieur and Madame Delande. Miss Hamilton's face was still ashen, and she looked as if she could not shake the horror of her discovery from her mind, or her eyes. Monsieur de Brassac went straight up to her, and spoke, in French which even I could understand.

"Won't you have a glass of port?" he asked, and when she had smiled a grateful acceptance he repeated his invitation to the two police officers. They very courteously declined, but Monsieur de Brassac's hospitality was undaunted.

"Perhaps afterward?" he said; and quite a pleasant human expression came into the face of the man at the table, before he turned to Miss Hamilton and politely and solemnly requested that she tell her story as a whole.

She spoke in French, but so slowly and clearly that I could make it out with little difficulty.

"I went with Mrs. Wilde to her room, about ten o'clock last night," she began. "That was the time she usually retired, and in her daughter's absence I wanted to see if she needed any help. She seemed to be feeling fairly well, but a little nervous—I thought she was perhaps a little upset by the prospect of spending a second night alone, and I offered to stay with her. But she told me that she was really all right, said good-night to me pleasantly, and, so to speak, sent me away."

"Did you see a hypodermic syringe, or any evidence of the use of morphine, in Madame Wilde's room?"

"No. I have never seen any such things in Mrs. Wilde's possession, nor any evidence which would lead me to think that she was addicted to drugs. I supposed that she must take some sort of medicine, since her health is so poor; and I knew that she had an alcohol lamp to heat water. That could have been used to sterilize a syringe, of course, but I never thought of that specific purpose. Naturally, I have never looked into the cupboards, or any place in Mrs. Wilde's room where such things as medicines would be kept. I went to my room last evening, after saying good-night, read a while, then went to bed and to sleep."

"One moment, please," the policeman interrupted. "Do you happen to know whether Madame Wilde locked her door when you left her?"

Curiously, Miss Hamilton hesitated. I had the feeling that there was something in her mind of which she was not sure that she wanted to speak, that she was pausing to decide what, or how much, to say.

"No," she answered, speaking more slowly than before. "I mean—I happen to know that Mrs. Wilde did not lock her door. That is—she told me that she was going to leave the door unlocked, as she had done the night before."

"Was that to save herself the trouble of getting out of bed to turn the key?"

"No," said Miss Hamilton again, and she spoke with more sureness now. "No, she left the door unlocked so that I could come in if she called."

The policeman frowned. "But would you have heard her if she had called?" he asked.

"No, I don't think I should," Miss Hamilton answered. "Not unless she had opened the door, and even then called rather loudly.

I suppose she thought I might perhaps want to look in during the night and see if she was all right . . ."

"And did you?"

"No."

"She had not actually asked you to go in during the night?"

"No."

"But she had explained that she was leaving the door unlocked so that you could?"

"Yes."

"And if you had gone in you would have seen the empty syringe on the table?"

"I—suppose so."

"Since Madame Wilde had so carefully concealed any evidence of the use of drugs, that seems odd," said the police officer.

"Yes," Miss Hamilton admitted wearily, "it seems odd."

"But in cases of drug-addiction," remarked the gendarme sententiously, "one expects oddities. Continue, if you please, Mademoiselle. You slept well?"

"Very well. I did not hear any sound outside my room, but once in the night I was disturbed by my dog. However, I went to sleep again almost immediately, and I think I slept until morning. About eight o'clock, as I was having my breakfast, the maid Aurélie came to my room and said that Mrs. Wilde did not answer her knock, and would I tell her what I thought she ought to do? I knew that Mrs. Wilde liked her meals to be served promptly, so I told the maid to knock again, more loudly."

Monsieur de Brassac, sitting beside me, had very kindly taken it upon himself to translate the gendarme's speeches for me. He acted as my interpreter now when an inquiry was made as to whether Mrs. Wilde's breakfast was usually brought without being rung for.

"Necessarily," Miss Hamilton explained. "There are no bells in the rooms in the *annexe*, and we always leave our breakfast order to be filled at some stated hour. Mrs. Wilde and her daughter always had their coffee and rolls taken to them at eight o'clock, and, as I said, Mrs. Wilde was very particular about having it on time. This morning Aurélie went back, as I had suggested, and knocked again. She pounded, in fact, so loudly that I could hear her on the floor above, with my door shut. Then she came back to me and said that she couldn't hear any sound in Mrs. Wilde's room at all.

"I said I would go into the room, but before I got downstairs I heard Mr. Braye come out of his room, which is directly opposite Mrs. Wilde's. By this time Aurélie was downstairs again and standing in front of Mrs. Wilde's door. And I had got to the top of the stairs myself as Aurélie spoke to Mr. Braye and tried to make him understand that she could not wake Mrs. Wilde. Aurélie was frightened by this time. Mr. Braye tried the door, and it wouldn't open. As I came down the stairs he bent down and looked into the key-hole—you understand, these doors have big old-fashioned keys: they are not patent locks.

"'That's funny,' he said to me. 'She's locked the door and taken out the key.'

"'Then Aurélie had better get the master-key and open the door,' I said. 'I am afraid Mrs. Wilde may be ill.'

"So Aurélie ran to get the master-key. Just then Mrs. Braye came out of her room, which is down the hall, and just under mine, and said something about their breakfast's not coming, and I told her about the delay. She said then probably they had better go over to the inn and get their breakfast there, and Mr. Braye said he thought so, too. But before they actually started, Aurélie came back, and Madame Delande was with her, with the key. Mr. and Mrs. Braye went immediately, without stopping to say anything at all. And as I had known Mrs. Wilde better than anyone else did, and thought that if she were ill she would rather see me first, I was the one who took the master-key and opened the door.

"She was lying in her bed. There was an empty hypodermic syringe on a saucer on her night-table, within reach of her hand. There was a little phial on the saucer, too. Its top had been broken off, and it was empty. There was no bottle marked morphine, but I—I suppose I just tried to put two and two together—I guessed it was that."

"Your conjecture was correct," said the gendarme, "but you did not actually *know?*"

"No," Miss Hamilton replied; and she looked, now, as if she were almost at the end of her endurance, "I didn't actually know. But I saw at once that she was dead. She—she had the appearance of being quite at peace. I—I was greatly shocked, upset. Madame Delande stayed with me while Aurélie ran for Monsieur. It just so happened that the doctor Montard was in the village, and he came at once."

That ended what had plainly been an extremely difficult ordeal for Miss Hamilton. The doctor had come meanwhile from the *pavillon*, and gave in detail evidence with which most of his hearers were probably already familiar. Again, Henri de Brassac acted as my unofficial interpreter.

Mrs. Wilde, the doctor reported, cautiously, pending the autopsy, had probably died from a lethal dose of morphine. There were marks on her body that showed the use of a hypodermic syringe. Yes, he thought the use might be habitual, but he refused to go on record as stating that she was a drug-addict. He insisted on pointing out the fact that the marks of injections were on her lower limbs, not her arms. He had found no morphine in her room. But he had had no opportunity for search. She might be addicted to the use of morphine; she might not; he had never seen her before; he could not say. All he was willing to assume was that it was morphine which had killed her. Would not her daughter know her habits?

I shivered. But I was not now allowed to sit silent and think of Christine. My story was called for next, and I told it in English, sentence by sentence, which Monsieur Delande, my host, now officially translated for the police. What with the necessity for translation and the gendarmes' careful recording, in longhand, of everything that was said, it was a slow story, with long pauses. And in the pause that followed my statement of my discovery of the sick man, Miss Hamilton turned dull, haggard eyes upon me, and said, as if she were learning of something which had a slight but totally unimportant interest:

"Oh, so you found Paul MacNeil?"

I had to go right on with my account of the night and the morning, and I was glad to be spared the necessity of answering. For I
was startled and shocked. I was even oddly bewildered. Miss
Hamilton had known about the sick man in the ruins! She had
known, and she had not done anything . . . And—this gave me the
greatest shock of all—she had lied to me! I had asked her, two days
before, if she knew of any other English-speaking person who was
staying in Neyronnes, and she had looked at me blankly and said,
"Why, no." And then she had, with playful casualness, suggested
that I might spend my evenings in some other way than prowling
around the crannies of these broken, ancient walls. I had asked
her a direct question—I had thought her the soul of honesty—and
she had told me a direct lie . . .

After my story came Henri de Brassac's, which corroborated a
part of mine. And then the Brayes were examined and had very
little to report—nothing beyond what Miss Hamilton had already
told of their movements. Mrs. Braye was nervous, over-ready to
talk and go on talking. Horace was blustering and rude, apparently
taking his routine examination as a personal insult, and making
childish references to the American consul.

He said that he had stayed at Neyronnes only until he could
get money on his letter of credit; that he had driven into the nearest city on the preceding afternoon and succeeded in buying francs
at a rate of around five cents apiece (which, also, he seemed to
take as an insult on the part of the French nation toward the United
States), and that he was now about to leave. He was going to
Marseille to find and board the first American ship bound for
America, he added; an addition which was totally irrelevant, but
which Horace insisted upon. And as a fine climax he thrust his hand
into his pocket, pulled it out full of not-very-large bills, and threw
them at Monsieur Delande.

"There's your money," he bellowed. "I'm leaving this hell-hole.
And if you say I owe you more than this you're a damned liar!"

Poor Miss Hamilton! It was proof enough of the collapsed state
of her nerves, of the tragic gravity of the situation, that this outburst brought no fire of indignation to her eye. No one, in fact,

paid the slightest attention to it, which must have been hard for Horace to bear. The money lay on the table where he had thrown it, and Monsieur and Madame Delande looked merely scornful and aloof. Horace sat down, snorting, and the gendarme at the table looked around at us, politely but with a little air of relief, as if he were glad to let us go now.

"I thank you for your courtesy, *Messieurs et Mesdames,*" he said. "And now before you go I will just look at your identity cards, to keep my records straight."

Automatically Miss Hamilton opened her purse and Monsieur de Brassac took something out of his breast-pocket. I saw what looked like little notebooks bound in lavender paper, as they handed them over to the police officer and he nodded, opened them, jotted down a word or two in his book, and handed them back.

"Identity cards!" Vaguely I remembered hearing of such things. But I had none . . .

I felt helpless and confused, when Monsieur Delande's kind, hearty voice spoke behind me. "Do not worry, Monsieur Armitage," and then to the gendarme:

"*Monsieur Armitage est en passage seulement: il est arrive de Génève il y a quinze jours.*"

I do not know much French, to be sure, but I could understand that and be grateful for it. And the gendarme smiled upon me with real good-humor, although he took no pains to disguise his pity for a foreigner who was only passing through France and had not been there long enough to require a *carte d'identité.*

"Then Monsieur will have the kindness to show me his passport," he said. And having attended to whatever formality was needed in examining that document, he turned to Mr. and Mrs. Braye.

Horace's face was purple. "I haven't got your damned identity card," he roared, "and if you don't like it you can lump it, that's all I've got to say. I haven't got an identity card, and what's more I don't intend to get one. I'm an American citizen, and you can go to hell!"

The gendarme did not wait for a translation of this speech.

"Then Monsieur will have the kindness to show me his passport," he said. And Horace handed out his passport and swore.

The police officer looked at this familiar piece of identification. He turned over its pages and looked it through. Then he laid it down, and addressed Mr. Braye very slowly and distinctly.

"I see that you debarked at Le Havre on the sixth of April," he said. "It is now the twentieth of June, and it seems that you have not been out of France in that time. Under the law you should have provided yourself with an identity card to become operative at least two weeks ago, Monsieur."

Horace began to bluster, but the police officer went on: "I am obliged to ask you to remain here until you have paid your fine and put yourself in accord with the regulations. And now Monsieur will have the kindness to show me the papers in regard to his car."

"They are in my room," said Mr. Braye. And to my surprise he spoke without profanity or abuse. The gendarme bowed.

"Monsieur will understand," he said, "that all France asks of foreigners is obedience to the laws of France. My friend will accompany Monsieur while he gets his papers."

And Horace went back with the other policeman to the *pavillon annexe*. I had the idea that he was really glad to have the officer with him. His door opened just across the narrow hallway from the room where Mrs. Wilde lay dead.

We waited almost in silence until he came back. And as I look back on my own feelings through that morning, I seem to remember nothing but confusion, from the moment when I first saw the bloodstains on the cobbles until the time of Christine's return. My first sense of relief, in regard to Christine, had vanished. I felt dazed and useless.

Horace Braye came back with a red portfolio under his arm and gave it to the gendarme without a word. The officer took out a large booklet, two small booklets, some loose sheets of paper; and carefully perused them all. Then he laid them down with a grimness that was obvious even to me, and said:

"I regret to discover, Monsieur, that your papers are not in order. You have not paid your tax."

"What tax?" Horace demanded. But there was no bluffing the gendarme.

"Monsieur knows what tax," he replied firmly. "That will have been explained to Monsieur by the Trans-atlantique. You have forgotten, Monsieur," he added, "that when you landed at Le Havre you took out a *laisser passer* for the circulation of your automobile for thirty days, at the rate of ten francs a day. I have here your *laisser passer*, good until the sixth day of May. It is now the twentieth day of June, Monsieur."

"All right. I forgot your damned tax," said Horace, and stuck his hand in his pocket. "Take your ten francs a day, for the love of Heaven, and let me get out of here."

Henri de Brassac smiled, and I thought that his eyes were not innocent of malice. But the gendarme's face was fixed in an expression of politeness and gravity.

"Monsieur is mistaken," he said. "The *laisser passer* cannot be issued for more than sixty days, and it can on no account be renewed. Beginning with the seventh day of May, Monsieur must pay the *taxe trimestriel*, which for a car so powerful as that of Monsieur"—he consulted Horace's papers again—"is at a rate which amounts to more than ten francs a day. Moreover, as Monsieur is in contravention, he must take the matter up with the proper authorities. You would not be permitted, Monsieur, in any case, to pay your tax to me; the *taxe trimestriel* must be paid to the *Bureau des Contributions Indirectes*."

"Oh, my God," groaned Horace, at the mere sound of this speech. When it was explained to him, he became more indignant than ever.

"You bloodsuckers!" he ejaculated. "You give me a pain in the neck! What right have you got to pile all these taxes on foreigners, I'd like to know? I'm an American. So I've got to have your damned identity card, and I've got to pay a tax on my car, and the Lord knows what else. I'm sick of this business of robbing strangers.

You bet Europe'll never see me again! My God, I'd rather be in Sing Sing, in America!"

I caught, at this, a rather pitiful little gasp from Rosalie, as if she thought Horace's rage was going beyond a joke. But she was the only person who seemed at all moved. From what I had heard of the excitability of the French temperament, I found myself looking for some fireworks to answer this explosion. But none came. With the exception of Horace Braye himself, everyone was absolutely calm, and absolutely solemn.

And calmly and solemnly, at this eloquent climax to Mr. Braye's oration, Henri de Brassac addressed first the gendarme with permission to speak, and then Mr. Braye. He spoke, of course, in perfect English.

"It is a little matter of misunderstanding," he said, with the utmost suavity, "and the gendarme will permit me to explain. There is no discrimination against foreigners, Monsieur. As the gendarme has already intimated, the French Government asks of you merely what it asks of every Frenchman: to be the possessor of the *carte d'identité* which is the guaranty of your registration in the country, and to pay the regular government tax on your automobile. The *laisser passer*, at ten francs a day, for any car, is a special convenience for foreigners; when your *laisser passer* expires, or in any case at the end of sixty days, you become subject to the ruling which applies to all French residents, and your car is taxed according to its horse-power."* His smile, guiltless of malice now, was really charming. "It is not the fault of France, Monsieur, that you are rich enough to have a forty-horsepower automobile."

Horace's great voice boomed forth with a great laugh. Once again his cherished sense of humor downed his rage.

"I'll say it isn't!" he bellowed, and having thus delivered a crushing retort, he was wholly pleased with himself again, while his wife

---

* To avoid misunderstanding, it may be pointed out here that the circulation tax on automobiles, long operative in France, was replaced in the 1934 budget bill by a new tax on gasoline. *Author.*

giggled dutifully. "But all the same, I'm asking you," he added, "what are these fellows picking on me for? Are they investigating a mysterious death, or are they trying to find out whether I owe ten cents to the French Government? Why don't they go about their business? Look here, Mister Brasstacks, or whatever your name is, that's just what we mean when we say that you people over on this side are inefficient. You've got brains. We don't deny that. Now if you just went in for real efficiency, you'd get somewhere."

"Where the United States is now, perhaps," Monsieur de Brassac remarked mildly; and before any reply was possible, continued: "Be that as it may, Monsieur Braye, we must, as you might say, remain with our lamb chops. This is not a comparison of American and European business methods, but a police inquiry. And it is a part of that inquiry to have clear records of all the persons who may possibly be involved."

"I am not involved," Horace flashed at him quickly. "What do you think I am, a dope-smuggler?"

Monsieur de Brassac ignored the latter part of this remark, but he said:

"You tried the door, did you not? You leaned over and looked in the keyhole. It was you who first pointed out that there was no key in the lock."

"Well, what business is that of yours? Who's conducting this dumb-bell inquiry, anyhow? It seems to me you're damned interested—"

Horace was getting ugly again. Monsieur de Brassac, unperturbed, shrugged his shoulders, and the gendarme re-entered the conversation and told Mr. Braye that he would be obliged to remain in Neyronnes, and that he would not be allowed to use his car, until the complications over his papers had been cleared up.

I suppose that this pronouncement would have been followed by more abuse, but at this moment came the interruption that I had been dreading for the last half-hour. An automobile horn, with the sound of which at least five of us assembled there were familiar, gave its warning at the corner. And a few seconds later, as we waited, Christine Wilde swung her big Packard into the *Place*.

VIII
MRS. WILDE MAKES A GIFT

Miss Hamilton was at her side in an instant, and it was she who told her, of course. I did not hear what she said: I was speaking with the Sherrills. But it was a scene far less confused, and therefore far less painful, than I had feared. Christine turned dead white, but she neither screamed nor fainted; much less did she become hysterical. Nor did she demand to be allowed to see her mother's body at once. She said that, since the police were there, she thought she would like to talk with them now, and get it over; and, refusing any assistance, she walked into the inn and sat down at the table, opposite the gendarme. The police officer asked his questions as considerately as possible, and she answered them calmly and quietly. And although I could not understand all that she said, I learned for the first time some details about the Wildes' background.

Their home, Christine said, had originally been in St. Louis, but they had spent all their time abroad for a great many years, and they were to all intents and purposes quite alone in the world. Since her father's death, four years ago, she and her mother had traveled about most of the time, but they kept an apartment in Lausanne which was the nearest approach they had to a home. Although they had been in the United States, briefly, in 1926 and again in 1930, they were officially residents of Switzerland.

About their financial position, Christine had no definite information to give. She said they had "never had to think much about money" until lately. But with the *crise*, and the failure of the St.

Louis bank, and the stoppage of important dividends, and now the fall of the dollar, her mother had talked about being worried. That was why they were staying in Neyronnes. But beyond that they did not seem to be obliged to economize very greatly, she said. She did not think that even with the bank failure they had become really very poor; it was more the fear of worse possibilities in the future that had been troubling her mother, she thought—the talk of inflation had been especially disturbing. But, Christine repeated, she did not know what property, or investments, her mother had, or even what their income was. Her mother had never told her. She supposed that their lawyer, in Lausanne, knew . . .

Then she was questioned about her mother's health.

Mrs. Wilde had been delicate for as long as Christine could remember, and her father had taught her from babyhood that she must always "think of mother first." But it was only when her father died and she was taken away from her school in Lausanne that she herself had felt her present responsibility for her mother's welfare. Yes, she supposed they could have had a maid, or a nurse, or a companion, but Mrs. Wilde had never wished to be taken care of by anyone but a member of her own family. No, there had been no change in her mother's health in recent years. The specialist was keeping the trouble checked.

"And what was the matter with your mother, Miss Wilde?" the gendarme asked.

"She was threatened with diabetes," Christine replied, in a low voice. "She did not want people to know, because it seemed so—so depressing. It seemed like an old person's disease, too, and my mother was not old, and she did not like to be associated with any ideas of growing old. She was young, and charming; and the doctor was keeping the trouble checked. He gave her insulin."

Elinor Sherrill, sitting beside Christine, made a very slight movement, but no one else stirred and no one spoke. Of course we all knew what was coming, and we sat there and dreaded it. But there was nothing anyone could do . . .

"Miss Wilde," said the police officer, "was your mother in the habit of taking drugs?"

But Christine did not look shocked. She looked merely puzzled. "Drugs?" she repeated. "I told you. The doctor gave her insulin."

"That is not what I mean," said the gendarme. "You must forgive me, Miss Wilde, but it is my duty to make my report as conclusive as possible. Was your mother addicted to habit-forming drugs, to narcotics—specifically, to morphine?"

"*What?*" cried Christine. She sprang from her chair and stood facing the police officer in a sort of white passion, which, for an instant, could find no further word to say. She looked around the room, looked at us all. "*Morphine?*" she repeated. "Did my mother die from *morphine?*"

I thought I understood the horror in her face and voice, but I was very far from guessing the truth, quite unprepared for what was to follow.

"I thought, from what Miss Hamilton told me, it was a heart attack," Christine said. "If it was morphine—"

Her voice broke off dramatically, and then she seemed to be gathering all her strength for what she must think out, for what she must say.

"My mother never touched morphine. She never could take it. She had an idiosyncrasy, the doctor said—all opiates were a deadly poison to her." She swayed a little as she stood there, but she went on and finished her statement.

"If my mother died from morphine poisoning," she said, "someone meant her to die."

. . . She staggered, and almost fell, but she did not faint. It was poor, insignificant Rosalie Braye who fainted; and as she was easily the least important person there, no one paid much attention to her, except Madame Delande, who somehow got her out of the room and saw that she was taken care of. Poor Rosalie; she was always inept, always feckless, the kind of person whom nobody ever took into account. Now she just fainted, and no one took any notice. But Christine's astonishing accusation had changed the entire nature of the inquiry. Moreover, we were sitting in the public dining-room of an inn and it was lunch-time—the Auberge de Vieux

Neyronnes had its own proper business to transact. The police investigation was abruptly adjourned, and we were all directed not to leave the village and to hold ourselves in readiness for the continuation of the inquiry when the *juge d'instruction*—a French local magistrate, I gathered—should so decide.

Christine made one further remark before the police left the room, a mere emphatic repetition of what she had already said.

"If you think that my mother was a drug-addict, you are very much mistaken," she declared. "I know beyond a shadow of a doubt that she was not. But I cannot ask you simply to take my word for that. I am going to telephone at once to my mother's physician in Lausanne and ask him to give you his evidence. I will ask him to come here to-morrow morning, if possible. And now may I go to—may I go to my room?"

She went to look at her mother's body, and Margaret Hamilton and Elinor Sherrill went with her. John Sherrill and I followed them, and one of the policemen accompanied us. The other stayed behind to talk with Horace Braye—poor Monsieur Delande being still held in service as interpreter. Horace, I learned later, was required to drive his car, with the gendarme in it, to the headquarters at Jeanniot, and there to leave the automobile pending the regularization of his papers. . . .

When we reached the Wildes' room in the *pavillon annexe*, we found that two other policemen were on guard there and had been all morning. And I realized for the first time that since the instant when Miss Hamilton, Madame Delande, and the maid opened the locked door with the pass-key, there had been no moment when at least two persons had not been with the body in that room. I learned, too, that there had been an examination for finger-prints. Had these non-committal gendarmes suspected from the first that the case might not be so simple as it seemed or had all this been mere routine? I did not know then, and I was never to know. My own opinion at this stage was that Mrs. Wilde must have committed suicide. Menaced with the progress of an all but hopeless disease, seriously worried about money—the suicide theory seemed natural enough . . .

It was a dreadful afternoon. It was dreadful because of Christine's suffering and the necessary and heart-sickening inconvenience to which she was put. Her mother's body was taken away at once for post-mortem examination, and she was told that the room must be sealed, and that she must, therefore, go somewhere else immediately. The gendarme stayed with her while she pulled a few dresses and a coat off the closet hooks, snatched up some shoes and a hat.

"I'm ready now," she said. "The hotel is almost full, but there's a little room I think I can have."

"Oh, no, Christine," Miss Hamilton broke in very gently, "there is someone there now. Mr. Armitage," she added, "has found Paul MacNeil and brought him to the inn."

Christine turned suddenly to me, where I was standing in the doorway waiting to see if I could not be of some use. And to my astonishment she smiled, a very sad smile, but a very human one. For the first time in the two weeks since I had heard her voice outside my window on the day of my arrival, Christine Wilde looked at me as if I were a real person like herself, a real acquaintance, almost a friend.

And in the light of that smile I saw clearly for the first time what had been true since that day and would be true for all the rest of my life—that in my heart the sun rose and set, and the clouds scudded across the sky or piled up their storm threats, and the stars sang in their courses, for Christine Wilde and for Christine Wilde only. To bring her happiness, to save her sorrow, to serve her and belong to her all my life, to watch her face and listen to her voice and to win her smile, and to hold her in my arms against the twilight and be her comrade forever—that was all I wanted, so long as my life should last. And this, I told myself with a kind of wonder, this was what love was: this consecration, this curious uplifting, this sudden inexplicable joy and this intolerable pain . . .

I tried to smile back at Christine, but to my shame I felt near to tears. Her face was so kind, however, it showed no consciousness of my shortcomings.

"You brought Paul to the inn?" she echoed. "Oh, I am glad."

For me that was piling mystery on mystery. But this was no time to be even mildly interested in that.

"You had better take my room," Miss Hamilton added. "I can easily move to the other house."

"Oh, no," said Elinor Sherrill. "It will be much better, Margot, if Christine takes my room. John's is quite large enough for two beds. And I have been here so short a time, it will be much easier for me to move the few things I've unpacked. Then no one will be made uncomfortable."

"All right," Miss Hamilton agreed, and Christine thanked Mrs. Sherrill and said, yes, that was what she would do. So they changed their rooms, and Christine moved up to my corridor with the Sherrills and Miss Hamilton, so that the Brayes and Monsieur de Brassac were left to occupy the first floor beside the sealed door, with the sick man as neighbor.

Everything was settled within half an hour, and although the afternoon had already set in, we tried now to eat some luncheon. To our surprise we succeeded. Even Christine ate a little, I was glad to see. And Miss Hamilton seemed to have recovered something of her poise, although she was still white and haggard. We were all sitting at luncheon together—the Sherrills, Miss Hamilton, Christine, and I—when word was brought to Christine that the Lausanne call had come through, and she went into the little back room where the telephone was installed.

She was gone a long time, and when she came back she looked stronger and more sure of herself. All she said was, "Dr. Lavigne will be here tomorrow morning." But I had the feeling, as I had begun to have it, in less degree, when she spoke of the morphine, that she was somehow becoming, herself, the master of the situation. And that brought relief and comfort to my heart.

I had seen Christine Wilde, at the beginning, as a girl who was completely dominated by an unscrupulously self-absorbed mother; a girl of bright mind and quick reactions, whose spirit was caged, whose individuality was crushed, whose intellect was in grave danger of being stunted. Except in foreign languages, she had had very little education, as I understood that term. Her whole energy and thought were concentrated on the care of an utterly selfish, semi-invalid mother, with the one sole outlet of driving, and looking after, a motor car.

There are invalids and invalids, as I knew better than most: my own mother had been almost completely bedridden for years before her death, and life with her opened windows on wide horizons not only of courage and high-spirited self-forgetfulness, but of beauty and interest and intellectual resource. But that was not the kind of invalid that Mrs. Wilde had been.

With her, all windows that opened outward were closed and barred. And for her daughter, lovely and kind and helpless and imprisoned, I had feared actual arrest of mental development. Only once had I felt any vividness of movement behind those too-bright eyes, and that was when I found her cleaning her car, and she said that she liked a dirty job because it made her "feel free." And yet, I remembered, that was the only time I had had any real talk with her. It was very odd, when I came to think of it, how rarely, in those two weeks in this tiny village, I had even seen Christine!

Now, she seemed quite different already. Shocked and sorrowing as she was, she moved among us as a free creature, as one of ourselves. And her eyes were not too bright now: they were sad, but they were soft and thoughtful, and very beautiful . . .

Later in the afternoon, Mr. and Mrs. Sherrill got special permission by telephone from the gendarmerie, and drove in to the city to do some conventionally necessary shopping for Christine. In the morning, she was up and about early, waiting for the doctor to come from Lausanne. But a telephone message came instead to tell her that he had stopped to see the *juge d'instruction* on the way. It was not until after luncheon that a rather elegant car with a Swiss license plate drove into the *Place*, and its chauffeur held the door open for two strangers.

The Sherrills and Miss Hamilton and I were in the *galerie*, and Christine was with us, with her eyes on the road. We were seeing very little of Henri de Brassac and the Braye couple. But the Frenchman had told me that he was taking care of Paul MacNeil, of whom I still knew nothing whatever beyond his name and the fact of his illness, although I had called briefly to see him several times. And as for the Brayes—to whom nobody gave a thought, I am sure, except to be thankful for their absence—Horace was probably sulking somewhere, with or without his wife. As the strange men stepped out of the automobile, Christine said:

"There is Dr. Lavigne; and Mr. Williamson is with him."

And Miss Hamilton gave a startled little exclamation.

"Why, that is the man who came to see Mrs. Wilde two weeks ago," she said. "Who is this Mr. Williamson, Christine?"

But Christine was already on her way to greet the newcomers, and did not answer. It was obvious that she had not heard Miss Hamilton's question. And when she had greeted the two men, she turned and walked with them up the curving *ruelle* toward the *pavillon*. She was fairly sure of privacy there, I knew, in one of the rooms downstairs. But as she disappeared from view, she called to us over her shoulder:

"Please wait, all of you, until I come back."

We waited half an hour or more. It occurred to me, as we sat there, what a wonderful thing it must be to have money—not millions, but just enough to meet emergencies without thinking of the cost. As simply as if she were merely buying a new pair of gloves, Christine had summoned an important specialist to come all the way from Lausanne, and with him another man who also looked important, to take time from their busy lives to do her bidding at Neyronnes: their bills would be enormous . . .

When she came back, she introduced the strangers and asked them to sit down with us. Dr. Lavigne informed us, without wasting any words, that he had already been able to assure the investigating officials that Mrs. Wilde was not a drug-addict, that opiates were poison to her system, and also that in his opinion it was altogether improbable that she should have taken her own life. She was not of the temperament for suicide, he said; and she had talked constantly with him about plans for the future.

"But I have asked Mr. Williamson to come with information of another kind," Christine added. "Mr. Williamson has been my mother's lawyer, and mine, all my life. He knows all about our affairs, everything that my mother never told me. I felt that I must find out at once, you see, how I stood. So far as I know, I am entirely alone in the world. But I have never even known the terms of my mother's will—I mean, I have known only a little about how she was leaving her money, and nothing about how much she had to leave. As you heard me say yesterday, I have never known what our income was, much less the principal. I have asked Mr. Williamson to come and tell me."

She looked around at us, a little wistfully. "You are all my friends here," she went on, "and I have no family, or even any neighbors. I should like Mr. Williamson to tell you about my affairs, too—I have asked him to tell me in your presence . . ."

It was a little formal. It was very practical. It was wholly businesslike. And it seemed to me like a dream. For I was not used to money, or to talk about money in large terms; and the lawyer's explanation had a kind of unreality to my unaccustomed mind. He talked of investments, of interest and dividends, of stocks and bonds, of losses and depreciations and residues and hopes of amelioration. I did not understand it all. I even found it hard to listen to it. But he caught my attention in a torturing grip when he began to speak of these matters in their immediately personal aspect.

"As you will see," he pronounced, "Miss Wilde, named as the residuary legatee, is almost her mother's sole heir. And in spite of shrinkages in Mrs. Wilde's estate, she is left very comfortably off. I may add as my considered opinion that the further shrinkages feared by Mrs. Wilde need not cause her daughter grave concern, if indeed they ever take place, which in fact I doubt. It is probable that Miss Wilde's estate will grow larger instead of smaller, if the principal is well husbanded during the immediate future. And, as you will see, deducting the moderate bequests to charity in the original will, and the substantial trust fund established by the codicil, Miss Wilde is left with an income at the present time of roughly thirty thousand dollars a year."

Thirty thousand dollars a year! Christine, whom I knew that I loved; Christine, whom I had longed to help, whom I wanted to stand beside and shield from all future disaster—I with my miserable job as a junior teacher in a boarding-school! I thought with a dull nausea of pain and humiliation of the life I could have offered Christine, its meagerness, its poverty, its round of prosaic duties and circumscribed enjoyments—how she would have laughed at me if she had known! How they would all have laughed . . . I knew now that the lawyer was reading Mrs. Wilde's will, but I could not listen. It was all a daze of misery. Through that daze, through that chilling, hopeless fog, I heard his precise voice, going on and on; and at last, once more, it gripped my attention:

"This codicil which I drew up for Mrs. Wilde seventeen days ago, is as follows:

"And I direct that a trust fund be established to provide a permanent annuity, in token of my appreciation for all her kindness, of the sum of seven thousand dollars a year throughout her lifetime, to my friend Margaret Joyce Hamilton . . .'"

Behind me sounded a long, strange wail, as if despair itself cried out from depths that only the desperate knew. And in the next instant I was staring at a threadbare coat sleeve, where the shabby middle-aged spinster had fallen unconscious on the dirt floor.

IX

I LEARN THE SECRET OF THE RUINS

At a signal from Christine the Swiss doctor helped John Sherrill
and me to get Miss Hamilton to her room, and the lawyer came
tagging along after us. I had a horrible sensation that he had determined, as long as he should be in Neyronnes, not to let Miss
Hamilton out of his sight. But he did not obtrude his presence. He
merely followed us, with his precise little trot that might have
amused me under happier circumstances. The doctor and Mr. and
Mrs. Sherrill went into the bedroom, and the rest of us stood at
the door or in the hall. And a trivial thing happened which seemed
to me rather curious. As the unconscious woman was laid on her
bed, she came to herself again, opened her eyes, and looked about
her; and what she said, in a voice that was beautiful even in its
extreme weakness, was:

"Doctor—will you please look at Paul MacNeil?"

Mercifully, at that moment of returning consciousness, Miss
Hamilton had not remembered the situation which she must face
for herself. And that recollection was postponed a little further, I
hoped, when Christine spoke from the doorway in an even and
matter-of-course tone:

"Yes, doctor, we shall be very glad if you will examine Mr.
MacNeil while you are here. He is in the inn, very ill. I will tell you
about him."

"Presently," said the physician.

And with that as our dismissal, we all, except the doctor himself and Elinor Sherrill, turned and trooped down the narrow

stairs—to walk into Horace Braye as he emerged from his room on the first floor. Christine headed our little procession, of which the lawyer Williamson brought up the rear.

And at sight of Christine Mr. Braye stopped in the hallway, blocking our path directly at her mother's door. He held out his hand.

"I have not yet had an opportunity to offer you my condolences, Miss Wilde," he said. "Permit me to express the deep sympathy of myself and my wife in your bereavement."

The bounder! The unspeakable bounder! I could have sworn that he was deriving immense pleasure for the chance to be oratorical, to show off. And if I could have smitten him to earth with one blow I should happily have done so. What I did instead was foolish enough, in all conscience; for it merely brought more annoyance to Christine and moved Horace to rage.

"This is hardly the time to make a speech, Mr. Braye," I broke in.

And although I knew that nothing made a man more angry than a public reproof to his manners—especially from the young and inexperienced, as well as poverty-stricken, person that I knew myself to be—I was surprised by the ugliness of Horace's face in its contortion of fury.

"Mind your own business, you damned pup," he said to me. And of course I realized that I had acted like a silly child! My own behavior was no better than Horace's.

Christine's voice fell very gratefully on my ears. "Thank you, Mr. Braye," she said, and took his still outstretched hand. "Please thank Mrs. Braye for me, too. But, as Mr. Armitage says, I can't talk about those things now."

She smiled at him with faultless impersonal politeness, and as he backed awkwardly into his room, she turned and smiled comfortingly, bless her heart, at me. She knew what an utter fool I was, I said to myself, and she was willing to forgive me.

No one spoke again as we went down the stairs and out into the small *place* opposite the war memorial. But after we had turned into the village street, on our way back to the inn, and had passed under the Brayes' windows, the lawyer addressed Christine.

"Who is that man?" he asked.

"His name is Horace Braye," she answered. "That is all I know about him."

"Do you know that?" the lawyer insisted. And Christine shook her head.

"I only know that that is what he calls himself," she admitted. "I haven't seen his passport."

"I have," I put in. "His name is Horace Braye, unless his passport is false."

"That wouldn't be likely," said Mr. Williamson, "but it seems queer."

"What seems queer?" Christine asked.

"Just that his face seems familiar to me and his name is not. I can't place him. I have no recollection of ever having met anyone called Horace Braye. But I have a distinct conviction that somewhere, fleetingly, in the United States, I have seen that man. Did your mother know him, Christine?"

"No," she answered, quite positively, "I am sure she did not. She had never heard his name and she had never, so far as she was able to remember, seen his face. She didn't know his wife, either. The reason I am so sure," she added, "is that on the evening the Brayes came, and he first spoke to us, Mr. Braye looked at mother as if he thought he might have seen her before; and she spoke of it afterward to me, and said he must have been mistaken, because he was a complete stranger to her. And mother had a very good memory for faces."

"I should say that it was not entirely reliable," the lawyer objected, in his precise way. "Your mother remembered people whom she met socially, even people with whom she chatted casually in hotels. But unless there was some such personal interest as that, I should not consider her memory for faces altogether dependable."

"Well, we have certainly never met the Brayes," said Christine. "And I am quite sure that I have never seen him before. I don't like Mr. Braye, and I should not have forgotten him. I dare say he might have seen mother somewhere in the United States long ago: he would be more apt to remember her than she would him," she added, colloquially but none the less emphatically.

"He does remember faces, I'll wager," John Sherrill remarked. "He has that look in his eye—gives you a quick hard glance when he meets you, and stores notes away in his head, for future reference.

"Since you are interested in Horace Braye, Mr. Williamson," he continued, "we had better tell you that he has been providing our comic relief here in Neyronnes since Saturday evening. He has his American bootleg bar with him, and he thinks all foreigners are robbers, and he doesn't see why the old houses of Neyronnes aren't torn down to widen the road—you know the type. He is one of those coarse, clownish, ill-tempered, incredibly ignorant American bounders that you read about, and that occasionally you do actually meet. Foreigners hate them, of course; but no foreigner could possibly hate them with the concentrated fury of aversion which they inspire in their suffering fellow-Americans—their squirming fellow-Americans, I might say. Horace is one of those king-fishes, and we laugh at him and loathe him and wonder what offensive imbecility he is going to bring forth next. But all the same, Mr. Williamson, Horace is no imbecile. I think he knows his own stuff, and I think he has pretty keen brains, of his own kind. When he asked Mrs. Wilde about her finances, he knew what he was talking about."

"Oh," ejaculated the lawyer. "So he asked Mrs. Wilde about her finances? What did he ask?"

"He asked her how she had lost so much money, and when she said a bank had failed, he asked what bank."

"And did she tell him?"

"Of course she told him," said Christine, "and then he told her to cheer up, everything would be all right, and pretty soon he and his wife went to their rooms."

"Oh," remarked the lawyer again, this time with an air of rounding up the subject. "Now tell me, Christine," he began again, after a brief pause, "it has never been made quite clear to me—how long have you and your mother known this Miss Hamilton?"

"About two months," Christine answered. "She was here when we came in April, and mother was feeling particularly wretched. She was tired from the trip, and when the country went off gold she was so terribly upset. Miss Hamilton was very kind, right from the beginning. Mother told her how worried she was . . ."

"I," put in John Sherrill, very clearly and firmly, "have known Margaret Hamilton for many years, Mr. Williamson. And although naturally I have not had a chance to ask her permission, I think I may take it upon myself to say that I am prepared to represent her legally. I am a member of the New York Bar, although I have not practiced for some time."

This was news to me, and I felt heartily thankful for it. I myself was all confused: I did not know what to think about Miss Hamilton. But whatever she might or might not have done, it was clear that she needed a lawyer as well as a friend. Mr. Williamson made a formal little bow—exactly the kind of bow one would have expected from hearing him speak and seeing him walk on the cobblestones.

"Ah, I am glad of that, Mr. Sherrill," he said. "That is quite regular, and as it should be. We will talk of this, privately, in detail."

"We will, indeed. And I may add that I think it is a very good thing we are both here." John Sherrill, too, had an air of dismissing the subject.

But I was not surprised when, as we got back to the *galerie*, he said to me, "Try to persuade Christine to have some tea, Armitage, or a glass of port. I'm inviting Mr. Williamson to go for a little walk."

"Thank you," said Christine. "I shall be glad to have tea with Mr. Armitage, right away."

She waited while I ordered the tea, and the others walked slowly across the *Place* and down the hill toward the rampart promenade. Then she said:

"I want to talk to you. I—I feel that I can talk to you now. Mr. Armitage, I am so terribly worried about Miss Hamilton. I can see that Mr. Williamson suspects her of having killed my mother. That is so horrible—I can't even think about it. I knew that my mother was leaving her some money—I don't know whether she knew or not—I never thought of it this way. I can't believe such a terrible thing of Miss Hamilton—she was always so kind to mother. But someone killed my mother, Mr. Armitage. There was someone, here in Neyronnes, who wanted her to die. And there must have been some *reason* . . . Miss Hamilton— Oh, what do *you* think?"

Strange that the first direct question Christine had ever asked me should be one to which I could give no direct answer . . . For I did not know what I thought. Or rather, I did not know how to differentiate between what I thought, or felt, and what I knew. And the more I pondered over it, the more strong grew the realization that although what I *thought* and *felt* might be in Miss Hamilton's favor, what I *knew* pointed dreadful fingers of accusation against her. What I thought was that I liked Miss Hamilton, enjoyed her conversation, admired her spirit; what I thought was that she was intelligent and courageous, that she was an aristocrat who had fallen upon evil days, that she was kind . . .

And even as I formulated the last items in my mind, I saw how they themselves were items of accusation. An aristocrat who had fallen upon evil days—a gently nurtured woman, unused to poverty, untrained to any profession, without commercial experience or ability, without much physical strength, a woman middle-aged and desperate. And kind. Oh, so terribly kind! So terribly too kind! Damningly, I heard again Henri de Brassac's casual sentences:

"She is kind, that lady. Why should she be so kind to this Madame Wilde? She is the good neighbor, *n'est ce pas?*"

Could one think, now, that she had been merely the good neighbor? Or must one read a new and sinister significance into those next casual words that Monsieur de Brassac had spoken—"She is very intelligent"?

Before I could frame an answer to Christine's question, Elinor Sherrill and the doctor came into the *Place*, and Henri de Brassac was with them. But when Mrs. Sherrill's voice fell upon my ear, it was not of what she said that I was thinking. It was of another voice, low-pitched, beautiful, somehow poignantly *living* in its quality, speaking in the fragrant summer darkness sentences which I would have given anything in the world, now, not to have heard:

"I'm just finished, done for, Elinor, unless something turns up
. . . It's all just swallowed up, disappeared . . . When one is quite
desperate, as I am . . . A sense of desperation seems to sweep away
everything, somehow, one's sense of values, even one's sense of
right and wrong . . . I'm not going to sponge on my friends; theft
or murder seems more self-respecting than that . . . Sometimes I
feel as if I understood the strangest impulses . . . It almost frightens me . . ."

Oh, they were terrible sentences to be remembering now, to be
unable to forget, to be haunted by, along with that low wail of an-
guish and the sight of a threadbare coat sleeve on the dirt floor! At
the time I had thought them almost heartbreakingly sad; but now
they were terrible! Then, as she and her friend finished their conversation, I had admired her courage so greatly, I had thought her
words of valorous acceptance so fine, so utterly sincere. And she
was almost old enough to be my mother, this tired and lonely
woman with the beautiful voice. Yes—another thought came to torment me—she was not young; she had been living in Europe for
several years, ever since the crash came; the Sherrills had not seen
her for some time; with all their loyalty and old affection, how could
they really know to what dark depths her spirit might have sunk
under the pressure of those lonely desperate years? How could even
they know? How could anyone know? What was I to think, how
puzzle through it all?

Well, at least I knew what I was going to do—or, rather, what I
was not going to do. I was not going to tell anyone that Miss Hamilton had lied to me about Paul MacNeil, or that she had cried out to
me that Mrs. Wilde had taken an overdose of morphine when—as
she had been obliged later to admit to the police—she had no way
of actually knowing what the drug in the hypodermic syringe had
been. Certainly those first words of Miss Hamilton's to me, repeated there in the doorway of the inn, had been precisely the right
words to 'plant' the impression that Mrs. Wilde had died acciden-
tally after taking too much of an habitual narcotic; if Christine had
not made her surprising revelation about her mother's idiosyncrasy
in regard to opiates, that impression, I thought, would most likely

have prevailed . . . I shuddered. But I had made up my mind. Let them all find out for themselves, if they must. I was still sorry for Miss Hamilton; I was more sorry for her than ever. I wasn't going to tell.

And upon these thoughts in my mind fell Elinor Sherrill's voice, as calm and sweet and even as if nothing of what had happened could hurt her friend in any way.

"Monsieur de Brassac has been kind enough to offer to change rooms with Margaret," she said to Christine and me, "so that I can stay with her at night, or she can have a nurse if she needs one. But I have just been telling him that it is not necessary for us to take advantage of his generosity. Dr. Lavigne has given her something to make her sleep, and he says she will be all right soon."

"Oh, I am glad," Christine cried, with a spontaneity for which I heartily admired her. "And that was very good of you, Monsieur de Brassac. Miss Hamilton," she added, with no effect of challenge, but firmly withal—so that I realized that, with no assistance from me in answering her question, she, too, had made up her mind— "Miss Hamilton is my very good friend."

"And mine, I hope," said the Frenchman, with his grave smile. And,

"I am sure of that," Mrs. Sherrill answered him.

Well, I was glad that they were rallying to her defense, that Christine was going to befriend her. At the same time, I felt a sense of relief from tension as Mrs. Sherrill turned to Christine and spoke again without allowing any time for interruption.

"Will you tell the doctor what you know about this Mr. MacNeil?" she asked. "He is going to see him, but he would like to know something of his history first. And won't you tell the rest of us, too? We are all completely in the dark, you know. And that seems hardly fair to Monsieur de Brassac and Mr. Armitage, who have been so kind."

"Oh—didn't Miss Hamilton tell you about him?"

Christine seemed surprised, and I allowed Henri de Brassac's negative to serve as answer for the two of us.

"Then I will tell you about him, of course," she went on, at once. "It's no secret, now. And it is all very simple . . .

"Paul MacNeil is an American, who has been living for several years in a village in the Vaudoise Alps, because of the state of his lungs, and who came here in May. My mother and I met him in Lausanne two years ago, and, curiously enough, it was he who told us about Neyronnes: he had known this place, and loved it, long ago. But we never had much acquaintance with him—as a matter of fact, he seemed to us a very solitary sort of young man, who loved English poetry more than anything else. He knew heaps and heaps of it, and he used to recite long poems to himself, he told us, to pass the time. For, you see, he was very poor, and very ill. I mean, he had consumption badly, even then, and he had had it for years. The woman who introduced him to us said that his condition was probably hopeless, and had been ever since they found out about it; but of course nobody told him that; and he always seemed cheerful, the few times we saw him.

"It seems that he had a very small income, and he had come to Switzerland and was living in a *pension* in the mountains for five Swiss francs—one dollar—a day. And once in a great while, when he had saved a little money, and was feeling better, and the weather was good, he would go down to Montreux or Lausanne—once, I think, even as far as Geneva—on a holiday, to keep in touch with ordinary life, he said. And then his little income began to shrink. And this spring, when his dollar wasn't a dollar any longer, he simply didn't have the money for his board in the *pension*. He got the idea, then, of coming back here, and he worked out a plan."

"Couldn't he have gone home?" asked Elinor Sherrill.

"No, I think that wouldn't have been possible. In the first place, I am quite sure that he had no home to go to. It was the paper he had worked for that had raised a fund to pay for his fare to Switzerland in the first place, and he hadn't the money, now, to pay his passage back. But more than that, I doubt if he could have stood the long journey back to America and the uncertainty and loneliness when he got there—it isn't easy to find board anywhere for a dollar a day, and his strength had failed very greatly. He was much more ill, even when he came here, than he was when we met him in Lausanne. And, you see, he wanted to come to Neyronnes. He remembered how beautiful it was, and how peaceful. And he had a good plan."

Christine was telling her story primarily for the doctor's benefit, and she addressed him directly now.

"I don't know much about tuberculosis," she said, "but it seems that the form of disease from which Mr. MacNeil is suffering is a special, and rather rare, kind, which is not contagious until the very end. Our acquaintance in Lausanne, who introduced him to us, explained it to mother, because even then anyone could have guessed that he was a consumptive, and she did not want mother to be worried about infection. That was how it was that he could go about as freely as he did then, and could live in a *pension* in a village where ordinary tubercular patients were not received, and could plan to come here. You know all about that, Dr. Lavigne, of course."

"Yes," said the physician. "That part is quite simple. You are speaking of what we call 'dry' pulmonary tuberculosis. There is no discharge from the lungs until the last stage of the disease is reached, and therefore there is no danger to other persons except under conditions of great intimacy. But the last stage is that of hemorrhages, Miss Wilde; and although naturally I cannot make any specific diagnosis until I have seen the patient, I should warn you, I think, that the last stage is usually very brief. Is Mr. MacNeil having hemorrhages?"

Henri de Brassac had been listening with the most absorbed attention to everything that Christine and the doctor said. It was he who answered the latter's question.

"He has had at least one, and it was very severe indeed. Since then, he has seemed to be simply exhausted. He has not been able to talk to us."

"He is very ill," said Christine. "I tried to see him this morning, but he was too ill to see me at all."

"It is no wonder that he is very ill if he was in a leaking shed through a hard night's rain," the doctor commented sternly. "Monsieur de Brassac tells me that that was where Mr. Armitage found him, and that his clothes and bed were soaked through. Why was he there, Miss Wilde? If he must come to Neyronnes, why did he not come to the inn? And why has there been—I gather from Monsieur de Brassac that there has been—such secrecy about him?"

The physician hurled these questions at Christine, not unkindly, but in the authoritative manner of one who must be told everything. And then he added another query, which, like its predecessors, had been in my mind, too.

"Did he come to Neyronnes because you were here?" he asked.

But on this point Christine seemed as innocent as a child. Small chance she had had, I reflected, to so much as think of any romantic suggestion in connection with young men, or to suspect them of a sentimental interest in herself!

"Why, no," she answered. "We hardly knew him. We had not seen him since that time in Lausanne, long ago. And we did not know he was coming here. We have scarcely seen him since he came. Mother did not like me to talk with him, or to talk with him herself. In spite of what people had told her, she could not get rid of the fear of contagion. That is why there has been so much secrecy, don't you see?"

"Oh," the doctor commented briefly, "I see. But why was he living in those ruins?"

Christine looked as if she thought that the answer to that question, too, must be obvious, and her voice was very gentle and sympathetic when she spoke.

"He was so poor," she said. "He was poor, and his illness was worse, and the dollar was falling, and he loved Neyronnes and knew it well; and so he made this plan. We thought it was a good one."

"We?"

"Mother and I, in the first place. And of course Monsieur and Madame Delande—they have been very kind. And then Miss Hamilton. Mother did not approve of his being here—I think that if she had not been so worried and felt so poor, she might have sent him to a sanatorium, or somewhere, herself. But after we had talked it over, she did consent to his staying in Neyronnes, so long as he wasn't in the inn. The village people knew about him, of course; they didn't mind at all. But mother was afraid that the fear of contagion might get about, and so she told the Delandes that they mustn't allow anyone else to know about his plan. So Monsieur and Madame agreed to that, and so did Miss Hamilton."

"But what was this plan of his, Miss Wilde?" the doctor persisted.

"That was his hut in the ruins—his living there," Christine answered. "He thought it up himself, and at first he enjoyed it. He said that it was like camping out, and that it was absolutely the best thing in the world for him: it was like living outdoors, when those shutters were opened. He thought it was a good idea."

"That is true until it rained on him," the doctor commented, "but it is certainly not good for a sick man to get wet."

"I know," Christine agreed. "It was terrible—the rain coming in. I don't understand that. I never went into the shed myself, after he settled there, but mother told me it was water-tight. The rain must have been unusually hard that night. I wasn't here."

She turned pale as she spoke, and it occurred to me suddenly that this questioning was a little cruel: it was on that night that Mrs. Wilde had died—Monday night; and we were talking in this cool historical fashion on Wednesday, with the mystery of her death unsolved. But Christine went on with her story:

"Monsieur and Madame Delande arranged that he should have the free use of one of the ruined old houses—the one with the best roof and shelter—and they did everything they could to make it comfortable for him. They gave him a camp bed, and blankets, and candles, and every day they sent him a good meal. He paid for the meal, but they wouldn't let him pay for anything else. And they would have done more for him if he had let them, I know. I think that they were always rather worried about him, and I think they are glad to have him in the inn now. Then Miss Hamilton arranged with one of the farms to send him eggs and milk. He insisted on paying for that, too, but the farmer's wife only charged a few sous. At first, for two weeks or so, he was quite free, and I think he was happy. But when other guests began to come, mother thought it would be better if he kept more or less concealed. She was always worried about contagion, and she never wanted his being here to be known. And when she talked about it with the Delandes and Miss Hamilton, they agreed. I thought it was hard for him. But of course the most important thing for me was that mother shouldn't be worried."

She broke off abruptly, and turned again to address the doctor.

"Do you think that he can stay in the inn now, Dr. Lavigne? I mean, is his condition contagious now—"

"He can stay in the inn with perfect safety to everyone if the proper precautions are taken," the doctor answered. "If he is having hemorrhages his disease is contagious. But of course, as you must know, Miss Wilde, the danger of contagion from tuberculosis is not the deadly thing it once was: we know now, you see, what precautions to take."

"I will assume responsibility for all safeguards," Henri de Brassac put in quietly. "If you advise it, I will see that a good sanatorium is found for him. But when you talk with him, doctor, I think you will realize that he would greatly prefer to remain here, where he feels himself among friends. Myself, I am extremely sorry that I did not know all this when I came—I might have been of service to this unfortunate young man in time to save him much suffering. As it is, I can only ask you to command me now. I wish to befriend him to the best of my ability."

It was not the first time that a quiet remark from this grave and scholarly gentleman had made selfishness seem very ugly, and presumptuousness very childish, and ill-temper very crude and coarse. I felt extremely sorry for Christine at this moment: she had been accustomed all her life to accepting everything her mother did as right and everything her mother wanted as desirable, without any reflection of her own; but if she had not realized her mother's callous selfishness and niggardliness as she told her story, she certainly must have some inkling of it now! She would very gladly have taken entire charge of Paul MacNeil herself, I know—indeed, I think she had been planning to do just that—but naturally she was in no position to dispute the matter with Monsieur de Brassac! And I was glad that Miss Hamilton was not there, to listen to this story of her acquiescence in selfishness and neglect.

She had been very kind to Mrs. Wilde. But, in spite of the eggs and milk, it seemed to me that she had not been kind to poor Paul MacNeil . . .

That young man's pathetic story was unimportant enough, perhaps, in the sense that he himself was unimportant, poor lad. But it was not unimportant in what it had to tell us about the outstanding figures hi this other story with which it was so oddly joined. Nor, as a matter of fact, was it unimportant in regard to myself; but I did not know that until later. I was thinking, now, about the story itself.

I believed that Christine was telling the truth as she herself saw it. But I did not for one moment believe that her mother had really been afraid of contagion from a case of fibrous consumption, and still less did I believe that Margaret Hamilton felt any such fear. Mrs. Wilde had kept Paul MacNeil at a distance, and virtually imprisoned, had not allowed Christine to pay any attention to him, because she wanted to concentrate all attention—her daughter's and everyone else's—on herself. And Miss Hamilton had fallen in with her callously selfish designs, had followed wherever Mrs. Wilde had chosen to lead—why? It was an ugly thought that threw a dark shadow over my old vision of Miss Hamilton as generous and kind. And then, on the heels of that, came another idea, a curious idea, but a little less ugly: if Miss Hamilton were really, at heart, as humane as she had seemed to be, the sheer inhumanity of Mrs. Wilde's self-absorption might have offered, to those 'strange impulses' of which it frightened me now to think, something of excuse . . .

All these thoughts were ugly, and this story had been cruel. I was glad that Christine went off at once with the doctor, on his way to visit Paul MacNeil, and that, asking Mrs.. Sherrill to accompany her, she left me alone with Henri de Brassac.

And yet, it seems strange to me now to remember that I felt such a comforting sense of peace in being left there alone in the *galerie* with Monsieur de Brassac. For there was no peace in Neyronnes, and no comfort. And what was to come later was more dreadful than anything that had gone before.

X

I RETURN A HANDKERCHIEF

"The roof was already leaking," Monsieur de Brassac said.

I jerked my thoughts back to Paul MacNeil.

"What do you mean?" I asked.

"The roof leaked before this last rain," the Frenchman answered. "This unfortunate young man may have been drenched many times before this. He may have had other hemorrhages. He seems unable or unwilling to talk much, but he did tell me that rain had been getting into his shelter—that this was not the first time. He said that Monsieur and Madame Delande had been extremely kind: I suppose that they did the best they could, and they probably believed that the shelter was waterproof—they could not have been expected to watch over him constantly: they have their own work to do. But surely Madame Wilde might have informed herself."

"Or Miss Hamilton," I reminded him sadly. "Miss Hamilton might have looked after him, poor boy."

"Yes," Monsieur de Brassac agreed, "that is true."

Then, as we caught sight of John Sherrill and the Lausanne lawyer coming up the hill, he changed the subject.

"The *juge d'instruction* is coming tomorrow to hold his first inquiry," he said. "Madame Wilde's physician will remain to repeat his testimony. I understand also that the lawyer will arrange, if possible, to stay in Neyronnes as Miss Wilde's legal representative —fortunately there are still a few rooms free in the main building of the *auberge!* And Monsieur Sherrill will do what is necessary to protect Miss Hamilton's interests, is it not so?"

I nodded, and he went on, again with his air of pleasant comradeship: "Madame Sherrill will do whatever can be done to make life less difficult for Miss Wilde, and also to take care of Miss Hamilton, while you and I, my young friend, have our invalid to look after. That leaves only Monsieur Braye unemployed—and, yes, I had forgotten, his wife is still somewhat *fatigué*; he will, perhaps, occupy himself with her."

"Perhaps." I answered his grave smile, and then I said—conscious of feeling shy, and yet anxious to put myself on record—"If there is anything at all that I can do for Miss Wilde, I shall be most happy—"

But the Frenchman ceased to smile, and his face was troubled.

"Will you allow a man who might almost be your father to give you a word of advice, my friend?" he said. "I would not devote myself too conspicuously to Miss Wilde, if I were you."

And John Sherrill and Mr. Williamson came within earshot before I had time to answer him. Even so, I might have said something if I had not at that moment caught sight of Horace Braye, just coming around the *ruelle* and into the *galerie.*

As the narrow *ruelle* curved between the old houses directly to the *galerie* entrance, he was already nearer to me than were the two men who were walking up the hill and across the broad square. I could not even be sure that he had not heard Monsieur de Brassac's mysterious warning. But he gave no sign, if he had. Nor did he show me any ill-will as a result of the unpleasantness of our last meeting. He sat down beside us and lighted a cigar.

"Rosalie still feels rotten," he grunted. "A hell of a mess we got into, coming to this place. Hullo, Sherrill, how's the arm of the law?"

John Sherrill made some appropriate reply to this sally, and I was pleased to notice that the attorney from Lausanne was not regarding Horace Braye with too great attention. If he had any personal interest in him, he was keeping it quite successfully to himself. And Horace went on:

"I'm glad we've got two American lawyers here, anyhow. That means we'll get something done. A nice chance there'd be of solving the mystery if we had to leave it to these fool French, hey, Mr. Williamson?"

Henri de Brassac looked merely amused by this remark, but the precise lawyer took it very seriously.

"You are mistaken, Mr. Braye," he said. "'Foolish' is the last adjective which can be applied to the French. It is true that I have my own practice in Switzerland, and not in France. But the efficiency of the French police is famous the world over. All lawyers know that."

"'Efficiency'!" echoed Horace, with a roar of his ready laughter, which, like his outbursts of ill-temper, seemed to be always on tap. "Well, I'll be blowed! *Efficiency!* The *French!* Well, when I drove my car into this tumble-down dump-heap of a place, and I was growling about that damned street, my wife said maybe the people were just too poor to tear down that gate and those houses and make a real road that you could drive a decent car through. *Poor!* And now comes a lawyer and tells me they're efficient! The French poor, and the French efficient! What's the next fairy-tale for little Horace's bedtime story?"

Here was the 'comic relief' of which John Sherrill had spoken to Mr. Williamson. But for the first time it seemed to me that Horace's laughter was a little forced, and his joking a little self-conscious, even laborious. Perhaps the big bounder was really upset about his wife, I reflected—or, more likely, about his automobile and his own position as a law-breaker.

"Have you got your car yet?" I asked him. And it was not a question likely to keep Mr. Braye in good-humor.

"No, I haven't got my car yet." His roar was not of laughter this time. "I can't get my car until Saturday, damn them! What's more, I've got to pay a fine. I offered to hand out the money for the tax and their idiotic identity card, and they had the nerve to say I'd have to pay a fine on top of that! Look here, Mr. Brasstacks"—he turned suddenly to Henri de Brassac and bellowed at him—"I've got nothing against you personally—God knows you're quiet enough—but you're French, and I'd just like to tell you here and now that I'm not going to stand for this without a protest. You God-damned foreigners think you can get away with anything, as long as it's an American you're picking on—well, you can't: not with Horace Braye. I'm going to get my car on Saturday, and I'm going straight to the American Ambassador, and I'm going to see that he knows about this. You'll see!"

"*Volontiers*," replied Henri de Brassac, with real alacrity. Then he looked Horace up and down, aloof and frigid. "Monsieur Braye, I have no personal interest in your affairs or in your automobile. And I have no wish to pronounce an oration. But since you have chosen to address me as the scapegoat, so to speak, of the French nation, you must forgive the candor of my reply. I hope with all my heart that you will make a detailed report to your government representatives at the earliest possible moment. The American officials in France, Monsieur Braye, are gentlemen who know the laws of France and respect them. It is your misfortune, and ours, that one cannot say the same of you."

There had been no emphasis whatever upon the word 'gentlemen,' and indeed I did not know, then or ever, whether Henri de Brassac, speaking in what was to him a foreign language, realized the ambiguity in his use of that term. But Horace turned purple. And I—although my intentions were good in desiring to create a diversion—did not improve matters much by the tool which I now threw into the disordered machine.

I stuck my hand into my pocket and pulled out the square of white linen that I had picked up in the corner outside Mrs. Wilde's door, the morning before.

"Here's your handkerchief, Mr. Braye," I said, and added, unnecessarily, "I found it on the hall floor, near Mrs. Wilde's door yesterday."

The purple color of rage ebbed away from Horace's fat face and left it looking pale and oddly flabby. But he did not take the handkerchief from my hand.

"That isn't mine," he said. "I didn't drop any handkerchief in the hall."

I opened up the folded piece of white linen, and I am afraid that—since I disliked him so heartily—I took a certain pleasure in the thought of Horace Braye's discomfiture, as well as a certain satisfaction in withdrawing his attention from Monsieur de Brassac and from the pastime of insulting all foreigners.

"It has your initials in the corner," I said.

Mr. Braye took the handkerchief from me then, and looked at it, and at the neat embroidered letters, 'H. B.,' to which I had called his attention. The color came back to his cheeks and he no longer appeared flabby. And when he spoke it was without bluster or rage, and totally without discomfiture, in a voice that was no bellow, but surprisingly clear and calm and cold.

"That is not my handkerchief," he said. "Those are not my initials. I mean to say, my initials are H. B., to be sure, but not that H. B. I suggest that you return his handkerchief to Mister Henry Brassac."

The Frenchman shrugged his shoulders. "Monsieur is mistaken," he said. "If I may borrow the terseness of Monsieur's remark, those are not my initials. I mean to say, my initials are not H. B."

"It's your handkerchief, all the same," Mr. Braye insisted, with a slight return of his braggadocio. But the Frenchman only shrugged his shoulders again. "Well, anyhow, it isn't mine," said Horace flatly.

John Sherrill reached out his hand. "I guess I'll take charge of it, if you don't mind," he said. "It may possibly prove to be interesting. Our neighbor's name is de Brassac, Mr. Braye."

Horace grunted. "Sounds pretty phoney," he muttered, "but have it your own way. You can't pin anything on me, that's one sure thing." He got up. "I'm going to look after my sick wife," he said, "and I'll thank you to have some consideration for her, the whole damned lot of you."

He strode belligerently up the *ruelle* toward the *pavillon annexe*.

"Not a nice man, as Reggie Fortune would say," said John Sherrill. "I wish we had Reggie Fortune, or one of his ilk, here right now. Well, Mr. Williamson, you have seen our Horace in action, and I hope you hate him as much as I do. Now you and I are antagonists, in a way," he went on seriously, "but I know we are fair and friendly antagonists. And I want to say this: I can only really protect Miss Hamilton's interests by finding out the truth about Mrs. Wilde's death, and it is the truth I'm after—the truth, the whole truth, and nothing but the truth. We know that the police have been busy. Tomorrow we shall have a formal inquiry, and we shall probably find out what concrete evidence there is to date. Tomorrow, too, I hope to have an answer to a cablegram I have sent. Until then, Mr. Williamson, shall we declare a kind of truce?"

And with that speech—which, curiously enough, began with an appeal to one of the famous detectives of fiction—John Sherrill seemed to enter upon a new avatar, become a different kind of person, in my regard: John Sherrill was going to investigate this sorry business, and he was going to do it well. And I must confess that John Sherrill was about as unlike my image of a crime investigator as could be imagined. I did not know anything about actual crime investigation, to be sure, but I knew certain detectives in stories; and I had been impressed with the fact that, much as they differed from each other, practically all of them had one characteristic in common: they were creatures of conspicuous mannerisms. Mannerisms were precisely what John Sherrill lacked. Indeed, he had seemed, up to that moment, rather a negative personality, so far as personality went . . .

He was a quiet person, inconspicuous in appearance, voice, dress. I could see him as the successful novelist which I knew him to be. I could see him as the lawyer which I had just learned that he was. I could not see him in the activities of a detective, at all. His spare, lank person, his already sparse brown hair, his attentive dark eyes deep-set beneath his broad forehead, his long hands with their rare gestures, his pleasant, unobtrusive manners with their quick thoughtfulness, the occasional boyishness with which he swung his long legs in and out of his little car, or expressed himself in some racy or slangy bit of speech—all these were the attributes of a likable American gentleman, which was just what John Sherrill was. He could get, on rare occasions, outrageously

angry, but he could see a joke; he was not self-conscious; he neither bragged nor tried to show off. Modestly, with a characteristic
quiet gusto, he went his way. He was widely informed, widely traveled, I could see that he was widely and keenly observant. But his
novels were primarily character-studies—never stories of crime,
or even of adventure; and I did not know then, as I did later, that
he had been a newspaper reporter in New York City, and that in
that maelstrom of strange mysteries he had solved more than one
problem which had "baffled the police." Now, as he went about his
self-appointed task in solving the mystery of Neyronnes, he was
very far from calling attention either to his activities or to himself.

"The police have been busy," he told us on this Wednesday
afternoon, the day after the discovery of Mrs. Wilde's body. When
the formal inquiry was opened the next morning, the whole affair
had entered, I realized, upon a new phase.

XI

WE HEAR TESTIMONY

The inquiry was held in the big game-and-banquet room on the ground-flour of the *pavillon*, and it was more formal, more serious, and more disquieting than the first meeting with the gendarmes had been. Mrs. Braye was not there, and her husband reported that she was still very weak and asked to be excused; the question was left in abeyance, I gathered, pending the development of any fact or situation which might make her presence desirable; as nothing came up which seemed to demand any word from Rosalie, she was not sent for. Somewhat to my surprise, Margaret Hamilton appeared promptly: she sat between John and Elinor Sherrill, and although she was extremely pale and more than a little haggard, she looked not unlike her usual self. Christine sat on Mrs. Sherrill's other side, with her lawyer next to her. I, to my discomfort, was assigned a chair beside Horace Braye, but it was some relief to have Henri de Brassac on the other side of me.

In spite of myself, I found that I was interested in the proceedings just as a spectacle—although, as a spectacle, it was very bare. We sat in a horseshoe formation of chairs in the big plain stone-floored room, the line beginning with Mr. Williamson on the right of the magistrate's long table and swinging around to Henri de Brassac on the officials' left. It was like a magnet, with the police table as its bar. And behind the magistrate and his assistants, I could look through the windows out to the garden . . . An official interpreter had been brought this time from the city, together with a police stenographer who also seemed to understand English. The

testimony was all given very slowly, and Henri de Brassac's oblig-
ing pencil made it possible for me to follow it fairly easily, without
waiting often for the formal translations.

Madame Delande and the maid Aurélie testified to the finding
of the body, and were immediately excused to go about their sadly
interrupted business. And I want to say right here that my hat will
always be off to the Delandes and to their servants, for the quiet
efficiency with which they managed to keep the inn going in its
accustomed way and to meet all the extra demands upon their time
and thought as well; when the news of the tragedy had become
public it must have been especially hard. After Madame's testimony
came that of the local doctor as to the morphine in the syringe and
the cause of death—the autopsy had borne out the original diagnosis—and then the Lausanne specialist took the stand.

He repeated the statements he had already made: that Mrs.
Wilde was not addicted to the use of any drug, that she had an
idiosyncrasy which made any opiate a poison, and that the self-
administration of even a small quantity of morphine would be tan-
tamount to suicide.

"Speaking as Madame Wilde's physician, would you consider
suicide probable?" he was asked; and his reply, as we had expected,
was an emphatic negative.

"I should consider it all but impossible," he said. "In spite of
her ill-health, Mrs. Wilde enjoyed life. Her financial worries were
not serious. If her daughter will pardon my saying so, I may state,
with all respect, that Mrs. Wilde was the type of woman who enjoyed dramatizing herself. She made a drama of her ill-health, to a
great extent. She quite distinctly dramatized her financial losses,
knowing that although they were considerable she was still wealthy;
she was able thus to get a certain amount of not unpleasurable
excitement out of the picture of herself as one of the victims of the
crise. I think that her coming here to 'economize' was a kind of
game, and a new sensation.

"I say this in no criticism of Mrs. Wilde," he declared, "but
merely in recognition of her type of temperament and in accen-
tuation of my conviction that her circumstances were certainly not

driving her to the consideration of any desperate act. On the contrary, she was full of thoughts and plans for the future. She liked to think and talk about what she would do next year. She was deciding upon a new car, for instance. The last time I talked with her she asked me about winter resorts—she thought of trying Malaga for this next season, and she was already thinking about what clothes she would need for that climate and—er—social life. She enjoyed that sort of thinking ahead. I feel sure that she did not kill herself."

The *juge d'instruction* frowned a little, looked at his notes, and said:

"It is not usual for a lay person to own a hypodermic syringe. Madame Wilde evidently owned one, and used it frequently. Will you enlighten us on that point?"

"Certainly. For some time Mrs. Wilde, under my directions, has been taking insulin, by subcutaneous injection. And the syringe which was found at her bedside, which had contained the morphine which caused her death, was not the kind of syringe which is customarily used for morphine and other ordinary *piqures*, but was of a size and type especially adapted to the administration of insulin."

"But one can administer morphine with this syringe without difficulty?"

"Without difficulty, yes. But not in a very large dose. I cannot picture a drug-addict using such a syringe habitually."

"Do you suggest that the morphine was administered to Madame Wilde by someone who knew of her idiosyncrasy in regard to opiates—or who at least knew that she was unaccustomed to the use of opiates and that a small dose would be fatal?"

"I suggest nothing. I think it quite possible."

"Do you know how long Madame Wilde had herself been aware of this idiosyncrasy?"

"For many years. An extremely small dose of morphine nearly killed her, many years ago. She always told doctors and nurses of that experience, to avoid all danger of having an opiate given to her again."

"Then she made no secret of it?"

"Oh, no. Generally speaking, Mrs. Wilde was not a secretive person. On the contrary, she was in the habit of talking very freely about herself. But she never told anyone that she was threatened with diabetes, and I think that almost no one knew that she took insulin."

"Then it is possible, is it not, that an individual who knew that Madame Wilde kept the nature of her disease a secret might have administered the morphine with homicidal intent, and trusted that her death would be attributed to an accident of drug-addiction?"

"It is quite possible," the doctor replied. "I should say that it was probable. It would have been a stupid chance to take, but murderers do take stupid chances, as you know, Monsieur *le juge*. Since I feel personally convinced that Mrs. Wilde did not commit suicide, I can see no alternative to murder. And it certainly leaps to the mind that a woman in a mysterious state of ill-health—particularly, perhaps, a woman of Mrs. Wilde's temperament—might be suspected of drug-addiction and that her death might be set down to that. As I said, it was stupid," he went on. "It was either very ignorant or very careless, or both. But it may have been what happened." He took it upon himself to bow to the magistrate. "Such a plan would only have been carried out, in my opinion," he added, "by a man or woman unaware of the efficiency of the French police."

The *juge d'instruction* bowed in return. "I thank you, Monsieur *le docteur*," he said. "You will permit me to remark that that also leaps to the mind. But now I must inform you, Monsieur *le docteur*, of a strange thing: finger-prints were found upon the hypodermic syringe; but they were all Madame Wilde's own finger-prints. The broken *ampoule*, also, which had contained insulin—"

John Sherrill leaned forward in his chair. His eyes were very bright, but when he spoke his voice was even quieter than usual.

"May I interrupt with a question, Monsieur *le juge?*" he asked. "The broken *ampoule*—it had not contained morphine?"

The magistrate consulted his notes again. "No, Monsieur Sherrill," he answered. "The broken *ampoule* had not contained morphine. That fact has been established. The broken *ampoule* had contained insulin."

"Thank you," said Sherrill. "Might I ask that the *ampoule* itself be explained to us, Monsieur *le juge?* It is not a term, or a usage in medicine, with which most of us are familiar."

"But certainly," the magistrate replied affably. Even in a murder inquiry, these French officials gave the impression of having all the time in the world. "Monsieur *le docteur* will make it clear if he will be so kind."

"Willingly." The Swiss physician was equally polite. "The term *ampoule* is applied to the small glass container which is used to hold, say, one dose of medicine. Insulin is one of the medicaments which is distributed in these small *ampoules*, as a matter of better preservation: it is, I may add, distributed in one of two forms—either as a powder and a liquid, of which virtually each dose must be especially mixed, or as a liquid already prepared for the syringe. I prescribed it for Mrs. Wilde in the latter form, as it was more convenient, and she usually gave herself the injections. That was still the case, was it not, Miss Wilde?" he added. "Your mother continued to take her medicine herself?"

"Almost always," Christine answered. "I generally sterilized and filled the syringe for her, but sometimes she did that, too."

"It appears that she gave herself this injection," said the magistrate. "As I was saying, no finger-prints were found other than Madame Wilde's own. And the fact that her finger-prints are plentiful and clear on the syringe would seem to show that no one handled it—with a glove or a handkerchief—after herself."

A handkerchief! I shot a glance at Horace Braye, stolid beside me. But his gaze, fixed upon the interpreter, never wavered, and his face was expressionless.

John Sherrill addressed the presiding official again.

"I should like to ask Monsieur *le docteur* another question, if you will be so kind as to permit it," he said. "It is rather a delicate and difficult question, but I am sure that I shall not be misunderstood . . . Dr. Lavigne, you were speaking of Mrs. Wilde's 'temperament' a few moments ago—should you say that she was a person of uncertain moods, that she was subject to moments of great anger?"

I did not dare to look at poor Christine, but of course I realized that questions like that had to be asked. The doctor's answer was calm and even.

"Yes, Monsieur Sherrill, she was. She was subject—I think I must put it so—to attacks of rage, which were always ungoverned, usually unprovoked, and sometimes very cruel. She was often very unreasonable in her demands, in her likes and dislikes, so to speak. Mrs. Wilde was not gifted with much self-control—you understand that her health had been delicate for some years; she had been indulged in every way. I dislike saying these things, Monsieur *le juge*. But if you agree with me that someone must have murdered Mrs. Wilde, you will wish to uncover all possible motives to crime." He shrugged his shoulders. "Mrs. Wilde was a woman of wealth, of charm, but of no self-discipline. She suffered, too, from the curse of jealousy."

"Thank you," said John Sherrill again. "That is what I wanted to know."

The magistrate spoke now, first to the doctor, and then to the company at large.

"We do agree with you that someone must have murdered Madame Wilde," he said. "Your character evidence against suicide, Monsieur, is borne out by one simple, concrete, and I think we may say conclusive, fact: Madame Wilde's door was locked, and the key has disappeared.

"The lock was of the old-fashioned kind," he continued, "which cannot be fastened without a key. The key was one of the large implements with which, in an old house like this, we are familiar. It was not easy to mislay, or even to hide; and the room has been thoroughly searched. Moreover, no one had an opportunity to take away the key after the body was discovered. If Madame Wilde had locked her door herself, the key would have been in her room: to assume any other possibility is to ask too much of coincidence, of possibility itself.

"It appears, however, that Madame Wilde's own hand was the last to touch the hypodermic syringe in which the residue of morphine was found. We are then forced to consider the probability

that Madame Wilde was in some way deceived, and was thus persuaded to give herself this injection of deadly poison—in other
words, that she took an injection of morphine in the belief that
she was taking her customary injection of insulin. On the face of
it, this probability would appear to narrow the field of our inquiry:
for so far as our present knowledge goes, the number of persons
who could thus have deceived Madame Wilde is limited. But our
present knowledge, *Messieurs et Mesdames*, does not go very far.
This investigation is only beginning. There may have been influences at work of which we know nothing, as well as motives of
which we are unaware. I need not remind you all that most of the
witnesses in this case are foreigners, that the victim was a foreigner, that the possible interrelations of one with another among
you are unknown to the French police. We are glad to welcome the
co-operation of Monsieur Sherrill, an American whose reputation
has preceded him to France"—he bowed, and John Sherrill bowed
in response—"and we thank him for his courteous assistance. Before this inquiry is continued at its next meeting, we hope to be in
possession of certain specific information which we at present lack.
Meanwhile, we continue with what is at hand . . .

"Monsieur *le docteur*, I thank you for your most generous aid,
and I am glad now to be able to excuse you so that you can return
to your important duties in the very friendly country from which
you come. We will proceed now to the next witness: Miss Margaret
Joyce Hamilton."

The beneficiary of Mrs. Wilde's surprising will was deadly pale
now, and her hands were trembling. She understood perfectly, of
course, that in spite of the magistrate's careful warning against
premature judgment, the evidence that had been given thus far
pointed directly toward her; and information which might come
from America, laying bare her financial losses and her desperate
need of money, could not be expected to help her . . . She had a
great deal of courage, Margaret Hamilton, and the poise of a duchess; but these were not enough, now, to conceal the fact that she
was suffering from what was certainly shock, and might well be
remorse or even fear.

I looked from her to her friend Mrs. Sherrill, anxious and watchful beside her; to Christine, unmoving and expressionless in her grief; to Henri de Brassac, whose sensitive face showed real pain; and around to Horace Braye, to note with some astonishment that Horace's coarse cheeks were marked with nervous red blotches, and that his eyes, a minute ago so fixed in their gaze, were roving restlessly about the room. Was he beginning to feel this as a real human tragedy, I wondered? Or was he only tired and ill-tempered and in want of a drink?

Then, very low, hesitant, still lovely, Miss Hamilton's voice fell upon my ear.

Her evidence brought forth, however, practically nothing that was new. She was obliged, of course, to repeat the damaging admission that Mrs. Wilde had left her door unlocked so that she, Margaret Hamilton, could gain entrance to her room, "to see if she was all right" during the night. Her story, as a whole, Miss Hamilton told exactly as she had told it before, except that she was interrupted from time to time with a question that was in effect a demand for more detail. Thus, it was brought out for the record that the door of her room was directly at the top of the stairs and the door of Mrs. Wilde's room directly at the bottom, and that on the night of the crime the rooms above Mrs. Wilde and opposite Miss Hamilton had been empty, because Mr. and Mrs. Sherrill, who occupied them, had been away. Except Horace Braye, no one could have had such easy access to Mrs. Wilde's room as could Miss Hamilton.

It was also made clear for the record that the space under the Wildes' room, on the ground-floor, was given over to the hot-water heater and a sink, and was never used except when an extra serving-room was needed for banquets in the *pavillon*. Miss Hamilton told again of the maid's visit to her room, of the vain effort to wake Mrs. Wilde by pounding on the door; she told of seeing Mr. Braye come out of his room just opposite Mrs. Wilde's and of hearing his remark about the key; she told of finding Mrs. Wilde's body. And she surprised me a little by telling, under detailed questioning, of seeing me come from the other side of the *Place* and hearing me ask help for a sick man.

"But I could not think of that," she said. "I could not even grasp what Mr. Armitage was talking about. All I could think of was that Mrs. Wilde was dead from an overdose of morphine."

"You said that to Mr. Armitage?"

"About the overdose of morphine? I—I don't remember. I may have. It was what I was thinking."

"But you did not *know* it was morphine?"

"No. I—I think I must just have taken it for granted in that first moment. I had never known what Mrs. Wilde's illness was, and I had never known that she took insulin. She had been a person of moods, sometimes very gay and animated, and at other times nervous and—er—irritable. She was exceedingly restless, also. When I said good-night to her the evening before, she had seemed nervous, and I thought she was anxious to be left alone. When I saw the hypodermic syringe beside her bed, I jumped to the conclusion, Monsieur *le juge*, that she had been a victim of the drug-habit."

"Then you did not know of her idiosyncrasy against opiates?"

"Certainly not, Monsieur. If I had known that I should not have thought she was a drug-addict."

The *juge d'instruction* frowned.

"Madame Wilde had an affection for you, had she not?"

Miss Hamilton's white hands closed tightly, and opened, and clenched again, and she did not reply at once. Then she looked straight at the magistrate from eyes that were swimming with tears, and said:

"She must have had. I never knew."

She was asked then whether she had expected a bequest from the dead woman, and she denied all knowledge or thought of such a possibility. She said that a little over two weeks ago she had seen the Lausanne lawyer in Neyronnes one day, in conversation with Mrs. Wilde, but she had never learned who he was nor why he was there.

"You were fond of Madame Wilde?" the magistrate asked. And it seemed to me curious that Miss Hamilton hesitated before answering, and that even then she gave no direct response.

"I was very sorry for her," she said. "At the beginning, I was under the impression that she had had very serious financial losses, like—perhaps like my own. And she had an illness of which she was unwilling to talk, except to say that she suffered. She told me that she had no real home, and that she was alone in the world except for her young daughter; and she required so much attention from her daughter, I thought that she must be much more ill than she seemed. I—I thought perhaps she had cancer, Monsieur, or something like that, and I was very sorry for her. I myself have had grave financial losses, Monsieur *le juge*, and I myself am alone in the world; but I am not ill. When Mrs. Wilde came to Neyronnes to live quietly and cheaply, I felt that here was someone whose situation was far more serious than my own—and I wanted to help her all I could."

In Miss Hamilton's low and beautiful voice, this was a very moving little speech, and I knew that it might well be true. From the bottom of my heart I hoped that it was true. But was it really convincing? That, I simply did not know. Certainly the magistrate's next question betrayed no sympathy: it was a question of ambiguous purpose, though it was gently put.

"When you found your friend's body, and concluded, correctly, that she had died from a lethal dose of morphine, you were glad to think that her death had been painless, were you, not?"

It was gentle, but Margaret Hamilton understood what its significance might be, and for the first time a wild horror gazed from her tortured eyes. She raised one hand with a queer, helpless gesture as if she were trying vainly to ward off a dreadful blow. But before she had time to answer, John Sherrill was on his feet.

"I beg that you will excuse my interruption, Monsieur *le juge*," he said. "It is not for me to criticize the conduct of such an examination as this. But if this were a trial by jury, Monsieur, I should as Miss Hamilton's lawyer object to that question and instruct her not to reply to it. Since this is not a trial but a mere inquiry, I do not enter my objection in that way. But I consider the question prejudicial, Monsieur *le juge*."

I expected the magistrate to show some vexation, but he did not. He replied with perfect suavity:

"I do not consider the question prejudicial, Monsieur *l'avocat*. Certainly I have no wish to persecute the witness. And I may suggest, Monsieur, that you are at this stage ignorant of what is in my mind. I have warned you all against premature judgments; I warn you all again. Miss Hamilton, I will withdraw my former question, and I will inquire concerning only one point further, this morning. Will you tell me whether you slept well? Did you hear any sounds in the house? Were you disturbed at all?"

Remarkably, she was almost calm again. "I slept well. I heard Mr. Armitage come in, but no noise in the house after that, although I did hear the rain in the night. But I was disturbed once: my dog growled."

"When was that?"

"I do not know, Monsieur. I did not turn on the light to look at my watch. But it was still raining—it seemed to be raining harder than ever, or else the wind had changed—and I had the feeling that I had not been asleep long."

"And your dog? Does he often bark in the night? Is he quiet by nature?"

A little smile flitted surprisingly across Miss Hamilton's face. "He is very quiet. He almost never disturbs me. He sleeps on the floor beside my bed, just inside the door, and sometimes I disturb him, but he never makes any fuss. Occasionally he barks when someone knocks at my door. But this was not a bark: this was a growl."

"Thank you, Miss Hamilton," said the *juge d'instruction*. "We will pass on to other testimony. Monsieur Horace Braye."

He rapped out his next questions with the nearest approach, thus far, to speed.

"Monsieur Braye, did you have a quiet night? Your room is opposite Madame Wilde's—were you disturbed by any noise?"

"I was." Horace's fat face was still mottled, but he spoke with a bellicose firmness. "I heard this young Armitage prowling around the house in the middle of the night."

Mr. Braye, of course, spoke in English. This remark hit me head on. The magistrate, when it had been translated, repeated most of it.

"Ah. Monsieur Armitage—prowling around the house in the middle of the night? How did you know it was Monsieur Armitage?"

"Because his room is just above mine and I heard him go into it."

"Yes—Miss Hamilton heard that also. But you, Monsieur Braye: you heard Monsieur Armitage moving about elsewhere in the house? In other rooms? In the corridors?"

"Well, no—that was the funny part of it," Horace answered. "I didn't really hear him until he got upstairs. I—I had sort of felt there was someone out there, prowling around the halls. And when I heard this whippersnapper go into his room, I realized that he had been wandering around and keeping mighty quiet while he was doing it."

Through my indignation I found myself conscious of amusement, for the interpreter very politely translated 'whippersnapper' as *jeune gentilhomme* . . .

"Ah," said the magistrate again. "And what time was this, Monsieur Braye?"

"Sixteen minutes past twelve," replied Horace promptly.

"You looked at your watch?"

"Sure I looked at my watch."

"You turned on the light?"

"No!" roared Horace, "I didn't have to. My watch has a radium dial."

"And after that you went to sleep?"

"I did. I went to sleep, and I slept all night."

"Then you did not hear the dog when he disturbed Miss Hamilton?"

"No, I didn't. I'm a sound sleeper," Horace answered, and went on with a rather surprising willingness, I thought, to add details. "But my wife did. My wife has the room just under Miss Hamilton's. She said this morning that she had heard the dog growling, and she thought it was funny, because she hadn't heard him do it before."

"Madame Braye will tell us her story later, when she has recovered. Now in the morning, Monsieur Braye—"

But the rest of Horace's testimony proved to be merely a repetition of what we had already been told. Once or twice the *juge d'*
instruction looked at a piece of paper which he held in his hand
throughout the examination of Mr. Braye, but the examination itself was merely formal. And after that we adjourned for a queer,
strained, hurried luncheon.

Henri de Brassac was the first witness called at the afternoon
session, and it seemed to me that he was being questioned in a
good deal of detail about the finding of Paul MacNeil. I thought,
too, that the Frenchman looked a little worried—as if his mind were
troubled by some new anxiety—when the magistrate finally spoke
the word of thanks which concluded his examination and turned
to me. And I was asked for the complete and minute story of that
night: naturally, after Horace Braye's silly and malicious insinua-
tion, I had expected that!

So I told them all about the sounds I had heard in the ruins of
Neyronnes, the inexplicable English word that had struck my ear
in the midst of unintelligibility, the return to listen for other
sounds, other words. I told about hearing the poetry on Monday
evening; I did my best to describe the state of perplexity in which
I had gone back to the house; I confessed my worry and my now
conscience-stricken inaction over the rain in the night.

Then I went on to the morning, my early departure from my
room, the discovery of blood on the cobbles, the trail that led to
the sick man. Up to this point, I was allowed to tell my story in my
own way, as a straight and uninterrupted narrative; but here I was
taken back, by a question, to the night before—what time was it
when I came in?

I replied that I did not know exactly—unlike Mr. Braye, I had
not looked at my watch—but that I felt sure it was somewhere
around midnight. And, I added, emphatically, I had not been
"prowling around the house"; far from it! I had taken especial pains
not to make any sound as I passed Mrs. Wilde's door and went up
the stairs just outside her room, but there was nothing unusual in
my going up those stairs at a late hour: although I did not often
stay out until after twelve o'clock, I was in the habit of strolling

about Neyronnes in the evening. I told about hearing Miss Hamilton's dog growling at some time during the night, and repeated
my first statement that after that disturbance I had slept well until daylight. I told about my hurried return to the house, after finding the sick man, to look for help, and about my encounter with
Miss Hamilton at the inn door. Except for Miss Hamilton's denial
of the presence of an English-speaking stranger in Neyronnes, I
told them now everything I could think of. My one desire was to
keep nothing back.

And, yet, I felt that I did not tell my story very well.

I was heartsick, anxious, upset. The whole difficult situation
made me feel self-conscious, and I know that I spoke stupidly: I
found myself hesitating, forgetting things and having to go back.
My one purpose was to tell the whole truth, simply and clearly,
keeping to myself only that one falsehood of Miss Hamilton's,
which might have hurt her, and which was, I said to myself, quite
irrelevant really. But after I had been thanked for my courtesy and
was allowed to relapse into silence, I found myself wondering, as I
had wondered about Miss Hamilton's testimony, whether my true
and simple story had really sounded convincing at all! For the first
time, I was conscious of a sort of envy of Horace Braye: in spite of
the silliness of his accusation against me, that big bounder had
said what he had to say clearly, unhesitatingly, exactly, and well!

What with the need for translation, my examination took a long,
long time. When it was over I was tired, and I thought that everyone must be; I was not surprised when the *juge d'instruction* stated
that he was about to dismiss us for the day.

"I shall want you all to meet with me again, as you understand,"
he said, "but not tomorrow. I may tell you now that there are points
in this situation which are far from being clear. We cannot solve a
problem like this in terms of what we have seen only today, or yesterday, or in the past two months. We must look for a past beyond
that brief moment, *Messieurs et Mesdames*.

"And if in so doing we subject some among you to inconvenience, hold some of you here against your will, investigate matters which our very investigation proves to have had no concern

with this tragedy—in such case I must pray that you will be patient, and that in so far as possible you will give me your willing aid. Some individual, *Messieurs et Mesdames*, has been guilty of murder. The innocent must to some extent suffer with the guilty until the guilty person has been identified. But you must remember that innocence has nothing to fear.

"I ask you, then, to return to this hall at half-past ten o'clock on Saturday morning—the day after tomorrow. By that time I hope to have received certain information by cable from the United States."

I had heard a slight sound out in the hall during this speech, but I was concentrating all my attention on the effort to understand the magistrate's sentences in the original French; and it was not until the translation was finished—when the slight sound had ceased—that I turned my eyes toward the door. I was shocked at what I saw. Rosalie Braye was leaning weakly against the jamb of the doorway, and she was staring at her husband with eyes that looked utterly panic-stricken, above the scarlet dabs of rouge and lipstick that stood out like dreadful scars in her dead-white face.

XII

I EXPLAIN TO A FRENCHMAN

Horace looked at his wife, and saw that we saw her.

"My God, Rosalie, do you want to kill yourself, coming down-stairs when you're so sick?" he cried out. "This is terrible—look at her, all of you! And, here, someone lend me a hand to get my wife back to her bed." He glared at us all. "Now you understand why I asked to have her excused from the hearing; and I hope you all see how sick she is," he said. "Look at her—white as a sheet. Hold on, old girl, don't faint again. There, now, you're all right. Your old man's got you."

Without taking advantage of the assistance which was instantly proffered by every man in the room, he supported his wife across the hall-lounge and toward the stairs. But in spite of her husband's physical aid and his noisy words of comfort, the expression on Rosalie's insignificant, not-quite-pretty face did not change at all. She certainly did look ill. But she looked more than ill, I thought. There was certainly a suggestion of terror where there was usually placid and good-humored stupidity. Was there something that Rosalie Braye knew, or suspected, something that frightened her?

Whatever questions of this kind the others might have shared with me, no one showed anything but complete acceptance of Mr. Braye's explanation and complete sympathy for Mrs. Braye's ill-health. But after Horace and Rosalie had gone up the stairs and into their own rooms, the *juge d'instruction* handed to John Sherrill a paper which I recognized as the one he had held in his hand during Horace Braye's testimony.

"Thank you, Monsieur," he said. "I am very glad, indeed, to have your co-operation. Let us hope that the succeeding cable messages will be more detailed."

"Yes, this one is a disappointment," Sherrill replied. He took another paper out of his bill-fold and handed one to Henri de Brassac and one to me.

"You fellows would like to see these," he said. "They are the French and English versions of the cable I told you I was expecting: the one you have is the original, Armitage. It doesn't tell us anything, but we are looking for another soon."

I read:

SHERRILL NEYRONNES—JEANNIOT—HORACE BRAYE WELL-KNOWN IN CLOAK-AND-SUIT TRADE NEW YORK NINETEEN-TWELVE TO NINETEEN-TWENTY-TWO STOP MADE CONSIDERABLE FORTUNE IN SIXTEEN-DOLLAR SUITS MEN AND WOMEN STOP BAD REPUTATION WITH FACTORY INSPECTORS CONSUMERS' LEAGUE UNIONS STOP IN NINETEEN-TWENTY-TWO RESIGNED PRESIDENCY HOBRY MANUFACTURING COMPANY AND APPARENTLY DISAPPEARED STOP RETURNED TO NEW YORK FEBRUARY NINETEEN-THIRTY-THREE STILL PLENTY OF MONEY WHEREABOUTS IN INTERIM UNEXPLAINED STOP SAILED WITH WIFE AND LINCOLN CAR CHAMPLAIN MARCH THIRTY-FIRST STOP INVESTIGATIONS CONTINUE END OF MESSAGE GREGG

"So the question, Who is Horace Braye, is not yet satisfactorily answered," Sherrill said. "Apparently Horace Braye is simply Horace Braye. But there was no connection between Mrs. Wilde and a sweat-shop proprietor who got in wrong with the Amalgamated, that's sure! We'll hope for more news soon."

It occurred to me that the *juge d'instruction* might make a caustic comment on the first of these remarks. I half-expected him to ask, "Who is Margaret Hamilton?" Or even, "Who is Wayne Armitage?" And I remembered suddenly that I, like Horace Braye, had no identity card. But the magistrate only smiled politely and took his departure. The lawyer Williamson hurried away, too. And I yielded to the warmth of a comfortable feeling that Horace's accusation against me might have acted merely as a boomerang for himself. It was decidedly Horace Braye of whom I was thinking as I walked over to the *auberge* with John Sherrill and Henri de Brassac.

"Did you see how Mrs. Braye looked?" I asked them—a foolish question, for everyone must have noticed Rosalie.

She had evidently come downstairs to see whether the hearing was almost over and to find out whether her presence would be required before it was adjourned, and she had overheard the translation of the magistrate's remarks about awaiting further information. So much was apparent to everyone.

Sherrill and Monsieur de Brassac both nodded.

"Our ugly braggart," said the Frenchman, "is not lacking in quick thought."

"Horace," said John Sherrill, "is nobody's fool. We all see that his wife is in a panic over something, and does he try to cover it up, or distract our attention? Not he, the old fox! He points it out to us, and explains it, as quick as a flash and as natural as you please. By George, it might even be true! But I'll bet he beats her when he gets her upstairs!

"So far as I am concerned," he went on, with a complete change of tone, "that inquiry did not go badly. It established two points which are important, though they are both negative. One of them I'm not going to call attention to at this moment, but the other we can certainly talk about: it was not Christine who killed Mrs. Wilde."

We had reached the sharp turn of the road under the overhanging corbels of the beautiful fourteenth-century house at the entrance to the *Place*, and I stretched out my hand toward the wall in a queer impulse to steady myself.

"*Christine?*" I echoed blankly. "*Christine?* How could it have been Christine? How can you say such a thing?"

Sherrill looked at me almost pityingly.

"You haven't *thought* much about this affair, Armitage," he said. "You've felt a lot and thought very little. Up to this point this point in the inquiry—there was not one of us here who could be held free from the suspicion of having killed Mrs. Wilde. And until the establishment of those two facts about the key and the *ampoule*, Christine was one of the most obvious suspects. I have not doubted her myself, any more than you have, Armitage, but look here . . ."

We walked across to the outspreading linden tree and sat down. "It's the cocktail hour," said Sherrill. And—for the sake of relaxation, as we all recognized, and not because we wanted a drink!—we all ordered *apéritifs*. Then Sherrill began:

"You can't get away from the good old rule of motive, means, and opportunity, Armitage. That's the three-pronged fork with which you spear your murderer. And to look for motive, means, and opportunity, in searching for a murderer, is more than a rule: it's an instinct. Motive, means, and opportunity—and the first of these is motive. Who had the biggest motive for getting rid of Mrs. Wilde?"

"Miss Hamilton," I replied.

"Miss Hamilton may have had the most immediately obvious motive, and she did have a big one," Sherrill agreed. "But it wasn't the biggest. No, Armitage, the person who gained most by Mrs. Wilde's death was Mrs. Wilde's daughter."

He looked at me a little queerly, I thought. "*You* know that," he said.

"But Christine was devoted to her mother," I stammered.

"Was she?" Sherrill raised his eyebrows. "She was a very dutiful daughter, and she went through all the paces of devotion, as she had been taught to do all her life. Christine Wilde had been trained to walk in a treadmill, poor child, and she kept on walking in it. But I very much doubt if she felt any real devotion—any warmth of human affection and comradeship—for a mother who treated her like an African slave, and never even let her call her soul her own.

"Good God!" he interrupted himself, "that girl's life was a thing
to make your blood boil! She never had any fun. She hadn't a cent
of money of her own. She had no chance to make friends of her
own age and no freedom in choosing her acquaintances. She hadn't
had any education to speak of. She wasn't allowed to so much as
read a book to herself, or ever to choose any book she wanted to
read. All this petty slavery in addition to having to be at her
mother's beck and call every minute of the day and night. We found
out a good deal about Christine's existence on that trip, and it just
about made me want to go out and kill Mrs. Wilde myself! She was
tied for good and all, too: her mother would never have allowed
her to marry. In fact, she would have started in with some special
torture, I'll wager, if Christine had ever shown any signs of a girl's
simple normal human interest in a young man."

"Yes," said Henri de Brassac.

As for me, I groaned. It seemed worse even than I had imagined. Monsieur de Brassac shot a quick glance at me, but Sherrill
continued:

"And Christine Wilde was an heiress. Thirty thousand dollars
a year is a lot of money. Even if the dollar drops to fifty, at home
and abroad, thirty thousand dollars is still going to mean a lot of
money. With her mother's death, Christine gets that money with
not one string to it."

I felt like groaning again, but of course I didn't. I growled at
Sherrill, instead:

"Good Lord, do you think I don't know that? It's terrible!"

Henri de Brassac stared at me now, but Sherrill gave a not unkind little laugh.

"Terrible, is it? A nice unselfish thought that is! Terrible for
you, maybe, if you look at it that way, but not for Christine! Christine, who has been a slave, is free. Christine, who hadn't a penny
of her own, is rich. What's more, her mind and spirit are set at
liberty, just as her actions are. She can make decisions and choices,
think things out for herself. And do you mean to say you haven't
noticed that she is doing that already—and enjoying it? Christine
was a dutiful daughter: she is doing her duty now, and she is loyal

to her mother's memory and anxious to clear it from any stain. But she isn't overwhelmed by grief, Armitage.

"Christine," he added, "is a capable young American girl who is going to live her own life from this time forth and forever—and it's going to be a good life, what's more. I like and admire her enormously."

Henri de Brassac was still looking at me in what seemed to be perplexity, and before I had a chance to ask the question that was trembling on my tongue, he addressed me with a query of his own.

"Monsieur Armitage, you said that Miss Wilde's fortune was 'terrible.' Perhaps I did not understand you aright, but that was what I thought you said. And Monsieur Sherrill said, 'Terrible for you, maybe.' Will you not take pity upon my ignorance and explain these incomprehensible remarks? Is there something here which has been kept from me? Is there another detail of this mystery which I do not know?"

Sherrill laughed again, the short friendly little laugh that was characteristic of him, and somehow full of understanding. And I felt, myself, a little perplexed, and also more than a little ashamed.

"I am not such a selfish cub as I sound, Monsieur de Brassac," I answered. "Indeed, I am very glad that Miss Wilde has inherited a fortune. When I said that it was 'terrible,' I was speaking from a selfish and childish impulse, and I am extremely sorry. Mr. Sherrill has already rebuked me, justly. I hope that you will not misunderstand me."

I looked from one to the other of the two men, intelligent, thoughtful, sophisticated, older than I, yet surely my friends . . . They had been very kind to me, John Sherrill and Henri de Brassac: Sherrill was ten or twelve years my senior, and Henri de Brassac must be nearly, if not quite, fifty; they were men of the world, men of assured position, and I must be, in their eyes, no more than a boy; but there had been a real companionableness in their attitude toward me. And to Monsieur de Brassac, for his ready, unquestioning help in the matter of poor Paul MacNeil, I felt a deep and personal gratitude. I felt that I was not talking to mere acquaintances, casually met in travel, but to friends, as I continued:

"I am very, very glad, for her sake, that Miss Wilde is rich, and free. But of course you can see for yourselves that her being so great an heiress makes me feel a little—well, a little dashed. Even in this short time, Monsieur de Brassac, Christine Wilde has come to—to mean a great deal in my thoughts; you can understand, surely, what my dreams must have been. And you can understand what it is that I feel now, since her fortune has shut me out, on the other side of a high wall . . ."

"No," said Henri de Brassac, "I do not understand. But, Monsieur Sherrill, you need not try to explain it to me." His movement gave me a quick comprehension of the term 'Gallic gesture,' so vivid, so significant, did that little flicker of his hand seem to be. "I have read it, in books, of the English and the Americans, this feeling about marriage. Now I see it. Monsieur Armitage wishes his bride to be poor, not rich: it is he himself, he alone, who will build the house, who will set the fire upon the hearth; it is what he earns from day to day or from year to year, that and that only, which will keep the fire burning. And when he finds that the young lady of his choice is rich, then Monsieur Armitage sees an insuperable obstacle between himself and his happiness.

"No, my friends, I do not understand. I cannot see logic there, nor common-sense, nor a frank facing of the realities of life. It is not so with us: in France, Monsieur Armitage, when a man finds that the young lady who attracts him is an heiress, he does not regard it as 'terrible.' It is not to him what you call it—a high wall to bar him from happiness for himself. No, it is a door, on the contrary, which opens for happiness for the two together and for their children, since it assures security for the family.

"I think our way is best, Monsieur. But I am glad to have seen yours, in its sincerity. And I believe what you say, Monsieur Armitage. I believe what you say. At this moment, that is important.

"And now that you have been so courteous as to bear with my ignorance and permit my interruption," he added, "shall we ask Monsieur Sherrill to solve the riddle of how Miss Christine could have had the 'means' and the 'opportunity' of which he spoke?"

I felt definitely grateful to the Frenchman for the formal speech which gave me time to recover myself after my outburst; and grateful, too, for the way he changed the subject by bringing it back to the question that had been in my own mind.

And Sherrill went on as if there had been no interruption:

"You see, Mrs. Wilde was not really very ill—not nearly so ill, for instance, as Miss Hamilton thought at first. She was not strong; she had the first threatenings of diabetes, for which her doctor was already giving her insulin, and which he was already able to control and might well have been able to cure. But a large part of her ill-health, I am convinced, was in reality a pretext for having life made easy, for getting her own way, for keeping in the center of the picture. And she was comparatively young—only in her early forties.

"What I am trying to emphasize is the fact that Mrs. Wilde would probably have lived for years, keeping her daughter chained to her side until Christine's own youth was past. And Christine is not stupid. On the contrary, she is an ingenious girl. I think she is quite ingenious enough to have got hold of a small quantity of morphine, and to have found a way to substitute that drug for insulin in one of those *ampoules*, so that her mother would have taken a deadly poison when she herself was somewhere else."

Upon my speechless horror and amazement fell Monsieur de Brassac's voice, calm, interested, impersonal:

"But in that case would she have called attention to the fact that her mother was not a drug-addict, that she could not take opiates?"

"I think not," Sherrill agreed. "But one can't be sure of that. A clever murderer might possibly have taken just such a step, with the idea of provoking just such a reaction as yours has been. But of course it is not necessary for us to fash ourselves over that question: the *ampoule* had contained insulin; there was nothing in the room which had contained morphine. The poison was put in the hypodermic syringe by someone who was on the spot. And the murderer locked the door on the outside and took the key away with him; that second piece of evidence came out after my question about the *ampoule*. By one, or both, of those items, Christine is eliminated as a suspect. As are also," he added, with a little smile, "my wife and myself."

"Then the rest of us are under suspicion?" Henri de Brassac asked.

"In a sense, yes."

"What do you mean by 'in a sense'?" the Frenchman insisted.

On at least two occasions afterward I was to recall that scene, as vividly as if I had been watching it all in a play: the picturesque old *Place* in the soft light of a late afternoon in June, the ancient mellowed walls of the building that had become the inn, the leaning upper story of the museum above the broad *galerie*, the little old house that was now the garage, and the other little old house beside it where vines climbed upward to a painted sundial, and just beyond this the narrow turning road; the majestic linden tree in the center of the square; and ourselves sitting under it discussing this tragedy, while John Sherrill told us that we were all under suspicion "in a sense," and Henri de Brassac asked, "What do you mean?" Here in Neyronnes was beauty, a remarkable scenic charm, and that strange quality of 'picturesqueness' that comes to dwell upon ancient walls which have found peace after turmoil, that is the legacy of old forgotten far-off things and battles long ago.

"'In a sense'?" Sherrill repeated. "Why, I mean that one must use one's reason, that one must consult the triumvirate of motive, means, and opportunity—and character as well. We can rule out the Delandes and their servants, for example. But I do not think that we can rule out anyone else, except as I have just been telling you."

"But what about motive?" Monsieur de Brassac asked, again. "Surely not every one of us had a motive to put Madame Wilde out of the way?"

"Some of us had, very obviously. About the others, we really don't know very much, as yet."

"You think the *dossiers* will tell us?"

Sherrill got up. "Perhaps," he said. "Look here, it's almost dinnertime. If you want me to, after dinner, I'll tell you more of how I've reasoned it out so far. I shouldn't mind talking with you both about Margaret Hamilton . . ."

"I shall be very glad," said Monsieur de Brassac, with more animation than he had yet shown. "You seem so sure . . . That other piece of evidence you spoke of, Monsieur Sherrill—the second point which was established at the inquiry today—does it concern Miss Hamilton?"

But Sherrill shook his head. "I'm not going to say anything about that yet awhile," he declared. "But I will talk with you both about—well, about things, if you will come and have a liqueur with me after dinner."

Each of us accepted the invitation with alacrity. But when the tables had been cleared and Elinor Sherrill and Christine had gone back to the house—Margaret Hamilton had not come to dinner— and the three of us were having our coffee, the hope of a talk about "things" was doomed to disappointment. Out from the main *salle à manger*, where he had dined alone, came Horace Braye.

He came straight at us, a little like a charging bull; and it was plain to be seen that he was in a very bad humor. Without so much as a "Good-evening," still less an invitation to join us, he pulled up a chair and sat down.

"I'm about fed up," he said.

Henri de Brassac regarded him with distant politeness.

"Oh," he remarked, "is it that you have not eaten sufficiently well? You should speak to Monsieur Delande about it."

Horace glared at him. "Trying to be funny, are you, Mister Brasstacks? Or just pretending you don't understand the English language? Well, it's a little late for you to pretend that. I said I was fed up, and when I say fed up I mean fed up, and you know damned well what I mean. My wife's sick with all this damned trouble that's been wished on her, and I'm stuck in this hell-hole giving evidence to your fool detectives, and I say I'm fed up. Not your handker-chief, eh? My handkerchief, was it?" A look of cunning mixed it-self with his air of ferocity and made his ugly expression uglier still, and he went on:

"Well, suppose it was—that's no hanging matter. But you know what is a hanging matter, and what I say is, when is this conspiracy of silence going to end? There's been a murder committed in this place, and you know damned well why it was committed and you know damned well who committed it, and I say, when are you going to tell what you know?"

Monsieur de Brassac met this outburst with entire calm, as by this time I knew him well enough to expect. But what did surprise me was that he was a little pale, as he answered, coldly and very disdainfully:

"I am totally ignorant of what it is that you are trying to express, Monsieur Braye. I do not know what you are talking about. I suggest that you endeavor to control yourself."

This, of course, was pouring oil on the fire. "You do, do you?" Horace bellowed. "Well, I can do a little suggesting too, you damned French popinjay. I suggest that you stop trying to get by with a highfalutin manner, and come clean. And I suggest that it's about time. Do you get that, Mr. Accessory-after-the-fact?"

He paused for the fraction of an instant, and then raged on:

"You know who stood to gain by Mrs. Wilde's passing out so quick and easy. You know who was really going to get the money, and who couldn't have got it in any other way. You heard Mrs. Wilde laying out her daughter because she spoke a friendly word to a real sweet young man, and you heard her call the young man a fortune-hunter and you heard the girl crying and you heard the man's name. Yes, and what do you do? You turn up at just the right minute after the murder to give him just the next thing to an alibi and a good alibi, too, I'll say, all artless and kind and sweet. Maybe you can fool these French dicks with that little tale of stumbling over a sick man and being so good to him, but I'll say that sick man was found at a mighty convenient time!

"And you know all about it," he continued; but strangely enough he was not bellowing now. His voice had taken on that clear coldness with which he had denied ownership of the handkerchief. "You heard, and you guessed, and you know. You're French, you mercenary coot, and it's natural for you to stand in with a fortune-hunter, I'll bet; maybe he's planning to split with you—I don't know that. But what I do know is as plain as the nose on your face. Slick young man sees easy money with a rich wife; mother steps in and pans the petting; young man murders mother, comforts girl, gets the cash, and the girl's just enough of a nitwit to fall for it. Then he chums up to you, and you help him out—you're French, and you were born with your eye on the main chance, I'll say. But I'm not French, damn you, and I'll be hanged if I let Mr. Smarty Amitage get away with murder. Sherrill can tell these dumb policemen about it—I can't talk their damned fool gibberish, but they can't put one over on me—I'm an American —"

John Sherrill pushed back his chair so that it fell with a bang against one of the iron tables, and stood over Horace Braye with a look on his face that was almost frightening. His fists were clenched, and his eyes were burning coals in furious whiteness.

"Yes, you're an American, God help us," he said, in a voice that was low and terribly distinct in its rage and bitterness. "You and your kind are the worst liability America has—and about the worst disgrace, you beast! 'Fed up,' are you? Well, I'm 'fed up.' I'm fed up with your greed and your meanness and your selfishness and your ignorance and your coarseness and your vile temper and your brag. I'm fed up with your silly insults to other countries and your childish profanity and abuse. I'm fed up with the meanness that suspects everyone else of meanness and dishonesty and self-seeking, and that doesn't know kindness or ingenuousness when it meets them face to face. A pig in the barnyard has a better standard of right and wrong than you have.

"An American, are you? Well, there are certain qualities that we like to think of in America, that we're proud of in our history, and you wouldn't recognize them if you fell over them in the street. *You?* You're a bully and a sneak and an ignoramus and an empty-headed braggart and a beast, and I'll swear you're a crook, and the only place where you really belong in America is behind prison bars. You'd better believe I'm fed up! An American—my God, you've got your nerve! Wayne Armitage is an American. I'm an American—and you ask me to pull your dirty chestnuts out of the fire, you big loathsome brute! I'll see you in the frozen limbo first: that's where I'd like to see you, Mr. Horace Braye!"

He made a gesture with his hand as if to push the very thought of Mr. Braye far from him, and strode out of the *galerie*. But Horace sat limp and red-faced in his chair for a full minute, while no one spoke. Then he got up slowly, and lumbered across the *Place* toward the *chemin de ronde*.

XIII
A FRENCHMAN EXPLAINS TO ME

"Monsieur Brays has never read Dante," remarked Henri de Brassac dispassionately. "Monsieur Sherrill would have done better to use the only language he understands and to tell him to go to hell. But no—Monsieur Sherrill has done enough!"

His eyes were fixed reflectively upon Horace's back, as that completely deflated personage all but stumbled across the square. And the phrase, "go to hell," as the Frenchman spoke it, was really funny. But I was not listening. I was not at all interested in Horace Braye's collapse into silence and flabbiness. I was engrossed in my own affairs.

"Monsieur de Brassac," I demanded, "is this true?"

"Is what true, Monsieur Armitage?"

"Is it true that I am suspected of the murder of Mrs. Wilde? And what is all this about her warning Christine against me? What did that bounder mean?"

Henri de Brassac answered my first question, and his voice was grave.

"I am afraid that it is true, my young friend," he said. "You are one of what Monsieur Sherrill has called the 'obvious suspects.' And no one has known—I myself have not known—that you were unaware of Madame Wilde's opposition to your—er—acquaintance with her daughter."

"There was never anything for her to be opposed to," I muttered. "I've hardly spoken three sentences to Christine Wilde. If I've thought about her a lot—well, her mother didn't know that."

"No. It was not your thoughts that her mother was interested in. It is quite possible that her mother guessed that she might be thinking about you. It seems to me that you are too modest, Monsieur Armitage—too modest for your own good, and also too romantic. But we must remain with the facts. Here, then, is the fact which you have not hitherto known: Madame Wilde forbade her daughter to hold any communication with you beyond the demands of the most casual courtesy to a fellow-guest who was, and would remain, a stranger. She told her daughter that you were undoubtedly a fortune-hunter, that you wished to pay your addresses to her for the sake of her money, that you were—forgive my repeating her words—an unscrupulous adventurer, a nobody, looking for a rich wife."

"And did Christine believe that?" I cried out.

Monsieur de Brassac smiled.

"I am inclined to think that she did not," he answered, with a certain amount of compassion and forbearance, I realized, for my state of mind. "She cried. She cried very miserably, Monsieur Armitage, and she told her mother she was sure she was mistaken. But she obeyed her mother, as you have probably noticed."

So that was why I had seen so little of the Wildes. My mind went back quickly to that early day—how many lives ago! when first Miss Hamilton, and then Christine herself, had welcomed me to Neyronnes as a person who would help to keep an invalid entertained. "I am hoping," Margaret Hamilton had said, in that beautiful voice which, like a magic wand, touched slang with piquancy, "that your coming will pep her up a bit." And Christine had greeted me with "You will give her a new interest." I had been irritated by the prospect of sacrificing my treasure of privacy and quiet to the business of pepping up Mrs. Wilde, but I had been pleased, naturally, by the hope of becoming acquainted with Christine, even though all she seemed able to talk about, in those first moments, was her mother's ill-health.

Then I had had that pleasant little exchange of a few sentences with a charming, wide-awake, dirty-fisted girl in overalls at a garage door and after that I had scarcely seen the Wildes at all. My irritation had had nothing more to feed upon, my hope had not

been fulfilled; and I had occupied my time with other matters, although the thought of Christine had never been far from my mind.
I had scarcely seen either of them—now I understood why! Christine
had told her mother about chatting with me, and the result had been
this string of silly accusations; and Christine had cried . . .

"How do you know this?" I demanded. "How does everyone
know?"

"I overheard it, alas," Henri de Brassac answered. "I do not
know the source of Monsieur Braye's information, but I suspect
that Madame Wilde herself talked about it to Madame Braye.
Madame Wilde seemed to welcome the Braye couple as congenial
acquaintances"—he made a little grimace—"I have asked myself
whether that would not have been unpleasing to her daughter: one
can see that the Wilde and the Braye families are not of the same
social standing in the United States, is it not so?"

I nodded. "But Mrs. Wilde was excruciatingly bored," I said,
"and the Brayes were the kind of people she could impress. How
did you overhear all that talk about me, Monsieur de Brassac?"

"Too easily. My room is next to the large one which the Wildes
occupied. Although the walls themselves are thick, one keeps one's
windows open on a warm June evening and words leap to one's
ears. Madame Wilde was given to moods of excitement in which
her voice was less low than in ordinary conversation. And you
may remember, Monsieur Armitage, during the first days after my
arrival, Madame Wilde had no reason to know that I understood
English."

Yes, I remembered. I remembered the scene of the Brayes'
arrival, and Mrs. Wilde's preposterous demand of our French
fellow-guest. I remembered the coy persuasiveness with which she
had addressed him in his language, and the icy, rigid obstinacy
with which he had answered in hers. How they must have loathed
each other after that brief exchange of courtesies, Mrs. Wilde and
Henri de Brassac! And it came over me suddenly, for the first time,
what a curious mixture of raw human emotions we had, as civilized creatures and as complete strangers, stirred up in each other
in a very few days!

Mrs. Wilde and Henri de Brassac hating each other. Mrs. Wilde taking a bitter and cruel dislike to me, and persecuting her daughter miserably because of it. Myself angrily resentful of the woman's selfishness toward Christine, and John Sherrill confessing that he could "just about want to kill Mrs. Wilde" himself, for the same reason. Then Horace Braye and I, flaring out at each other into an actual enmity; and John Sherrill losing his temper when his detestation of that big bully—especially his detestation of him as a disgrace to John Sherrill's country—burst the bounds of conventional self-control.

And Margaret Hamilton—what had she been thinking and feeling, through these last weeks? Under the avalanche that had fallen upon my own unhappy person, the thought of Miss Hamilton had been battered clean out of my mind. For the matter of that, too, what about poor ill Paul MacNeil, whose recitations of English poetry to solace himself in the ruins I had heard at such an inopportune time for myself? And what about Henri de Brassac—what was really going on in the clear mind behind that mask of French calm?

Well, at least I could go on asking questions of Monsieur de Brassac . . .

"Then you suspected me," I said. And I could not help noticing that his reply came not only a little wearily, but with hesitation.

"I would not say that," he demurred. "But Miss Christine's tears told me that she did feel an interest in you, and from that it was surely only the next step to see that you might have had a very strong motive for wishing—forgive my rude phrasing—to put her mother out of the way.

"Moreover, Monsieur Armitage, it seems to me important in this connection that you should remember that you are in France, and not in the United States of America, I have no way of knowing how generally your idealistic conception of the best foundation for a marriage is shared by the young men of your country; that it is universal I find it difficult to believe; but that is not the point. The point, my romantic young friend, is that just as it had not occurred to me that you would regard Miss Wilde's independent fortune as an obstacle to your courtship, so it will not occur to the police. The police, I fear, will not—will not easily credit it."

"Oh," I said flatly. "Go on."

He went on:

"Also, Monsieur Armitage, there are one or two little things which were, I am willing to believe, mere unfortunate coincidences, but which do not look very well. In the first real conversation which I ever had with you, it was a little noticeable that you made a special point of telling me that Miss Christine had never had a chance for independent intellectual development. When you ran to me for aid for poor young Monsieur MacNeil and told me your story of having heard him in the ruins in the night, it is quite possible that you might have been, as this person Braye charged, attempting to establish something in the nature of an alibi—not an alibi in actual strokes of the clock, but something more subtle: the impression that you were a young man of very gentle and sensitive nature, who had spent the night in contemplation of a work of mercy."

"But I wasn't!" I interrupted. "I don't know anything about alibis, but I hate myself for not having rushed right out to find that poor boy as soon as it began to rain. If I had done that, I'd have an easier conscience—and a real alibi," I added, a little bitterly.

"If you had done that, you would perhaps have met the murderer in the hall," said Monsieur de Brassac gravely, "or, possibly, heard sounds as you passed Madame Wilde's door."

"I wish to Heaven I had," I muttered. And then I had a sudden thought.

"Look here, Monsieur de Brassac," I said, "didn't you hear any sounds at all in Mrs. Wilde's room that night—after you had been able to hear all that conversation before?"

"No," he answered, still gravely, "I heard nothing. And that is not so strange as it seems. The walls of those rooms are very thick—the police have been testing for noises, I believe—and one cannot overhear anything but the loudest sounds, through the wall. The conversation to which I was unwillingly obliged to listen came through the windows: out one open window and into another. On the night of that hard rain from the west, my own windows were

closed, and Madame Wilde's must have been. Also, the rain itself
was noisy, and could have drowned light sounds."

"Oh, I see." I felt as if I had been a little stupid, not to grasp that
obvious fact for myself. "Well, are there any more clues against me?"

"Not clues exactly, Monsieur Armitage." He smiled again now.
"Not clues. But you know I have already warned you against the
obviousness with which you began to devote yourself to Miss Christine as soon as her mother was dead. And, although this last has
no apparent bearing upon the death of Madame Wilde, it is something which may be thought to require explanation—your footprints
have been found in the dust of the unfinished room in the *pavillon*.
One may ask oneself, what were you doing there?"

"One may ask me that," I remarked none too politely. And
somewhat to my surprise Monsieur de Brassac's smile became more
friendly.

"These are small things," he said. "Perhaps I should not have
mentioned them at all. They are small, and obvious. Too obvious.
Monsieur Sherrill would tell us that the too obvious clue is probably no clue—that anyone clever enough to commit a murder would
be too clever to leave a succession of aids to identification behind
him, or to throw out helpful hints to his pursuers from day to day.
If it is any comfort to you, Monsieur Armitage, I do not believe
that you murdered Madame Wilde. I know that Monsieur Sherrill
does not believe it. But it is possible that you may have to undergo
further police examination before the real murderer is found."

He sighed. "Myself, I am no investigator. I am a quiet scholar,
of no particular distinction and no particular talent, who has been
drawn much against his will into these lamentable events. As I once
pointed out to you, I am almost old enough to be your father, and
I am your friend. And since I have been caught in the currents of
this tragedy, I am interested, Monsieur Armitage. I lack the skill
to inquire into the mystery—that is not my *métier*, it is Monsieur
Sherrill's—but I am interested. I am interested in you, my young
friend with the illogical modesty and the romantic ideas in regard
to marriage and love. I am interested in Miss Christine, whose life
is just beginning—who can awake now like an embryo that is for

the first time touched by the light. I am interested in Miss Hamilton, that American lady whose fortune has fallen from her, but who keeps her pride. I am interested in this poor afflicted young man whom it is so easy for everyone to forget in his affliction. I am even interested, Monsieur Armitage, in Monsieur Horace Braye and in his wife."

"Horace and his wife?" I echoed. "Oh, are you? Well, I'm not." But as soon as I said that, I knew it was a brainless remark. As a matter of fact, I was still feeling stunned—too stunned, too bruised and sore, to think clearly.

And Monsieur de Brassac seemed to understand that.

"*Et puis alors*," he said, "have you any theory about this crime, Monsieur Armitage? Myself, I am offering no opinion," he added, "but we must face the fact that one of our number here in Neyronnes is a murderer. Will you permit me to ask you—who do you think killed Madame Wilde?"

"Not Horace Braye's wife, anyhow," I answered.

"No? And not Horace?"

I shook my head, not as a negative reply, but in sheer perplexity.

"I don't know. It has occurred to me that he might have done it. I think, as Mr. Sherrill says, that he's a crook. And he seems to be doing all he can to frame me. But he doesn't seem the type for that kind of murder—that big bragging bounder. And what motive could he have? He and his wife seemed, as you said, to be making friends with Mrs. Wilde."

"There is no type for any particular kind of murder, I am afraid," Monsieur de Brassac said soberly. "And I think that Monsieur Braye's mind is more subtle than it seems. Motive? We do not know now what motive he, or anybody, may have had. We cannot place too much dependence at this moment upon motive, I think. The clue of motive, Monsieur Armitage, leads to you."

"The clue of motive," I said, "seems to lead to Miss Hamilton."

"Ah, yes, Miss Hamilton . . ." Henri de Brassac looked worried, and for an instant he did not speak again. Then he went on:

"Myself, I know little or nothing. But there is one thing in which I find myself somewhat interested: the handkerchief. The handkerchief which might have been used to keep the murderer's fingers from leaving any prints, even on the door-knob in Madame Wilde's room. Why did Monsieur Braye deny ownership of the handkerchief you found?"

"I have thought about that handkerchief myself," I agreed, "but it would have been so easy for Mr. Braye to drop it there when he leaned over to look in the keyhole, in the morning, or when he was trying the door. Indeed, he might have dropped it when he was passing by—his own door is just across the hall. I don't think there is anything incriminating about the handkerchief's being there."

"Exactly," Monsieur de Brassac declared. "There was nothing incriminating about the handkerchief—then why deny its possession so emphatically? Especially since Monsieur Braye was so eager to disown it *before* it became known that something of the sort must have been used to prevent the leaving of fingerprints. To say it was my handkerchief! It was not my handkerchief. But if it had been my handkerchief, I should have seen no reason for disowning it. It appears to me that there may be something not quite right in Monsieur Braye's conscience.

"And now," he said, "I will tell you a little fact which I think you do not know. This affair—it is not now in the hands of the local police. You have seen gendarmes and detectives here in Neyronnes ever since the murder was discovered, and you saw with them the *juge d'instruction* this morning. One of them, Monsieur Armitage—the tall one with whom you have perhaps seen Monsieur Sherrill speaking—is Monsieur Reynal of the Sureté."

"The what?" I said. And for the first time in our talks together an expression crossed the. Frenchman's face which seemed to betoken some impatience with my ignorance of the things of France.

"The Sureté Générale," he answered, "from Paris. I understand that in the United States you have no such central government bureau to investigate crime, but you are probably familiar with the corresponding office in Great Britain. The Sureté, my friend, is the Scotland Yard of France; it is our Criminal Investigation Department, so to speak.

"And now," he continued, without pause, "permission has been given to remove the body of Madame Wilde, and tomorrow her daughter, with Monsieur and Madame Sherrill, will go to the city, where there will be a funeral service and temporary burial. They will remain until Saturday morning.

"And on Saturday morning the second meeting of the inquiry will be held. By then, surely, something will have happened."

In that, he was right.

XIV

MRS. BRAYE COMES TO DINNER

After I got over feeling dazed, I found that it was impossible for me to take the suspicions against myself seriously, in any practical way. When I tried to imagine myself being arrested for the murder of Mrs. Wilde, it seemed simply ridiculous. It was true that Christine's wealth—which had filled me with such consternation—might contariwise be argued as inciting me with a motive to crime. It was true that I had had—like everyone else in the place—the opportunity to kill Mrs. Wilde on the night when she slept alone in a hotel room behind an unlocked door. Probably someone would be able to think up a way in which I could have got hold of the means—though where and how I could have laid my hands on morphine, whether in France or in my own country, I had not the slightest idea! But none of that was real evidence! And I felt too firm in my complete innocence to be worried. I even concluded that Monsieur de Brassac who had said he was my friend, had meant to speak a word of comfort and reassurance when he told me that the case had been put into the hands of the highest police. They would find out the absurdity of accusations against me!

But did Christine herself suspect me? That was another question. She had been so kind, in these last few days. I had had very little opportunity to talk with her; I had not even seen much of her. But at this time, when she was certainly awakening to a real life of her own, she had been cordial and even companionable in her attitude toward me. Was she only pretending? Could she suspect me of responsibility for her mother's death? That seemed too terrible. I did not believe that she could.

And as, in the night and early morning, my mind went back over the conversation with Henri de Brassac which had closed the events of that crowded day, it was not false accusations or suspicions of murder that troubled me, but the true accusations that came from my own conscience. What was it the Frenchman had said? "I am interested in this poor afflicted young man whom it is so easy for everyone to forget in his affliction . . ." Yes, I, too, had forgotten Paul MacNeil. I had listened to his voice in the night, in the ruins; had traced him and found him, drenched with the night's downpour in his flooded hut, and desperately ill; had brought him to the inn; and had had the definite idea of taking care of him; and then in this press of tragic events I had all but forgotten his existence.

Henri de Brassac had remembered him constantly. Margaret Hamilton and Christine Wilde, each of them deeply involved in this tragedy, as I was not, had thought to send the Lausanne doctor to him. Someone—not I—was seeing to it that he had whatever care he needed. And yet—of course this was the thing which made me feel so miserably remorseful—he was really *my* responsibility. If I had only taken the trouble to find him in the ruins *before* he had lain there all night in the rain!

Of course that was not the first time that the rain had come into his shelter; but it probably was the first time that it had come in such force and quantity as to drench him through and through. And I had known that it was raining, and known that he was there. Although I had not known that he was ill, I had heard the note of weariness in his voice as he said over the poetry that he loved, in the darkness. I had marked the dragging tempo that made the final lines so sad, even though the last words were those of the beautiful cadence of the Shakespeare sonnet—

"All losses are restored, and sorrows end."

And when I had got back to my own comfortable room I had been pricked and troubled by the thought of the strange man in those crumbling ruins, in the rain. I had questioned then whether I should not go and find him and bring him to a surer shelter. And in the morning it had been too late! And I found no comfort in the sorry realization that Paul MacNeil was a doomed man anyway, and that the end could not have been far off in any case, even though it was the pelting all-night downpour which had caused his present collapse. Dr. Lavigne had intimated unmistakably that there was little chance of his living through the summer and autumn—"Consumptives die in the autumn," an old saying came back to me—but he might have spent these weeks of midsummer with less suffering if he had not had that night in the rain . . .

That was the thing that was haunting me. And some people were saying that my discovery of Paul MacNeil was an attempt to establish a sort of alibi! What a strange irony!

My conscience was making me so unhappy on the subject of the sick man that, when I went to see him immediately after breakfast on Friday morning, I was surprised to find him sitting up in bed, clad in a red bathrobe, and looking actually gay. There was a volume of Alfred Noyes's poems, *Tales of the Mermaid Tavern*, lying on the counterpane beside him, and his eyes were bright and dancing.

"Hullo, here's my rescuer," he greeted me. "I say, these Noyes things are great, aren't they? I had read them before, but I didn't remember any of them well enough to say off to myself. Mrs. Sherrill got me this book when she went into town the other day. Wasn't it good of her? And wasn't it queer, and lucky, that she could find this in such a funny job-lot of English books as they had there? Not much poetry, of course. Mostly novels. I don't like novels. I don't like modern poetry much, either—I mean, Robinson Jeffers and T. S. Eliot and Cummings and Ezra Pound and those chaps that do the woozy stuff. What I like is a good swinging rhythm, something that sings itself to you in the night. Or else a sonnet. There's nothing in the world like the beat of a sonnet, is there? And the old ones are glorious. Listen:

"'Earth has not anything to show more fair . . .'"

I had a curious feeling that I could almost have wept, as, sonorous in the very faintness of his tired voice, the noble words swung out upon my ear. Like the rise and fall of a great wave, it was, line after line—sweeping to its climax, ebbing far away, lost now in the sea. . .

    "'And all that mighty heart is lying still!'"

He smiled at me. And, thinking of the wave, I remembered how lovingly his voice had dwelt on the lilting rhythms of 'The Last Chantey,' and the Masefield poem.

"But don't you like the ocean best?" I asked.

"Oh, yes!" he cried, like a boy. "I love the sea. I never get enough of it. I never get enough of it in poetry, and I have never got enough of it in life. They tell me, now, that I shall never see the ocean again. And so I think of all the poetry I know about it, and say it to myself. Do you remember Kipling's 'The Sea and the Hills'? That's not so well-known as some of his others, but it's great.

    "'Who hath desired the sea . . .'"

He went on, and recited the whole long poem. And in his voice, in his manner, in his quick eager smile, there was not one hint of self-pity, of sadness, of regret for the life that he must leave, and the loneliness and poverty in which he was leaving it. He was feverish, of course—that was a part of his illness—but this was no fever, this gallant acceptance of life and death, this bright serenity . . .

Nor did he dramatize himself and his plight. I know that my face is a very self-revealing one, and as I sat there by Paul MacNeil's bed I think he must have guessed what was in my thought. I had expected that he would make some sort of reference to it, that he would recite or quote a poem which might show a personal significance for himself. I was almost bracing myself for

    "'Home is the sailor, home from the sea,
     And the hunter home from the hill.'"

But no such relapse into conscious pathos came.

"Old Matthew Arnold had some grand phrases," he said. "But I never could get anything out of Swinburne: the stuff isn't *real*."

I agreed with him. He quoted 'Dover Beach.' Then he quoted some of Swinburne's sea stanzas, from 'The Triumph of Time,' with so much of joyous and clever burlesque in his sing-song that I burst out laughing in delight. And then it was easy enough to say:

"You look very perky. In fact, you look fine. Don't tell me you got that scarlet bathrobe off Monsieur de Brassac!"

He laughed at my mild effort. "Oh, no. This bit of tarnished splendor is my own. Gaudy but not neat. But Monsieur de Brassac had been most extraordinarily good to me," he added seriously. "So has Miss Hamilton. For all she has felt so ill and—and troubled herself, she has been so very kind to me, ever since you brought me to the inn. And Monsieur de Brassac treats me as if I were his own—he told me once that I made him think of a nephew, who had died. Now, what do you think, he is getting me a new suit! And he is so kind and fatherly I don't mind his doing it. He looks after me just as if I were a baby. It's grand!" He chuckled again. "Pull aside that curtain, and see how he has arranged my princely wardrobe."

I held back the cretonne curtain that had been hung in front of a row of hooks to make a closet in the tiny room, and I was impressed, just as Paul MacNeil had wished me to be, with the orderliness with which his few bits of clothes had been hung there: his two shirts laundered, a necktie solitary on a coat-hanger, a worn pair of boots mended and polished and set into shoe-trees on the floor. It was all neat and practical, and it showed that someone was taking good care of the sick man. But on the hook farthest from the bed, where he himself could least easily see it, hung the old gray suit in which I had found him: the trouser-legs looked rough around the edges, and on the jacket were pathetic dark splashes, still. I was in the act of dropping the curtain for I had guessed by this time that any reminder of that hemorrhage distressed young MacNeil—when I noticed something else, which swung my attention painfully back to a tragedy more terrible than his. One elbow of that coat was threadbare, and a fringiness was beginning to appear about the cuff: it was like Margaret Hamilton's . . .

He was marvelously quick, I knew already, at reading one's thought, putting two and two together. I have never known whether his eyes followed mine and he grasped the association in my mind, or whether his next remark was mere coincidence. But he reached out to the night-table, as I let the curtain fall, and handed me a book, an old book, much worn, much read, in a blue cover.

"Look," he said. "Miss Hamilton has let me have this. It is one of her treasures. I have never been able to buy it, because it is an expensive book and now she has let me have this."

It was the *Oxford Book of English Verse*, in the thin paper edition. And on the fly-leaf, in a girl's writing, immature but by no means without character, I read, "Margaret Joyce Hamilton, Vassar College, April, 1907." Perhaps I was sentimental over this sudden glimpse of the young Margaret Hamilton a girl of Christine's age or less, beginning life with a promise, a background of stability and of consideration, which had been denied Christine, and coming now to—what? Perhaps I was too sentimental, as Monsieur de Brassac had told me that I was too romantic. But it seemed to me that not even her cry of despair when she fainted had been more sad, more fraught with disquiet, than the sight of this book which had been "one of her treasures" such a long time ago . . .

I was glad when Paul MacNeil changed the subject.

"When my new suit comes—maybe today—I'm going to surprise you," he burst into gaiety again. "I'm coming to dinner. Oh, yes, I am, like a real gentleman, or a Bright Young Thing. I'm going to have a festive evening at the Auberge de Vieux Neyronnes!"

So I chaffed him about that, and the things we should eat and drink, and I kept the conversation as light as I could, and left him soon. I had been very careful not to mention anything that might have reminded him of the tragedy among us, and I had tried not to tire him; but I felt that he had talked as much as was wise. I went back, myself, to the inn.

There, in the *Place*, I found a surprise.

To be exact, I found two surprises. The first was Miss Hamilton, wearing an old-fashioned blue cotton dress, and looking stronger and more natural than at any time since Mrs. Wilde's death. But the second—and more noteworthy—was Horace Braye. The Sherrills were just about to set out with Christine on their sad errand to the city. Henri de Brassac had apparently been having some conversation with Elinor. And, as I arrived, Horace embarked upon a voyage of apology.

He apologized abjectly. He apologized profusely. He apologized to Henri de Brassac, to me, to John Sherrill—who certainly owed an apology to him, and who had no intention of making one! He apologized for his belittling references to the French police and his offensive remarks about the French nation. He apologized to all the countries of Europe for having accused them of cheating Americans; and I thought he was going to take the grand final step of apologizing for his traveling American bar. But he stopped short of that. He evidently still considered it entirely natural that he should bring his American bootleg liquor to France, just as he considered it entirely natural to wonder why the old houses of Neyronnes had not been torn down to make a wider motor road. He apologized for everything he could think of, but there were some things which were beyond the reach of Horace's thought.

And I confess that I disliked him even more when he was wallowing in humility than when he was strutting around as a natural-born bully and hitting the eagle to make it scream. Horace bragging, Horace blustering and losing his temper, Horace insulting other people and other countries, was genuine. This cringing, crawling Horace was a slimy coward.

He assured us that he had not been quite himself the evening before—in fact, he added, he had been pretty well spiffed—and although we knew perfectly well that this was not true, we all duly accepted his apologies, and I envied the Sherrills for being able to get away from him.

"You'll be back tomorrow?" he asked them, with a great show of geniality.

"Tomorrow morning, early," John Sherrill announced briskly. "The hearing is called for ten-thirty."

"Oh, yes, yes, so it is. And now I am sure that the whole matter will be cleared up, and that we can go our ways—go our ways," Horace repeated, as if he had got hold of a highbrow phrase that pleased him. "I've been thinking, as a matter of fact, it was most likely some passing thief that killed poor Mrs. Wilde—doped her to keep her quiet while he robbed her. She had jewels, you know."

"All of which were found in her room," John Sherrill said. "Good-bye, Armitage. Good-bye, Margaret. See you in the morning. Monsieur de Brassac, if anyone asks for me, will you be so kind—"

"Yes, but the thief might have got scared and run away without his loot," Horace interrupted. "Miss Hamilton's dog—"

Sherrill had already put the car in gear—they were taking the Packard, but he was driving—and it was on the point of moving. But he put his foot on the brake, turned, and looked straight at Horace Braye.

"Yes," he said, with an emphasis which I was at a loss to understand, "Miss Hamilton's dog. Good-bye."

The car shot forward, around the corner, and out of sight. Fergus, as if he had recognized the mention of himself, gave the sharp little bark with which he sometimes said good-bye to his friends, and Miss Hamilton leaned over and scratched his ear.

"Well," remarked Horace, to everyone and no one, "I'll say it's good to have a car. I'll appreciate mine for the rest of my life, you bet! I'm going down to get it early tomorrow morning, and drive back to the hearing in style."

Nobody paid any attention to him and he went into the inn. Miss Hamilton and Henri de Brassac walked across the *Place* together and down the sloping path toward the Promenade des Lices. A little girl with a tall copper pitcher came out of one of the smaller old houses and got water at the faucet-pump on the opposite corner of the square. The *gardien* of the little *cité*, a courtly white-haired old army man who was curator, cicerone, and caretaker for

all the mediæval Neyronnes, came out of the museum in a blue
denim apron, with a broom made of long fagots, and began sys-
tematically to sweep up the already clean cobbles under the great
linden tree. And two little boys came running up the hill with a
hoop made of an old bicycle tire. In the distance sounded an ear-
piercing shriek which I recognized as heralding the approach of
the baker's car from Jeanniot; but not even a motor klaxon, and a
bad one, could break the sense of peace which seemed to lie over
Neyronnes when Horace Braye had removed himself and I was left
there in the *Place*, alone with the village's ordinary daily life. How
restful it was! And how natural, in its ancient beauty! When the
sadness of today was over, and the ordeal of tomorrow, might it
not even be possible for Christine to find a little quiet, a little heal-
ing here at Neyronnes?

And through the rest of that silent and almost completely solitary day, my own spirit found some guerison. When Rosalie Braye
came to dinner with her husband, and they elected for the first
time to be served in the *galerie*, I was not disturbed by Horace's
nearness, or even by the sound of his voice and his laughter. And
when Miss Hamilton and Henri de Brassac appeared in company
with Paul MacNeil, proudly dressed in his new suit, and suggested
that the four of us dine together, I was glad.

Paul MacNeil's eyes had the pathetic brightness of the consumptive, and fever burned, almost scarlet, in his wasted cheeks;
but he walked without support or assistance, and he seemed very
pleased to be there. It was easy to see that he felt an actual dependence upon Monsieur de Brassac, and a very deep gratitude to him
and also to Miss Hamilton. And no words were necessary to make
plain the tacit determination which we three well people shared,
that the evening should be made wholly light and pleasurable for
Paul MacNeil's sake, and that we should behave like a happy normal
group of friends whom neither mysterious death nor hopeless illness
had touched. The sick lad was very quiet: he ate little and drank nothing and talked scarcely at all; but his smile was happy; and he
seemed richly contented just to sit there with his friends and look
out across the *Place* to that unfailing spectacle that was Neyronnes.

"I am so glad you love it as I do," he said, once, to us all. "Isn't it odd that Miss Hamilton and Monsieur de Brassac and I have known Neyronnes, and loved it, for years and years, and that it was I who was responsible for the Wildes' coming here?" He smiled at his own speech. "Don't misunderstand me," he said. "I should not be likely to have influenced the Wildes to do anything! And I had no idea they had ever thought of coming here. But when I met them in Lausanne that time, I got to talking about Neyronnes: how picturesque it was, and how sweet, and what a good inexpensive inn it had. And then when the United States went off the gold standard, and Mrs. Wilde wanted to get the most for her francs, she came here. Isn't that funny, really—the near-millionaire Mrs. Wilde, and the near-pauper me, coming to the same place at the same time, for the same reason!"

"And Mr. Armitage," said Miss Hamilton, "and I. That is, I have been coming for years, to spend part of the summer; but this year, as soon as the country went off gold—or rather, as soon as I could get any money out of any bank—I came straight here." She smiled at me, and I wondered if a great effort lay behind the return of her old roguish gaiety. "I, Mr. Armitage, changed my dollars at twenty-three. And you, Monsieur de Brassac—don't think we can't see that you are finding it hard to eat this delicious *poularde de Bresse* at this moment, because you are struggling between your native politeness and your desire to burst into howls of mirth over the fall of the mighty dollar and the squirms of the Americans as they choke over their own medicine, so to speak."

She made a grimace that was pure comedy. "Go right ahead," she said. "Don't mind us. We are not amused."

I forget what Henri de Brassac said in answer. But I remember how light-hearted our chuckles would have sounded to any stranger passing by . . .

Then Miss Hamilton continued, "Mr. and Mrs. Sherrill came here to economize, too. And—I wonder . . ."

Obviously she had been thinking of the Braye couple, wondering what had brought them to Neyronnes. But they might have overheard any mention of themselves, there in the *galerie*, and it seemed safer to change the subject. It was only a few minutes after that that Monsieur de Brassac announced firmly that his charge must go to bed, and arose and walked with him up the *ruelle* toward the *pavillon*.

Miss Hamilton and I smoked in silence for a few minutes, and I watched a little sadly as the gaiety faded from her face and left the traces of fatigue and anxiety behind. She had been 'keeping up,' so that the sick lad might have a pleasant festival. Now that he was gone, she looked suddenly very tired. But she seemed to have made up her mind to cast the mantle of sociability over the whole evening, for soon, with a companionable little smile to me, she got up and walked down to the table that was set at the other end of the *galerie*.

She addressed Mr. and Mrs. Braye with what seemed to me to be, in the circumstances a beautiful graciousness. "Won't you come and have your liqueurs with us?" she said. And a rather pathetic blush of almost too evident pleasure swept over Rosalie's face and showed wherever it could through and around her make-up.

"Oh, thank you! We'd just love it!" she cried, and jumped up promptly.

Horace lumbered to his feet. And again the blushes chased each other across Rosalie's cheeks as Miss Hamilton exclaimed in genuine delight and admiration,

"Oh, Mrs. Braye, what a beautiful piece of lace!"

It was a scarf of exquisite *point d'Alençon*, thrown around her neck in the opening of her fussily smart summer evening dress; and it gave Rosalie the utmost of grace and charm that she would ever, I thought, be able to achieve. I was annoyed with Horace when he scowled at her.

"It's worth a fortune," he grumbled. "She hadn't any business to wear it tonight, at a place like this. When I pay a lot of good money for lace, I want it to be taken care of."

Rosalie giggled. "Oh, Horace," she said, "you've given it away!" She giggled again. "I don't mean that you've given away the lace, Horace; I mean you've given away the secret." She turned to Miss Hamilton. "Horace keeps saying that I must tell everyone that this is ancestral lace. And I guess it must have belonged to somebody's ancestors; but they weren't mine! Horace bought this for me at some family sale in St. Louis."

"You shut your mouth!" roared Horace. His face was purple again, and I thought he was going to burst into one of his tirades of abuse. But he controlled himself, and apologized to Miss Hamilton, not to his wife.

"I hope you will excuse me," he said. "That is a very valuable piece of lace, as you can see—I got it in Louisville, Kentucky, not St. Louis—and I am naturally upset over Mrs. Braye's wearing it here. There is no sense in dressing up so in a little place like this; and, as I told Mr. Sherrill this morning, I feel more and more sure that there are thieves about."

Poor Rosalie had turned quite white, but she pulled herself together again. Miss Hamilton had asked them to have liqueurs with us, and have liqueurs with us they did. And Miss Hamilton talked to Mrs. Braye with sweetness and with charm. But Horace scarcely spoke, and all Rosalie's pleasure had been spoiled. Horace had the air of being somewhat crushed, if not actually repentant. But he was still disagreeable. And the brutality of his public insult to his wife was something one couldn't forget.

XV

A WITNESS IS LATE

Christine seemed to feel much better when she came back to Neyronnes in the morning, and I thought that the Sherrills had been wise to suggest staying at a hotel in the city overnight. They had picked up the lawyer, Mr. Williamson, who had come from Lausanne by express train, and had brought him with them from one of those numerous junctions; and Christine was driving when I looked out of my window and saw the big Packard swinging the four of them through the arch of the ancient gate. To my surprise and delight she caught sight of me and waved her hand. After that I did not see her again until she came, still flanked by her attorney and Elinor Sherrill, into the inquiry room. John Sherrill followed with Miss Hamilton. We sat down in the same horseshoe of chairs, in the same order. But it was Rosalie Braye, not her husband, who was seated at my left.

She looked anxious and haggard, almost ill. In deference to the subject of the meeting she had put on a dark gray dress, which was of heavy silk, and had the appearance of being stiflingly uncomfortable on a warm June day. And in a praiseworthy but mistaken attempt to conceal the fact that she did not look well, she had piled more make-up than usual on her face, and had a strained and indeed almost ghastly expression in consequence. Poor Rosalie! She looked as if this inquiry frightened her. And that, certainly, was not a good way to begin . . .

She assured everyone, nervously, that Mr. Braye would be in very soon, surely in a few minutes. She even made a bright little remark to me about a possible puncture. But nobody paid any attention, and, with Horace Braye still absent, the hearing began.

It began with the reports on who and what and whence we were, those 'bundles of papers' that we had been promised or threatened with. But the first *dossier* was one which the police must have had in their hands all the time:

"Henri Maurice Robert Veyrin de la Palud de Brassac, third son of the Marquis de Brassac, brother of the Comte de Brassac, born August 22, 1885, in the Château de Brassac, near Sarlat, Dordogne—" and so on with his education, his war record, his decorations and marks of distinction, his achievements in the authorship of several erudite works on prehistoric man. Our French neighbor had certainly done well to refer to himself as a 'scholar,' although he was, as certainly, wrong when he said he was not a distinguished one. Since he did not use the courtesy title that belonged to him, he evidently wished what renown he might have to rest upon his work alone. We all listened to his record in respectful silence, and then the *juge d'instruction* laid down the first paper and picked up the second:

"Margaret Joyce Hamilton, only daughter of Philip Wainwright Hamilton, Judge of the Supreme Court of the State of New York, born April 18, 1888, at 12 East Eleventh Street, New York City, educated at Vassar College, Poughkeepsie, New York—" and then some unimportant facts about Miss Hamilton's no doubt charming and interesting, but on the whole quite unimportant, life. Her financial ups and downs, which of course the police knew, were not read to the assembled company, but uncertainties in her career could easily enough be guessed; for it was noted that she was an orphan, without near relatives, with no 'permanent' address except Morgans' in Paris, and with a list of abiding-places for more than three years in which the only alternative to cheap *pensions* was an occasional country inn, equally cheap; one could guess, too, that the selections of these had been getting cheaper.

It was Mrs. Wilde's own *dossier* from which we next heard chosen facts, but these facts were not new to us now. And then came Christine's—the short bare record of the existence of a girl who had been born in Honolulu and had wandered about the world in a fashion which seemed as aimless and intellectually meager as it was uprooted and emotionally poverty-stricken, for all her twenty years. I wondered whether the short and simple annals of the poor Wayne Armitage would be given to the public next. But after Christine's life story the magistrate laid aside his *dossiers*. He began again to question Miss Hamilton.

He questioned her in new detail about her acquaintance with Mrs. Wilde, her knowledge of Mrs. Wilde's financial circumstances, the possibility of her having expected any legacy. The facts of her own devastating losses, her extreme poverty, came out now. The questions were put considerately enough, but it was a cruel ordeal, and Miss Hamilton showed plainly that she was suffering under it. Whether or not the officials believed her continued stout denials, it was of course impossible to tell. She stated again, emphatically, that she had known nothing of Mrs. Wilde's finances, nothing of Mrs. Wilde's will; that a bequest for herself was the last thing in the world that she could have seen any reason to expect. Then she was asked once more to tell the story of the night and morning: her good-night to Mrs. Wilde, the arrangement about leaving the door unlocked, the almost unprecedented occurrence of her dog's growl in the night, and then the discovery of the body.

Christine's testimony, which came next, helped Miss Hamilton in one way and hurt her in another.

For Christine came firmly to her support in the matter of the will, and she had a good deal to say about it. She averred that she had known all about the will except the actual figures; that she and her mother had discussed the establishment of the trust fund for Miss Hamilton and had been in complete accord about it; and that her mother had directed her not to mention the proposed legacy, as she meant it to be a surprise.

"Miss Hamilton had been extremely kind to my mother, from the very first," Christine said, "and when my mother learned that she had become very poor, after having always lived in comfortable circumstances, she wanted to do something for her. My mother was so uneasy about her own losses that she did not feel that she could make a gift of any sort at this time, but she decided to leave her a substantial bequest in her will. She did not tell me the figure, but she told me its general proportion, in relation to my own income, I mean, and explained that after Miss Hamilton's death the principal would revert to the estate. I knew that she had made the arrangement with Mr. Williamson."

"But it was not strange that your mother, of her own free will and with no suggestion from outside, should have thought of making so large a bequest to a stranger, to the detriment of her own family?"

But Christine shook her head as the magistrate asked this question. As she answered it, it occurred to me that her knowledge of the French was not confined to their language. She realized that any danger of "detriment to the family" was something that needed explaining, in this land.

"No, Monsieur *le juge*," she said, "it was not strange. It was not to the detriment of her own family. My mother had no family, except myself. Miss Hamilton, also, had been left by circumstance alone in the world. I think that this similarity in their situations appealed to my mother's heart, Monsieur. I am sure that you can understand fully, Monsieur *le juge*, that a woman who had lost all her family except one daughter would be moved to great sympathy for a woman who was quite alone . . ."

It seemed to me that in that moment I saw the mature Christine Wilde—clear-thinking, perfectly poised, gracious—just as in the moment in the garage I had seen the girl who longed for activity and freedom, just as in her smile when I found Paul MacNeil I had seen her kindness and loved her for the gentle, thoughtful nature that looked from her beautiful eyes. I saw a woman, not a mere girl, in Christine now, and I felt that I loved her more than ever for this glimpse of her clear mind. But how clearly her mind was working at this moment, and how cleverly, I had not at the time the slightest idea . . .

"Then, too," she went on easily, "my mother enjoyed surprising people, making things dramatic. From the point of view of her health, her physician has told you that. It was as true from other points of view. She did not have many pleasures; making things dramatic was one of them. Sad as it may seem, Monsieur, I know that my mother got a real pleasure out of the thought that Miss Hamilton would find her kindness to her so surprisingly rewarded, when she was gone."

If Christine's testimony had ended with this matter of the will, it would have left a very good impression for Margaret Hamilton. But the magistrate changed the subject and asked her a question for which she was quite unprepared: did her mother often sleep with her door unlocked?

"No," Christine said, and added: "I was always with her. We locked the door."

"Why do you think she left it open on this night?"

"Miss Hamilton has told you that." Christine's voice was very low.

"Had your mother mentioned to you her intention of leaving her door unlocked?"

"Yes, Monsieur."

"For the reason Miss Hamilton gave—so that she might be able to enter her room in the night?"

"Yes, Monsieur."

"What exactly did your mother say to you, Miss Wilde?"

Christine was very white, but she answered the question with a certain brave casualness, as if she did not consider it important:

"She said that since I was going to be away overnight, and she disliked to feel herself entirely alone, she was going to leave her door unlocked and ask Miss Hamilton to look in during the night, to make sure that she was all right. That was Sunday night, of course, not Monday."

The magistrate thanked her, and recalled Miss Hamilton. Had Madame Wilde requested her to visit her during the night?

"No, Monsieur." Miss Hamilton's voice was firm, and not casual.

"She did not ask you to go to her room, either on Sunday night or Monday night?"

"No, Monsieur, she did not make any such request. She said that she was leaving the door unlocked so that I could go in if she called. She did not call."

"And you did not go into her room?"

"No, Monsieur, I did not go into her room."

That, somewhat to my surprise, marked the end of Miss Hamilton's questioning at this time. The magistrate thanked her with unwavering politeness. Then he looked over his papers again, and said:

"Monsieur Horace Braye."

Horace's empty chair stood staring at everyone in the room.

"He hasn't got here yet, Muhseer," said Rosalie weakly.

"*Pas encore arrivé*," I heard someone else remark. Whether in French or English, it seemed unnecessary.

Horace's non-arrival was patent to all.

"*Arrivé?*" echoed the magistrate, sharply. "*D'où?*"

This was too much for Rosalie. "Do? Do what?" she cried almost hysterically. "What can I do? He isn't here. He went downtown to get his car. He hasn't come back."

The *juge d'instruction* spoke in a low voice to one of the gendarmes. Then he frowned. He sent the gendarme out of the room, and he looked long and steadily at Mrs. Braye. After that he spread out a sheet of paper before him and read it through to himself, very carefully. He did not speak, and his silence was stern and terribly impressive: I guessed that it must be shattering to Rosalie's nerves. No one spoke. At the end of perhaps three dragging minutes the gendarme came back and whispered to the magistrate, and the official eye fixed itself again, pitilessly, upon poor Rosalie Braye.

"Madame," said the *juge d'instruction*, "according to the permission given him by the authorities, and upon receipt of his corrected papers, your husband took his car from the police garage at Jeanniot at four o'clock yesterday afternoon. He did *not* go this morning to get his car. Why has he not come to this inquiry?"

More appallingly garish than ever, the carmine makeup stood out again like the gashes of ugly wounds in Rosalie's dead-white face, and her hands opened and shut with the convulsiveness of an automaton.

"I—don't—know," she whispered, and her voice was ghastly.

"Madame," said the examining magistrate, and curiously it did not seem odd to us that the next words were spoken in English, *"where is your husband?"*

Rosalie gave a wild little shriek and sprang to her feet.

"I don't know where he is!" she screamed. "I don't know where he is! Why can't you let him go? He never hurt you! He never hurt any of you! He never even hurt you, Christine Wilde. Let him go— let him go—let him go!"

Her voice rose to the frantic shrill outcry of hysteria, and she rushed out of the door. No one stopped her. A gendarme silently followed. There was perfect stillness in the room.

But if I allowed myself for one moment to think that the inquiry might be adjourned, I was mistaken. I believe that most of us had some idiotic idea of rushing out ourselves in search of Horace Braye; of finding him and dragging him back in triumph, to thrust him into the jaws of the guillotine. With the shock of Rosalie's revelation, too, I realized how deep-seated my fear of Miss Hamilton's guilt had been, and how the more earnestly I had longed to believe in her innocence, the more difficult had such belief appeared.

In reality, it seemed to me up to this moment, nothing that had come out in anyone's testimony, no circumstance, no clue, had weakened the possibility that Margaret Hamilton, middle-aged, solitary, desperate, had ingratiated herself into a rich woman's good graces, worked cleverly upon the hope of a future generosity, and murdered her benefactress at the first opportunity when that generosity was assured. Not the loyalty of the friends who had known her before the plunge into poverty had changed her life and taught her "strange impulses"; not her own graciousness and poise (that least of all!); not this new assurance of Christine's about the will—nothing had really lifted the burden of suspicion that lay on Margaret Hamilton's sloping shoulders, that threatened its hideous brand upon that lined forehead under her graying hair. And now came Rosalie Braye, to shriek out her wild demand that the law let her husband go . . .

I had suspected, of course, that Horace's past was not all that it should be. But even in that moment when his wife listened panic-stricken to the threat of "information from the United States," or later when Henri de Brassac insisted that there was "no type for murder," I had not really thought that this big bully was guilty of this rather subtle and clever crime. Now, in my reaction of relief over Miss Hamilton, I could have pushed Horace Braye, with gladness, down the stone trap-door in the *Salle de Justice* of some mediæval donjon, into some forgotten *oubliette* beneath a robber baron's keep . . .

What happened was that the magistrate sent two of his officers from the room, and the rest of us, with his eye upon us, just sat still. And in fearing that we should hear no more from Rosalie for the time being, I had reckoned without the gendarme. The French gendarme, of course, is no mere cop, and it is not for him to be confused with the *agent de police* whose whistle stops a motor car that is making a wrong turn. A member of the National Constabulary, the gendarme has his place in the French army; he is a very real person, and when occasion requires he can behave like a real personage. Rosalie's screams continued for a few moments only. We caught the sound of the gendarme's voice, calm and determined, from the lounge outside. He could not speak a word of her language, and she knew nothing whatever of his, but he plainly had the Latin gift for expressing himself clearly, even when words failed. And under his methods, whatever they were, Rosalie Braye snapped out of her hysterics in an astoundingly short time.

Incredibly soon, as it seemed to me, the slammed door opened softly, and she walked into the room, followed by the gendarme in an attitude of the most complete deference. Mrs. Braye went back to her chair and sat down.

"Do you feel able to talk to me now, Madame?" asked the magistrate.

And she said, weakly but willingly, "Yes, Muhseer."

But it was the interpreter who next addressed her directly. He had a paper in his hand.

"It is requested that you listen to what I am about to read you, Madame," he said, "and that, having heard it, you tell us whether or not it is true."

"Yes, Muhseer," Rosalie murmured.

"Very well," said the interpreter. "I will now read:

"Horace Braye of New York identified as Howard Bretton of St. Louis, Vice-President of the defunct Marquette Trust Company, wanted by the Missouri police for fraud, embezzlement, and mis-appropriation of funds."

"Is that true, Madame?"

"Yes, Muhseer."

"The *juge d'instruction* suggests that you tell what you can, in your own way, of your husband's life and—er—operations."

"Yes, Muhseer. I don't know much about his operations, but I know about his life. He made a lot of money. He was smart," said Rosalie.

"Please continue." The magistrate spoke to her now himself, and although his words were French, they were so simple that she could hardly fail to understand them. His manner was not at all unkind. I think that at this time everyone was sorry for Rosalie Braye.

"Yes, Muhseer," she repeated dutifully. "He made a lot of money in the cloak-and-suit trade in New York. He started a company to make suits to sell for sixteen dollars retail, and he called it the |Ho-bry Company—"

"What was his real name?" asked the magistrate.

Rosalie looked surprised.

"Why, his real name was Horace Braye," she answered, "and he called his firm the Ho-bry Company and his sixteen-dollar suits the Ho-bry suits—don't you get it? He was clever like that. He was always smart. He made a lot of money, and he made it fast, too—big profits right from the first. But after while he sort of got sick of it. The unions were always making trouble—you know, the Amal-gamated: they're a bunch of Bolsheviks, and he used to say sup-pose they did take away all his money and give it to a lot of kikes, the way they wanted to, how much better off would anyone be?

But the trouble with the fire inspectors in the lofts was the worst. Fellows used to come snooping round and send in reports that he wasn't safeguarding his workers and things like that. He used to talk to me about it. He had a hard time, and it wasn't fair. He was so smart, and he kept right on the job, and yet they were always jumping on him about something, trying to do him out of his profits just because he was smarter than other fellows. They tried to make him do all sorts of things to the lofts, because they said they weren't safe for the workers— Gee, it was only those dumb working girls that anybody seemed to be thinking about! And of course he tried to get the best of all those snooping inspectors and people, but he couldn't always succeed. Things got so hard he was just fair sick."

Rosalie gave a reminiscent sigh. But she was deep in her subject now, and needed no prodding to make her continue.

"I guess you don't know much about America, Muhseer, and maybe you don't want to," she said, finding relief and forgetfulness in words, "but I'll tell you here and now, that Perkins woman has made a lot of trouble for men like Horace. And now she's Secretary of Labor, and you can just see what the country's coming to—all this talk about working people— Gee, America won't be worth living in for people like Horace, if things go on this way! Well, Muhseer, about ten years ago Horace got sick of it, and he decided he'd clear out." Nobody stopped her, and she went on:

"Besides, he'd always had a sort of a yen to be a banker. He liked doing things with money. He was smart that way. And, you know how it is, when you've made a lot of money in the cloak-and-suit trade, you aren't satisfied, somehow—not if you're ambitious, like Horace. He wanted to be a gentleman. We moved to Park Avenue, but that wasn't enough."

She had another flash of realization that she was talking to a foreigner, and she delivered herself of a few sentences that would, she seemed to think, make everything clear.

"I suppose you aren't used to anything but Europe, Muhseer," she said. "You are the slaves of the class system, here—I'm not so ignorant as you may think, I've heard about those things—and you don't know what freedom is, like we have it in America. America isn't like Europe, Muhseer. America is a democracy. Anybody can be a gentleman in America if he's just got money enough and is smart enough to put it across. Being in the cloak-and-suit trade isn't being a gentleman. But if you're a banker, you are . . ."

John Sherrill, that genuine patriot, grinned a lemony grin. Christine's expression was one of shocked bewilderment, and Margaret Hamilton had a light of satiric amusement in her eye.

Henri de Brassac turned his courtly gaze toward me, and smiled.

"That kind of democracy is not unknown in Europe," he murmured.

The *juge d'instruction*, too, seemed less shocked than were Rosalie's compatriots. And it came over me suddenly that there were Horace Brayes in every country, in this modern age.

"So Monsieur Braye became a banker?" the magistrate prompted.

"Yes, Muhseer. It was easy, easier than you'd think. Horace was rich by this time. We moved to St. Louis, and he gave himself a new name. He never had liked the name of Braye—of course you wouldn't understand it, but it made you think of a donkey—and he always wished he had changed it before. So now he called himself Bretton—Howard Bretton is right, like that cable says. First he was going to make it Brereton, but that seemed kind of extreme, and he thought Bretton was safer. Nobody would ever think Howard Bretton wasn't his own name. And nobody ever did. And he got into the banking business very easily and in just a few years he was Vice-President of that bank, and everything was hotsy-totsy, just like he said it would be.

"But then the depression came and everything sort of got different. For a long time he kept saying that it was only psychological and prosperity was just around the corner and the bottom had been reached and we were already on the upgrade—nobody ever could say that Horace wasn't an optimist. But after while I could see he was worried. And then one day last winter he came home in an awful state and said we were going right back to New York in a hurry and he was Horace Braye again, and so we did, and he was, and the next day the bank closed its doors, and that's all I know about it, until we came to Europe. May I have a glass of water?"

Her attendant gendarme got the water for her—she was really a little breathless by now—and the magistrate remarked, in a leisurely fashion:

"Surely you can recall a little more than that, Madame? The return to New York—that could not have been easy?"

"Oh, yes, it was! Horace had kept a lot of his old acquaintances in the cloak-and-suit trade, and he was just good old Horace Braye again. Horace was very smart, just as I've been telling you, Muhseer. And people liked him. He was always jolly, except when something made him mad. And he always had a joke about everything. And when he went back without his business and wasn't always having trouble with those Bolsheviks, he was always cheerful and out for a good time. And he had one of the best bootleggers in New York City, too—people were always crazy about Horace's liquor. Oh, yes, Muhseer, things went all right for a while. You see, there wasn't any warrant out for his arrest for quite a long time—Howard Bretton's arrest, I mean. Horace had been awfully smart. He almost got away with it. You see, he was only the Vice-President, and those people in St. Louis had a good deal of trouble with what they called placing the responsibility."

She took another drink of water. "By the time they'd placed it on Howard Bretton, Horace Braye was having a nice easy trip to Europe, and that was that.

"Then we came here and saw Mrs. Wilde . . ."

Mrs. Wilde's lawyer scribbled something on a piece of paper and handed it to the magistrate.

"I am reminded," said the latter gentleman to Mrs. Braye, "that Madame Wilde lost the sum of sixty thousand dollars in the collapse of the Marquette Trust Company."

"I don't know how much she lost. I don't know anything about business," said Rosalie. "I'm telling you the truth, just what I know and that's all. But I know that Christine Wilde is still rich, and if Mrs. Wilde had told on Horace she'd have been a skunk."

"Did she intend to do that?"

"How do I know?" Rosalie was turning sullen again. "I don't even know whether she recognized Horace—she never acted as if she did. But she had met him a couple of times in St. Louis, and he remembered her all right, because she had such a lot of money in the bank, and right away when we got here she told him how broke she was and he was worried. He didn't know what she might have up her sleeve."

"And so—" said the *juge d'instruction*, and stopped.

"And so," said Rosalie, "when Mrs. Wilde passed out so mysterious, and the police were all over the place, and stirring up trouble in America, he thought he'd better make his getaway while he could."

"Ah," said the *juge d'instruction* reflectively, and left an impressive silence before he asked, "Can you not tell us more? He got his car yesterday afternoon . . ."

"He hid it at the foot of the hill somewhere. He made me go to dinner with him last night, and sit where everyone could see us, and act normal, he said. Then in the night he sneaked out to take a suitcase to the car and see that everything was all right, and he said he was coming back to get me and another suitcase; and I was all ready to go with him. But he never came back. Maybe he got scared. Maybe he never meant to take me along. You just can't tell. He never came back." She turned suddenly dead white again. "That's all I know," she said.

Her gendarme handed her the glass of water without being asked, and the magistrate gathered up his papers.

"Thank you, Madame," he said. "All that you have told us is most interesting. We will now have our luncheon and consider matters further. Will you all be so good as to return to this place this afternoon at half-past two?"

Curiously enough, there was no conversation at luncheon, and there was no approach to even a comforting semblance of sociability. Rosalie had something sent to her room. Christine ate in the main dining-room with her lawyer. On the *galerie* the Sherills and Margaret Hamilton occupied their usual table, but talked very little, and Henri de Brassac and I each lunched alone. Since it was Saturday, there were country visitors about and a few French tourists: if they noticed us at all, they must have thought us a silent bunch! I was not hungry—who could be?—and I was trying to make up my mind to eat a bit of cheese at the end of the meal when a gendarme came and spoke to John Sherill, and I thought he looked rather disturbed when the officer had gone. No one said anything to me. And I decided that I did not want the cheese, and went back to my room. I had some vague idea of 'resting,' of trying to collect my thoughts, before the second session of the day's hearing was called.

But I felt restless. Solitude didn't seem to be the right thing. I started out again, this time with the notion of endeavoring to get into conversation with Monsieur de Brassac. I walked slowly down the hall to the head of the stairs, and stopped.

. . . I shall never know what moved me to open the door of the unfinished room. Some driving force from the oppression that had lain for days over us an, some feeling that here in this ghostly chamber with the cobwebs thick on its barred windows that oppression might reach a climax in my own spirit and so bring me rest—some urgency, some impulse—I do not know. It was not that Henri de Brassac had spoken of finding my footprints on that dusty floor: I never thought of that at all, indeed I had forgotten it. But when I came to the door of that room, I opened it.

And there must have been something that, subconsciously and inexplicably, I was expecting; for I felt a strange little shiver of surprise to see that the room was exactly as it had been before.

I glanced at the shuttered windows, at the veils of dust and cobwebs, at the staring white walls with their blue chalk marks. It was all as before. Exactly as before, I looked into the room and felt a strange sense of terror. Exactly as before, I saw a giant spider in his web, another making his way across the floor. Exactly as before, my eyes followed the hideous insect as he scuttled along the dusty baseboard, around the wall, to the attic door opposite.

But that did not look quite as it had looked the last time. Beneath the closed door, reaching only a very little way into the room, spread a small stain. It was dark and reddish. It glistened as only wetness glistens.

I dashed across the empty room and flung open the attic door upon the strangely sprawling body of Horace Braye.

XVI
WE WAIT FOR ROSALIE

He was lying directly at the top of the stairs, his legs and feet slop-ing down over the upper steps, his head just inside the door which led to the unfinished room. Even to me it was unmistakable that he was dead. But not much blood had flowed from the wound in his forehead, and most of it must have seeped under the door, where the ancient crooked boarding of the attic floor slanted to-ward what had been the outer edge of the original old house.

It was the fact that this storage annex was in another house which had dulled the sounds that must have accompanied Mr. Braye's murder, for I was sure that there had been some struggle, however slight. Through the thick stone wall and the heavy oak door no noise had come to us in the *pavillon* itself. And I remem-bered that the maid who usually slept alone, in this ancient 'lean-to' had been given a week-end holiday before the heavier work of the July season should begin. To all intents and purposes, this annex was an empty house. Horace might even have cried out for help without being heard. But I fancied, somehow, that neither he nor his assailant had spoken. And that assailant—had the attack been made in murderous fury or in self-defense?

Horace Braye had been killed by a blow on the right temple, which had broken the skin, but, I thought, had not actually crashed in the skull. And the weapon that had killed him was lying beside him—a large iron monkey-wrench, such as forms part of the tool-kit of an automobile. All this I saw in an instant. And almost in the same instant I saw the dusty stained rag that lay on the floor beside the monkey-wrench, as if it had been wrapped around it when the blow was struck. I saw all this, and touched nothing. I was there only a few seconds. I backed out of the door into the unfinished rooms, and as I backed away, with my eyes still on the dreadful scene before me, some trick of light, some sharpening of my vision, showed me a detail which at first I had not noticed. The torn rag that lay beside Horace Braye's dead body, with Horace Braye's blood dark and dirty upon it, was a piece of *point d'Alençon* lace.

There is no use of my pretending that I did any thinking at this time. I felt as if I had fallen into some black morass of horror, where only my body could struggle automatically, where my mind could not work at all. I ran back to the *galerie*, where I had a confused vision of the Sherrills and Miss Hamilton, sitting at their table peeling oranges. Henri de Brassac was not there.

As I stumbled across the dirt floor, I heard John Sherrill say, in the reflective tone that was natural to him:

"Rosalie Braye is a strange creature. I think she is completely a-moral."

And I rushed up to him like a man demented. "She has killed her husband!" I cried.

Afterward I realized that he, too, was deeply shocked, and that the inconsequential speech with which he greeted my announcement was a deliberate attempt to bring me back to the beginnings of calmness. It succeeded, too.

"Well, I wouldn't put it past her," was what Sherrill said. He got up quickly, but without giving any impression of restlessness or disturbance.

"Come on, Armitage, snap out of it!" he said, in a very different tone. "I'll go with you to tell the police."

Neither Elinor Sherrill nor Margaret Hamilton spoke a word— I had already learned that these were no women to buzz and hem and haw—and John Sherrill and I crossed the *ruelle* and went into the main dining-room where the police group was just finishing its excellent and somewhat elaborate lunch.

The gendarmes and the interpreter were at a big table. The *juge d'instruction* and the detective from the Sureté were set apart in the elegance of solitude. Every man among them had the air, which seems so universal—and is so enviable!—among the French, of being able to set aside all the cares of the world and the deceitfulness of riches and battle and murder and sudden death, and devote all humane motion and energy to the rich and satisfying enjoyment of a good meal. From this lunch they would all return, I knew, refreshed and clear-thinking, to give keen concentrated attention to the business in hand, without getting frazzled over it. Not for nothing does all activity in France pause for two hours in the middle of every day! And although, of course, I was not making any of these reflections at the time, it is true that through all my horror and confusion I was conscious of a sense of relief when I saw that the magistrate and the detective had already reached coffee and liqueurs. We should not, then, be really interrupting them. . .

"Don't tell them that Rosalie has killed her husband," was almost all that Sherrill took time to say to me. "Just tell them what you saw. Tell them in English, old man: I'll translate, if necessary."

It was not necessary. The detective understood, and spoke, English perfectly, and the *juge d'instruction* was by no means ignorant of the language, as we already knew. Of course that made my task easier. I told them, as clearly and quietly as I could, exactly what I had discovered. And they did not seem particularly surprised.

"We sent you word, Monsieur Sherrill, that Monsieur Braye's car had been found in a shed at the foot of the hill," said the detective Reynal, "apparently where he hid it when he took it from the garage in Jeanniot yesterday."

"Yes, I got your message, thank you," Sherrill replied. "But surely he would not have been able to get far away, in any case?"

"I should not make any such positive statement," Reynal demurred. "If he had succeeded in getting out of Neyronnes itself in the middle of the night—say at two in the morning—he would have had more than eight hours, on a clear road, before his absence was sure to be discovered. No general alarm had been sent out. His papers were in order. He could have got across the Swiss frontier as soon as the Douanes opened. By half-past ten, with a car like that, he could have been well on his way to Bale, and so to Germany—in spite of the fact that there are speed limits in Switzerland. He was clever, that Monsieur—and then someone killed him."

He sighed, almost as if he regretted the world's loss of a clever criminal. Then he went on:

"I think that we must try to look into the mind of this Monsieur Braye, to make plain to ourselves what his plans were, thus perhaps to understand why he was killed as he was. We will go now to see the body, to perform the necessaries. After that we will sit down quietly and do some thinking, Monsieur Sherrill. By thinking we may discover some matters which now seem hidden from our eyes."

He bowed politely to John Sherrill, and with the *juge d'instruction* he rose from the table. Then he turned rather sharply to me.

"You will remain with us, Monsieur Armitage," he said, and his remark was neither request nor query, but a flat statement of fact. I remained with them. The gendarmes came, too.

As we went through the first-floor hall on our way upstairs to the unfinished room, and the attic, I noticed for the first time that another gendarme was sitting on the window-sill outside the Brayes' doors. He sprang to salute as we passed, but no one spoke. The official investigators went into the unfinished room and across it, and I followed with John Sherrill, silently, thankful, I confess, that I need not again face that dreadful scene alone.

What came next was one of those quiet and thorough examinations that I had read about, that are universally, I suppose, a part of police routine. And before its quietness and thoroughness my own mind and spirit grew more calm. The investigators looked, they examined, they measured. For a long time they said almost nothing.

After a while the detective Reynal held out the piece of torn lace to me.

"You have seen this before?"

"Yes." I did not know whether I ought to go on or not, but a second question at once prompted me.

"When? Where?"

"Mrs. Braye had it around her neck at dinner last night," I said.

"Was it torn then? Or soiled?"

"Oh, no. It was very beautiful. Miss Hamilton noticed it, and spoke to Mrs. Braye about it. Mrs. Braye seemed pleased, but Mr. Braye did not like it." I stopped, because I had an idea that the police disliked volunteer attempts at giving evidence, but the detective said sharply:

"Monsieur Braye did not like it? How do you know? What did he say? Please continue."

So I told them the whole story of the conversation about the lace scarf, and when I came to Horace's snarl of "You shut your mouth," John Sherrill interrupted me.

"I think perhaps I can explain better than Mr. Armitage at this moment that that was an almost unbelievably insulting expression for any man to use to his wife in public, even Horace Braye," he put in. "Of course we can understand now that Mr. Braye was in a panic over her mention of St. Louis, and he, so to speak, reverted to type. But even so, it was astounding."

"Did she seem upset?" the detective asked me.

"Yes, she did," I answered. "She seemed upset all the rest of the time they were with us."

"Miss Hamilton also was there during all this time?"

"Oh, yes."

"Did they stay with you long?"

"No," I replied, "not more than twenty minutes. Mrs. Braye said that she was still not feeling well, and that she wanted to go to bed early. So they both went back to the house."

"Did you see them again?"

"No. I did not see Mrs. Braye again until she came to the inquiry this morning. I never saw Mr. Braye again until I found his body."

"Did you hear them?"

"No."

"Your room is directly above Monsieur Braye's. Did you not hear them talking?"

"No, Monsieur, I did not hear a sound from their rooms. The walls and floors of this old house are very thick, and I almost never heard any sound from Mr. and Mrs. Braye's rooms—only once in a while when he roared at her."

"You heard him roaring at her?"

"Sometimes."

"Not often?"

"Not often. Occasionally in the morning or the late afternoon they seemed to have er—discussions."

"Did you hear any words?"

"No, I never understood any words from their rooms. I only heard the sound of his voice once in a while, roaring the way he sometimes did when he was angry."

"I see. Now, on this night in question—last night, Monsieur Armitage—you heard no sounds, at any time? No voices? No movements? Not anywhere?"

"No," I began. And then a faint memory stirred within me. I had slept very well. Had I slept all night? Had I slept, and dreamed the careless dreams of sound sleep, and forgotten them, to remember disconnected, troubling bits again? Or had I been at one time half-awake? Was there a sound that I had heard?

"Wait a minute," I said. "Wait a minute. Just wait. Maybe yes, that's right. I've got it. I did hear a sound in the night. I heard Miss Hamilton's dog."

"Ah." The detective was interested. "The dog? He barked?"

I saw that John Sherrill was watching me very closely, and I wondered why. But I was sure of my ground now. Fleeting as it was, the memory had come back, and it was sharp enough.

"No," and I could answer positively, "I remember now. I did hear the dog. But he didn't bark. It wasn't as loud as that, not that kind of sound at all. He just gave a little growl."

"If it was as slight a sound as that, how do you know it was this dog?" the detective insisted.

"Why," I said, "I know this dog. It was in the next room to mine, the sound, and it was Miss Hamilton's dog that made it. I am sure of that. He growled that same way, only louder, the night Mrs. Wilde died."

John Sherrill never took his eyes off me. The detective asked another question.

"If it is so difficult to hear sounds through walls so thick as these, how can you feel sure of a noise like the 'little growl' of a dog?"

I was beginning to feel somewhat on the defensive. "A dog's growl is a penetrating noise," I replied. "And besides, I have occasionally heard sounds from Miss Hamilton's room. She seems to move very quietly, but once in a while I have heard her walking about, and sometimes I have heard her talking to her dog."

John Sherrill smiled at that, and himself took up the conversation, easily.

"I think I can explain the difference in sounds, if you will permit me, Monsieur Reynal," he said. "This old house, as of course you know, has very thick walls, within and without. The doors, too, are heavy, and exceedingly well fitted. But the small single rooms, such as Monsieur Armitage's and Miss Hamilton's—such also as my wife's and mine—have been made in more recent years by putting a partition across one large chamber, to divide it in two: these partitions are not so thick, not so sound-proof, as the other walls on the house. Monsieur Armitage could hear noises from Miss Hamilton's room more easily, therefore, than from any other room or even the hall."

He turned swiftly from the detective to me:

"Was the dog's growl the only sound you heard last night?"

"Absolutely."

"And you are unquestionably sure that you heard that?"

"I am."

The detective thanked me, and returned to his examination of Horace's body and of the scene of the crime. After a few minutes he led the way back into the unfinished room, shut the attic door, gave an order to the gendarmes, walked over to one of the unshuttered windows that admitted their tempered light from the garden side of the house, and, regardless of dust and cobwebs and spiders, sat down on the wide window-sill. The *juge d'instruction* sat down beside him, but he dusted the boards with his handkerchief first, and I thought he looked at the cobwebs with some distaste.

"I am thinking," said the detective Reynal, "of Madame Braye. No one has told her of this discovery?" He was looking at me, so I answered,

"Not that I know of."

"When Monsieur Armitage found the body," John Sherrill added, "he came straight to me, and my wife and Miss Hamilton and I were alone in the *galerie*. I do not think that anyone else knows. And I feel sure that neither Miss Hamilton nor my wife would have taken it upon herself to tell Madame Braye that her husband's body had been found."

"That is something to be thankful for," said the detective genially. Then he called one of his henchmen, and there was no geniality left in his voice.

"Bring Madame Braye to me," he ordered, and leaned down to remove a large gray cobweb from his blue trouser-leg.

I think that I shall never forget anything that happened in connection with the murders at Neyronnes—certainly I shall never be able to forget any detail that had to do with the murder of Horace Braye. But it sometimes seems to me that of all the dreadful moments in all those dreadful hours, the most dreadful was not the moment when my eye followed the spider's scurrying flight toward the dark stain on the floor, not even the moment when I flung open the door upon that horrible thing that sprawled at the top of the stairs, but the moment when I stood with the police officers in the unfinished room and waited for Rosalie Braye. . .

Was she going to be confronted with her husband's body, I wondered? The attic door was shut. But in any case she was about to be told that his body had been discovered—and her eyes would find, I knew, the small dark spot that was not yet completely dry upon the floor . . .

We waited while the gendarme's boots clattered down the stairs, the gendarme's knuckles pounded on Rosalie's door, the gendarme's voice spoke first to his colleague on guard and then to Rosalie. He had left the door wide open, and we could hear everything. And then, as I for one had expected, we heard Rosalie shriek.

"I won't!" she screamed. "I won't go into that ghastly room! It's full of spiders. I won't go, and you can't make me! If that French detective wants to talk to me, he can come to my room like a gentleman. I tell you I won't go up there . . ."

I felt a nervous desire to laugh, of which I was ashamed until I glanced at John Sherrill and saw that he was smiling quite frankly. Rosalie stormed and bellowed in a manner that was worthy of Horace's teaching and example, but she did, surprisingly soon, walk up the stairs. She did come through the open doorway of the unfinished room and stand looking at the detective and the magistrate. She had no make-up on, and that gave her an appearance that seemed oddly unnatural.

There was no chair to offer her, of course, but the two officials— the only men who were not already standing—politely rose from the window-sill.

"Madame Braye," said the detective, speaking in his perfect English but with no attempt at 'preparation' for the blow he was about to strike, "I regret to be obliged to tell you that your husband is dead."

Rosalie did not scream: she only gasped. But that gasp seemed somehow far more terrible than any of her howls of anger or her frantic outcry in hysteria. She gasped, and tottered a little on her high-heeled 'cut-out' shoes, but she did not fall. She had fainted when Christine Wilde had first called out the undirected accusation that her mother had been murdered, but she did not faint now. She mustered her strength with a visible effort, and out of her bluish-white lips came her voice with a strange hard clearness.

"Have you killed him?" she asked.

"No, Madame," the detective answered calmly. "Someone else has killed him. Would you like to see?"

She found the bloodstain then. For her eyes wandered wildly around that gruesome dusty room, paused at the attic door, fell upon the dark spot on the boards beneath it. Her body was perfectly still, but I could see that the muscles of her throat moved as if she were trying to swallow, and the tip of her scarlet tongue shot out to moisten her dry mouth; she looked like a trapped animal.

She gazed at the detective and the magistrate, and we all gazed at her. Then she spoke, rather oddly.

"What is going to happen to me?" she said.

I did not know, myself, whether it was a question, or just a moan. I heard the *juge d'instruction* say, *"Assez,"* in a very low undertone, and when I saw the detective nod his assent I was glad that he, too, thought that this was enough . . . He spoke gently, now, to Rosalie Braye.

"You will go back to your room, Madame," he said. "The maid will bring you restoratives. I suggest that you go to bed. There is nothing now that you can do for your husband: his body is at this moment being taken away. You will go back to your room, and if you are quiet no one will disturb you in any way for the present. A police officer will be in your husband's room, making necessary investigations, but it will be best for you to try to rest."

"Yes, Muhseer," said Rosalie, and made no further sound as the gendarme led her out of the room and down the stairs.

XVII

THE DETECTIVE THINKS ALOUD

"And now, Monsieur Sherrill," said Reynal, "we will go downstairs and hold a little consultation—or, shall I say, a little meeting of thought? We have made for ourselves a small bureau in the *auberge* itself; there is no necessity that we remain here in the *pavillon*. We will sit down quietly in this small bureau and do some thinking together, Monsieur Sherrill. It will be well, perhaps, if the lawyer of Madame Wilde is also present. And Monsieur Armitage will remain with us. Monsieur *le juge* is so good as to permit that I do the greater part of the talking, since he is unduly modest on the subject of his English speech. If you will be so kind as to find this Monsieur Williamson, and bring him to the little private dining-room of the *auberge*, where we of the police have our bureau, we shall be most grateful. No one else is to be present—only we five."

We filed back to the main building of the inn, myself obediently following in the others' train. I had long since ceased to try to do any thinking myself, and I admired them for the ease and competence with which they could plan at just this time to "sit down and think." But all that was their business, of course. And besides, I reminded myself, it was no wonder that I, more than the others, was still feeling dazed and stunned and sick—none of them had had that dreadful experience of discovering Horace Braye's dead body where a spider's trail led through the cobwebs of that dim and dusty emptiness upstairs . . . John Sherrill found Mr. Williamson very quickly. We all went into the little room behind the main dining-hall (it had a vaulted thirteenth-century ceiling, and a spinet stood, dainty and incongruous, in the corner beside the fireplace) and sat down around a big table.

"We must try first to look into the mind of this Monsieur Braye," the detective began. "And before I ask you to do that with me, I will recapitulate for you what we already know, and what has already been done, in the case of this Monsieur.

"When your friend in New York received your cablegram on Wednesday, Monsieur Sherrill, inquiries were at once set on foot in regard to this Monsieur Braye, especially to discover what association he could have had in the past with Madame Wilde or her affairs. And to that association her mention of the failure of the Marquette Trust Company of St. Louis had already given us a clue—which, naturally, was made stronger by his immediate and quite unnecessary denial that he had ever been in that city, and which was also helped by our knowledge of the dates upon which Madame Wilde herself had been there.

"As you directed in your second cable, Monsieur Sherrill, your friend Monsieur Gregg of the New York police sent the results of his investigations directly to us. But we did not receive until this morning the cablegram which was summarized and read to Madame Braye at the hearing, and we did not broadcast a general alarm—an order to hold Monsieur Braye if he should try to escape—until that cablegram was received. We did have a local guard around Neyronnes itself, and that guard received special orders yesterday to look out for Monsieur Braye and his car.

"By not driving his car up the hill, he escaped bringing the automobile itself under the guard's attention, and there is a slight possibility that he could have got away under cover of the darkness last night. That is what I was thinking of when I spoke to you of the possibility of successful flight, a little while ago. No one was sufficiently near the empty shed to hear him starting his engine, and such a car as his is very quiet. I think that we erred in not watching the car more closely; I think our own movements were not sufficiently correlated, probably. But as we saw Monsieur Braye in Neyronnes at five o'clock yesterday afternoon, and several times during the evening, we supposed that everything was satisfactory.

"Indeed," he added frankly, "Monsieur Braye's failure to bring his car up the hill and into Neyronnes yesterday was not in itself a thing that would arouse our suspicion. It is extremely difficult to get an automobile of that size through the double gate, with the curve in the road between the two arches, and it is also difficult to traverse the street of the village and get around into the *Place*. Monsieur Braye has complained loudly and repeatedly of this difficulty, and when he took his car from the police garage he complained more loudly than ever, and said that he would leave his car outside if he knew any place to leave it.

"All these considerations are academic merely," the detective went on. "We know that Monsieur Braye did not go to his car at all last night. He started, but he did not arrive. At the same time, I think it is helpful to us to try to establish in our minds what his plans must have been, and how far he was able to get in carrying them out. We must remember, however, that it is unlikely that he had any way of guessing how much was known of his criminal record, how much of a guard had been placed upon his movements, how free a road he might or might not have to the frontier. He cast himself upon the mercies of fortune. But ourselves, at this moment, let us go back to our scrutiny—shall I say, our meditative scrutiny?—of Monsieur Braye's record, his possible plans, before we try to ask ourselves who could have met, or followed him as he tried to escape from Neyronnes, in the middle of the night."

Sherrill nodded gravely. "The failure of the American police to get hold of him, thus far, is not so strange as it may seem," he said. "When Horace Braye retired from the cloak-and-suit business in New York in 1922, after making a fortune and just barely managing to get by with the Factory Commission and the union, he quietly moved away from New York and nobody paid any attention to him. When Howard Bretton's bank failed, eleven years later and a thousand miles away from New York, there was a hue and cry in the State of Missouri over Howard Bretton and even that didn't start for some time—but there was no hue and cry in the State of New York over Horace Braye. And the old fox had covered up his tracks from the St. Louis end in the first place. The only footprints that he left were around New York, in the life of Horace Braye, not Howard Bretton. And it was only when an investigation was begun to find out what had become of old Ho-bry, who hit the Amalgamated below the belt and tried to fool the factory inspectors and got out from under in time to save his skin—it was only then that the trail to the smash of the Marquette Trust Company in St. Louis began to show. You see, Messieurs, these speculations of his seem to have been entirely local matters. The Marquette Trust Company was not a national bank. It was not even a very large bank. And in February, 1933, Messieurs, the failure of one small bank in one big city was not so conspicuous or unusual a happening that the United States Government as a whole was likely to get excited over it!"

"Yes, Monsieur Sherrill, I understand that," said the detective. "This Bretton's bank closes in St. Louis just a few weeks before the general closing of all American banks by order of the National Government. This Braye goes back to New York, where he is known as a business man who never had any connection with banking. And he is quite clever enough to have found a plausible way of accounting for his absence to those of his old friends whose companionship he now seeks."

"Quite," remarked John Sherrill, with a wry grin. "I can just hear him making jokes about his successful escape from the Factory Commission."

"And now he has no business to worry about," Reynal continued. "Returning to New York in February, he makes his presence there somewhat conspicuous. As I understand it, no one could possibly suspect Horace Braye of having anything to conceal, in those weeks between the middle of February and the first of April. He even sailed to France with a certain amount of *réclame*. But before the warrant was actually sworn out for Howard Bretton's arrest, Horace Braye had left Paris and was driving about in the French provinces, in districts which are not usually visited by tourists.

"I think it likely," he added, "that Monsieur Braye came to Neyronnes with the idea of staying some time—until his eye fell upon Madame Wilde."

"I think so, too," Sherrill agreed. "Horace didn't come here to economize. He came to hide. When he found all the rest of us here, seeking refuge from the dancing dollar, that tore it for Horace."

The detective frowned. He disliked to admit any gaps in his perfect English, but he wished everything to be quite plain.

"Monsieur says?" he suggested. And Sherrill, without a smile or a word of apology, replied:

"I said that when he discovered other Americans here, trying to live as cheaply as possible because of the devaluation of the dollar, Mr. Braye's hope of finding privacy in Neyronnes was destroyed. As you point out, when his eye fell upon Mrs. Wilde, he became at once seriously worried."

"Yes. And immediately, I think, he began to make new plans . . ."

"He set to work at once, in a way which I think was very clever," Sherrill said. "I have been thinking a great deal about Horace Braye—and his wife, too, for that matter: she played up well—and I have been going over his conversation in my mind, even on that first evening. I feel pretty sure that he was genuinely glad to see some Americans, in the first place: he had been driving that car around in provincial France, with no knowledge of the French language, and with the tactful and persuasive manner of a grizzly bear. I think he was beginning to feel a little worn and frazzled; and I hope you will not misunderstand me, Messieurs, when I say that I think that Horace did by this time heartily dislike France and the French people. A foreigner who tries to get along by bullying usually does. But he was clever enough to adopt exaggeration as a disguise. It was the kind of disguise he could make convincing, and he pretty nearly did."

He turned to me. "Do you remember, Armitage, as soon as he found out that we were Americans, he began to talk about how he was going right home—fed up with Europe and all that sort of thing? He was on his way to Marseille, he said, to take an American ship back to America. I thought that was a little odd, at the time, for although there are two lines of American ships that run to New York from Marseille, the ships are very small, not Horace's type at all; and he could just as easily have taken the big new *Manhattan* or *Washington* from Havre. As a matter of fact, Horace had some plan of a destination which would take him out of here on a south-bound road —"

"Greece, probably," said the detective, with a grimace.

Sherrill chuckled. "Probably. And he never once let an opportunity slip, Monsieur, to tell everyone in sight how he loathed Europe and all Europeans, how fast he was hurrying home. And all that was absolutely in character. He was a big braggart jingo of the worst type. He enjoyed insulting other nations. But he wouldn't have done it quite so much, he wouldn't have dragged it in all the time, *naturally*. He was trying to get an effect, to impress us with his deep determination to get back to his own country—where, as a matter of fact, he wouldn't have dared to set his foot. He deliberately overdid it, just as I did the other night, when I turned around and insulted him."

"What!" I ejaculated. "Weren't you really angry?"

And Sherrill chuckled again.

"Angry?" he echoed. "Of course I was angry. I was livid with rage. But usually, Armitage, when I am angry I have the self-control not to make myself conspicuous, at least. No, I was doing that on purpose; I 'let myself go.' I made myself as objectionable as I could be, to see how Horace would take it. I called him a crook, right straight out. And what did be do? Did he punch me in the jaw, literally or figuratively? Not he! He crumpled up like a stewed cabbage, Messieurs, and the next morning he came around and apologized."

"I see," said the detective reflectively. "That is interesting, Monsieur. And we know, of course, that he was planning to leave Neyronnes at once—early on the morning following Madame Wilde's death. You, unfortunately, were not here at the preliminary hearing, when it was still believed possible that Madame Wilde's death might have been an accident, or suicide. Unfortunately, again, I also was absent. But we have the stenographic report of those proceedings, and we also have other reports.

"The baggage of Monsieur and Madame Braye was packed," he continued. "The reservoir of their car was filled with *essence*, even the money which Monsieur Braye so rudely cast in the face of the good Monsieur Delande was the correct amount of his bill, with the ten per cent service charge added. If Monsieur and Madame Braye had been able to get away early that morning as they had planned, they would have been across the Swiss border before it was even surely ascertained that Madame Wilde had been murdered . . ."

"It was stupid of him to get in wrong over his papers," Sherrill commented. "I don't see how he happened to do that—I suppose it was just the one stupid thing a clever criminal is so apt to do. But then, I don't see why he hung around so long in France, anyway. Indeed, I don't see why he came to France in the first place."

Surprisingly, the detective permitted himself, at this, the luxury of gesticulation. He flung his arms far from his somewhat stiff and military body and shrugged his shoulders at the same time.

"Why did he come to France, you ask? Monsieur Sherrill, I tell you—they all come to France. All *émigrés*, all *proscrits*, all refugees—they all come to France, Monsieur. Russians fleeing from Bolshevism, Italians fleeing from Fascism, Germans fleeing from Hitlerism, Spaniards fleeing from revolution, Americans fleeing from Prohibition—they all come to France! Fugitives from justice also—they come to France first, even if they know that they will be obliged soon to leave France and seek refuge in Greece. They all come here, Monsieur! *Ecoutez*, if the man in the moon should be threatened by a dictatorship on the part of his lady, what is it that he would do? *Figurez-vous*, Monsieur, he would make the grand leap into France!"

He groaned. "And when they murder each other, Monsieur, we must find the murderer. They have no *cartes d'identité*, they have no *dossiers* with their own police, many of them have not even any *foyers* in the place from which they come. The American, I am convinced, Monsieur, lives hopping from branch to branch, like a crow! And we—we must find out all, all! We must uncover their hidden pasts; we must solve the criminal mysteries of their present; we must dispatch them to a future in hell by way of the guillotine— *Mon Dieu*, Monsieur, I ask you—is this just?"

He all but tore his hair. And I watched and listened with a good deal of interest. I had always shared the prevalent American notion that the French were an excitable people; and through every step of this murder mystery I had been impressed by their supreme and unshakable calm. In their investigations of the serious problem which confronted them, and us, all these Frenchmen, from the *juge d'instruction* to the youngest gendarme, had been self-controlled to the point of frigidity, and as solemn as owls. Keen, quiet, self-contained, they had gone about their grave and gruesome business like perfectly-moving automatons, and one had the feeling that nothing could ever upset their absolute poise. Now, over a mere rhetorical question as to why Horace Braye had chosen France to flee to, the extremely calm and capable detective from the Sureté burst into torrents of answering rhetoric and beat upon the air about him with gestures of despair!

Then, before anyone had a chance to break in upon his speech, he smiled at John Sherrill with extraordinary sweetness, and said, in a tone whose sincerity took away all suggestion of grandiloquence from his words:

"But in this case we have the great benefit of your generous and brilliant assistance, Monsieur. With all my heart, I thank you . . ."

And he arose suddenly and shook John Sherrill's hand. Then, with perfect simplicity and again with complete calm, he went on with his recapitulation:

"It now appears that we can with assurance say that we know that Monsieur and Madame Braye were greatly frightened in recognizing Madame Wilde, who would not be likely to rest idle if she discovered the man who was responsible for such a large loss in her fortune. We will for the time being pass over the night of Madame Wilde's murder, but we can with assurance say that the Braye couple planned to flee from Neyronnes the next morning. When they were held here and their car was taken from them, Monsieur Braye made a new plan. It appears that that involved the effort to lay at least the suspicion of guilt for Madame Wilde's murder at the door of one of his fellow-lodgers. You can probably see more clearly than we what went on in Monsieur Braye's mind, Monsieur Sherrill, in this regard."

"I can make a pretty good guess," Sherrill said. "It seemed to me from the very beginning that Braye was trying to distract suspicion from Miss Hamilton, who appeared to a number of people to be the 'logical suspect' at first. And I wondered at that—until I realized that Miss Hamilton's fortune had been entirely lost in the financial crashes at home. He didn't know where, or how; and in all probability he did know that she had not had any money in the Marquette Trust Company; but all the same, he didn't want any more financial hornets' nests to be stirred up, if he could help it. I think his first idea, as a victim in his effort at framing, was Monsieur de Brassac—he would naturally want to hit out at a foreigner, he's that kind. But then it occurred to him that this was the foreigner's own country, and he himself didn't know its way or its language, and he got scared. So then he fell back on Wayne Armitage." He smiled at me, and went on:

"Monsieur Armitage, I am sure he will permit me to point out, is the perfect choice for such machinations. He is a school-teacher who has never been concerned in financial affairs, and has not lost money because he has had none to lose: all he has suffered in the *crise* has been a couple of salary cuts. He is young, ingenuous, of scholarly tastes but unsophisticated in practical affairs, and with no talent for the concealment of his feelings. He speaks only a little French."

I was squirming a bit, naturally, but John Sherrill's smile continued to be very friendly, although now it ceased to be gay.

"Monsieur Armitage has shown all too plainly that he finds Miss Wilde attractive," he went on seriously. "Miss Wilde, also, has seemed to like him. Unfortunately, Madame Wilde had objected to the development of any friendly acquaintance between these two young people. I have been unable to find the slightest evidence which would seem to connect this young man with Madame Wilde's death," he added, with emphasis, "but for a person bent upon finding an object of suspicion, as was Horace Braye, it must be admitted that the situation in regard to Wayne Armitage played into his hands. Naturally, he took advantage of it."

"I see," said the detective. "Of that, I think, we can feel assured. The next step in Monsieur Braye's new plan was to call the attention of all his compatriots—not, you notice, of the police—to his intention of getting his car on Saturday morning. Having received special permission—and being of course watched, although he may not have realized that—he got his car on Friday afternoon, and hid it in a shed.

"Then," Reynal continued, "when he had, as he thought, quieted his wife by the promise to return to get her, he attempted to leave the house in the middle of the night. One point leaps to the mind: one cannot believe for one moment that Monsieur Braye intended to return for his wife. He had decided to leave her behind. And she probably knew it."

"Yes," said John Sherrill gravely. And I shivered.

"Then, as I reconstruct the affair," Reynal's quiet voice went on, "Monsieur Braye sought to leave the house by the back exit, through the storage-room, so as to avoid the danger of being seen from any of the other houses which front on the Place de l'Église. By leaving through the storage annex, he could come out on the village street opposite the kitchen of the inn and the other small buildings which the hotel uses as woodsheds, service offices, and the like; thus he would run comparatively little risk of being seen: he could slip around the corner and get out of the village by the little back lane without passing another occupied house until he was well beyond the village wails. I say that he 'could' have done this: I think that he could not have done it; I think that our guard would have caught him. But he unquestionably hoped that he could do it. As I said, he cast himself upon the mercies of fortune. But, certainly, he would not be likely to run the second risk of returning for his wife!

"Now, Messieurs, I enter the realm of conjecture. I have studied the plan of the *pavillon annexe* very carefully; and in passing into the storage addition, where he was killed, I do not know whether Monsieur Braye chose the direct way from his own chamber or the upper route through the unfinished room. He sleeps on the first floor. His body was found on the second floor. I think there is no one in Neyronnes who is strong enough to have dragged the dead or dying body of Monsieur Horace Braye up the rough, steep, and somewhat unsteady stairs of that old house, if he had been attacked on the floor below. And in the middle of the night no one, for fear of making a disturbance, would have tried. Beyond doubt, Monsieur Braye was slain where his body was found. And naturally I ask myself, how did he come to be on the second floor, when he was on the way out of the house from his first-floor room?

"This could have happened in one of two ways, Messieurs. Either Monsieur Braye deliberately chose the roundabout way up the stairs in the *pavillon* and through the unfinished room, as being less likely to arouse anyone in the house; or else he was in some way lured or attracted or urged to mount from the first floor to the second when he had got as far as the storage annex. The first is quite possible. We have tested those stairs and the halls for any creaks or moving boards: there are none; the entire house is quiet; the doors, as well as the halls, are thick. Without his shoes, any individual could move quietly through the house without arousing a normal sleeper, or even attracting attention from a person lying awake beyond a closed door. The second is equally possible.

"I find myself unable to determine what Monsieur Braye's choice would have been. Would he have taken the straight route past the doors of Monsieur de Brassac and the sick man Monsieur MacNeil, or would he have climbed the stairs and passed the door of Miss Hamilton and that of Monsieur and Madame Sherrill? He would have chosen the way he thought less dangerous. I do not know how he would decide.

"His suitcase was found on the first floor; but that means nothing. The floor of the unfinished room is dusty, but there have been too many footprints there lately to distinguish them surely, or in any case to depend on them for any clue. The question of how he happened to be on the second floor where he was killed remains, then, one for us to answer, along with the related question—if it follows—of who lured him upstairs, and how . . ."

He paused, and looked gravely around at us all.

"There is one question which may come to your minds which I can immediately answer," he said. "Monsieur Braye was killed, it seems plain, by a blow on the head with a heavy instrument, and it may seem to some of you that only a strong arm could have dealt such a blow. That is not correct, Messieurs. The blow which fell upon Monsieur Braye's temple could have been struck, with that spanner, by a child.

"Now," he continued at once, "we will pursue our investigations, and it is better that we should do this alone." He bowed formally to John Sherrill and to Mr. Williamson. "I shall be at your disposal, Messieurs, for any questions you may wish to ask, and I shall welcome your collaboration with gratitude. Monsieur Armitage, it is possible that we may wish to talk with you further. It will be well if you do not go far away."

Both the representatives of French law rose from their chairs and smiled upon us in courteous but firm dismissal. They had evidently taken time long since to spread the news that there would be no afternoon session of the meeting of inquiry. With Sherrill and Mr. Williamson, I walked out across the main dining-room of the Auberge de Vieux Neyronnes, and so into the broad Place des Halles.

It was later than I had thought. Already the shadows were slanting as the sun made its slow midsummer descent behind the old houses, and on the side of the square farthest from the linden tree the cars of Saturday afternoon visitors were already parked. The maids in their pretty peasant costume were serving *gouters* at tables under the tree, and people were passing in and out of the museum and up and down the path that led to the lower Gate and the Promenade des Lices. As always, it looked as if it were part of a play—but the play was gay and attractive, not like the grim drama of death and fear and greed that was really being staged there . . .

"I seem to be kept under surveillance," I muttered discontentedly.

But John Sherrill only shrugged his shoulders.

"You are rather an important witness, you know," he said. "They can't let you get out of call. You found Horace Braye's body. You have heard Horace 'roaring' at Rosalie in their rooms, and you were present when he first scowled at her and then insulted her in the matter of the lace scarf. You found Horace's handkerchief outside Mrs. Wilde's door on the morning after her murder. It was you whom he tried to accuse of that crime. You were here on the night Mrs. Wilde was killed, and you heard Margaret Hamilton's dog growling on both those nights—look here, Armitage, did you ever hear that dog growling in the night, at any other time?"

"I don't remember that I did," I answered slowly. "You know how this hotel is—or rather, how it has been lately: a certain amount of movement in the halls, people going in and out, up to half-past eleven or so, and then everything quiet after that. Fergus seems to be quite used to hearing some slight noises in the halls before midnight, but to resent any sounds after that—or does he smell people, instead of hearing them? Anyway— Oh, wait a minute! I did hear him growl once. I think he was growling at me."

And I told John Sherrill how I had heard a low growl from Miss Hamilton's dog as I was walking through the corridor very late on one of my first nights at Neyronnes. He seemed mildly interested.

"But after I had been here longer, and he had had time to get accustomed to me, he never made a sound if I passed his door late at night," I added. "You know on the night of Mrs. Wilde's death I had been out in the ruins until midnight, on that strange trail of poor Paul MacNeil, and when I came in there wasn't a whimper from Fergus, although Miss Hamilton said she had heard me."

"Horace Braye heard you, too," Sherrill remarked, with his friendly smile, which in itself heightened the effect of his changing the subject. "Poor young MacNeil is worse today," he said. "Going over to the inn to dinner must have been too much for him. I suppose that is why we have seen so little of Henri de Brassac—he is staying with his invalid as much as possible."

"I am so glad Monsieur de Brassac is so kind to him," I responded. My conscience still troubled me on the subject of the sick boy.

"Yes, so am I," Sherrill said. "You know about his nephew, don't you—the Comte de Brassac's son?"

Then, as I shook my head and looked puzzled, he continued quickly:

"It is no secret, certainly, and it has nothing to do with our mystery, but it is interesting. Henri de Brassac, who has never married, was very fond of his brother's oldest son, and the boy was horribly gassed in the war and died of quick consumption not long afterward. Ever since then, Monsieur de Brassac has taken a very great interest in the prevention and relief of tuberculosis, especially among young people. He has given a great deal of time and energy and money to that work. When he found that Mrs. Wilde's stinginess and selfishness had kept a very ill consumptive lad alone down there in the ruins in the rain, he was very indignant and very much disturbed. As you know, he has made himself a sort of guardian to this poor young man. That's why."

"Oh," I exclaimed. "I'm glad to know that. Neither of them ever told me."

"Well, Monsieur de Brassac doesn't talk much about himself, as you've noticed. And Paul MacNeil is shy, and doesn't talk much about anything, except English poetry. Perhaps he doesn't know, anyway. It was Margaret Hamilton who told me about it in the first place and then I asked Henri de Brassac himself." He sighed. "Look here, Armitage," he said to me suddenly, "I know you are having a raw deal at the present moment, but it won't last. You haven't really anything to worry about."

The lawyer Williamson had not spoken at all during this colloquy. Now he addressed me, in his precise fashion.

"All will shape itself satisfactorily, Mr. Armitage: we can see that already," he said. "I confess that I have been entertaining the gravest suspicions of Miss Hamilton in connection with the death of Mrs. Wilde—"

"Did you feel that way before, or after, you had listened to the evidence?" Sherrill interrupted sharply, and the lawyer looked perplexed.

"Both," he replied. "It seemed to me, Mr. Sherrill, that most of the evidence was of a nature to intensify the gravity of my suspicions, although, on the other hand, Miss Christine's testimony in regard to her mother's will made me feel more hopeful. But now, of course, everything is changed."

"Yes," Sherrill agreed, "everything is changed. Mr. Williamson, you are not a criminal lawyer, and you have told me that a case like this is very distasteful to you. But we cannot forget that it was you who started us on the trail of Horace Braye in the first place. Everybody owes you a rising vote of thanks."

Mr. Williamson's cheeks reddened with a surprising sudden blush, and he made a little sound that made me think of a purr.

"Ah, thank you, Mr. Sherrill, thank you," he said. "And now, will you and Mr. Armitage not join me at tea?"

He included me very graciously in his invitation, but I felt that the two lawyers would much prefer to talk over the situation alone. And I had a craving for solitude, myself. I went back to my room for a few moments only—there was complete silence from the Brayes' suite below me, although I passed two gendarmes in the first-floor hall—and then I decided that the late afternoon was too beautiful to be wasted indoors.

There was little privacy to be found inside the walls of Neyronnes on a Saturday afternoon, but I went out through the towered Upper Gate and around by the outer rampart toward the west, where the meadows sloped up to the very fortifications of the ancient citadel. I could see several guards standing about, and I knew that they could see me, but no one stopped me or spoke to me, and I did not mind being watched so long as I was not disturbed. That is, I did not mind much . . . I sat down on the grass, under a tree.

XVIII
WE PLAN TO GO HOME

This was an aspect of Neyronnes and the country around it which I knew far less well than the Promenade des Lices, or the *chemin de ronde*, or the changing view toward the mountains far away. Indeed, from where I was sitting, I did not see Neyronnes itself at all. Directly in front of me the meadows fell away in pasture-land where sheep were grazing, and on the other side of a tree-bordered lane the hill rose again, gently, in grain-fields that were already golden between their green hedges in the ripening warmth of late June. On both sides, and all around me, were these low rolling hills, these twisting lanes; these thick and tangled hedges, and in the little vales between the soft rises of harvest-land narrow dirt roads ran among the farmsteads or met the stream at some mill.

Over to the north I knew that there was a castle, the ancient feudal keep of Jeanniot; but the trees grew so luxuriously in its park that even on its hilltop I could not see it; nor could I see, to the south and behind me, the mediæval church of pilgrimage that crowned another hill. The picture that lay spread out before me was of old, old things, but they were the old continuing things of the earth and of man's simple living, not the things of changing civilization and war-stained history farmsteads, with great barns and smaller houses, with sheep grazing in the fields and cows already starting home to be milked at the end of the day; ploughed fields that had almost come to their summer fruition; here and there men moving, small faraway figures, about their immemorial toil. Wild clematis scattered its white stars in the nearest hedges, and from a garden wall behind the ramparts wild honeysuckle cast its old familiar fragrance on the air.

The light was changing, even as I sat there, and a golden glow was taking on a rosy tinge in the western sky. It was a lovely scene, not magnificent, not spectacular, not 'picturesque' or strange. It did not look, to my unaccustomed eyes, like Europe. It looked like home. And suddenly, with a passion of nostalgia that literally swept me to my feet, in the meadow under the Neyronnes ramparts, I wished that I was there . . .

It was not that I felt worried, or resentful, over any treatment which I had received. I knew that suspicion must fall, for a while, on the just and the unjust alike; and it seemed to me that the French officials had been uniformly fair, as they were uniformly courteous and competent. I felt, too, that I had made a valued friend in Henri de Brassac. And I liked Monsieur and Madame Delande and the pleasant-mannered servants of the little inn. I liked the inn. I liked Neyronnes. I liked France. No, it was with no sense of personal dissatisfaction or disparagement toward France or the French that I felt suddenly almost unbearably homesick; but after all, this was France—a beautiful country, but not mine . . .

These were foreign people, who lived here, people with points of view that I could not always understand, with a language that I could not speak. And in this remote spot which had never even seen more than a handful of Americans, among these habitants who were so completely foreign, a dreadful tragedy had overwhelmed us, had engulfed even me. I felt suddenly bewildered, lost, terribly alone.

It was different, I told myself, with the others. John and Elinor Sherrill belonged to that class of sophisticated and highly cultivated Americans, relatively small as a class, which takes 'going abroad' as a matter of course: not to try to get ahead of the Joneses, or to boast of crossing on the *Rex* or the *Ile-de-France* or the *Europa*, but to see beautiful and interesting things that they were fond of, to keep in touch with a life they enjoyed, people like the Sherrills came every year or so to Europe, and returned happily— not expatriate but cosmopolitan—to their American homes.

Margaret Hamilton was of that class, too, and she had lived that kind of life until she lost her money: now, after nearly four years of poverty which had closed more and more tightly about her, of that restricted existence of penury in foreign pensions which threw her back more and more upon the resources of her own spirit, Margaret Hamilton did not care, I knew, where she lived; she could be happy, or she could starve to death, anywhere. The same was true, for a different reason of poor Paul MacNeil, whose brief candle was burning out so fast. They all spoke foreign languages. They all knew foreign ways. What was 'foreign' was not necessarily bewildering; they could deal with it.

And Christine—Christine was equally at home in all civilized countries, because she had a real home in none. It had been a sad and difficult and unsatisfactory life: she had been a lovely bird carried about in its cage. But she was free now. The bird could fly— anywhere. She would fly, of course, far away from me . . .

There would soon be no mystery about her mother's murderer. The story was nearing its end. Christine Wilde would soon drive her big Packard down the narrow, curving street and out of the towered gate of Neyronnes and along the broad road of the valley; and I should never see her again. With her wealth and her beauty and her new freedom, with that strength and resourcefulness of which she herself was just becoming conscious, Christine would go out into the world. And it was not my world.

My world was small and simple: its views were such views as those that lay before me now; its routine was humdrum, its horizon limited, its rewards a little pinched. But it was a world not without beauty, not without interest, not without its own lovableness and its own challenge to valor in living and maturing keenness in thought. I should never see Christine again. But I would go home. I would go home to my job . . .

Yet suddenly, as I thought of my job, of workaday duties, I was smitten again with the realization of other tasks that were being carried out at this moment behind the fortress walls of the ancient village on its hill. I did not know—and I have never known—how much of the police 'third degree' was permitted in France: that dreaded successor to the rack and the thumbscrew, which is forbidden in England and still talked of in the United States. I was unable to guess what might be happening to Rosalie Braye. But I shuddered as I recalled the detective's quiet statement, "We will pursue our investigations, and it is better that we should do this alone." It had been an ominous quietness, I thought. And I had a sick sense of having stumbled upon almost a modern analogy, as I remembered the stories of the torturing of witches in the mediæval prison-tower.

Almost against my will, I turned my face away from the peaceful comeliness of the farming land before me and the shadows that were growing longer in the brightening glow of the sky, to look back toward the ancient houses of Neyronnes, huddled still protectively behind the massive walls of the town. I looked back with a feeling that I should find something terrible in the scene, some visible reminder of death and brutality and remorse and defiance and punishment. And what I saw was beautiful—old ramparts grown mellow in the tawniness of their ancient stone, the rich verdancy of clambering vines touched here and there with starry clematis or white and yellow honeysuckle, the crimson of rambler roses 'flung riotously' against the walls of houses and gardens; an old, old village that had lived its life for more than a thousand years and that was beautiful still . . .

It was not terrible. It was beautiful. Whatever might be happening to Rosalie Braye, whatever horror might have come upon us all, Neyronnes remained beautiful and lovable. I was still homesick. I still felt lonely and strange. But Neyronnes itself spoke kindly and comfortingly to me, from all its changing centuries . . .

And as I looked at it in the loveliness of the sunset, Christine Wilde came through the gate and along the road to where I was sitting.

"I saw you out the window," she said conversationally. "I thought I'd come and talk with you."

She sat down on the grass beside me, under the tree.

"I have heard what has happened," she said. "The police are with Mrs. Braye now, but it is perfectly quiet. It is so still it is frightening. I was glad when I saw you here, because it is so nice to sit here peacefully like this. Everything is always so beautiful at this time of day. And one can get away from things . . ."

She broke off suddenly, but before I had a chance to speak, she went on:

"Get away from things or face them. Wayne, I want to ask you . . . You are young, like me, and I'm not afraid to ask you . . . Do you think I did a wrong thing to my mother to leave her like that?"

She was so earnest, so pathetic, so troubled, that my little thrill of gladness was only subconscious when she called me by my first name. What I was consciously thinking was that I wanted to comfort her; but I did not want to offer any careless consolation, to try to 'cheer' her with a reassurance merely superficial.

"No, I don't think you did wrong," I answered. "I think you did right. Your mother was feeling better when you went away. There was no reason why you shouldn't have left her for two nights."

"I hadn't gone away from her like that for years," she said sadly. "It was dreadful, Wayne—a dreadful coincidence somehow. And the most dreadful part of it all is that I know I don't feel so sorry as I ought to feel . . ."

She clasped her hands over her knees, and went on, without looking at me:

"I can talk to you about it—you are young, like me. The others—they are all so kind, but they are so much older. I never could be sure that they would understand. And if they said nice gentle comforting things to me, I shouldn't know for certain that they meant them—I'd be afraid they were just trying to make me feel better, the way one does to a child that's been hurt. But I'm not a child. And, oh, Wayne, the trouble isn't that I am hurt. It's that I'm not."

"I know," I said, as softly as I could. And I did know. "My mother was buried yesterday in the Protestant Cemetery in the city," she said. "Perhaps in time I shall take her body back to St. Louis, or perhaps to Lausanne. It isn't important, because she had no real

home. But when we came back here, after my mother was buried—
even when I went to the hotel with Mr. and Mrs. Sherrill last night—
I didn't feel sad. I didn't think about sad things. I thought about
glad things. I thought how now she will never grow old, or be unimportant, or be afraid of my leaving her, or of people's not liking
her enough. It wasn't being ill that troubled her really. She was
not very ill, and I think she could have got well, probably. And of
course she knew there was no danger of her being poor. But she
was afraid of growing old, of not being pretty any more, or making
friends easily.

"She was only forty-one years old," Christine added; and remembering the radiant vision of Mrs. Wilde as I had first seen her,
I was not surprised. "And she was so pretty, and always important, the center of things, in spite of her ill-health. But lately she
has not been happy. She has been so restless, this last year, even
more restless than she used to be. And lately she has been unhappy
about me, in a new way.

"She was always afraid of my leaving her, and she would never
let me get well acquainted with any young people. She was jealous
about me, you see—that was natural enough, for she wanted me
always to be with her and take care of her. But lately it had been
worse than that: she seemed to be getting jealous *of* me, too, in
such a sad way. Because I am young. And she was so afraid of getting old. She would not let me talk to Paul MacNeil, and she would
not let me talk to you—that was natural enough. But she would not
let me talk to Miss Hamilton either. And when Mr. and Mrs. Sherrill
came and seemed to like me—I mean, seemed to like me as much
as they liked her—she was unhappy. I was miserable about it. But
what could I do?"

She turned and looked straight at me, and I saw that her brown
eyes were full of tears, though her voice was as clear and unwavering as a silver bell.

"I know that my mother was selfish, Wayne," she said. "I know
all about that. But she was not happy. I saw her unhappiness better than anyone else could see it, and I could forgive her selfishness better than anyone else. Perhaps selfish people are never really

happy. I don't know. What I do know is that now it is all over. And I don't feel sad. I can't feel sad. All that I feel is a kind of perplexity and questioning of myself, and a kind of lostness."

I don't remember what I said. I only remember that it was sincere and quite candid, and that it seemed to comfort her. I did understand how she felt—it was natural, poor child, and simple enough—and I was glad that we could sit there under the tree in the meadow and talk it out, not having to explain much, but really seeing into each other's minds, as if we had known each other for years. And after we had exchanged a few sentences, she said, with a sudden change of expression:

"But I don't know what I am going to do now. It all seems strange. What are you going to do, when this is all over?"

"I?" I answered. "Why, I'm going home. I'm going back to my job."

"Oh," said Christine, "I remember—you teach history in a boys' school, don't you? But—where is your home?"

"In the Chester Valley," I replied. And as she looked quite blank, I added quickly, "The Chester Valley in Pennsylvania. It is very beautiful."

"Oh," said Christine again, and she leaned forward and looked at me rather curiously. "Wayne," she continued, "do you live in the place where you were born?"

I laughed a little. "Well, yes and no," I answered. "I was born on a little old farm in the Chester Valley, forty miles or so from Philadelphia; my father was born there, too, and my grandfather, and my great-grandfather: it's the old Armitage farm, and I still own it. But after my father died, when I was still in my teens, we couldn't go on farming it; so we rented it; and my mother and I took a little house in one of the Main Line suburbs near town. And that is where we lived until she died, last year. After that I moved into the dormitory of the school where I teach, in Paoli. But I hate that: I mean, I hate living in the dormitory. I don't hate Paoli, of course. All that country is lovely.

"It is like this country, Christine," I added, "and there are box hedges and stone walls and honeysuckle. And out in the Chester Valley there are old farms, with old stone houses and big barns.

The barns are bigger than the houses, and some of the houses are beautiful."

"Is your barn bigger than the house, Wayne?"

"Yes," I answered, "and my old stone house is beautiful."

"Oh," began Christine again.

But the silver clarity of her voice broke suddenly, and she dropped her head on her hands and cried, as in all the shock and horror that had come to her I had never seen her cry before.

I let her cry, because I thought that was the best thing for her; and after a while she raised tear-stained eyes and said, with a wistfulness which would have made me very sad if it had not made me, suddenly, very happy:

"That is the most wonderful thing I ever heard of. I think it is the most wonderful thing in all the world. Could you get your farm back, Wayne?"

"Why, of course," I answered. "I—that's my home. Does it really sound wonderful to you, Christine?"

She laughed, surprisingly, a gentle, radiant sort of laugh.

"Sound wonderful?" she echoed. "*Home?*" Her hands flew out in a gesture that made me think of a bird's wings—how often, and in what different ways, Christine has made me think of a bird!— "Oh, Wayne," she said, "I have never had a home. I am very ignorant. But I am not really stupid. I think I could learn . . ."

For a long time we just sat there, talking quietly, with my arms about her, until the summer twilight began to dim the sunset, and the men and women started home from their work in the fields.

XIX
JOHN SHERRILL DISSENTS

Of course I wanted to tell everyone. I wanted to go shouting down the streets of Neyronnes, rousing new and joyous echoes in the ramparts! But of course I did nothing of the sort! Christine and I both agreed that this was no time to be talking of this miracle that had come into our lives. We went back and had dinner with our friends as usual. We were perhaps a little quieter than was our custom, but that was all. And yet, for awhile that evening, it so chanced that none of us spoke of the terrible things that had happened in Neyronnes, and I, for one, did not think of them.

When I got back to my own room, that night, it swept over me with the queerest sense of complete incredibility that I had become engaged to be married to Christine Wilde within seven hours of my finding the body of Horace Braye in the attic beyond the unfinished room in the *pavillon*. The most beautiful thing that had ever happened to me had followed directly on the heels of my life's most hideous experience. And I had forgotten the discovery of Horace Braye's body. I had forgotten that horrible tense moment when Rosalie came into the dusty haunted chamber to confront the officers of the law. The Braye couple and all that they stood for—murder and theft and ugliness and cowardice and greed—had been wiped out of my mind as if they had been marks made upon a slate. But the sponging had been only temporary: alone in my room at midnight, the marks came back . . .

It was John Sherrill's suggestion that we should go for a drive next day—Christine and Elinor Sherrill and Miss Hamilton and I.

It would do Christine good to get away from Neyronnes on a simple little pleasure drive, he said. And I realized that he and his wife had probably talked it all over (and got permission from the police) before the idea was mentioned to us. It was plain that a little pleasure drive would be good for Christine: it was also plain that John Sherrill wanted to be alone, or as nearly alone as possible, in Neyronnes. . .

I said I thought we should all enjoy having Monsieur de Brassac with us, and when the others agreed with me I went to his room and asked him if he could not come along. But he replied that he did not want to leave his sick boy—Paul MacNeil was less weak than he had been the day before, but he was still very ill indeed. And although Monsieur de Brassac's kindly courtesy was unchanged and his smile just as friendly as ever, I thought that he himself did not seem well: his manner was just a little preoccupied, and his eyes looked as if he had not slept.

John Sherrill, too, looked tired. I wondered why he felt it advisable—as I was sure he did—to do any more work over these last details of investigation, the rounding up of evidence, the completion of the story of a mystery when the mystery itself was solved. But was it solved? I remembered that John Sherrill was not occupying himself with the murder of Horace Braye. So far as that crime was concerned, I felt sure that he would be quite content to let the police take charge of Rosalie, and keep his own hands off. But in the murder of Mrs. Wilde, a crime for which suspicion had rested quite publicly on one of his friends, he was still very deeply interested. And was that problem solved?

In this last turn of affairs, I had taken it for granted that Horace Braye had been Mrs. Wilde's murderer; that after he had immediately tried openly to get away, with his wife, and had found the roads closed to him, he had decided to run off in the night without her; and that she, ill-treated, insulted, deceived, and deserted, had killed him with a blow from his own monkey-wrench as he tried to sneak out of the house. That was my own reconstruction of the crime, as we talked with the police, as we waited for Rosalie; and most of it continued to seem, to my mind, the obvious solution.

But as I thought it over again in the night, when the marks came back on the slate to haunt me in the midst of my own happiness, I was not so sure that all of my reconstruction was right. Might not Rosalie herself have committed the first crime, as well as the second? Or—more probably—might not Horace Braye have planned Mrs. Wilde's murder and forced or persuaded his wife to carry it out, to administer that deadly injection of morphine? Three possible solutions—yes, it was small wonder that John Sherrill stayed behind to work, alone or with the police, on what was still a mystery.

We took Mr. Williamson with us as far as the junction where he could catch a Lausanne express, and then we drove for hours. Christine drove, of course, but it was Elinor Sherrill who held the maps and gave the directions, and I have never to this day known just where it was that we went. We passed other walled villages on hilltops, not unlike Neyronnes. We drove along charming sunny slopes all covered with vineyards, bright green vines stained turquoise blue with the summer's spraying against phylloxera. We mounted into rougher hills, on smooth winding roads, and slipped along under the walls of magnificent feudal castles that thrust impregnable towers into the sky. Although we did not stop at all, except for luncheon, we saw, in passing, many picturesque churches and fine old houses, and went through more than one ancient town gate. We must have driven hundreds of miles, and it was all fascinating.

On the front seat, Christine and Mrs. Sherrill discoursed learnedly of roads and places and points of interest. But in the tonneau, with the dog Fergus sniffing the air between us, Miss Hamilton and I sat almost silent, in a quiet content that dowered us with its own sense of repose. We had a memorable luncheon at a commonplace-appearing hotel, and we got back to Neyronnes in time for a late tea. We all felt enormously better.

But John Sherrill, I gathered, did not feel better. His keen, sensitive face looked more tired and worn than before, and although he welcomed us gladly and ordered tea with an air of enthusiasm, we guessed that he did not want to talk about his day. Although it was Sunday, it was unusually quiet for a holiday, for the sky had been cloudy all day, and not many people from the country or the near-by towns had come to Neyronnes, even for *gouters*. By the time our tea was half over, almost all the visitors had departed and the rest were getting ready to leave. Christine went back to the *pavillon*, explaining that she wanted to inquire for Paul MacNeil; but the rest of us sat on in the *galerie*, as we so often did, and it wasn't long before we had the whole central square almost to ourselves and were sitting quietly there, as so often, looking out upon the scene that was so much like a play.

This, I could see, was bringing some repose to John Sherrill as our drive had brought repose to the rest of us.

And after a while he said, without being asked any question

"It has been fairly peaceful here. Curiously enough, Rosalie has been making a frightful fuss because she cannot have Horace's body cremated. Her howls about discrimination against Americans would have done credit to Horace himself."

"Why can't she have his body cremated?" Margaret Hamilton asked.

"The French law forbids it in cases of death by violence," Sherrill answered. "But it has been difficult to get that simple fact into Mrs. Braye's head. She insisted that someone was trying to put something over on her, as she said, because she is a foreigner. I tell you frankly," he added, "that I still cannot understand that woman. Morally, she is a moron: she has no normal sense of right and wrong. But is she mentally of the lunatic fringe, or is she very shrewd? I'll swear I don't know."

"Probably a little of both," suggested Elinor.

"Probably," her husband agreed. "Shrewd along certain lines of self-interest, and a moron otherwise. She has stayed in her room all day, and for part of the time the police have been talking with her. I saw her only that once, when she howled for me to come and 'represent' her. She has been actually under guard ever since her husband's body was found, you know. But now I think that the Sureté man Reynal is giving himself a well-earned rest, and has turned her over to the gendarmes. The *juge d'instruction* has not been here today."

We sat there very comfortably, the four of us, and the tension seemed to have relaxed a bit in all our minds. It seemed like old times, like those early days in Neyronnes when we all chatted together so naturally. I had hesitated this afternoon, to make any inquiries of John Sherrill or even to mention the tragedy that still cast its shadow over us all. But since he spoke himself, so candidly and so companionably, about Rosalie Braye, I plucked up courage to ask him a direct question.

I thought for a minute as to just how I should ask it, what form I should put it in, and I tried to decide upon the possibility which seemed likeliest in my own mind. After some pondering, I seemed to feel myself on fairly firm ground, and I said,

"Don't you think it was probably Horace who killed Mrs. Wilde?"

Sherrill looked at me without any sign of displeasure, but he did not answer at once. It was still broad daylight, but in the *Place* around the linden tree there were the unimportant movements of late afternoon among the village folk. An old peasant woman strode slowly across the square on the side farthest from us, a little girl came with her copper pot to the fountain, a child on his way home to supper dashed out of the *ruelle* and across the *Place* and so pell-mell down the hill. Passing him, and stepping aside to avoid collision with his impetuous speed, Henri de Brassac walked slowly up the sloping path and into the square, as he had done so many times in the days when we did not know him and he was only a stranger passing by, but this time he waved his hand as he saw us.

The picture was one that never failed to charm me, that simple scene of the life of Neyronnes toward the end of a summer day. I gazed out upon it as I waited for John Sherrill to answer me, but when he turned toward me, it seemed as if he had been looking at something far away, and very sad.

"No," he said slowly, "I don't think that Horace Braye killed Mrs. Wilde. I wish to God I did."

XX

WE LEARN OF A DISCOVERY

Before anyone spoke—I, for one, felt dumbfounded and utterly speechless—Christine came around the corner of the *ruelle*, a fresh and lovely picture in a white dress, and called out to Henri de Brassac.

"I was looking for you," she said. "How is Paul? I thought I might talk with him for a while—and you can have a bit of a rest."

"Thank you," he answered, and there was a note of real gratitude in his voice. "He insisted on getting up, just before you got back, and he is down in the *Lices* now, sitting on the bench by the Lower Gate. I didn't think he was strong enough to get out of bed, much less walk down that hill, but he seemed to have set his heart on seeing the view. If you would like to go and sit with him for a quarter of an hour, it would give him much pleasure."

He had approached the *galerie* now, and he bowed to the rest of us.

"Meanwhile, I will join our friends if I may," he added.

"Do," said John Sherrill. "I am going for a little walk—I seem to need to stretch my legs a bit. Come and let these people tell you about their drive, Monsieur de Brassac. They have had a glimpse of *la douce France* to the extent of about four hundred kilomètres, I believe, and Armitage's farming instinct has been aroused by the sight of the vineyards. Sit down and talk to them about grapes."

"Thank you," said Monsieur de Brassac again. He came into the *galerie* and seated himself, not in the chair which John Sherrill had left vacant, but in another, opposite, with its back to the *Place* and the sloping path down which Christine's white dress was already disappearing on her way to the *Lices* and the Lower Gate.

Sherrill walked across the square and out the road, under the beautiful fourteenth-century house at the corner, and down to the *chemin de ronde*, where he, too, was lost to our view and we could not see in which of the two opposite directions he had gone.

Monsieur de Brassac ordered a *vermouth mélangé*, smiled a rather tired smile at us all, and said:

"I am afraid that my knowledge of grapes is not very extensive. But we do make some good wine in the Dordogne country. We have a few hectares of vines on my own little place."

"I thought you lived in Paris," Elinor Sherrill remarked.

"Oh, yes, I do; part of the time. But my home is in the Dordogne country, Madame. I was born near Sarlat, as the police investigators insisted on pointing out; but my own little property is a bit farther west, not far from the château of Biron, not far from Monbazillac—do you know the wine of Monbazillac? The wine of Monbazillac comes from the Monbazillac estates, of course, but the grapes of my little property make a wine which is similar to that."

He made a little bow again, this time directed specifically toward Mrs. Sherrill.

"When your country makes the promised change in its Constitution, it will be a great pleasure to me to send you some of our wine," he said.

Perhaps it was because I had been thinking so much of my own little farm in the Chester Valley—and, too, because we had driven so far that day through rural France—that this quiet talk about vineyards and country places and agricultural products seemed so intensely interesting to me. I had never seen the Dordogne Valley; except for its association with the caves of prehistoric man and the vague recollection of having been told that it was beautiful, I knew nothing about it. I had never heard of the wine of Monbazillac. And although, of course, I was conversant with the life of the unfortunate Duc de Biron whose treachery to Henri IV led him to death on the scaffold, I had no acquaintance with the location of his ancestral home.

Like Elinor Sherrill, I had thought of Henri de Brassac as a Parisian simply. The vision of him living on an old farm in a valley, like me, loving his land, as I did, was a surprising and a curiously impressive one. And as long as I live I shall remember, with a strange and tragic poignancy, those few minutes that we sat there in the *galerie* of the Auberge de Vieux Neyronnes, Elinor Sherrill and Margaret Hamilton and Henri de Brassac and I, talking about life in the country, "talking about grapes . . ."

It was only for a few minutes, a quarter of an hour that was oddly peaceful, oddly serene. And then we saw John Sherrill coming back from the *chemin de ronde*. He was walking slowly, and I—sitting where I could see him more clearly than any of the others—noticed that he looked more tired than ever, more troubled: there was no spring to that dragging, measured pace across the square. He had one hand in his pocket, and as he approached us, unsmiling and so strangely somber, he kept it there. He came into the *galerie* and he was close to us all before he spoke.

"It is only fair to tell you that I have found the key, Monsieur de Brassac," he said.

Henri de Brassac sprang to his feet. The color had left his face, but his mouth was firm.

"I may reply that the key could have been planted," he said.

"Yes, you may reply that," John Sherrill agreed, "but you know that the key was not planted: you know that it would not have been planted in this place. The key was put there to be hidden, Monsieur, as you know—not to be found. And you cannot make such a reply to other things. There was no plant about the bloodstains. There was no plant in the evidence of the coat. I have even found the broken end of the *ampoule*, that bit of glass which had disappeared. I think, Monsieur de Brassac, that there is nothing that you can say."

His voice was sad and stern, and like the voice of doom. No one else spoke. For me, the whole world was whirling. This was something that I could not believe. Henri de Brassac! Henri de Brassac! How? Why? Henri de Brassac the murderer of Mrs. Wilde! How could that be? And why? Why?

Monsieur de Brassac looked John Sherrill full in the face, and then he bowed his head.

"You are right," he said. "There is nothing that I can say. There is nothing, now, that I can do. I think you know everything or almost everything."

"From the very beginning," said John Sherrill, "I have trusted you."

Yes, that was it. That was what made it so terrible. We had trusted him. We had all trusted him, completely. Far away, as in a daze, I could hear the voice of the *juge d'instruction*, telling us the bare facts of Henri de Brassac's life—"son of the Marquis de Brassac, chevalier of the Legion of Honor, author of—" No, it wasn't that that was important: it was the other things. It was the Henri de Brassac that we knew, Henri de Brassac who was kind to a sick boy, who was patient and courteous with a stranger, who was my friend: Henri de Brassac who had warned me of the suspicions against myself—but, wait, was that necessarily so friendly? And his suggestions about Horace Braye: had they been mere remarks made in a sense of companionship, or had they had—why, yes, of course, they must have had!—a purpose that was sinister?

We had trusted him. We had trusted him absolutely. And it was he who had murdered Christine's mother. It was Henri de Brassac ... And what was this about a bloodstain? A bloodstain? Why, then, he must have murdered Horace Braye, too. My brain was really whirling. I kept saying to myself, "This can't be! This can't be!"

"I know," Monsieur de Brassac said to John Sherrill. "You trusted me. I—I am sorry. I suppose it is too much to ask you to put yourself in my place . . ."

He seemed to be making an effort to pull himself together, and when he went on speaking, it was with some resemblance to his usual calm.

"Listen, Monsieur," he said, "I think you understand that this was no case of ordinary murder—that the motives were different . . ."

"Yes," said Sherrill, more gently than he had spoken before. "I know that. Sit down."

He sat down himself, in his chair facing the *Place*, and Monsieur de Brassac returned to his seat opposite.

"I think that in a way I do put myself in your place," Sherrill went on, as if he were trying to be his natural self again. "I can understand how a man could have yielded to the sudden impulse to mete out a painless death to Mrs. Wilde, when the opportunity was unexpectedly put in his way—a man who had heard, from your window, the selfish cruelty of her attacks upon her daughter, who had heard her daughter cry with such wretchedness, and had realized the hopelessness of her tears—the hopelessness of all the future for a girl with a mother like that. It would be apparent to that listener as it was not apparent to the rest of us, that Mrs. Wilde's self-absorption had entered upon a new phase."

He paused for an instant, and went on, more slowly still:

"For years she had been her daughter's jailer and slave-driver, and she had regarded her as a child. But just this spring it had become plain to her that Christine was not a child any longer—that she was twenty years old and very charming and likeable. And with that realization Mrs. Wilde began to look upon her daughter with bitter jealousy as a rival, almost as an enemy.

"She did not only forbid Christine to so much as make Wayne Armitage's acquaintance, when she saw that the two young people liked each other, and she could not face the possibility of being left alone if Christine should want to marry. She did not only do things like that. She turned upon the girl with fury when she saw that my wife and I found Christine more attractive than her mother; she had done the same when she saw the likelihood of pleasant acquaintance between Christine and Margaret Hamilton, and Margaret had found out about it and taken pains, afterward, not to arouse that frenzied jealousy again, for Christine's sake; but Elinor and I did not know in time.

"Oh, yes, Monsieur de Brassac," he added earnestly, "I do understand that. And all this was in addition to her cruelty to that poor consumptive, which was in itself enough to drive any man's indignation to white heat. Mrs. Wilde was a monster, Monsieur de Brassac. Christine will never tell anyone about it or confess what she has suffered: she is too proud. But I know that you knew."

"I knew, too," said Margaret Hamilton. "It was only in the very beginning that I was deceived. All these weeks—before any of the rest of you came—I have known that Mrs. Wilde was a monster . . . I have tried to do what I could to soften things for Christine, and for Paul, but nobody could do much. Mrs. Wilde was a monster, John: she deserved to die."

Henri de Brassac turned toward Miss Hamilton, and his white face was ravaged with pain.

"Oh, my friend, I have let suspicion rest on you," he said. "It is that for which I cannot excuse myself. Can you ever forgive me?"

"That needn't worry you," said John Sherrill quickly. "The suspicion, I mean. I'll talk about it later—"

But he broke off without finishing his sentence. For Margaret Hamilton interrupted him again, and it seemed now as if, even in this terrible moment, the surging tragedy about us must somehow be calmed by that beautiful voice.

"Oh, no," she cried, "there's nothing to forgive. I understand it. I know—everything . . ."

Henri de Brassac looked at her as if he knew that he need say nothing more. When he spoke again, after only a little pause, it was to John Sherrill:

"I think there is only one thing which you have not learned—perhaps a thing not large in itself, but in great degree an extenuating circumstance. I should like to tell you about that. I should like to tell you about everything . . ."

"Hush—not now!" And as Sherrill rapped out the words, hurriedly but kindly, the Frenchman turned to see what we had all seen before him. Walking very slowly Christine and Paul MacNeil were coming, together, up the hill.

She was very straight and tall and strong, like some white-clad goddess of youth and vigor—very strong and very beautiful as she came up the hill and across the square. But what I was noticing particularly as I watched her was not her beauty: it was the way she was walking, with her hand on Paul MacNeil's arm, supporting him with that fresh strength of hers, yet looking, to a stranger's eyes, as if he needed no assistance, as if, even, she were leaning a little on him. We were all struck silent—I had the feeling that for poor Henri de Brassac this must be almost a last straw—and as they came near us, Christine called out:

"We are coming to join you for a while. We have been having the most fascinating time: Paul has been reading *Tales of the Mermaid Tavern* to me, and it's lovely. But the light has faded, so he had to stop."

"Yes," said Paul, with a queer little smile, as they came into the *galerie* and sat down, "the light has faded, so I had to stop." His tone changed suddenly. "And now, Monsieur de Brassac, I am going to have a glass of port, and no one shall say me nay!"

His voice was gay, but it was very weak, and he looked more ill than I had ever seen him, except on that one dreadful morning when I found him in the ruins after the rain. The Frenchman ordered the drink for him. And I sat, stunned still and bewildered, and looked at the both and tried to think. Monsieur de Brassac's attitude toward the sick lad was so protective: no wonder he had been so ragingly angry over Mrs. Wilde's cruelty toward Paul MacNeil, no wonder that had added fuel to the flame of his pity for the hopeless plight of her own daughter, whom she was torturing in her imprisonment: this was no ordinary murder, as he had said . . .

Christine was talking about *Tales of the Mermaid Tavern*, and how beautifully Paul had read 'The Companion of a Mile' to her, and the other poem about the mariners who crossed the Atlantic; but I was scarcely listening to what she said. I was thinking—and in my thinking I felt as if I were trying to push away blackness from my eyes, in a blinded effort to see . . .

For there was something wrong here, something that didn't fit into the puzzle, that didn't make complete sense. Mrs. Wilde had been killed *before* Henri de Brassac knew of her cruelty to Paul MacNeil. And a faint memory stirred in my mind: I had heard sounds in the night; I had heard sounds in the night, in or near the room that was Henri de Brassac's, *before* the Frenchman came to Neyronnes . . . What was it that they had been saying to each other, John Sherrill and Henri de Brassac? What was it they had meant?

But I found myself listening now. For Paul MacNeil raised the glass of wine that had just come for him—

"I drink to that great inn beyond the grave —
  If there be none the gods have done us wrong—
  Ere long I hope to chant a brighter stave,
  In some great Mermaid Inn beyond the grave. . ."

He set down the wine-glass, untouched, and faced John Sherrill.

"I think you know everything," he said.

"I think I do," Sherrill answered. "And I want to tell you—if it can be arranged, my wife and I should like to take you with us to Geneva when we go."

Paul MacNeil smiled. "Thank you very much," he responded, "but I—must stay here. I am not afraid. And I do not regret what I did. Her death was merciful, to everyone. And his was accidental. I killed him in self-defense. I'll tell you the whole story . . ."

But on the instant his eyes, which had been bright with fever, turned dull, and the fire that had flamed in his cheeks left the gray of dead ashes where it had burned red. It may be that there was something theatrical in his instinct as he spoke again, but I think not. I like to think that at this moment his mind went quite simply to the great immortal English that he loved. For his smile, as it changed and deepened, was very sweet and very natural.

"'The rest is silence,'" he said.

As the thin line of scarlet showed between his white lips, Henri de Brassac sprang forward. But Christine was nearest; and it was she who caught him as he fell.

XXI
WE HEAR THE WHOLE STORY

Paul MacNeil died two days later. He was conscious until the end, and he talked a little to one or the other of us now and then although words came with difficulty and he could never say much at a time. He seemed to feel curiously at peace, curiously and mercifully content; and although his spirit did recoil from the horror of that blow in the night which had killed Horace Braye, I think that his attitude toward life was not quite normal and that he was incapable of feeling regret for what he had done. Mrs. Wilde's death he saw only as release—release for others and release for herself.

The rest of us did not talk much, among ourselves, of what had happened during those days. Both Miss Hamilton and Henri de Brassac spent a great deal of time at Paul MacNeil's bedside; and if I had not come to realize it long before, I should have understood fully then, how unjust my suspicion of Miss Hamilton's treatment of Paul had been. Through all those weeks she had done for him everything that it was possible to do, and one could see now that he felt a kind of devotion for her that was almost filial. It had been necessary for Miss Hamilton to conceal any kindness to the sick boy, as it had been necessary for her to acquiesce in the concealment of his presence, in order to prevent Mrs. Wilde's outbreaks of fury, which would have been directed, not against Miss Hamilton, but against Paul himself, and most of all against Christine. Little by little I had come to see that clearly now.

"I was sure that Horace Braye had been killed by his wife," Miss Hamilton said one day, when Christine was with Paul, and both she and Monsieur de Brassac were having tea with the Sherrills and myself in the *galerie*, "and yet, once one grasps the initial mistake about the key, one can understand what happened afterward."

Yes, it was the mistake about the key—Paul MacNeil's mistake about the key to Mrs. Wilde's door—which had precipitated later events and been responsible for the almost accidental death of Horace Braye. Paul had entered Mrs. Wilde's room quietly and easily, through a door not only unlocked but ajar. If he had left the door as he found it, the whole story of what happened afterward would have been very different. But he was in a thoroughly unnatural state of mind when he went out of that room where Mrs. Wilde lay dying of morphine poisoning: he was scarcely conscious of what he was doing; without noticing it, he locked the door and stuck the key in his pocket. And when he realized that he had it, he was afraid to go back.

He had hurried out of that house of death to seek his own shelter in the ruins. And his idea, on discovering the key, was to throw it down the supposedly bottomless well, on the grassy triangle near the prison-house. But he was really very ill and the rain was coming down in torrents. He ran by the shortest way to his refuge and flung himself upon his bed. In the morning he vaguely remembered that he had done something with the key, but he was too ill to think or even to recall clearly the main events of what had happened. Later, when he remembered his intention of throwing the key down the well, he supposed that that was what he had done.

But on the evening when he felt so much better, when he put on his new suit and dined with us in the *galerie*, recollection swept over him: he had had the key in his hand when he entered his hut; he had not thrown it in the well; he had hidden it somewhere in his shelter; he could not remember where. In the night he was seized with the conviction that he must go and find it, that he must fling it away for good and all. It was certainly not wise determination; but Paul MacNeil was not wise; and he was excited and already feverish . . .

So, in the middle of the night, when the house was quite still, he slipped out of his room and into the storage-room of the old 'lean-to' house, on his way out the back exit to the village street. And he almost walked into a man who was making a slow and laborious way down the stairs from the unfinished room, with a suitcase in his hand. He had been badly frightened, of course, and had slipped back into the darkness of the shadows—a little light was coming in through the dusty windows from the street lamps outside—but the man saw him, and when he got to the foot of the stairs, he dropped his suitcase and made a lunge at Paul with a heavy weapon of some sort which he held in his hand.

I suppose that Horace Braye was desperate and had completely lost his head. Certainly he flew at Paul with the enormous monkey-wrench that he was taking back to his car, and Paul thought that he was trying to kill him. He got panicky, too, and his only thought was to get away. He knew the storage annex, as Braye did not, and he managed to double back and run up the stairs to the second floor, thinking that he could reach the door of the unfinished room and so get back into the *pavillon*. But Braye rushed after him, still hitting out with the monkey-wrench, until he got to the top of the stairs, and there he stumbled and fell, dropping the big iron tool and the lace scarf. He was trying to scramble to his feet when Paul picked up the monkey-wrench, with the piece of lace around it, and struck out blindly. As Braye fell under the blow that hit his head, Paul ran out of the attic and back to his room.

It was Henri de Brassac who told us this story.

"He was very ill again in the morning," he added, "far too ill to think of looking for the key. And he did not know until Monsieur Armitage found the body, that Horace Braye was dead. Then he told me about it . . ."

There was silence for a moment, and then Miss Hamilton asked,

"But how did the lace scarf happen to be there? And why did Braye have the monkey-wrench?"

This time John Sherrill answered:

"He had the lace scarf with him because it was valuable, and he was sneaking it away, as a sort of loot. He had packed his small suitcase and was all ready to take himself off—there is no reason for thinking that he had ever really had any idea of burdening his flight with his wife's presence—and as he was about to leave the room, he saw the scarf. She says—and I believe her: it's the logical explanation—that she had thrown the scarf on a chair the night before and forgotten to pack it, and that when he noticed it he said, "I'll just take this along, and you won't have to bother." So he went out of the room with the scarf in his hand, and he threw it around the handle of the monkey-wrench, with some queer useless instinct (naturally, his finger-prints were all over the monkey-wrench anyway), when he tried to hit Paul.

"As for the monkey-wrench," Sherrill added, "it seems that Horace had wanted to mend something about his suitcase, and he didn't want to run the risk of attracting attention to his packing, at that time, by saying anything to the servants; so he got the big spanner out of his car. It is all very simple, isn't it?"

Christine came out to the *galerie* just then, and Miss Hamilton went to take her place at Paul MacNeil's bedside. We did not speak of these things before Christine. She, too, was with Paul a great deal, and I came to understand his feeling for her and to feel deeply touched by it. She was always to him what she had seemed to me to resemble as she walked with him up the hill and across the cobbles of the ancient *Place*—some lovely goddess of youth and vigor, very strong and beautiful, and gentle and kind. He did not 'love' her, in any ordinary human sense, but he felt a sort of worship for her, and personally, a sort of gladness that she was alive. It was like the last couplet of the Shakespeare sonnet that I had heard him reciting in the ruins: when he thought of her, his losses were restored and his sorrows were over, and that was all he asked. And he was happy now in the thought that she was happy.

And one day, just before he died, Christine said a strange thing. She said it to Paul—a few words which I, hearing, thought might be mere words of comfort. But she said it afterward to me, at more length, and I saw that it was quite true.

"I'm not sure that I can make you understand, Wayne," she tried to explain, "but, after all the shock and terror of my mother's death and the fear that those horrible Brayes had killed her, I feel so relieved, so at peace, now that I know how it really was. The thing that had haunted me was the thought that she had waked up in the night and seen that man's dreadful face, all hideous with fear and greed and hate, and had known that he was killing her, had died with that horror in her mind and in her eyes. That was the terrible thing, Wayne, that torture for her. And now I know that nothing like that happened. Nothing frightened her, nothing troubled her. She didn't know she was dying. There was nothing but gentleness about her, from the moment that she looked up and saw Paul's face until she just slipped quietly off to sleep.

"And you know," she added, "Paul never felt any resentment against my mother for her strange treatment of him here. I don't believe he ever thought about it. He didn't think much about himself: he was always sorry for other people."

He died very soon after that. That last sentence was Christine's epitaph on Paul MacNeil . . .

And not until after his death did Henri de Brassac and John Sherrill tell the story of Mrs. Wilde's death as they had learned it . . .

Rain had begun to seep through into Paul MacNeil's shelter only a short time after he had installed himself there. He had told Miss Hamilton, and she had told Monsieur and Madame Delande, and when they found that it was not possible to make the ruined but waterproof, they had given him a key to the *pavillon annexe* of the inn. There were very few guests at that time, and the hotel-keeper and his wife, who had known Paul for years, told him that in case of rain at night he could come into the house to sleep, so long as Mrs. Wilde was not allowed to find it out. No one was afraid of contagion; but Mrs. Wilde had already shown that she was capable of unpleasant scenes, and—largely for her daughter's sake—the Delandes, like Miss Hamilton, were anxious not to cross her.

On the night when I first heard sounds in the back part of the *pavillon*—the night of the party in the inn and the sudden hard shower—Paul MacNeil had slipped into the house early, as soon as the rain began, about half-past ten, and had gone into the room which was later Henri de Brassac's, the room which was nearest the top of the stairs on the side of the house which was on that night sheltered from the rain. He had been in that room before, and his demands for comfort were so simple that he never disturbed anything; nor, as a rule, did he stay long. He brought a blanket with him, laid it on the floor beside the window, and usually went immediately to sleep. When the rain stopped, he went back to his own shelter. He was always absolutely quiet, and he was personally neat and fastidious to the point of fanaticism; otherwise, of course, he would not have been given the freedom of the house!

But on this night he did not sleep. In the next room, just inside the open window, Mrs. Wilde and her daughter were having a conversation which he could not help overhearing and which made sleep impossible. He had heard Mrs. Wilde raging at Christine on other occasions, but he had never heard anything like this. For after she had worked herself into a fury on the subject of me, Wayne Armitage, and poor Christine's slight evidence of liking to talk with me, she suddenly switched over to Miss Hamilton. And Paul said, telling the story to Henri de Brassac, it was just as if she were mad . . .

She accused her daughter of trying to steal her friends, of setting herself up as a social rival to her mother, of plotting against her. She said horrible things. She laughed and shrieked and told Christine that she could never hope to be as attractive as her mother, and that she had no brains and no charm. She went on and on, Paul said, and the Frenchman interrupted his story at this point to tell us that he, too, had overheard such conversations— only worse, if possible, when the Sherrills came, and Mrs. Wilde accused her daughter of trying to snatch their attention and to make them think her mother was old and passé. Not only Henri de Brassac, too, but Elinor Sherrill, and of course Margaret Hamilton, corroborated Paul MacNeil's story of Mrs. Wilde's insane jealousy, and further reference to it came even from Rosalie Braye.

On this night, too, the legacy to Miss Hamilton had been spoken of—not at all as Christine had cleverly and loyally reported it, but as a harsh and bitter threat of punishment and revenge.

"You'll see!" Christine's mother had screamed at her. "You haven't a cent of money except what I give you, and you think you'll get it all when I'm gone. Well, you won't get it all. And it won't be you that Margaret Hamilton, at least, will remember. I'm going to leave her a trust fund, and a good big one. I've got it all fixed up already. You think you're so generous—you'll see!"

And at that, Paul said, Christine had stopped crying, and had shown unreservedly how glad she was. And curiously enough she had been able to quiet her mother then.

But it was a frightful scene, and he could not stay where it had been so close to him. He slipped out of the room and back to the storage annex. That was when I had heard him. He was breathing heavily because he had had such a shock . . .

Henri de Brassac came to that room the next morning, and on the hall floor just outside, in the shadowed corner by the door, he found the button of a man's coat. Knowing the scrupulous housekeeping of the Auberge de Vieux Neyronnes, he was surprised. And when he had brought Paul MacNeil to the inn, he looked at his coat-buttons and understood that he must have been in the house . . .

On the second night of Christine's absence, Paul again sought shelter in the *pavillon annexe* of the inn. His plan this time was to go to the unfinished room and spend the entire night, because the rain was getting worse every minute—one could bolt that door on the inside, and the plan seemed quite practical. The house was very quiet as he entered and went up the first flight of stairs, but as he passed Mrs. Wilde's door he noticed that it was a hair's breadth ajar, and from inside he heard the faint sound of moaning. He stopped, listened, pushed the door a little, and then Mrs. Wilde said,

"Is that you, Miss Hamilton? Please come in. I'm so miserable."

Paul MacNeil was naturally kind, and charitable in his judgments. He knew, too, that people who are ill are often unreasonable. He had never bothered his head about Mrs. Wilde's real cruelty toward himself. And he was genuinely sorry for her. He stood still for a moment, waiting to see if Miss Hamilton might be coming downstairs. But there was no sound or movement anywhere in the house, and he pushed aside the unlatched door and went into Mrs. Wilde's room.

"It's only me, Paul," he said. "Isn't there something I can do for you? I just came in for a minute, out of the rain."

She was so absorbed in the self-pity of the moment that she did not give a thought to the disobedience to her mandates, implied in Paul's presence in the house. She was too glad to have someone to talk to. And talk she did. He had shut the door tight behind him, and no one would hear them—she had just opened it a crack, she said, because she was thinking about calling Miss Hamilton. And she told him right away that it was very wrong of Christine to stay away two nights.

"She knows I need someone to talk to when I can't sleep," she said.

"Well," he suggested, "here am I. You can talk to me."

She really was lonely and nervous. She was angry with her daughter for leaving her, and the Sherrills' desire for Christine's company had been a bitter blow to her vanity. Her desire to dramatize herself ran away with her. She told Paul MacNeil not only that she was cursed with an undutiful daughter—which, of course he knew to be untrue—but that she was suffering from a painful and incurable disease. She had nothing but a slow and wretched death, she said, to look forward to. And he did not know that that was not true. It was his own state exactly, except that his disease was almost never actually painful. It seemed to him that Mrs. Wilde was far worse off than he.

"I told you, Monsieur Sherrill," said Henri de Brassac as he reached this point in his story, "that there was one thing you did not know, which was to me a greatly extenuating circumstance. This is it. Paul MacNeil did not look upon Mrs. Wilde's death only as a justifiable execution, but as a merciful release. He thought that it was for her the only way out of hopeless suffering."

"I thought that, too," said Miss Hamilton. "She told me the same thing, that evening. It seemed to me curious, but I believed her. When she first came, and talked to me about her mysterious illness and her great trials and misfortunes, I concluded that she must have cancer. Then I decided that I must have been mistaken. But suddenly, Monday evening, she began to talk just as she talked to Paul. And I believed her, just as he did. I think now that she was making a frantic effort to attract and concentrate attention, to get back to the center of the picture, no matter how. I suppose none of us can really understand how upset she was, Elinor, when you and John preferred her daughter to her and actually kept Christine with you for two days!" She sighed suddenly. "Perhaps I should have known better than to believe her but even the fear of hopeless disease seems so horrible . . ."

"Paul MacNeil, at any rate, did not know enough even to think of such a thing as disbelieving her," Monsieur de Brassac went on. "He felt only pity for her."

And after a little while Henri de Brassac was still telling the story—Mrs. Wilde said, "I haven't taken my medicine all day. I didn't want Miss Hamilton to know about it, and it's such a trouble to fix it for myself. Perhaps if I took it now, I might be able to get to sleep. I don't know where it is, but you find it, Paul, and get it ready for me . . ."

It was then that he thought of the morphine.

"Don't think I take drugs," he had said to Henri de Brassac. "That is something I would never do. But there was a newspaper man at home who knew that I had consumption and who felt sorry about it, and one day he brought me a little package, and said, 'There's nothing I can do for you, but if things ever get too bad, here's this. It's morphine, enough to send you over the edge for good and all. Keep it for emergency.' So I did. I never asked him how he got it, poor chap, but I kept the stuff in a little tin box in one of my inside pockets, so it wouldn't get wet or be lost—or found. And when Mrs. Wilde spoke of medicine, and 'getting to sleep,' I— I thought of it."

Monsieur de Brassac interrupted himself. "Of course that is almost all the story," he said, and turned to address John Sherrill. "Will you be so kind as to tell me how you traced this sorry business to Paul MacNeil—and why you were so angry with me for concealing what I knew?"

"I'll answer your second question first," Sherrill said. "I was very indignant because I had trusted you completely all along, and I thought that you ought to have trusted me. I had no intention of turning that poor lad over to the police; I would have helped you to do everything you could for him. I think that you and I must

hold out the hand of pardon to each other over that misunderstanding, Monsieur de Brassac. And before I answer your first question—
tell me when did you first suspect Paul MacNeil?"

"I had my suspicions from the beginning," the Frenchman replied, "but for a while I thought it was most probably Horace Braye.
After Braye's death, Paul told me, as I have already said to you,
everything. And you?"

"I began to wonder about him right at first," Sherrill answered,
"because of his clothes. If he had spent that night on his bed in the
ruins, either he would not have been dressed when Armitage found
him or else his suit, which would have remained in his waterproof
box until the rain stopped, would have been dry. That is what I
meant when I spoke to you of the 'evidence of the coat.' It seemed
queer. It seemed queer, too, that the big key to Mrs. Wilde's door
should have completely disappeared.

"But when we began to trace Horace Braye's footprints back in
his paths of crime," Sherrill continued, "I confess that my
ponderings concerned themselves chiefly with him. But even so I
still wondered about that key: if Horace Braye had murdered Mrs.
Wilde and taken the key with him from her locked door, I think
that the key would not have disappeared: I think it would have
been found in quite an accessible place, probably among the be-
longings of Wayne Armitage. Incidentally, no one would have
planted that key on Paul MacNeil! Then, after Horace was killed, I
realized that all the reasons for suspecting him were just as clearly
reasons for not suspecting him—reasons for believing that he was
simply trying frantically to get away. And the more I thought about
that complacently unmoral recital of Rosalie's, the more likely it
seemed to me that it was true—that left to herself and terribly
frightened, she couldn't think of anything better to do than to blurt
out the truth . . .

"So I went back to my first questionings about Paul MacNeil. I
made an excuse to look at his old coat, the one in which he had had
the hemorrhage, which had not been cleaned because you were
going to throw it away; I found a very small new bloodstain on the
right sleeve. Then I searched for the key, and found it, in a hole in

the ground under the pile of branches in his hut. The broken end of the ampoule was with it, wrapped in a handkerchief."

"I had already looked, without success," Monsieur de Brassac remarked. "I had almost come to the conclusion that he must have thrown it down the well, after all."

"Then, when Paul saw me coming from the direction of his old shelter, as he was sitting there with Christine at the gate, and re-membered that I had made an excuse that gave me a chance to see his old coat, he realized that I must have learned the truth, and he confessed to us all, as he already had done to you."

John Sherrill sighed, as he finished his story. But Henri de Brassac had another question to ask.

"I have been deeply troubled over the suspicions against Miss Hamilton," he said. "About young Monsieur Armitage here, I have not been troubled, because—as you and I have agreed, Monsieur Sherrill—he is plainly too frank and ingenuous to play a part suc-cessfully after a murder, even if he had been able to commit such a crime in the first place. But about Miss Hamilton I have been troubled. Yet you have intimated that my fears were groundless. Why?"

"For several reasons." John Sherrill smiled at his old friend. "To begin with, there was Fergus . . ."

The Kerry blue, hearing himself spoken of, raised his beautiful head and fixed his devoted, intelligent eyes upon his mistress, and she leaned over and stroked him, with more of open affection than she was usually willing to show. But Henri de Brassac looked puzzled.

"Fergus?" he echoed. "I remember that he made a noise in the night. But how does that prove anything, Monsieur Sherrill? A house dog, like this one, will often make a noise when his master or mistress goes out of the room. I had a dog once that always barked when I left him."

"Yes. But Fergus didn't bark. He growled. A dog will bark sharply at his master or mistress, to make a protest, to say any one of a number of things; *but he won't growl*. The fact that Fergus *growled* on both those nights is as strong a proof as one could wish for, that it was not his mistress who was in the hall, that someone else was there—someone, too, whom he either disliked or did not know very well. That was the second point of evidence I spoke of, that pleased me when it came out at the hearing," Sherrill added. "And I noted later that he had growled once when Armitage went through the hall late, but never after he became really acquainted with Armitage. I think that he never did become really acquainted with Paul MacNeil—did he, Margot?"

"No," Miss Hamilton agreed, but I thought she looked uncomfortable. "When I went to see Paul in his shelter, I always left Fergus behind. Paul didn't like dogs much: I think they were too active and healthy; they seemed to worry him, poor lad. But, John, Fergus's growl proves that someone else was in the hall: it doesn't prove that I was not."

"Not quite—but wouldn't that have been stretching the long arm of coincidence to the point of improbability?" He gave a little chuckle, and addressed Monsieur de Brassac again. "Besides, I think that Miss Hamilton was the one person in Neyronnes most likely to realize that Christine could not be deceived into thinking that her mother took drugs. And note this: if she had known what was coming, when Mrs. Wilde's will was read, and had killed Mrs. Wilde to get that legacy, I do not believe—knowing Miss Hamilton as I do—that she could have managed to faint with such dramatic genuineness when she heard the codicil." He turned to Miss Hamilton again, with his friendly smile that was no longer troubled.

"But I have always wondered, Margot, and I know that now you won't mind my asking you," he said. "Why did you faint?"

But Miss Hamilton was not smiling. And her voice was remote and frozen, as if a glacier spoke.

"I fainted because it was I who killed Mrs. Wilde," she said.

. . . John Sherrill and I sprang to our feet, aghast, and stood there staring at her, and Elinor Sherrill strangled a cry of horror and disbelief. But no one spoke. And Miss Hamilton, in a tone that was perfectly even and that gradually came to sound more natural, went on, quietly:

"Everything that you have said, so far, about Paul MacNeil is true. But it was not Paul who killed Mrs. Wilde. It was I. And I fainted because when I found that she had left money to me, it was more than I could bear . . .

"Paul insisted on taking the blame; and when I found that she had left me that horrible money, I did not know what to do. But now I have arranged that I need never even see a penny of the money—it is all to go to charity, of course—and I feel that I can face life normally again. So far as Mrs. Wilde's death is concerned, I am not sorry—I cannot be sorry. I was mistaken in believing that she was going to die of a terrible disease; but even so her death was a blessed release, for Christine and for herself, just as Paul said. I"—she looked around at us all—"I should like to tell you about it. I want you all to know the whole truth. Please sit down."

As her hand flew out in one of its old familiar gestures, Elinor Sherrill caught it, and I saw her press the long white fingers.

"You needn't tell us a thing if you don't want to, Margot," she said. "We all believe in you—"

"Thank you," said Miss Hamilton, and her voice was her own again. "But I want you to know. It is very simple . . .

"When Paul MacNeil thought of the morphine, as Monsieur de Brassac has told us, he did not think of it as you supposed he did. After he had listened to Mrs. Wilde's distressing and almost hysterical complaints and ragings, and heard her speak of a medicine which she did not want me to know about, and which would help her to go to sleep, he thought of the morphine—because he suddenly thought she must be a drug-addict. It seemed to him probable that her supply of drugs had given out, or something like that. And he was horrified and heartsick, and came to ask me what to do.

"My door was very slightly ajar, because I had gone to bed feeling very greatly disturbed about Mrs. Wilde, and after Wayne Armitage had gone to his room and the house was quiet, I had opened my door a trifle so that I could listen for any sounds from her room. So I knew that Paul was there, and as he started to come upstairs I slipped out into the hall and motioned him into the unfinished room—I was afraid that Wayne might hear us through the

thin partition if we talked in my room, and of course there was no
one next the unfinished room that night, John being away. Paul
told me what he thought, and told me about the morphine, and
said, 'What shall I do?'"

Miss Hamilton was speaking very slowly, but she did not pause
at this crucial point in her narrative.

"I did know about the insulin," she said. "Christine had told
me, before she went away. I knew about her idiosyncrasy against
opiates—she had told me that herself. I had been her constant companion for nearly two months, and I knew that she was a monster
of selfishness and jealousy, whose selfishness had become a frightful ingrowing thing that seemed as if it must destroy her reason
and would certainly wreck her daughter's life. That afternoon, from
the time that you telephoned, John, about staying overnight in
Cluny, I had listened to her frenzy of rage against Christine, and I
was sick with dread of the mental torture she would inflict upon
that child when she returned. And that evening she had told me—
in what I see now was a frantic clutch at self-importance—that she
ought always to be cared for and made much of because she was
hopelessly ill and doomed to hideous suffering. I thought it was
cancer. I went to bed and lay there for hours, trying and trying to
think of something to do, some way in which she might be persuaded to get a nurse, for instance. And then Paul came and asked
me what he should do. And I said,

"'I think that is just the right thing, Paul. But I had better give
it to her. You just stay here and try to get some sleep.'

"So I went to her room and got out the insulin and emptied the
ampoule and put the morphine in the syringe and gave it to her. I
had a handkerchief around my hand and I rubbed at the door and
other things that Paul might have touched. But I was not ashamed
of what I had done or afraid to face the consequences, so far as I
myself was concerned. I wanted to avoid a great outcry, and I didn't
want Paul to be involved in it at all. I went out of the room and left
the door unlocked, with the key in the lock, inside, and went right
to my room. No one heard me, of course.

"But Paul, poor lad, was too upset to sleep. He couldn't get the thought of Mrs. Wilde out of his head for an instant. And after a while he went downstairs and into her room, to see if she seemed all right. I didn't hear him at all, but it was then that Fergus growled, and that worried me a little. What Paul saw was that Mrs. Wilde looked as if she were dead—and the poor boy lost his head completely. He never had much mental stamina, you know, and he was very ill. He rushed out of the room and locked the door and ran to his hut, with the key in his hand, and he must have snatched up the end of the *ampoule*. And in the morning you know what happened . . .

"I had not thought out clearly what I was going to do. But I was not worried, not ashamed of what I had done. I thought probably I should be able to tell Christine, and since she must know that her mother's disease was so horrible, she would surely understand. In any case, I thought that the supposition of suicide or drug-addiction would stand for the world at large.

"Then came the disappearance of the key. And Christine, poor child, came in and blurted out that her mother must have been murdered. And she testified that her illness had not been serious. And the doctor verified that, and I knew that what Mrs. Wilde had told me could not have been true. I was troubled and confused, but I should have told the truth, all of it, and taken the consequences, if it had not been for that frightful will."

Miss Hamilton shuddered, now, and caught her breath in a little gasp, but she went on:

"I did not feel that I had much to lose in life. I had done something which at the time I had believed not to be wrong, which at the time I had believed to be merciful. I was willing to take whatever punishment might be necessary for that. But to be branded as a woman who had murdered for money—that I could not face. That I could not bear.

"From the first Paul had insisted, and pleaded with me, that he must take the blame. In a curious way, it seemed to be a point of pride with him. As soon as I could see him alone, after Mrs. Wilde's body was found, I told him just what it was that I had done. And he said, first, that if he had known what I knew he would have done what I did; and second, that he felt actually responsible in any case, because he had had the morphine and had called me into the situation, and then had made the mistake about the key. Of course these were not real arguments; but I did not know what to do; so I tried to conceal both Paul's part and my own, tried to behave as usual, tried to think of something to do.

"And then Paul had that wild idea of looking for the key in the night, poor boy, and he killed Horace Braye in self-defense, as a result of it. I never thought of his having had anything to do with that: I believed wholly that Horace Braye's wife had murdered him, until Paul himself told me what had happened. And then his strength had failed completely, and we knew that he was dying and he begged me not to tell my story until he was gone. I did promise him that. But I urged him to tell Monsieur de Brassac . . ."

She looked at the Frenchman, and he bowed gravely. "Yes," he said, "at the very end—yesterday—he told me all that you have told us now."

"You had never suspected the truth?" she asked him.

"No," he answered. "I had never suspected the truth. And now I beg that you will never tell this story to anyone else . . ."

"So do I," said John Sherrill. "A few of your close friends know and understand what really happened, Margaret; that is enough."

"And your own life must not be shadowed or troubled," Elinor added.

Well, I have written down this story—in deep shame for having suspected Margaret Hamilton of a dastardly motive for a crime. But these are my private papers. No harm will come to her through me.

"I think," she said now, "that everything will come right, in time. Christine is happy—I can see that already. Paul died in peace and real contentment. The money will go to charity and do some good. And you, John, have failed for the first time to solve a mystery, because the apparently obvious motive obscured the real one, and you knew your old friend could not be guilty of what would have been a hideous crime.

"But it is all a curious commentary on evidence, isn't it? You knew that it was utterly impossible that Margaret Hamilton should have ingratiated herself into a rich woman's affections and then killed her for the money she had made sure of getting in her will. So you ruled out Margaret Hamilton from all connection with Mrs. Wilde's death. And that was a mistake. For alone among all the people here, John, I had the *real* motive, and that was plain from the start. Not from a few conversations, or scenes overheard, but from day-in-and-day-out association with her for nearly two months. I had learned the kind of woman Mrs. Wilde was. I testified at the first hearing that I had believed her to have cancer; and that—like nearly all my testimony at the inquiry meetings—was true. And my own position was such that if I felt that her death was the right and merciful thing, I should not be afraid, myself, of anything to lose. It was that horrible codicil that changed everything—a bequest conceived in spite and malice to torment her daughter, a bequest that was devilish . . .

"And you saw nothing but the money motive, in so far as I was concerned." She smiled surprisingly. "If you will forgive the play on words, John, I may say that you ought to have abandoned the gold standard sooner, in your investigations.

"As a matter of fact," she added, "the only person who came near to guessing the truth was Christine . . ."

"Christine!" I echoed.

"Yes, Christine. She was bewildered at first, but when she thought it over, she came close to suspecting what had really happened. Then her suspicions were turned aside, toward Horace Braye."

"How do you know she suspected you?" I asked.

"Because she told me so," Miss Hamilton answered. "Christine knows everything now. It is with her that I have made the arrangement about the money—"

It may seem incredible, but we found ourselves talking normally again. None of us troubled our heads about Horace Braye, who had been killed instead of being sent to prison; and to all of us, I think, it was not his bank robberies which were most loathsome, but the piling up of his rapacious fortune in New York's sweat-shops and fire-trap lofts. And most of us did not think much of Rosalie. But we had not yet seen the last of her . . .

Paul MacNeil was buried on Thursday morning in the Protes-tant Cemetery in the near-by city. And Rosalie Braye, her car driven by a smart chauffeur in black livery, and herself clad in the most fashionable widows' weeds, appeared at the service with bowed head and downcast eyes. Nearly all of us were going to Switzer-land the next day, and we were about to have tea together for the last time, when Rosalie popped suddenly out of the main door of the inn and waylaid John Sherrill as he was on his way to join us.

"Oh, Mr. Sherrill!" she cried. "You are a lawyer—I do so want your advice!"

He made some excuse—they were busy packing, they were go-ing to Lausanne with Miss Wilde the next day—but she would not let him off so easily.

"But you see," she said, "I do need a lawyer to tell me just where I stand. I am so worried about Horace's money, Mr. Sherrill—the police being after him, and all, and now its all coming out about him being Howard Bretton, and that bank, and everything. And Mr. Sherrill, you are a lawyer, and you can tell me all about it—can they take the money away from me that Horace kept when the bank failed?"

"My dear Mrs. Braye," Sherrill began, in cold exasperation, "I have not the slightest idea—"

"But can't you *think?*" she insisted. Frigid formality was lost on Rosalie. "You can see, Mr. Sherrill, that is what has been wor-rying me all along—just as I said to those policemen, and they never answered me, I said, 'What's going to become of *me?*' I said. But you will know, because you're a lawyer; and what I want to ask you is this don't you think it will be all right? Because Horace was al-ways so smart, he put everything in my name. Of course he saw that the bank was shaky a long time before anyone else did, and he put it in my name before anyone could guess there was anything wrong with his affairs. He was always forehanded that way—he said if you were going to get away with it you always had to be looking ahead. And what I want to ask you is—even if they've found out everything, don't you think the money'll be all right for me?"

Sherrill's gesture was that of a man trying to shake off an annoying insect. And his politeness was less careful.

"I told you, Mrs. Braye, I do not know anything about it —"

"Yes, but can't you find out?" Rosalie interrupted brightly. "You're a lawyer, and I'd be so glad if you'd represent me, Mr. Sherrill—"

He was really shocked, and he showed it.

"Oh, no!" was all he could say, for the moment, and she went on:

"I'd make it worth your while. I always say if you want good service you've got to be willing to put up a good price. I used to say that to Horace when he grouched about spending money. I used to say, 'There's lots of things in life that can't be run like the cloak-and-suit business,' and I know if you want to get the law on your side you've got to pay the right price for it, or else you just get gypped in the end, and then where are you? There won't be any trouble about that, Mr. Sherrill. You're a lawyer—"

"I am not that kind of lawyer," he broke in rudely, and fled. In the *galerie* his wife was smiling broadly, and at this comfortable domestic sight his sense of humor triumphed over his annoyance and he joined in the laughter that somehow refreshed us all.

"Won't someone just throw her into the Atlantic Ocean?" he grumbled between chuckles.

And Miss Hamilton answered, blandly:

"Oh, no, John, not at all. She is going home on the *Rex*. She is going back, like everyone else, to the great open spaces where dimes are dimes. She has been waiting around here while a shopper in Paris provided her with heaps upon heaps of clothes in which to honor Horace's memory, and she has got a chauffeur to drive the Lincoln to Genoa, and she is about to have her heart's desire in crossing by the newest and fastest and smartest ship afloat. In spite of your rude rebuff, I think she is quite happy. And I'm glad she is. Poor thing, I've felt awfully sorry for her."

"You would," remarked Elinor Sherrill. "I'll wager you got her that chauffeur, and probably her steamship ticket—"

"I did not," Miss Hamilton retorted.

And Henri de Brassac laughed.

"She did not," he repeated. "I must rush to Miss Hamilton's defense, Madame Sherrill. She only told me she was sorry for that poor numbskull, and asked me if I couldn't help her out. So I did."

"Did you get her clothes, too?" John Sherrill demanded.

"No," said Margaret Hamilton, "I did that. I mean to say, I gave Mrs. Braye the address of a good shopper in Paris. It is an American shopper, and Rosalie liked that. She says she never can feel that foreigners are quite honest, somehow . . ."

We all laughed again. But Elinor Sherrill's voice was rather grave as she asked,

"And you yourself, Margot—have you made any plans yet?"

"Well, I expect maybe I'll go back to America and see what seven hundred real dollars a year will do for me." She spoke without any trace of self-pity, in a tone as matter-of-fact as her words were colloquial. "I've learned that there are worse things than extreme poverty, and I'm willing to take my chance—"

"The dollar will go down in this United States, too," Henri de Brassac remarked.

And Miss Hamilton's smile looked like her old self.

"You cannot teach a Frenchman to put his trust in inflation," she said.

It was evident that she did not want to talk seriously about her personal problems. So we just smiled, once more, with her. And as we smiled, Christine came out of the garage and walked around the end of the *Place* and into the *galerie*.

She had on her old denim overalls, and she was rather grubby and inexpressibly charming.

"Everything's fine, Wayne," she said to me. "The engine just purrs with delight."

She looked around at the others, a little shyly.

"We were going to make an announcement this afternoon," she told them, "but I think announcements are rather difficult things, so we'll just invite. Will you all come to our wedding, in Lausanne, very, very soon?" She spread out dirty, happy hands in a gesture that still made me think of a bird's wings, and that seemed to fly out to include all the world and all the future in our rejoicing.

"We are sailing in just a few weeks," she added, "to our home in the Chester Valley . . ."

I reached down, suddenly speechless with joy and with shyness, and scratched Fergus's ear.

COACHWHIP PUBLICATIONS

COACHWHIPBOOKS.COM

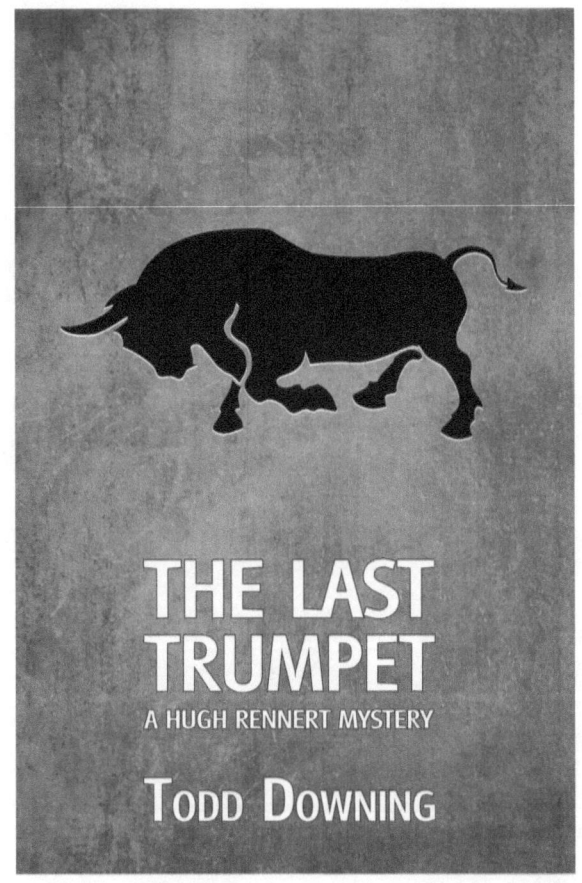

THE LAST
TRUMPET
A HUGH RENNERT MYSTERY

TODD DOWNING

ISBN 978-1-61646-152-2

COACHWHIP PUBLICATIONS

COACHWHIPBOOKS.COM

BLOOD ON HER SHOE

MEDORA FIELD

ISBN 978-1-61646-275-8

COACHWHIP PUBLICATIONS

COACHWHIPBOOKS.COM

THE
DARTMOUTH
MURDERS

THE
WAILING ROCK
MURDERS

CLIFFORD
ORR

ISBN 978-1-61646-323-6

ISBN 978-1-61646-250-5

COACHWHIP PUBLICATIONS

COACHWHIPBOOKS.COM

LOUIS F. BOOTH

THE BANK VAULT MYSTERY
BROKERS' END

ISBN 978-1-61646-326-7

Coachwhip Publications

Also Available

MYSTERY AT
LYNDEN SANDS

J. J. CONNINGTON

ISBN 978-1-61646-320-5